LAS HECHIZADAS

Anne Garcia

The occurrences in this book are intertwined
with the ebbs and flows of Mother Nature.
Each chapter is named after a particular plant
or flower that represents the essence of the story. It
is such, because without the life of these plants,
this story would not exist.

Pay close attention to how these plants
can influence one's destiny.

BOOK I

The
Unexpected Rebellion

BOOK 1

CHAPTER ONE

Begonia

Balance

The early years of the 21st century had passed. Men and women loved, lived and died. The world had changed, but not as much as one would think. There were still people fighting for power and money; children starving; men fighting wars and debating ideologies; and there were still some parts of the world that were striving for peaceful existence.

In one of these parts, on a chilly morning near the equator, two women from two generations knelt down in the soil, digging up the hardened crust to access the soft nutrients below. The older woman was teaching her granddaughter how to plant the gladiola seeds during new moon so that the plant would reap the energy of the lunar tides. "We have planted like this in the valley for thousands of years," she said.

"Why?" the young girl asked as she dirtied her hands with the earth's food.

The older woman stopped and sat back on her heels. "It's a long and complicated story," she said. "When I was a young writer I decided to take a trip. I packed my bags and headed south for Ecuador where I thought I would find the answers to all of my questions. What I found was a mystery unraveled and a peace I would have otherwise never known. I was

writing a book about a man named Juan Romero Rodriguez."
She sat cross-legged on the warm ground and began to tell
the child the long and detailed story about the person who
changed the destiny of the valley and her life.

"The pool of blood swirled around his head. The burning
in his chest was more than he could bear. The car raced away;
he could feel the mud as it splattered all over him. Sofia's arms
squeezed him; she was holding him to her breast. Her screams
became softer. He wasn't sure why he couldn't hear her. He
could feel the tears dripping onto his face. Where was Maria?
He managed to whisper 'Maria?' but Sofia didn't respond; she
just kept screaming. His body felt warm, tingling like when
he was awakening from a heavy slumber. He knew there were
other people around him. His father and his grandfather were
talking to him, telling him to get up. Telling him to be strong
and to stand tall. With his last bit of strength he did and took
his father's hand, but that is closer to the end of his story," the
old lady reflected. "I should give you more information about
his life."

"Who Abuela?"

"My father, your great-grandfather. It started when he
decided to leave home and come to the valley." The grandmother took the child's hand and they sat beneath the shade of
a wild cashew tree. "It's a story that is so fantastic it's almost
hard to believe," she began. "I sometimes don't even know if
it was real until I look down at you and breathe in the air of the
meadows filled with rich scents of all of the herbs and flowers.
It was a very long time ago my child." Her voice trailed off
and her mind wandered. Her eyes glazed over and she began
to see images floating across the screen. And after a few minutes of silence she began the story that shaped her life.

"Miniscule droplets of sweat dribbled down his face,
not from the heat, as much as from the humidity. His back
ached from the bouncing on the mule he had rented to traverse
the mountains. It had been a month since he left Arizona en

route to Aguas Puras. Abuela was waiting for him, had been
for months. Esperanza, my great grandmother, knew Juan
Romero would eventually join her in the village, even if for
just a short time. She had consulted the Milagros when his
father passed away. She chose the *águila*, eagle, the leader,
destined to change his life significantly with guidance from
others.

Francisco, his guide, set camp three hours from town,
claiming that the bridge crossing *El Rio Valiente* was not safe.
Juan Romero knew it was superstition. Abuela had told him
the legend of the river long ago. Valiente, the water God of the
local tribe, controlled the water in the valley. Several centuries earlier a drought scorched the countryside.

'Catarina was the daughter of Valiente,' began Francisco.
'One afternoon, in the dead heat of the drought she decided
to walk to the river in search of a cool haven. This notion was
unfathomable for many, because the river had been dry for
nearly 40 sunsets, but she insisted. Her father was not aware
of her journey thus a guard was not sent with her. Some say
Catarina left alone on purpose, as she had grown weary of the
constant oppression of being followed. Shortly before dark
she wearily made her way to the dusty bank. Parched, she
knelt down and reached out, seeking the cool water she had
once bathed in. As her fingers swept across the desolate riverbed, the pounding of horses moved the earth. She lifted her
eyes to see Coltamba's soldiers racing towards her. Coltamba
was Valiente's most violent enemy and would do anything to
destroy him. Catarina, without realizing, had in fact been followed. She sat down on her knees and awaited her destiny.
Coltamba's soldiers trampled her beautiful body into the arid
ground and as she lay between life and death, they ripped
her heart from her chest. There was a brief moment in which
the princess let out a high pitched sound, but not a scream. It
was a note of relief and rejoicing that rang clear in the mauve
colored sky. Many miles away Valiente heard the song of

his eldest child and rushed to her side. She was already dead despite his efforts to salvage her maimed body. In a fit of rage the God of water rose up and called all of the waters of the world to his powers. Within minutes the skies crackled with lightning and thunderous drums and the rains began. The riverbed filled as quickly as it could and the floods commenced.

Valiente sucked in the air around him and in one raging breath blew a wall of water 100 meters high. It raced toward the canyon where Coltamba's men had fled and drowned them instantly. Throughout the years those who have fallen at the hands of floods or drowning are said to have angered the Gods.'

Juan Romero was familiar with those souls, but was still not sure if their fates were controlled by an archaic myth. Men had fallen from the bridge during torrid rainstorms and drowned, while others had met unfortunate deaths after their homes were washed away in epic floods. Juan Romero rested his head on a bedroll made of T-shirts and stared absentmindedly into a sparkling sky. It reminded him of the desert sky at home in southern Arizona. His mind wandered into the dream world as nostalgia set in.

"YOUTH CITY ART SHOW" was painted in carefully scripted letters above the main entrance of the warehouse. Several spotlights hanging from a wire illuminated the sign in the dark alley. Brochures of the photographers' biographies were fanned across a makeshift plywood table at the entrance.

"Evening Juan Romero."

"Hey Shilo." They shook hands forcefully. He had been so nervous that night. His first real exhibit, all thanks to Rosa and Miguel, the owners of *Mi Tia*, a tiny, but exquisite, Mexican restaurant downtown where Juan Romero had been working to help his mother pay the bills. Shilo frequented the restaurant and Rosa pushed Juan Romero's photos on him as if he were the next Henri Cartier-Bresson. She didn't have to sell them, because Shilo took an immediate liking to them. He was a professor at the photography school at the university and promoted youth photography as an alternative to drugs and violence. These art shows served two-fold as fundraisers for the project and venues for young people who would otherwise never show their art.

"Your mother is already here," said Shilo as Juan Romero and his sister Silvia walked through the door.

"I thought *Mamá* had to work," Juan Romero said.

"She did," Silvia replied. They wove their way through the hallways covered with images ranging from landscapes to a low-rider car series until they saw their mother, standing almost petrified in front of Juan Romero's photographs. Tears ran down her face, but no noise escaped her lips.

"*Hola mamá.*" They both leaned in to kiss her. She barely moved.

"When did you take this picture?" Her eyes remained fixated on her husband, captured in a black and white print, sitting in his favorite rocking chair on the back patio of their old house, sipping the bitter green tea from his native Argentina, *maté*, from a silver *bombilla*, straw.

"A couple of days before Silvia's birthday."

"Can I keep it?"

"Of course, *mamá*. Whatever you want." She took it home as soon as the exhibition was over and hung it in the kitchen of the apartment. Having his photo hanging made the air easier to breathe. None of them were able to talk about him, but the picture was a start. Juan Romero fell into a peaceful sleep under the stars, thinking of home and his deceased father. He slept heavily, not dreaming, but in a complete trance.

Dawn broke and Francisco packed up camp before Juan Romero had a chance to finish his breakfast. They arrived at the bridge by early morning to their advantage, as crossing with such a large load would take a considerable amount of time. Only one team could cross at a time because the bridge wasn't sturdy. It had been built in the early 1800s and reinforced during the Social Revival Period, by the Federal government. Those were times when leftist dictators posing as compassionate socialists forced most of Latin America into economic ruin. The government had supposedly replaced the wood beams in the bridge with steel and hung new cables flown in from France, but a journalist in the port city where the materials arrived claims they are still rotting in the salty air, many, many years later, on a dock because there was no way to transport the ten ton rolls. Truckers refused to load it for the price being offered. For eight weeks government workers had the bridge closed and worked diligently on something, Francisco says. "In the end I think they added a few plates and shiny new bolts. Maybe they painted it," he said as he lined the mules up to cross. "Juan Romero, go in the middle," he directed. He gently pulled Maria and José out onto the first set of boards. Actually all of the mules were paired and named Maria and José.

"Religious?" Juan Romero asked Francisco.

"Superstitious," he replied. "Besides, what was I going to call them, Neutral One and Neutral 2," laughing at his own idiotic humor.

When it was Juan Romero's turn, Francisco gave Maria and José (the third) a shove from behind, clucking at them like a mad chicken. They in turn pushed Juan Romero out onto the bridge. It was at that moment that he felt the presence of Valiente. Not only was the river below roaring, but the cloud forest suddenly opened up in the canyon and Juan Romero could see the moisture pouring out of her limbs into the body of the river below. Waterfalls fell hundreds of feet, crashing at the cliffs' basin only to quickly regroup and rush to join the other waters flowing downstream. The fog encircled groups of plants and trees like mini halos, nurturing them so they in turn could nurture the rest of their environment. The heavy humidity on the narrow dirt trail where the plants soaked up every drop of water like sponges, was being swept swiftly upward by a warm, brisk breeze, forming rain clouds high above them that later that day would release their fury on the land.

He stepped cautiously on the metal slabs below his feet, aware of every squeak and whine his weight released. The mules were not as courageous as Juan Romero and refused to move forward. Francisco whipped their backsides incessantly, shouting and whistling, forcing them to face their fears. The clanging of their hooves snapped at the roots of Juan Romero's nerves. His legs felt heavy as he put one foot in front of the other and the other side of the bridge seemed further and further away. As he reached the midpoint of the bridge his face felt hot, sweat rolled down his temples, the wind spun around his head, and the light dimmed. He knelt down holding on to the cable and took several deep breaths. He heard Francisco in the distance yelling at him to continue, but the spinning kept getting faster and stronger. He looked down and saw the water below rushing in and out of the boulders. Between the spinning and the river flow he saw a small hole opening up in the eye of the motion. A clear, crystal blue circle opened its mouth and revealed an electric blue Morpho butterfly fluttering inside a small round glass container. Juan Romero reached down to lift the jar and the moment his hand met the glass the spinning stopped. It wasn't until then that he realized Francisco was standing next to him, firmly grabbing his arm.

"*¿Qué pasa, Juan Romero?*" Juan Romero looked up with butterfly in hand and oriented himself. The spinning was gone, his head clear and the air felt brisk. "I don't know," he replied.

"It looked like you fell." Juan Romero looked down into his hand while Francisco followed his glance. "What's that?"

"I found it here, on the bridge. When I became dizzy and nauseous I knelt down and noticed the butterfly."

"Just sitting in the middle of the bridge?"

"It was as if it came to me," Juan Romero answered. Francisco's eyebrows dropped, giving Juan Romero a suspicious look. Then looking at the butterfly, he pulled Juan Romero to his feet. "Strange color. It's almost too vibrant."

"I thought the same thing."

"Let it out," Francisco insisted.

"Here?"

"Why not? It's the perfect place." Juan Romero wasn't sure if he wanted to let the magical mariposa out of the jar holding it captive. She was so entrancing that he wanted to stare at her longer. Against his desires to hide her in his knapsack, he unscrewed the lid and let her loose. The breeze lifted her high above where they were standing and directly into the sun. Within seconds she was out of sight. Juan Romero tucked the glass container, which had been her home, into his bag and followed Francisco to the other side. When they reached firm ground Juan Romero found a rock to rest on and wait for the rest of the crew. He gulped down some lemon water sweetened with *panela,* a type of brown sugar sold in blocks. As he leaned over to Francisco to offer him a drink he saw the trip leader's eyes open widely and mouth to him "DO NOT MOVE." Juan Romero froze.

"What?" he whispered.

"Your butterfly has returned," he smiled. "Be gentle or she might fly away." Juan Romero turned his head to the right and sitting, with fluttering wings, on his shoulder was the electric blue creature.

"*Que bello,*" noted Francisco with a grin. "Strange, but *bello.*"

The blue butterfly continued to follow the ungraceful pack trekking through the cloud forest. Juan Romero was tired and ready to arrive in Aguas Puras. It had been three years since he had seen Abuela, since his father's funeral. It had been nine years since he had been to Aguas Puras. That time they took a bus, entering the range several hundred miles south where the mouth of the valley opens and the wetlands lap up against the base of the mountains.

He remembered very little about the trip, other than the fact the bus was packed with people and there was a woman trying to stow-away with her rooster and her pig. She had squeezed her plump body in the corner of the bench where Juan Romero and his father were supposed to sit—the rooster in her lap, the big, squealing *cochino* stuffed underneath her legs, hidden partially by her puffy white skirt. She was nervous and jittery, jabbering to the conductor in an Indian language Juan Romero didn't understand, though he assumed was Quechua. With the screaming pig, the lack of air and the tight quarters Juan Romero began to feel nauseous. The bus rocked back and forth on its wheels, rolling quickly across the high plains. His head started spinning. He could hear the ticket collector shouting, *"Boletos!* Teekets pleez!" but couldn't seem to focus on the actual person yelling at him and the woman. She began to speak faster and faster and then covered her face with a red handkerchief. Just as the man dressed proudly in a ragged blue suit leaned in, blowing his hot breath up Juan Romero's nose. Esmeralda asked her son, "Are you okay Juancito? You don't look so good. Gustavo, he looks pale." She went to grab hold of him and instantaneously vomit came flying out of his mouth, spewing all over Silvia, the pig and the tips of the ticket collector's shoes. The smell was so rancid that the man quickly removed himself from the aisle, pushing his way to the front, cursing and yelling to the driver to stop the bus so he could wash his shoes. The woman began laughing and grabbed hold of Juan Romero, shaking his head, rocking back and forth in utter elation. She wiped his mouth with the kerchief and let the pig free to feast on the boy's potato soup from the night before. Her gratitude exceeded traditional expectations, and the Rodriguez family arrived at Abuela's house with a live rooster.

The caravan rounded the last of the mountains it would have to traverse before arriving at the village. As it came into view, Juan Romero's mind filled with nostalgia and his pace quickened. The descent was steep and still muddy from the rains two days before, but he insisted on rushing. His feet pounded the wet ground and dodged the large rocks. He left the group far behind. His breath quickened. The path widened, as it grew closer to the town, its inclination slowed and signs of human life began to pop up. First a balled up candy wrapper, then a nippy malnourished dog defending his ditch and slowly a sporadic speckling of houses. One after the other, built with exposed adobe brick and red ceramic roof tiles, the houses led Juan Romero straight into Aguas Puras and its main plaza, *La Plaza de la Cala*. The center was still adorned with the most magnificent bronzed statue of Catarina, elaborately covered with lilacs and lilies, daisies and roses, any and every flower from the region. Her eyes, made of emerald stones, twinkled as they glanced at the village's most recent arrival. Awestruck once again, Juan Romero stared at the exquisite representation of history long gone, and history in the making. He felt a gentle hand on his shoulder, and the scent of gardenias floated into his nostrils.

"Hola Abuela," he secretly smiled then swung around and lifted the elderly woman as high as he possibly could. Her violet skirt swirled around, brushing his arms as he spun round and round.

"Stop!" she hollered. "I'm as dizzy as a horse on carousel," he slowed down and set her black rubber boots on the ground. "I saw you coming," she said.

"I let you know," he grinned. Abuela had a special gift in that she could sense people's presence. She was not clairvoyant, she could not read fortunes, but she did know if and when someone was coming or going by their scent.

"Where is Francisco?"

"I left them behind. They should be here soon."

"Then we shall get something to eat and toast your arrival until they come." She took his hand and led him to a small café on the north side of the plaza. The front was painted brightly with yellows and electric blues and in dark green letters above the three glass windows facing the street was its name, "Café Sofia."

"This place is new."

"You'll love it. A bit of the old world mixed with the new." The front door was made out of tiny glass window panes that were scrubbed so clean they reflected the sunlight and every image in their path. A blast of warm air danced around Juan Romero's head as he pushed through into the atrium. Delicate Flamenco was being plucked in the far corner by a gentleman who seemed twice Abuela's age. "That's Fernando. He's from Spain. Owns the tulip farm east of town. He bought it from an ex-military man. He left town rather quickly when his wife found out he was caressing and seducing the night watchman's daughter. She became pregnant and forced a surprisingly dramatic scandal. I surmise it was because he wouldn't recognize the child as his own, but his wife did. She took the young girl in and they are raising the child together. He's almost seven. The man was so disgraced that he rushed back to the city to be with his own mother, but before he disappeared he sold the farm out from under his wife's nose. Fernando didn't know any better. He would never have bought it, and especially not at such a high price, if he would have known that the scoundrel was planning to run with the money. Fortunately, Fernando is a kind man with a fortune. He apparently made his money dealing art in Europe. How those dealings occurred is still a mystery. Some say Fernando is *"El Gato"*—the most infamous art thief of recent times. *El Gato*'s last job was a Van Gogh from *Museé d'Orsay* in Paris. It was worth $200 million. Sofia is convinced it was Fernando. He knows too much about the layout and architecture of the most important museums and she says has an eccentric taste for expensive art, yet he does not own even one piece of art."

"Who is Sofia?"

"She owns this place. Look at the name—you are still living in *las nubes, m'ijo*."

"No I'm not, Abuela. I'm just so fascinated with everything that it's hard to concentrate on one thing. So what happened to the two women? Did Fernando give her the farm?"

"She and the girl and her son live in a second house that Fernando built on the farm. She and Fernando have become special friends. So special in fact, that it's driving them both mad. It shouldn't be too long before they explode and give in," Abuela smiled as she eyed Fernando and waved.

"*Bon jour*, Esmeralda," a heavy French accent overtook the rest of the noise in the restaurant.

"*Bon jour* Sofia," Abuela leaned over and gave the sensuous young woman the traditional four Parisian kisses, two on each cheek. Sofia's long red curls wound around the nape of her neck. Small beads of sweat glued the damp strands to her soft, pale skin. "This is my grandson Juan Romero." Her jade green eyes flashed his way. It was as if time had slowed down and she only focused on him.

"Pleased to meet you," she stuck out her hand. "Will you be staying long?" He didn't answer, but instead looked to Abuela for support. He couldn't think what to say nor could he move his hand away from hers.

"He does not know. It's the beginning of a journey."

"Welcome," she said, forcefully pulling her hand away to grab two menus. "Now why don't we get some food into you? Let's sit you by the window." She led them to a front table with a view of the plaza. "Do you want to drink something?"

"I'll have a chamomile tea and he'll have a *tisana*."

"*Muy bien,*" she rushed off to attend to other customers.

"You still like *tisana* don't you?"

"Yes of course," he answered, flustered. The rich mix of whole fruit intertwined with sweet juices was one of Juan Romero's all time favorites.

"How is your mother? We haven't spoken for awhile."

"She has been better. Money is still tight."

"Is she still working three jobs?"

"Yes, but it doesn't seem to do anything except make her tired and irritable. Silvia is trying for a scholarship to a school in New York. Public policy, I think. She knows mom can't afford to send her anywhere so if she doesn't get a grant or scholarship she can't study."

"And you?"

"I was taking those photography courses at the university, but they were getting expensive. I learned a lot, even sold a couple of my photos. I thought maybe later I might try photojournalism."

"Interesting. *Hijo*, you know your *mamá* is doing her best."

"I know Abuela. Maybe that's why I left, to lift the burden."

"Children are never a burden. They are like bright sun after a rain and a good *mamá* will never leave her son."

"But at least she doesn't have to worry about feeding me, and she can afford other things. I'm 21 years old now. It was time for me to go."

"She only has to worry about whether or not you are safe, when she will see you again, and pray she raised you with enough sense to survive."

"You're making me feel guilty."

"That's the point."

"Your drinks," Sofia leaned in and placed the order on the table. Juan Romero took a deep breath and stared at her freckled breasts. She spun around, smiling, in a hurry to attend to her other customers.

"She smells so sweet. Almost like rose petals."

"It's her signature symbol."

"And yours is gardenias. What's mine?"

"Only you can define that."

"A toast," Juan Romero grinned. "To a new journey!"

"And to its success," she added.

JOURNAL

The air is cold in the garden as I sit and write this morning. It is refreshing to breathe in crisp air and not feel suffocated by fumes. Abuela looks fabulous. Her silver hair hangs down below the middle of her back, woven carefully in a braid. I had never noticed how beautiful she was before. Actually, there are a lot of things about her I never noticed, like how she always looks me in the eye when she talks. It doesn't matter what she is doing, she'll get my attention and focus on me like a falcon on her prey, the entire time we are having a conversation. She has always been one of the only people I have felt has actually heard what I say. She doesn't interrupt me or ignore me. I feel calm near her. When I finish rambling on about politics and poverty she smiles, and the wrinkles around her plump lips shine. She says in a soothing voice, "I think you should follow your dream Juancito." I've just turned 21 years old and she still calls me Juancito. I tell her I don't know what she means and she answers,

"You've spent an hour and a half talking about injustices. Change them."

"How?"

"Share them with others."

"I do."

"I mean with everyone. It's like my paintings. I walk along my road for hours looking at the birds, the rocks, the snakes, the flowers. If I walk for too long or I let too many days pass by before I put those images on canvas I lose them. Do you understand?" Her black eyebrows lift high above her dark eyes as she talks. We eat in the garden under the moon. She uses gas lanterns instead of electric lights. It makes me think about the places in the world that don't receive electricity. How is it possible? I enjoy not being under the watch of fluorescent bulbs, but it still seems unnatural because I am so accustomed to artificial light. She doesn't seem to care. She says, "Electric lights burn my eyes and tire my mind. Fire, on the other hand, gives me a sense of peace within my stomach and I can eat without stress." At 70 she knows who she is and what she wants. It must take that long to figure everything out. I feel so far from that stage in my life, but for the time being I feel safe, tired and content with a belly full of homemade treats. My plans are vague, but I'm considering staying here for a few weeks and then determine a plan of travel. I've been gone for two and a half years. Despite the fact that my travels have shown me big cities and small villages, ancient ruins and violent volcanoes, and introduced me to people I had never before imagined existed and still don't feel anymore certain about the world than I did before. I feel scared that chaos will take over. It is a fear that my ancestors were well aware of. The chaos spreads. Sitting here, in this simple room, writing in my journal, quiets my mind.

CHAPTER TWO

Loveage

Confidence in taking action

Abuela's house was several kilometers outside of Aguas Puras. The salmon colored adobe structure was larger than she needed, but after Abuelo died she did not want to leave. Octavio, who had been with the family for years stayed on to help her. Abuela had not chosen calla lilies to harvest, but had inherited them from her mother's family. She would often tell her grandchildren the story of how she learned to work in the flower fields.

"My father was a very hard worker. He and my mother ran the farm. When he married her he knew she would never leave her farm behind so he decided to work by her side. They worked together day and night tending their crop and the few animals needed to sustain their way of life. *Mamá* became pregnant with me, but it didn't stop her from working. In fact, as her belly swelled, she became more determined to work and spent most of her time in the field. It was raining lightly the day she lay down in the field and Anna attended the birth. It was so fast that there was no time for anyone to help her inside the house. I was a fiery soul and wanted to be born out of doors. It was my destiny to be in the fields. It was in my blood, and from the moment my lungs inhaled the sweet air perfumed by the calla lilies I wasn't happy anywhere else. I spent my infancy on my mother's back or sleeping, bundled in a flower basket. When I was old enough to walk I followed her everywhere and began tending flowers. I haven't stopped."

Abuela never admitted to anyone that her heart broke when Esmeralda left the farm and migrated with her foreign husband, but Juan Romero sensed it. She did not have any other children. Juan Romero's mother was born with complications that left Abuela unable to bear more children.

Abuela brought mint tea out to the patio and put the tray on the terracotta ceramic table that sat in the middle of the garden. She poured the tea into delicate blue china cups and served her grandson lovingly. The sun was low in the sky and cast shades of lavender over Abuela's lavish garden.

"What are you looking for *cariño*?"

"What do you mean?"

"You seem lost."

"Maybe," Juan Romero replied, sipping his tea. "I think I just need some peace."

"You are in search of a project," she said.

"I think I need to stay here for awhile if that's okay."

"Maybe take some photos," she suggested.

"That's a good idea." Abuela called for Octavio to light the lanterns.

"*Mi hijo*, I have something for you," Abuela reached inside her pocket. "I've been meaning to give you these for a long time, but you weren't ready. I think you are ready now." She opened up her hand to reveal a dark purple, silk bag with a leather tie around the top. "They belonged to your great-great grandfather. He was a healer and somewhat of a warrior.

"I remember your stories of his courage when fighting the government for his land."

"He was a strong man, honorable."

"What is it that you have in the bag?"

"Talismans, *milagros*."

"Show me." Abuela pulled the tie and emptied several metal charms on the bed.

"They will protect you against illness, pain, and trouble. They will help you guide others and make savvy decisions. It is important that any knowledge you gain is transformed into wisdom. You are on a pilgrimage. Take each step one at a time and recognize the importance of each person, each day, and each message. When you are confused or you feel alone ask the *milagros* for assistance.

"How do I know which ones to ask?"

"Use this journal," she pulled out a leather bound journal from under her chair. "It has been kept by our family for a long time. It will teach you how to use them. You may add any insights you gain while on your journey."

"Why hasn't mother used these?"

"She didn't want them." Abuela turned her head and gazed into the night sky. "Your father was a good man Juancito, but when he took my Esmeralda north she lost many things. The north is a hard place where individuals rule themselves and forget about others. There is little opportunity to share with others because they are all running around working themselves into the ground. People don't mean to, it just happens."

"What does that have to do with the *milagros*?"

"Northern culture wouldn't accept them as legitimate. Instead they are *brujerias*, witch-like, or they are simple trinkets an old woman prays to. Esmeralda changed when she realized she had to in order to fit in. Imagine if she had cut you off from our culture, Juancito. Imagine if you couldn't speak Spanish or never would have come to spend summers. Tradition and family are important. For that reason I am turning this over to you. They are the mind, body and spirit of our ancestors, and are yours to protect." She stood up and kissed him gently on the forehead. Her old bony hands were surprisingly soft against his face. She walked so lightly her feet seemed to not touch the ground, and with her departure a warm wind rushed through the garden, blowing the silk bag off the table. As Juan Romero reached down to pick it up, a small, copper-colored hand fell from inside. He held it up to the candlelight. It gleamed slightly in the flame, tarnished, not polished. He set the journal next to the hand and untied the rope that held the leather cover and worn pages together. The paper was thin and the words seeped through each page, allowing only one side to be used.

"*Milagros Diarios*" and then a list of dates beginning with 1897. Each date had a name carefully scrolled next to it. The first name, Romero Andres Rojas, Juan Romero's great grandfather appeared on the first page. He was an intellectual from Quito where he had studied law in his youth when he began the journal. He stayed in the city for many years working. When he met Julia his life changed. She was *an Hechizada*. Her powers to interpret signs and symbols fascinated Romero and drew him to Aguas Puras where he bought the Calla Lily farm, *La Flor Poderosa,* which Abuela still runs today. He left the tending of the flowers to Julia and opened a practice in town.

The entries in the journal included the name of the author and a drawing of the symbol chosen. Careful descriptions had been penned along with advice for future action. *1932 Humberto Rojas. After the death of Alejandra during childbirth the Milagros gave me the Hand. It tells me to search for the power of compassion and seek out knowledge in order to share and experience truth. It meant to raise Esperanza to be as wise as she can so her power of peace will spread throughout the countryside.* He was talking about Abuela.

The next morning Juan Romero and Abuela decided to walk into town to buy supplies. Octavio had taken the truck to deliver a load of chrysanthemums to Baños, a town not too far from Aguas Puras. Normally Octavio accompanied Abuela everywhere. If not Juan Romero would feel less comfortable with her living on the ranch. As they walked down the dirt road toward town people began appearing from the fields on the side of the road.

"*Buenos dias, Señora,*" they would say nodding their heads.

"*Buenos dias,*" Abuela replied graciously. When Juan Romero asked where they were all coming from, Abuela giggled and said, "They live around here."

"Where? I didn't see any other farms nearby other than the Castañeda's."

"Their homes blend into the mountains. You will only see them if you know where to look." A few minutes later a wave of people walking very slowly appeared on the horizon. As they got closer Juan Romero saw a small man in the front of the group carrying a large wooden cross with red ribbons tied around it. He wore a white robe with no belt, which blew gloriously in the breeze as he walked. He was short, only about 5'6", and his bald head glowed in the morning sunlight. He had dark wisps of hair that curved around the base of his head and was neatly groomed. The group was singing, actually repeating after the priest. As they approached one another he stopped and nodded his head, "*Buenos días Señora. ¿Cómo le va?*"

"*Buenos días Padre Miguel. Estoy muy bien ¿Y usted?*"

"*¿Yo? Muy bien como siempre.*" The priest eyed Juan Romero in a way that was almost comforting and in English said, "This must be the grandson we've been hearing so much about. I was told he had arrived."

"*Sí.* Juan Romero, this is Padre Miguel."

"Nice to meet you," Juan Romero held out his hand.

"*Igualmente,*" he took the boy's hand and shook it once, very firmly, holding it for a long moment and looking Juan Romero straight in the eye, "I hope you will be staying awhile."

"A short while, yes, but then I will have to return to the U.S. I'm planning to start school eventually. I also want to travel a bit more."

"I see." He let go of Juan Romero's hand and turned to Abuela. "It was lovely to see you *Señora*. You should come by for a coffee. Bring your grandson if you wish."

"*Gracias Padre*. I will." They stepped aside to let the group pass and Juan Romero watched as this man led the throng down the road. His movement was slow, precise, so much so that the two could have watched him for hours.

"Abuela,"

"*Si hijo.*"

"Who is that man?"

"Padre Miguel is the local priest."

"Yes, but what I mean is that he seems to be so much more." She looked at Juan Romero and then looked away.

"He is." Then they walked in silence into the winding hills until they reached town. They didn't speak for a long time, both of them listening to the drips of the dew on leaves and the rising steam; smelling the fragrances that rushed passed them with every step they took.

Once they got to town Juan Romero followed Abuela around the village and into a small supply store run by a man named Pablo. He was extremely friendly and chatty. Juan Romero said almost nothing as he stared out the window, soaking in the town. It was old and somewhat rundown, but each building had its own character. Most of them were salmon colored or burnt orange adobe. Cracked walls showed the pain time had burdened the town with. People sat quietly on their porches watching each other and the day go by. There wasn't a busy feeling on the narrow stone streets. A woman on the second floor opened the shutters to water a red geranium. Its vibrant color lit up the windowsill. "Juan Romero," he heard someone calling his name in the distance. "Juan Romero," a hand touched his shoulder and he jumped. *"Hijo, ¿qué te pasa?"*

"What Abuela?"

"Are you okay? I've been calling your name and you didn't move. Did you not hear me?"

"No Abuela. I'm sorry, I was thinking."

"It's okay. Come," she took his hand. "Help me with these things. Let's eat before we head home. My treat."

"*Si Abuela.*" He lifted the bag and wrapped the handles around his back. "Jeez, this is ridiculously heavy. What's in here?"

"If you can't manage I'll carry it."

"Don't be silly." They walked several blocks to Sofia's.

"Stay here." Abuela went inside and came back with two beers. *"Aqui estás.* It's a hot one today, ¿no?"

"Sure is." They sat in the shade and swigged the beers, waiting for the food. When it came, Juan Romero could barely control himself it smelled so good.

"Aqui tienes la sopa de quinoa." A young boy called Manuel put a huge bowl of quinoa in front of Juan Romero, along with a bowl of steaming melted cheese and a basket of warm bread. Juan Romero had been sent to heaven. The cheese hung heavily from the wooden spoon as he piled it onto the bread.

"Where is Sofia, Manuel?" Abuela asked.

"She is at home resting. Something about having to tend to her flowers and plants."

"Good for her. We should stop by for a visit before we leave."

"Mmmmm. I haven't had quinoa for years," interrupted Juan Romero.

"That's what you get for not visiting for so long."

"I've been traveling."

"Family is first *hijo.* Don't forget that." Ever since Juan Romero's father had died it had been hard for him to imagine family, but he felt safe alongside Abuela and was beginning to feel a sense of family growing inside of him again. The warm air and the thoughtful pace of life in Aguas Puras were different from at home, where the understanding of living simply had been lost. He actually had time to enjoy his family here.

"¿Quieres postre?"

"What do they have?"

"Crème Caramel. It's Sofia's French version of flan."

"Of course I want flan. I love flan."

"No es el mismo, but it's good," she boasted. They ate the rich, creamy flan and sat for a while before Abuela was ready to walk back to the ranch.

"Shall we stop by Sofia's?"

"Okay." Abuela led Juan Romero back toward the store and stopped in front of the red door directly below where he had seen the woman watering the geranium. She rang the bell.

"She lives here?"

"Upstairs." Juan Romero felt a sense of guilt for having admired Sofia's bosom earlier. His face got hot and turned slightly red.

"Are you okay?" Abuela asked.

"Fine, fine. Just a little hot is all."

"¿Quién?" Echoed the intercom.

"It's me Sofia, Esperanza."

"Come up." The door buzzed open. They climbed a set of spiral stairs to the second floor and found the door open.

"¿Aló?"

"Hola. Pasa, pasa," Sofia's voice rang from a distance. "I'm just finishing watering my plants." Although Sofia did not have a farm, she too had fallen under the spell of raising flowers, herbs and plants. She had transformed her back patio into an elaborate greenhouse where she grew everything from tomatoes to dill. She used the fresh herbs in the recipes at the café and cut the flowers for herself and for the restaurant.

"Wow," Juan Romero's eyes bulged out of his head as they stood in the entry to the exquisite garden. "Did you do all of this?"

"Oui. I am guilty."

"It has taken a long time for Sofia to develop a knack for her gardening," Abuela noted.

"Remember when I first started?" They both began laughing. "Everything I planted died before it even sprouted."

"I think you were using fertilizers! Imagine that." Abuela began laughing even harder. "Who in God's name would think to spread chemicals on a living being?"

"It's how I had been taught."

"Foolish French," Abuela snorted. "You see my love, when you work with the land, breathe it, taste it, feel it, you don't need foreign substances to yield fruits from her. Mother Earth talks to us, some of us just haven't learned how to listen." Juan Romero smiled at his grandmother and her rich history of tending the land. He knew it was more than just growing plants. It was a way of being, a kind of spirituality that only a chosen few would ever embrace and understand. *Las Hechizadas* were beings not fully of this world, participating in it so they could attempt to save it. For generations, centuries in fact, they had passed their knowledge to one another, guarded secrets for the women of the valley to nurture and protect.

The only response Sofia could muster was "Can I offer you a coffee?" Abuela was right, foolish French, but she was still sweet. There was something about her that drew Juan Romero in.

"I would love one," Juan Romero replied. Sofia pulled down a tin of dark roasted coffee. "My friend Eduardo grows coffee in Venezuela. Shall we try some?"

"Wonderful," said Abuela. Coffee for Sofia was a culinary art and therefore she had equipped her kitchen with an espresso maker, which she packed the coffee in and brewed three cups of espresso while whisking a jar of milk, transforming the milk into a creamy froth. She gently poured the milk into the cups for three cappuccinos.

"Come, let's sit in the sun room. It's cool in there with the windows open. Sofia's apartment was an elegant mix of Paris and Aguas Puras. The high vaulted ceilings and bright colors gave it the European finesse it deserved, while the creaking wood floors and rattling pipes reminded Sofia of its South American ruggedness.

"I heard a rumor the other day, Madame."

"About?"

"The miners."

"What about them?" Abuela's mood immediately changed at the word miners.

"They are back."

"Who told you?"

"It is just a rumor, but a friend from the capital told me he heard they are working on a contract near Aguas Puras. When he asked me I told him I knew nothing about it."

"They are long gone Sofia. We got rid of them legally. They cannot come back."

"What are you two talking about?" Juan Romero interrupted.

"Several years ago there was a group from outside the country trying to open a mine up river," Sofia explained. "My feelings about mining in this region reflect those of most people here. It threatens our environment and way of life, and I am therefore opposed to the idea. It will strip the mountains of important plants that maintain the cloud forests, which in turn bring us this magnificent moisture. Without it our land will turn into a stripped barren wasteland and our flowers will not survive. Not only that, but our animals, such as the Tapir, will lose their habitat."

"We fought them in court," Abuela said.

"They were not gentle with the environment," Sofia noted.

"They were going to ruin the landscape and contaminate the water. Luckily the judge was a good friend of Padre Miguel's and ruled for the town."

"He is dead," Sofia said.

"What?" Abuela seemed surprised.

"Car accident. He was drunk and drove himself off the road."

"When did this happen?"

"A couple of months ago. It was common knowledge, I thought you knew."

"No, I didn't. So maybe what you are saying is true. Maybe they will try again."

"I think they might. From what I understand there have been no negotiations. They just started."

"Have you been to anyone else with this news?"

"No Esperanza, only you. I thought you would know best what to do with such information."

"I suppose we should talk with Padre Miguel." Sofia gulped her cappuccino and gently placed the cup on its plate.

"I don't mean to be rude, but I must go to the café. They will need me to help with dinner prep. You are welcome to stay and enjoy the sun if you like. Just lock up when you leave."

"Thank you Sofia, but we should be on our way too. We walked to town today and have a long journey home."

"Please come by again. I enjoy the company." She looked straight into Juan Romero's eyes and smiled.

Abuela and Juan Romero were so full after lunch and coffee that they decided to stop by the river on the way home and take a *siesta*. The water ran lazily around the bend, and they rested peacefully near the riverbank. Abuela gazed up at the clouds and tried to quiet her mind, but the worry about Sofia's news was wreaking havoc with her thoughts. She would have to go to Padre Miguel first thing in the morning.

JOURNAL

My thoughts are confused and I don't know if it is because of the potent lust I felt today after seeing Sofia on the street, or if it is my desire to run naked through the meadows as the rain comes pouring down on me. The air seems different, heavy and humid. Abuela says it is the changing seasons, but I feel something other than a climatic shift. The blue butterfly continues to cross paths with me—it landed here in my journal just a few moments ago and it was as if it was staring at me. It slowly moved its wings and for a brief moment I thought I heard a voice. My mind feels flighty.

We just planted Lemon Verbena in the garden today. Abuela says it is for Sofia, to help her put the past behind her and show her how to open up to new experiences. I'm not sure Abuela knows how open Sofia is to new experiences. Pedro, the mechanic, told me that Sofia was the one woman in town that almost any man could go to for pleasure. Oddly, she is not seen as the town whore, just a wildly sexual foreign woman. Her wanderlust is her way of seeking the uninhibited love she speaks of. She emits an odor of feminine sex that draws me into her sensuous personality. It is difficult to resist.

I spent most of the morning taking photos of Abuela. I want to document her life. Her strength, both of body and mind, amazes me. She is unlike anyone I know. Her passion for life and her ability to interpret my thoughts leaves me in awe of her and her wisdom. I'd like Silvia to keep them and compile a book. I just sent her a letter and will have to wait to see what she says.

CHAPTER THREE

Cosmos

Speak the truth

His hands trembled like an arthritic old man as he struggled to wind the film into the canister to develop. He could barely breathe. His adrenaline pumped through his veins so quickly that his hands bulged. He had to purposefully inhale because he was so nervous that his body was forgetting to breath. The dim red light of his makeshift darkroom was just enough to allow him to see. Abuela had cleaned out an old storage shed behind the house for Juan Romero to fix up as a studio. It was only 10'x8', but there was enough room for Juan Romero to develop his images. He had taken a few days to explore the mountains at Abuela's suggestion. He was feeling restless and wanted to explore. He had packed a backpack with enough provisions for a few days and shoved his camera in a makeshift waterproof bag. It was on the third day he had come across the mine. It was totally unexpected. He had heard of an abandoned mine, from years ago, that had been shut down because of protests from the townspeople, but this was a fully functioning, working, loud, destructive mine. The sides of the mountains were raped of their lush green blankets, baring the innards of an exposed earth that was not meant to be seen by the sun. The noise of machines and the stench, he was not sure what that stench was, saturated the air, interrupting the sounds of the forest.

One by one the images of men recruited from the slums of the cities surgically removing vegetation from the earth's skin burned themselves onto the photo paper. Men with fair skin and light hair wore hard hats and goggles, carrying clipboards in hand. Gargantuan tractors carved chunks of life out of the mountainside. Juan Romero carefully printed every photo and gathered them up into a manila envelope, marking it "Canadians." He tucked the envelope under his arm to protect it from the light rain and threw his rubber boots and slicker on. He ran to the truck, which coughed as he tried to start the engine. The wipers squeaked and the lights barely cut through the thickening fog, but she slowly chugged down the dirt road towards town. Juan Romero had the accelerator pressed heavily on the floor, but she would not go any faster. She moved at the same speed she always had—leisurely and peacefully. He pulled into the parking lot and scanned the church offices for a light. Padre Miguel's office was illuminated.

"Padre!" he shouted from the truck, not wanting to soak the photos. "Paadreeee!" A figure appeared in the window and Juan Romero flashed the headlights. Padre Miguel waved and disappeared. Juan Romero grabbed the photos and bolted for the door. The large wood door creaked as the priest opened it.

"*¿Esperanza, eres tú?*"

"No padre. It's me, Juan Romero."

"*Pasa, pasa.*" He grabbed the young man's arm and pulled him in. "You're soaked."

"The rain comes down hard here doesn't it?"

"Always has. It's cleansing."

"It is also inhibiting."

"That is the point. One can't be cleansed if one is moving too frantically through life. What can I do for you, Juan Romero? It seems that something important must be on your mind to force you out into God's shower."

"There is something. It's something that I felt couldn't wait."

"Come in and sit down. I'll put water on for coffee."

"Thank you." Padre Miguel led Juan Romero down a dimly lit hallway to a sitting room warmed with a crackling fire.

"Sit. I'll be right back." Juan Romero made himself comfortable in a large red armchair and placed the folder on the coffee table in front of him. His eyes scanned the room, absorbing the images of the Catholic Church displayed sparsely on the walls; a hand painted ceramic cross strung with a wooden rosary, a photo of Pope John Paul II on his last visit to Latin America, and in the corner a stone statue of Saint Francis with dried rosebuds adorning his feet. On the far wall a painting hung of a young woman kneeling in front of a basket of calla lilies, her back to the painter.

"You like that painting?" Padre Miguel entered the room with a tray of steaming hot coffee, cookies, milk and sugar.

"It's beautiful in a haunting way."

"Haunting?"

"The fact that you can't see her face."

"That's his style."

"Whose?"

"I'm surprised you don't recognize it. It's Diego Rivera."

"Now that you mention it I do."

"It's an original."

"Where did you get it? It must be worth a fortune."

"It probably is, but I've never asked. It was a gift from my days in México."

"I didn't know you lived in México."

"It was a long time ago, before I became a priest. I left my home as a young man and traveled, much like you are doing. I ended up working for a wealthy rancher in central Mexico. I was there for several months and started helping manage things. I became very close with the family. His wife was an avid collector. I'm not sure how she acquired the collection she had, only because it was so vast and exclusive. One evening I was vaccinating the cattle when I heard screaming coming from the stables. I ran to find their daughter, lying in the hay about to give birth."

"What was she doing in the stable?"

"She was visiting her mare, Capitana. She would spend hours grooming and spoiling her because she was not permitted to ride her. She told me once that her one passion in life was not her marriage, but riding."

"What happened?"

"She was not able to move, so I simply sat there, trying to placate her. At first I was going to go for help, but the main house was more than two miles away and she did not want to be left alone. Her contractions were coming one on top of another so I found a clean horse blanket and helped her onto it. An hour later her son was born. When I arrived at the house with news of the birth, *el jefe* almost had a stroke. He immediately sent a car for her and she and her child, Miguel, arrived safely. They were so thankful it embarrassed me. I only did what any decent person would have done, but *la Señora* asked me to choose any painting in her collection."

"So you chose the callas."

"Yes."

"Good choice."

"I thought so. Do you take sugar and cream?"

"Sugar thanks."

"What is it that you've come to see me about in the middle of a downpour?" He held the hot cup of coffee out for Juan Romero.

"It's about the mines. I have proof they have started up again." Juan Romero opened the envelope, pulled out the photos and plopped them on the table.

"They are here?" Padre Miguel's bald forehead crinkled as he reached out for the black and whites.

"What are these?" He lifted the photos and pulled his glasses down off of his head.

"I took them today, while I was hiking."

"Where?"

"*Valle Bonito.*" Padre Miguel flipped through the stack of pictures, carefully examining each one.

"Here, use this." Juan Romero pulled a loupe out of his coat pocket. "Look at the name on the side of the truck." Padre Miguel held the lens against the photo.

"Maple Mining. Damn!"

"It's the same company?"

"Of course." His hands fell heavily in his lap and his eyes looked up at Juan Romero. "I will call a town meeting for tomorrow night. Can you blow these images up?"

"Sure."

"Bring them to me tomorrow night at 6:00. We'll meet at Sofia's." He stood and extended his hand, "Thank you."

"What will we do?"

"I need time to think, Juan Romero. Be off. I'll see you tomorrow." Juan Romero found his way down the hall to the back door. The rain had stopped. His mind raced in one thousand directions. When he arrived at *La Flor Poderosa,* Abuela was up drinking tea. He left his muddy boots in the entry and joined her.

"*Buenas noches Juancito.*"

"*Buenas noches Abuela.*" He bent over to kiss her on the cheek.

"We missed you at dinner. Did you eat?"

"No. I had to see Padre Miguel."

"Yes, I know." He was perplexed and stared at her in wonderment. "I saw this in your darkroom." She pulled out a photo he had left on the counter. "He was the only person you could have seen."

"He's going to call a meeting tomorrow."

"Good. We'll all go." She stood up and kissed him. "I'm going to bed. The water is hot if you want tea." She disappeared down the hallway and he sat, waiting for the last flame of the candle to burn out.

The next morning Esmeralda did not wait for Padre Miguel to call a meeting. She arrived at first light with a basket of warm baked bread, smoked cheese and a thermos of hot black coffee, sweetened with sugar. She knocked gently on the door despite her anger. She had sensed that Padre Miguel had known about the mine and had not said anything. He was afraid and tired. While he was one to fight for the people, the years had begun to take their toll and his dealings with the government had become more incestuous. The heavy door creaked open.

"*Buenos Dias* Esmeralda, I was expecting you." He nodded to Juan Romero.

"Buenos Dias Padre Miguel. May I come in?" He motioned for her to pass and she headed straight for the sunlit patio where she carefully laid out the breakfast.

"Come, we must talk." He sat down with his back to the purple *trinitaria* that blossomed on the top of the stone wall and served himself a cup of coffee. Several minutes passed as Esmeralda carefully cut the bread, methodically spread butter and blackberry jam, and filled her cup with hot coffee.

"We cannot sit here as bystanders and watch these mining companies try to take over again Miguel." Abuela was firm in her statement.

"I know Esmeralda, but what would you expect me to do? It is not necessarily about will. It is about money and power, neither of which I have."

"That is not true. The will of this town is greater than any greedy CEO will ever be able to fathom. We have spent generations of people healing and curing people of emotional and physical ailments. You think something like this will stop us? What we need is a leader. We need someone to stand up and say to the people that he will take them to their destiny!" Juan Romero had never seen his grandmother so passionate.

Her face was red with fire and her eyes were lit like the tail of a comet racing through the black night sky.

"How long have you known about this?"

"Several weeks."

"And you said nothing."

"I couldn't. I didn't have enough information."

"Have you spoken with the ministry?"

"*Sí.*"

"And?"

"*Y nada Esmeralda. Nada.*"

"They know nothing?" she asked with a tone of disbelief.

"They know plenty. They say nothing."

"They have already signed the deal then."

"They've done this before, it doesn't mean they'll get away with it."

"I don't care how long it takes. We must get rid of them. It's going to be a long fight." Abuela took a step toward Padre Miguel and pressed her nose to his. "We have no other option." She forcefully added. "Do you understand? Do you realize what could happen? It isn't just about us, it is bigger. It is about the health of the universe. It is about the future." She grabbed Juan Romero's shoulder and pulled him closer to her. "It is about my grandson." She shook him gently as these words left her lips.

JOURNAL

Abuela spoke forcefully today and after leaving Padre Miguel we went for a coffee. It was then that she filled me in more deeply on the Padre's perspectives. He is a Liberation Theologian. Liberation theologians explore the relationship between Christian, most often Catholic, theology and political activism, in areas such as social *justice, poverty and human rights. Apparently this is not the first time Padre Miguel has been in a place where his role in the church and his role as an activist have crossed and in fact he has embraced the two as one. I suppose it's not so odd to fathom a priest who is in the streets with the people working for them. Isn't that what they should be doing instead of gathering enough wealth to be a small nation and then tell others to forgive debt?!*

All of this mining only reminds me of the eternal greed of the human race and how life hasn't changed much. How many hundreds of years have gone by since Spaniard Francisco Pizarro captured Incan leader Atahualpa, extracted a handsome ransom paid in gold, and then executed him under the guise of politics? Today gold is extracted under the guise of business. Is there a difference?

CHAPTER FOUR

Lavender

Devotion, loyalty

The enclosed glass mudroom gave Abuela room to line her boots neatly under two opposing benches. The sun hats hung floppily on the hat rack next to the door, and Abuela's tool bag was carefully stored on the stone shelf at the back of the room. She had prepared a new tool bag for Juan Romero and placed it, and a pair of black rubber boots, next to hers. After a strong cup of black coffee they geared up to work in the fields. They sat on the benches with the morning sun trying to peek through the dripping dew on the windows.

"We will be adding lavender to the composted soil today," said Abuela.

"What does that do?" asked Juan Romero.

"Each herb or spice we add to our soil will eventually come through in the scent of the petals. Lavender is calming and it is time for balance to blossom." Juan Romero tightened his tool belt around his waist and Abuela began organizing tools. "Here is your gentle spade to nurture the soil and move her from one place to another." She held up the yellow handled spade. "Remember, she will always come full circle; you will never eliminate earth, only shift it. Come." She opened the door and walked down the path through the garden to the yellow gate and out into the meadow. She stopped at the first greenhouse to check in with Edgar, the second in command after Octavio."

"*Buenos dias Señora.*"

"Hello Edgar. I'm going out to the fields to do some tilling. I need you to bring ten bins of compost soil out to me."

"Yes *Señora*. What are you adding today?"

"Lavender."

"One of my favorites. Lifting the spirits, eh?"

"As always. *Pacha Mama* calls for it." Abuela lifted a large wicker basket and swung it over her back. "Juan Romero, take the other basket please." They left through the back door and walked through the fog that was beginning to burn off. Juan Romero felt the hissing of the plants as the emerging sun sizzled off droplets of dew. The path wound around and through three hills, over a gurgling stream, into a small patch of cloud forest, and back down to a clearing where Abuela finally stopped. She set her basket down and signaled for Juan Romero to follow her. She sat, crossed-legged in the middle of a dirt patch, and closed her eyes. They stayed that way for a while.

"*Ven mi hijo.*" Juan Romero followed suit. Abuela stood up and walked into an opening where a straw mat covered a small hole in the ground. She leaned over and untied the rope holding the mat down. She then lifted the mat and uncovered the hole, revealing a set of spiral stairs. She descended and turned her head. "Help me down here Juan Romero." He slowly stepped to the edge of the hole and peered down. It was difficult to see anything except for the tiny light Abuela had lit to illuminate her path.

"Abuela?"

"Come down *mi amor*. It's okay." He hesitantly made his way down the dark passage until he finally reached the bottom where Abuela was carefully pulling bottles of lavender out of her backpack.

"Lavender oil in the soil will give the earth a sense of inner freedom." She carefully placed three drops of essential oil into the compost. "It will help release anger so we can make balanced decisions." The underground cavern was much larger than Juan Romero expected. The floor was lined with wood pathways that connected several small compartments, each containing the materials for creating the compost. Gas lanterns and locked closets lined the walls. Juan Romero knew that inside those closets *Las Hechizadas* had hidden their own kind of weapons—venoms, recipes, salves and even a handful of traditional defense mechanisms (guns and machetes) for those times when the others just didn't work, or there was no time.

"Why not just plant the seed?" he asked, redirecting his thoughts.

"It will not grow here. It isn't dry and barren enough. This lavender grows in high, dry, rocky mountains."

"Where did you get the oil?"

"Sofia brought it to me from France. She occasionally travels to Europe to see her family." Juan Romero was once again reminded of his intention to visit Sofia and promised himself he would stop by to see her today. Abuela slowly mixed the compost with her hands and sang a song Juan Romero recognized from his childhood. *"Que bonitos ojos tienes, debajo de estas dos cejas. Que bonitos ojos tienes."*

"I remember that song," he said.

"It brings me peace," she replied.

"Where will this batch of compost go, Abuela?"

"The roses. Estela specifically asked for them."

"When did you talk with her?"

"I didn't. She simply asked." Juan Romero had known that Abuela was special, but they had never spoken of her ability to hear others' thoughts. If another *Hechizada* wanted to communicate with her she could easily hear them from far away without a word being uttered. Estela was one of the

Hechizadas that had been sent away to sell flowers abroad. It was part of the system that the group stayed together and handled the growing, shipping and selling of the flowers. They did not trust anyone else to handle the business. Partially because the *Hechizadas* were suspicious, but predominately because they believed that they had to know what kind of plant each person needed before selling it to that person and only *an Hechizada* could do that. "Help me load these sacks. We need to set to work before it gets too hot."

"Do the others know what to send Estela?"

"Of course *mi hijo*. We all communicate with her. It's not so difficult if you practice. We could all do it if we tried. *Las Hechizadas* have been taught to listen to the earth and the wind and the water and the sky. It's like learning another language."

"How many are left?"

"Thirty-two. There are six of us without heiresses to teach." Her eyes saddened thinking that her daughter would not know the truths the planet had to offer. "Help me lift these onto the platform. Edgar will be here soon with the llamas to transport the soil." They lifted in silence. Juan Romero knew it was best not to push any further about his mother, although he wanted to tell Abuela to save her. He wanted to shout at the top of his lungs that his mother was miserable living in the U.S. and that she shouldn't stay. Her life had deteriorated since his father died. She had worked three jobs, sold the house, and lived in a perpetual state of worry about how she was going to pay for simple things like milk, or gas or the phone bill. The wild spirit that once graced her home no longer existed and the warmth that was once her aura had transformed into a layer of indifference.

"Why don't you invite my mother to come stay awhile?" Abuela looked up, her eyes saddened.

"I have, many times. She doesn't want to come." In his mind Juan Romero knew it was that she couldn't, because of money and because of pride.

"Invite her again, Abuela."

"Maybe you should invite her *mi hijo*." He didn't respond and the conversation ended, but the idea still lingered.

CHAPTER FIVE

Heliotrope

Grief Stricken

Abuela climbed the stairs to Sofia's second floor apartment. She had missed work for a second day in a row, which was not like her. Abuela rang the bell.

"*¿Qui?*"

"*Soy yo, Esperanza.*" The door swung open but there was no one there. Abuela walked in to find Sofia sitting near the window staring at her geraniums. "Sofia, are you all right?" Abuela was cautious because she immediately realized it was not a physical ailment that was affecting Sofia. The young French girl turned her head to reveal her swollen face, one of deep sadness.

"*C'est ma mere,*" she muttered.

"Is she okay?" Abuela asked, knowing that she wasn't.

"*Elle est morte.*" Abuela approached Sofia and held her head in the warmth of her maternal belly as the tears of profound sorrow flowed. She did not have to ask. She knew it had been the cancer. Sofia's mother had been ill for more than a year and a half. It started as breast cancer and then moved into the rest of her body slowly. The treatment she was given prolonged her life, but she was in so much pain there were times Sofia prayed for a quick death. When a woman can no longer function, it is time for her to go. Sofia hoped that when death knocked on her own door she would not be afraid to embrace it and walk with her head held high into the darkness.

"I miss her so much. I should have been with her."

"You are happy here *mi amor*. She knew that."

"But she was my only family, Esperanza. Now I feel I have nothing."

"I know," Abuela whispered, thinking about the death of her beloved. She sighed and took Sofia's face in her hands. "But we must go on. You have a life in which you must participate. There are many things in this world's future that will need you. You must rise up after you have shed your tears and find the light to lead you forward. Your heart wants to give you permission to shine."

Sofia stood up and hugged Abuela with all of the strength her weakened spirit could muster. "*Te quiero Esperanza*. You are always here for me. Gracias."

"There is no need to thank me. We are family. We have always been such; it's just only now that we are able to be together. Now sit. I brought some food. Let's eat."

"And let's open a bottle of *ma mere*'s favorite—*Chateau Suplice*."

"Good idea."

As she rummaged through her mini-wine collection Sofia said, "So tell me about your grandson. He seems intriguing." Abuela smiled.

"You find him intriguing?"

"Yes. He is different. It's like a mix of American and Latino rolled up into one wild traveling package. He shows up here for vacation, I assumed, and now he is engulfed in the community as if it were his own."

"In a way it is. His mother is from here, I am from here, and the entire lineage on his mother's side is from here. It was his father who broke the line, and sometimes when that happens a child feels lost. I think Juan Romero knows that he has no true home, but this is as close to one that he has found so far."

"Home is where you make it Esperanza, not a place that makes you."

"Perhaps. In your case it seems to be. You're very at home here, but you've still brought things from your other homes, right?"

"Some, yes. I couldn't live without them."

"Thus you prove my point."

"But is that home or is that culture?"

"They are intertwined. One is not separate from another. Your home is part of your culture."

"If that is the case I should have stayed in France."

"No, because you also yearn for this culture. Not everyone fits into a box, into only one culture. Most of us do, but there are some who need variety. You, Juan Romero, perhaps my Esmeralda."

"Do you miss her?"

"Every minute of every day. When she left I tried to let go, but I couldn't. I've never been at peace with her leaving. Then when her husband was killed I was less at peace. She has struggled so hard to have a happy life and then they take love from her. She is in a place that is foreign to her, to me, to all of us, but she has chosen to stay there. I told her she could come home, but she refused. She has always been stubborn. When she did that I wondered if it was because she was happy there, but Juan Romero tells me she is not. That she works herself to death."

"I can understand that. Once you give up your childhood home it's hard to go back during difficult times. She is proving something to someone, maybe to herself. I think that's why I went home so rarely. I do regret it in some aspects, mostly because of mother. I would have liked to have learned more from her. She was an interesting woman, despite the alcoholism. That's why I ultimately left."

"Because she drank?"

"Because she didn't know where she was, who she was, and couldn't take care of me anymore. I remember when I was eight I came home from picking lavender in the fields. It was maybe two or three o'clock in the afternoon. She had been drinking for a couple of hours with one of her male friends. One of the ones who paid to drink with her," Sofia's eyes looked at Abuela with an expression of 'If you know what I mean.' "I put the flowers on the table and she flew into a rage. Half naked, she lunged for my neck and pushed it down on the table. The skin on my cheek split wide open. She hissed in my ear 'Why are you trying to steal my trick, *putain*?' I didn't move. I just let her hold my head, pressing it harder and harder onto the wood table until the man finally distracted her and she let me go."

"Doesn't seem like a peaceful place to be."

"It wasn't, but when she wasn't drunk she was wonderful. She liked to write poetry and read it to us. We would have poetry night every Tuesday night. We would sit around the fire and all listen to her lyrical poems. They were delicate, like dew on a petal after a soft rain. Nothing like her brusque personality as a drunken horror. Some nights she would even make fondue and we would devour the oozing warm cheese from its pot."

"If you had to do it over what would you change?"

"I would have brought her here to live with me."

"And if she didn't want to move?"

"I don't know. I'd like to say I would have gone back, but I don't think I would have. I love it here. This is my home now, regardless of where I was born. You're right."

CHAPTER SIX

Hibiscus

Femininity, sexuality, and warmth

The café wasn't busy when Juan Romero arrived in search of Sofia. He found her sitting at a table in the back of the room folding cloth napkins that she had just finished ironing.

"*Buenas tardes señorita,*" he ventured. Her round, green eyes rose from the table, but were in a distant place. "May I sit?" he asked.

"Hello Juan Romero. Yes, please sit. I could use the company," Sofia's hair was pulled back with one lone Hibiscus.

"My grandmother told me about your mother."

"She was very ill."

"I'm so sorry."

Sofia did not reply. A single tear rolled off her cheek and wet the napkin.

"There is nothing I can do now."

"Grieve."

"Odd advice," she said snapping her fingers for a second bottle of wine. Eduardo, a young employee rushed to the table and opened the bottle. "Do you like Beaujolais?"

"I don't know." She placed a glass in front of him and poured the pale red wine gently, pushing the glass into his hand.

"Try this." Juan Romero carefully sipped the wine and progressively took deeper gulps.

"You like it?"

"It's good."

"It is said it should be enjoyed soon after harvest to fully appreciate it."

"Where do you buy your wine, because there isn't much around here?"

"I bring it from Europe mostly, but I have a Chilean friend who ships cases from down south."

"I wanted to see you to tell you something," he said.

"What?"

"It's important not to block your emotions about your mother."

"I'm not."

"Maybe not, but please believe me, it's best if you share your pain with others. I didn't for a very long time and I suffered—and so did my friends and family."

"What happened?"

"My father was killed when I was 16."

"How did he die?"

"He was murdered." Sofia set her glass down and reached across the table for Juan Romero's hand.

"When?"

"I was 16."

"I'm sorry—what I meant was, how did it happen?"

"They think it was a gang, could have been a robbery."

"You don't sound convinced."

"There are strange circumstances surrounding his death, but they are more aligned with my own doubts and fears."

"What do you mean? What fears?"

"I never trusted my father's colleagues. They pretended they supported his work, his research, but he was too vocal. He wrote and lectured about disparity in politics and ethnicity, about despair, and he did not fear the corrupt people whom he criticized."

"What did he write about?"

"His primary field was Latin American politics. He focused on corruption and how it has infiltrated institutions to a degree, which he believed was ultimately irreconcilable. There were people in México who did not agree with his opinions. It would not surprise me to learn someone had him killed."

"I don't quite understand why."

"He was making connections that were not wanted to be made public. His research mirrored an investigative reporter more than a professor of Political Science. He meddled with information about relationships between government and corporations, which isn't looked upon fondly by Big Brother.

"American corporations are so powerful, more so than I first believed."

"Not just American, Sofia. Corporations are like mini governments wherever they are. Like the Canadian mining company coming into Aguas Puras to set up shop."

"It all seems like paranoia of the old men in this town, wanting to make something worse than it really is. We don't know what they are doing exactly."

"Don't underestimate the schizophrenic states, because often times they are closer to reality than one would like to believe."

"The company has very little support within the community and government circles."

"That hasn't stopped multinationals before."

"Maybe not, but I just don't believe it's worth their time and money."

"I guess we'll have to wait and see."

"It would ruin the flowers."

"What?"

"Mining. The seepage would contaminate our water supply and kill all of our flowers. Imagine, the harsh minerals gnawing at the life roots of the *flores hechizadas*."

"That's true."

"It's disgusting." An uncomfortable silence followed. Juan Romero changed the subject.

"So why didn't you go back to France?"

"No need really. Mum had everything arranged. She had been sick for so long." Sofia stood up and put a CD in the stereo.

"But don't you want to pay your respects? Visit her final resting ground?"

"No, not really. The truth is that my guilt is more about not being present for her passing. It's too late now.

A sweetly sad Argentinean tango fluttered through the windows, under the tables and chairs, and up through the pit of Sofia's stomach. She took a deep breath and pulled a pack of cigarettes out of the bag hanging on her chair, slid one into her hand, and lit it. Her next deep breath filled her lungs with sinfully juicy smoke. She held it inside for a brief moment and then released it slowly, one round cloud at a time.

"The world is shit Juan Romero," she said as she sat back down. "We're born, we suffer, and then we die."

"We live," he added.

"Not all of us. At least not fully. To live fully is to love in every aspect of our day. Uninhibited love of each quest we undertake, every person we encounter. There are not many people who do that."

"*Permiso* Sofia," interrupted Eduardo. "I'm finished and will be leaving now."

"Thank you, Eduardo. Could you lock the door behind you please? We'll be staying awhile."

"Of course," Eduardo left and the two of them sat in silence for several long moments. Juan Romero simply sat still with his thoughts, trying to discern whether or not what he had just heard had any merit, or if it was just the babble of a depressed woman. He looked at her hand caressing her wine glass, and his eyes followed the line of her arm up toward her supple breast and the exposed neckline. Her lips were pursed around the cigarette, the thin border of her nostrils flared, and her bedazzled green eyes penetrated him.

"What about you?" she asked.

"Not yet."

"But you try."

"Let's just put it this way—my failure to do so is not the result of a lack of effort."

"To love. Without inhibition, without discretion, without malice." Juan Romero ignored her and leaned in, slipped his hand around the nape of her neck, gently pulling her in to him with his other hand on the small of her back. He pressed his lips against hers, carefully whisking his tongue against hers. Slowly their mouths opened, consuming one another with a fury so desperate it was as if they had never known such passion. They tore at one another's clothes, knocking over chairs. Sofia pushed Juan Romero down onto the table and finished undressing him, slowly, with erotic movements of her hands, unbuttoning his pants and dropping her own. The heat irradiating off their bodies soaked the other with sweat, but they continued to eat each other up. The thrusts and the moans were so volatile that those living in the plaza were awakened with orgasmic smiles, trying to imagine, in their elated states, what it must have been like to have sex like the two young lovers. As they reached climax, Juan Romero began to cry and after releasing a shrilling scream, Sofia held his face to her mouth, kissing his cheek, licking his salty tears. As she swallowed she felt a sudden sense of peace in the images that came to her mind. They were images that only a pure soul can emit when it has opened itself up to another. She could see who he was, where he was going, and why in that moment she decided not to leave his side. She didn't utter a word, but she silently made a promise to herself. They lay together for a long time, holding each other.

"I have to go. Abuela is hosting a meeting tonight about the mines."

"Who will be there?"

"I'm not sure. Do you want to come?"

"*Oui*. Yes, I do actually." Sofia had an old beat up Honda motorcycle that chugged along its way through the misty evening. Juan Romero hung on to the back with his long legs pointing upwards toward the sky. Sofia rocked the bike back and forth around the rolling, winding road. Both of them were lost in thought—thinking of their lives in other countries, trying to work out what it was they missed and what it was they liked so much about this place.

When they arrived to Abuela's the driveway was lined with cars. The energy coming from the house was pulsating. Juan Romero could feel the anxiety. Sofia parked the *moto* near the front gate and they both stood, looking in at what must have been ninety women, sitting quietly in deep meditation. Abuela sat near her altar; the room was filled with natural candlelight. It was the loudest silent voicing of intention either of them had ever witnessed.

"It's '*Las Hechizadas*.'"

"Do you see any other men?" Juan Romero asked.

"Here we are son." A voice rose up out of the shadows. Padre Miguel and several other of the town's male residents were sitting in the garden smoking rolled tobacco and waiting. "We're not allowed in until they are finished. It's always been like this. Take a seat, they're just about through."

"What are they doing?"

"We don't really know. It is a kind of offering. That's all they will tell us."

Juan Romero approached the window to try to peek in but the closer he got, the harder it was to see. A thin veil of sage smoke filled the room. As he pressed his nose against the glass a bright blast of light exploded. Juan Romero jumped back and fell.

"I told you to just wait," chuckled Padre Miguel. "They don't like us to meddle."

"I was just curious."

"That was your first mistake, *mi'jo.*"

Shortly thereafter the front door creaked open and Abuela appeared in the shadows. Steam rose from her head and shoulders. She waved the men and Sofia inside. There was a hesitance at first, then Juan Romero stepped forward and the others followed.

"Sofia, I didn't know you were here. You could have joined us."

"I've just arrived Esmeralda, but gracias." The men filed in and found chairs or cushions to sit on. Juan Romero stood at the back of the room near the kitchen. Abuela made her way to the front, turned and raised her arms as if to embrace each person in the room. "We are here to save our valley," she began. "It is as simple as that. Those of you who are with us may stay. Any doubters should leave, because we have no room for wavering." She waited a moment or two, took a deep breath and let her arms fall to her side. "What kind of plan shall we initiate?"

"I was thinking we could negotiate with the mining company," began Padre Miguel.

"Negotiate what?"

"I've heard they aren't really strip mining," he replied.

"Did you not see the photos?" Juan Romero spoke up. "From what I've seen, they are strip mining, sir. No disrespect, but we cannot assume they are being courteous and respectful of the environment. It goes against their nature."

"What do you suggest Juan Romero," Abuela asked.

"I think we should protest, but go directly to the source. Block roads, stop work. We don't mess around. If we do they will walk all over us."

"And who will go all the way up to the mine for this?" Padre Miguel asked mockingly.

"I'll go," Juan Romero announced.

"I will too," said Sofia. And with that volunteer after volunteer signed up to trek into the mountains and directly confront the mining. Others volunteered to work the route through the capital and target politicians. The group began with its plans, making lists of supplies to take to the mountains, contacts to begin calling and writing, brainstorming different ways to attack the problem. There had to be rotations on the mountain, who would be in the thick of the mining operation protesting daily, support teams, political targeting teams, and media. The hum of the voices buzzed over the mountains.

"Sofia," Juan Romero motioned her over to him.

"What's up?" she slipped her hands in his.

"I don't want you to go to the mountains with us." Sofia pulled her hands away and her immediate reaction was one of anger.

"Why? Why do you not want me there? Do you think I'm too weak, incapable?" she raised her voice.

"Calm down," he whispered. "It's not that. I'm sure you are perfectly capable, but I'm worried about Abuela. With Octavio coming, she won't have anyone to count on. I am asking you to be that person. She is the most special individual in my life and I can't risk something happening to her." Sofia looked up in his eyes and realized he was telling the truth. Perhaps there was part of him that didn't want her to go, but his preoccupation with his grandmother was genuine and so she accepted. She would stay in town and work on the politicians.

CHAPTER SEVEN

Dogwood

Durability, life-giving power

It rained the first day the group began walking. Juan Romero estimated it would take them three full days with as many people that had joined. There were twenty-five men and ten women, including himself. Each person carried a small backpack with enough food for him/herself, a sleeping pad and bag, rain poncho, and one other communal piece of equipment—gas, parts of the stoves, tarps, etc. It was not an expedition, but they had to be prepared for the mountains. The trucks had dropped them at *kilómetro 9* on the river where they were to hike up the path to cross. They arrived at the cable-crossing where a solitary metal and wood cage dangled above the river. Only two people at a time would fit. Octavio would cross first and Juan Romero, last so they could assist in the coordination and physical work needed to pull the cage across with the long ropes hanging from either side. Two by two the group loaded and crossed, the rickety cage swinging back and forth above the river. Water rushed over rocks and the deafening roar let everyone know it had returned after a long dry season. What should have taken 15 minutes for a small group took an hour and 15 minutes. Juan Romero realized that every step of this journey was going to suck a small bit of energy from his source. Once on the wide path following the river up valley, however, he was rejuvenated by the appearance of the blue butterfly, and the light all of the sudden seemed brighter on that foggy day.

The trekkers were in good spirits, grabbing walking sticks from the brush and singing. It was as if they were on a camping trip together rather than embarking on a journey to save their way of life. That night the team found a series of caves to rest their heads. The largest was designated the cooking cave, and a small fire in the entrance kept their damp bones warm. Edgar prepared a soup of potatoes, quinoa, and chicken broth to evaporate the wetness of a long day's hike. Juan Romero remembered the flavor from somewhere else.

"I made it for you long ago," said Edgar.

"When?" replied Juan Romero.

"It was when you were a very young child, maybe two or three that you came to visit with your mother."

"I don't remember."

"Well your stomach does," Edgar smiled. His family came from the Quechua Indians, his father pure, his mother *mestiza*. His father worked as a tour guide in another part of the country, carrying equipment for adventurous men and women from abroad in search of God on top of the mountains. They often found that higher power they were looking for in the throat of a sleeping volcano or the gut of a solid ice crevice and discovered that the power of Mother Nature could connect their busy minds with the calming essence of their souls. While the tourists were weighed down with the most modern gear available, Edgar's father was adorned with a traditional hand sewn poncho and a wool cap. His feet were protected by rubber sandals.

The dawn came quickly and the team set out once again in the rain. They had to climb more than 2,000 meters in order to make it to the next campsite. It was cold and the altitude was slowing the pace, but Octavio did not let any of this dampen the spirits of the group. He began singing to keep everyone's mind off the freezing rain and slippery rocks. Lunch was impossible because there was no shelter to take the food out without soaking everything, so he passed out wads of coca leaves to suppress the appetite and buzz the body. Eleven hours after leaving camp they arrived, in the dark, to *Las Corrales de Gavidia*, named after a shepherd long gone. There was an old hut with a fireplace inside. The roof leaked so the group quickly hung tarps to stop the water from getting through. A fire was built and another soup was prepared.

"How much further?" A voice from outside floated in. Sofia's shadow stood in the doorway.

"What are you doing here? Is Abuela okay?" Juan Romero raced towards her.

"She's fine, but I can't stay away. It's my valley too. It's time I decided that. I'll only stay as long as it takes to see with my own eyes what is happening. I feel like I will be able to be stronger in my plight with the government if I know in my heart the destruction that is being done. Esperanza is fine. She as much sent me herself. I won't be gone long. So how much further," she stared him down so sternly that he was obligated to answer.

"We should be there by midday tomorrow."

"I hope it stops raining. The mountains can be so cold."

"I saw a hole in the sky," Octavio reassured her with a wink. "It will clear up." Juan Romero put an old sheepskin he had found in the corner around her shoulders.

"It's full of dust, but it will warm the skin." She pulled it up and wrapped it around her chest.

"Thank you." She brushed her hand across his cheek and accepted the mint tea, sipping the calming herb slowly, staring at the fire, trying to recall how she left Europe and why she was drawn to this man wrapping a dead animal skin around her, high in the mountains of the southern hemisphere. It was no longer a childish whim, an adventure to be had. It was deeper. She had stayed. She had a business and her mother was gone.

"This is my home now," she repeated.

"I know," Juan Romero said staring at her. His youth did not betray him, she thought.

"I'm 26," she said. He simply smiled, leaned over and gently kissed her cheek, then got up to help Octavio serve the rest of the group their meal. For as young as he was he did not act as such. His thoughts were restless, but concentrated, purposeful. The energy surrounding his body was powerful, attracting followers like a magnet. This power filled Sofia's body each time the essence of his body crossed her path. The clamor of people eating and talking snapped her out of her solitary daze, and she went outside to go to the bathroom.

Octavio was right. The sky had cleared and the moon was high in the sky, illuminating the wet rock and earth. Sofia made her way around the hut and squatted to pee. In her efforts to aim precisely and not urinate on herself, she hadn't had the chance to absorb the view, but as she began to settle in she lifted her head. Down valley, glowing like a white fire stood Chimborazo, the majestic volcano that was so large it seemed just a few steps away. She stood, pulled her pants up and gazed in awe.

"She's beautiful." Juan Romero came up behind her and put his arms around her waist; she settled into his embrace.

"More beautiful than I've ever seen her," she said, spinning around to face him. He slowly pulled her close to him, leaned in and kissed her so tenderly that her entire body fell into his arms.

CHAPTER EIGHT

Quatre Saisons Rose

Grown in Aphrodite's garden to be the true identity of love even amidst upheaval and change

The morning came more quickly than either Sofia or Juan Romero wanted. The warmth of their bodies snuggled next to one another was enough after the last coals of the fire had extinguished. Juan Romero's lingering kiss on Sofia's lips had kept her body warm all night. Octavio had already started the coffee when Juan Romero awoke. Several of the others were stuffing their backpacks.

"Heavy sleeper, aren't you Juan Romero?" Roberto said with a smile. "I haven't heard a snore like that since my days in the Amazon with the jaguars. You woke me up. I thought another one of those beasts was coming after my throat." Roberto ran a small *posada* in Aguas Puras, but he hadn't always been a businessman. It was after the attack that he returned to the village and opened shop. Roberto was a biologist by trade. He was on an expedition in the jungle to study the life cycle of the mahogany trees, when one night while he slept on the barge an adolescent jaguar made its way on board. Most probably nothing would have happened if he and one of the crew wouldn't have awakened, but they did and scared the animal. Actually, Roberto woke first to the sound of the cat scratching at one of the crates. The yellow eyes in the black night startled him and he jumped. The cat growled when he saw a crew hand, who trying to sneak up from behind Roberto with a rifle, scared the cat. Instead of fleeing, the jaguar leapt at the freakishly large shadow, tearing Roberto's abdomen and leg. It bit down on his shoulder, and took a chunk from his arm before the other man was able to shoot.

"*Perdón Don Roberto.* I am not always aware of the noise I can make," Juan Romero apologized.

"Don't worry son. It was too damn cold to sleep well last night," he winked at Juan Romero.

"We should get going if we're to make it all the way to the mine by nightfall."

"We eat and then hit the trail," Octavio said, not being one to miss a meal. The group was lucky on that third day, for the weather had cleared and the sun beamed down on the wet ground. Steam rose as the earth warmed and dried out. The trail was not as difficult, because they had climbed to just under the mine's altitude the day before. They wound their way along a narrow path, dry and relatively barren except for the *frailejones*, which speckled the mountainside with their silvery mint colored leaves, soft as velvet. It was rare to find them in this part of the country, but only near the valley could one be blessed with their presence thanks to a time when the *Hechizadas* decided to transplant some from the North. Shortly before dusk Octavio stopped in his tracks. "Do you hear that?" Everyone froze, hushing those coming behind. A dull hum filled the air, interrupted by the burps of a diesel engine.

"The trucks and bulldozers," said Juan Romero.

"Where are they, Juan Romero?"

"If I remember correctly they should be just over that mountain."

"We're too close." Octavio began scanning the hillside. "We must go back to the boulder field. We will spend the night there. Roberto, can you and Gerardo take everyone back?"

"Yes."

"Set up camp subtly. No tarps. If it rains we put them over our heads. Juan Romero and I will go scout out the route for tomorrow and meet you back there." They left the group and scaled the large rocks that had nestled themselves into precarious positions after falling from above. The noise grew louder and voices of men yelling to one another became apparent. They reached the top of the ridge, crawling on their bellies. Octavio peeked over first, and Juan Romero saw what must have been the same expression that bewildered him a week earlier. It was in-between shock and anger, enriched with a deep sadness. Octavio fell back behind the ridge and lay on his back.

"I don't understand why anyone would want to do this."

"Money, my friend."

"Money is not worth destroying the spirit of life on the planet."

"Not everyone understands what that is, Octavio."

"How can you not? If you've ever taken a breath of air or seen a creek rushing over rocks, or even heard a bird chirp, you have experienced her. These men have no excuse. They may be from cities, but look around us. Look at the pulsating of the forest and its animals. The clear sky, the driving rain." Tears ran down his cheeks as his monologue continued in a voice just louder than a whisper. Juan Romero lifted his head when he heard one of the workers shouting.

"It looks like they are calling it a day. Let's wait here until dusk when we can take a better look." The group sat in silence for almost forty-five minutes while the workers packed up their equipment and piled in the bus to go down the mountain. As the light dimmed, they made their way down to the site and crawled around like thieves scouting a building for a heist. They did not find much, except for what Juan Romero had already seen and taken pictures of. Access to the camp wasn't difficult. There were several paths that led in and out from the mountains. For cars, however, it was more limited. There was only one road in and out of the mine. Juan Romero noticed this immediately.

JOURNAL

Our "assault" on the mines was more violent than I had expected. We had not intended on having to physically interact with the workers, but the manager was aggressive. He began beating the herbalist, Lucas, Mariana's son, as soon as he sat down in front of one of the bulldozers. We screamed for him to stop but they kept coming at us, so we fought back. I suppose we should have sat there, in Gandhi-like style, but our natural reaction was to fight back. Metal tools and knives flew through the air. Shouts echoed through the valley. It all happened so quickly that it's hard to remember who was where and what was happening. I do remember the blast of a gunshot ringing in my ears and an instantaneous freezing of motion.

"¿Quienes son ustedes?" A booming voice broke through a small bullhorn. "¿Qué hacen aquí?" I moved forward with one arm in the air as the representative of the group.

I told him we were from Aguas Puras. His hat hid the light colored hair and pale, sunburned skin from far away, but as I got closer I realized he was not a local. "What do you want?" he asserted, shooting an eerily familiar demeaning glance at me.

"We are here to stop the mining." I remember proclaiming this as if I were declaring war.

The power I felt running through my veins was exhilarating. There was silence until his arrogant giggle rolled off the back of his throat into the early morning air.

"We have permits, everything is legal. You can't do a damn thing."

"My understanding is that the townspeople of Aguas Puras did not grant consent to this project."

"But the government of this country did and the landowner of this region is the federal government. I suggest you take your pathetic band of campesinos and leave the pits before someone gets hurt." His voice was stern and I believed him. I was about to turn to the group and tell them we should go, that we would re-group, when Sofia, sitting quietly next to one of the bulldozers lifted her hands in defiance. She began singing gently, a song by Mercedes Sosa—Gracias a la vida, que me ha dado tanto. Thank you to life, that has given me so much, and the chains wrapped around her waist and arms jingled and clanked against the metal she had connected them to. The foreman began screaming at her, and she simply smiled and kept singing. Others joined her chain and the man, who I later found out was Shawn Girlain, a Canadian in charge of the mines, began screaming orders for workers to attack us, to get us off the dozers, but at the first move we surrounded those chained to the machines and stood our ground. I'm not sure why the workers didn't move on us. It could have been the passion and fury in our eyes, or a sense of compassion, I'm not sure. All I am sure of is that an overweight man from the coast waved the workers back to their trucks and work. The team on "our" dozer was sent back to work with another group.

"You will not get away with this!!!!" Girlain yelled and stormed off toward a trailer in the distance. The man who had sent the workers back came up to us and told us we should back off, that things could get ugly. I told him how the mines would ruin everything the people of Aguas Puras live for. He knew the legends of the valley, but was convinced they were just that, legends. "I cannot protect you from him." He looked toward the trailer. "There is a lot of money here. Money is dangerous, you know?" I thanked him and extended my hand and shook the rough, fat hands of this gentleman who I knew would one day have to choose. We had to regroup. Those chained to the bulldozers stayed. After four days of confrontation Padre Miguel arrived.

CHAPTER NINE

Oleander

Caution, beware

"Juan Romero, I've been in touch with the Environmental Minister. He says there is little he can do. This company has paid off everyone and anyone. It doesn't matter what we do, corruption runs deep." Padre Miguel's eyes were red and puffy from lack of sleep.

"There must be something."

"We can file an injunction to stop the mining, but it could take months, even a year to do so. Even then, there is no guarantee."

"File it," Juan Romero said. "We at least have to look like we are trying to take legal means to stop this environmental rape."

Padre Miguel went to visit Carlos Santos, the town lawyer, in order to begin the legal process of stopping the gold mining, despite the fact that he knew this would do very little. Simultaneously, he gave Juan Romero the phone number of a man in Quito who was an expert in small, yet powerful raids. Jack O'Rourke was a former Irish Republican Army (IRA) bomb specialist, but had been self-exiled to South America after the murder of his daughter. Once before he had been to Colombia, recruited by guerillas to train them in urban warfare. He left the country shortly after an avid American photojournalist snapped his mug in the jungle, but the rawness of the untamed continent stayed in his blood and when he broke down at the sight of his family's feminine bloodshed he fled.

Padre Miguel knew him through a mutual friend in Quito—another exiled terrorist from the Basque country. Oddly, despite taking aliases and lying low, these men all knew one another and at times did contract work. Juan Romero traveled to the city, despite serious reservations, not knowing what to expect, or even what he was asking for. Sofia and the others were still in the mountains, chaining themselves to more pieces of machinery, enduring daily beatings. So far it was just a back and forth of powers of force and no one had been seriously injured. They had established radio contact, and he had sent supplies, but his anxiety levels were rising each day. He did not want her there. He wasn't sure why, but he knew she needed to be in town.

He met Jack at a bar called *El Corazón Frio*. It was dark and damp, lit only by gas lanterns running along the walls. It was lined with small round tables cramped together and was packed. He had been instructed to sit at the end of the mahogany bar closest to the bathrooms. When he arrived there was an overweight woman in a light blue dress sitting at the end of the bar. There was no one close to the description Padre Miguel had given him—extraordinarily tall, brownish-red curly hair that hangs around his shoulders, usually smoking a pipe full of sweet cherry tobacco. Juan Romero saw only the woman in the blue dress, so he took the stool next to her and ordered a whiskey on the rocks. An hour passed as Juan Romero awaited this mystery man, fending off irrelevant questions from the lonely woman. When he could no longer stand to wait any longer, (two and a half hours had passed), he asked for the check and left. He stopped at the door and felt someone behind him. As he went to turn around a voice said

"You're patient, but not enough. If you want to attack subtly you need to learn patience."

"And I suppose you will teach us that?"

"I cannot teach patience. It comes from free-will, which I assume you have or you wouldn't be here."

"We need help, that's why I am here. We are up against something that has no ears, no conscience."

"Government."

"Multinationals."

"Worse. Come, walk with me." They walked out into the rain and down the block while Juan Romero filled in the holes for Jack.

"You need non-lethal tactics," he interrupted.

"Preferably. Will they work?"

"You don't want to kill anyone?"

"No."

"Then they'll have to do."

"What do they entail?"

"Bombs, but set in places to destroy things, not people. The idea is to scare, not to do harm. If the workers are deterred the mining cannot move forward." Juan Romero stayed with Jack that night discussing tactics until it was decided Jack himself would travel to Aguas Puras, to help and he would do it for free.

"It's not often I offer my services for free, but Padre Miguel has helped me out of some difficult situations." Jack would travel within the week. Juan Romero returned to recruit more people to take into the mountains and to block the road, which is what Jack would hit first.

Abuela was mixing a remedy for a neighbor when Juan Romero returned to the house. It smelled of orange essence and honey. She moved a long, wooden spoon slowly around the edges of the earthenware pot. She sprinkled in a hint of mint right before removing it from the heat.

"She has a deep cough and hot rash," Abuela said without turning around.

"I'm glad you're still able to help."

"The water is turning rancid. What did you find?"

"They have begun mining, with the government's consent."

"They paid."

"I assume."

"We can't pay."

"We shouldn't have to." Abuela turned, her eyes angry and wet with tears.

"Life is not about shouldn't or couldn't, it just is."

"Abuela," he crossed the kitchen and held his grandmother. "We're doing what we can. Padre Miguel has some influence. We've started the blockade. Octavio and Sofia are there now."

"How is he?"

"He'll be fine. He's strong."

"He's been with me for so long. I don't want to lose him," her pain deepened with these words.

"Why would you lose him?"

"Money is power, which can be evil Juan Romero."

"The point is to stop it before it gets out of control."

"It seems to me that women chained to bulldozers is already out of control."

"I'm sending reserves in the morning. I've also written a letter to Silvia to see if she can help us get some international environmental groups involved. If we can get some press coverage it might help."

"I just want peace. This valley has a history of bloodshed. It isn't often, but every several generations there is fighting, which leads to death."

"There will be no death, Abuela. We want peaceful protests." He didn't mention Jack to Abuela, although he suspected she knew. He didn't want to have to use Jack, but his gut was telling him that the pressure it would put on the company would be much more forceful than townspeople protesting.

"It always starts that way, but the human ego gets out of control and forgets the value of life," she whispered.

"I'll do what I can." Juan Romero tried to reassure Abuela, but there was little he could say to convince her. He didn't believe what he was saying himself, and she sensed as much. He did mail the letter to Silvia with high hopes she would be able to get someone to pay attention. Included in the padded envelope were some of his black and white prints.

Dear Silvia,

It has been several months since I last wrote. I can only ask you to forgive my inconsistent communication. You'll be happy to know that Abuela is well, but the town is struggling. I have learned so much about who the people are and how they have survived all these years without depending on subsidies or industry. The truth is that I never thought about any of these things before I left home. My reality revolved around our own family, our own politics, economy, and education. We were rarely exposed to anything outside our sheltered lives and at some level I am grateful to mamá for that. All of her struggles after papá died were to protect us, and she continues to do it. Life is impacted by one's surroundings and we believe that those surroundings are our entire world. I've come to understand that each pocket of people, each community, has an impact on another. For this reason I write.

There is conflict in Aguas Puras that cannot be resolved by one person. We are in the midst of trying to stop a Canadian mining company from cutting away the mountains, therefore contaminating the resources that support the flower industry and habitat in the valley. The company, Maple Mining, has bypassed local authorities' wishes to NOT mine gold from the mountains and has paid the federal government large bribes to obtain access and permits. About a month and a half ago I was hiking and accidentally stumbled upon the mine. I took photographs and brought them back to town. The uproar has ignited a passion to stop the mining. Somehow I became directly involved by volunteering to lead a group to the site. None of us knew what we were going to do, but when we arrived a fight broke out. The workers, who are from all over the country, but not this area, were not happy about a local rebellion. Could be they know how dangerous a group of rural people can be to a project and thus fear losing their work, or maybe the company has brainwashed them into thinking the mines are the best source of income for the local economy. I really don't know, but I do know that whatever it is, they believe their jobs are more important and are willing to defend them. As I write to you several of Abuela's friends and neighbors are chaining themselves to machines high in the mountains. No word of whether Maple will talk with us has come through, despite several efforts by a local priest. I am afraid this is going to be a longer and more difficult struggle than anyone anticipated.

With all of this in mind, I need for you to find anyone from any willing environmental group to listen to this story. I've enclosed some photos so you can convey the gravity of the environmental destruction. I think contacting the media liaison for a green group would be the most direct route. This must all seem so abstract to you, but if we don't do anything Abuela could lose everything. All of her herbal remedies and recipes will become part of a book, but never realized again. Her flower harvesting will cease to exist. Everything she lives for will dissipate slowly, like a low hanging fog fighting the sun's heat. There are many like her who will also lose their means of income, their way of life, their happiness.

My intuition tells me that Maple will not go bankrupt without this mine. Gather as much information as you can on them and send it to me ASAP. I'm leaving for the mine in two days' time, but should be back no later than three weeks from today. Thank you for your help Silvia. My selfishness in not inquiring about you is only precluded by my obsession with justice. I hope, however, that you are at peace.

Love,
Juan Romero

CHAPTER TEN

Snapdragon

-Presumption, desperation

The fog was hovering low in the valley following the afternoon rain. Padre Miguel had just been to the bakery to pick up the bread for communion the next day. The bell on the door jingled as he left, his arms full.

"*Chau Angelica.*"

"*Chau Padre.* See you tomorrow."

"*Hasta luego.*" He walked slowly down the street inhaling the fresh air that crisply penetrated his lungs. It was so clean, pure like an untouched mountain stream. He rounded the corner after crossing the plaza and was walking home when he heard someone call him.

"Psst. Padre Miguel." Standing in the dark doorway of an apartment was a young man with a tan bolo hat and a light brown, tattered cotton jacket. Padre Miguel turned.

"*¿Si?*"

"Can you come in? I need to talk with you about something."

"Who's there? Do I know you?"

"No sir, I'm from out of town, but I need a priest's advice and was told you could help." Instinctively Padre Miguel was uncomfortable going in, because it was rare that he did not know someone in the community. He should have told the young man to follow him to the church, but he didn't. He stepped inside the doorway and was instantly grabbed from behind. A heavy hand slammed him on the head and wrapped an arm with a snake-like grip around his neck, covering his mouth with a handkerchief. The bread fell to the ground, some of it rolling into the street. He was shoved from behind and felt several sets of hands on him, grabbing him, dragging him down the hallway. A door opened and illuminated the hall, and he was shoved head first to the floor, ripping his trousers at the knee. The door slammed behind him.

"We were sent to order you to stop these ridiculous protests," rang a voice from behind Padre Miguel. He looked up to see four men with pantyhose covering their faces.

"Who are you?"

"I told you." A swift kick to the priest's ribs quickly established the objective of the visit. "We were sent to make it clear that the protests must stop or things are going to get bad."

"They aren't going to stop." Another kick, but this time in the stomach. Padre Miguel curled up, groaning.

"The mining will continue, fool. There is too much money for them to have to give it up for a bunch of peasant flower farmers."

"This valley has special friends, and it will not die without a fight. I cannot control the will of the people."

"You will control it," the voice said as another man lifted the father's head and repeatedly slapped his face, "or you will die, sir." They hit him several times in the face and head, painting bloodied and bruised pictures of the cowardly work. They continued to beat him until the vocal priest lay almost unconscious on the floor. "We will be back in a week," Padre Miguel heard before he blacked out. The men removed their makeshift masks and the one who had lured the activist clergyman into the trap signaled for the others to bring the limp body to the entrance. They propped him up and left him in the cold night air to bleed. If it weren't for the fact that Pablo, the town's only drunk and vagrant, was wandering down the street and stumbled upon the scattered bread, Padre Miguel might have died that night. As Pablo knelt down and gnawed on the holy sacrament, his eyes wandered and fell upon a leg sticking out of a door jam. He crawled over to find the priest lying beaten and alone. The normally inebriated bum was shocked into a sobering mode of crisis management. At first he tried to wake the man covered in blood, and when there was no response he began screaming at the top of his lungs.

"*Auxilio!* Help! Padre Miguel is dead! He raced as best he could up and down the street until lights flickered on and people funneled into the street. He grabbed the first person he saw and hysterically repeated, "He's dead! Come, come. I think he's dead!"

The gentleman followed Pablo, believing he was so drunk he was hallucinating, but Pablo was utterly distraught and this made the neighbor curious. As they approached the door, the man saw the same leg that had set Pablo off. He ran toward the priest.

"It's true," he shouted. "It's Padre Miguel, but he's not dead, just badly beaten. Someone help me get him to the clinic." The people banded together instantly to help the priest. They loaded him in the back of a yellow pick-up and raced to the clinic. Socorro, the only nurse in town, was on duty, but Doctor Perez was not. He was out of town visiting relatives in the North. Socorro quickly cleaned and dressed his wounds while the crowd outside began to grow. Padre Miguel was still unconscious. When Sofia heard the news she made her way to the clinic and pushed through.

"Socorro," she hollered in hysterics. "What happened?"

"He was beaten, Sofia. He hasn't regained consciousness, and it's hard to say if he has internal bleeding."

"Who did this?"

"We don't know. Pablo found him. *El doctor* returns tomorrow. I'll try to keep him stable until then. He seems okay. His blood pressure is normal; so is his respiration. That's all I can do."

"Can I stay?"

"Yes. Of course." Socorro left Sofia with Padre Miguel to tell the crowd outside his status. Sofia sent for Abuela who brought a salve to cover the cuts. A message was sent to the mountains. It took several days for Juan Romero to reach the clinic and by that time Padre Miguel was out of danger, but still very weak.

"Juan Romero," Padre Miguel spoke slowly and softly.

"I'm here, Padre. I came as quickly as I could."

"I'm fine. Thanks to your grandmother and her charms." Abuela had spent a day and a night with the injured man, washing his forehead with *neroli* oil to soothe his exhaustion and brought ginseng root and lotus flowers to inspire clarity of thought in hopes he would remember. She bathed him in sweet chamomile to ease his aches and she read poetry from her own works to keep his thoughts from repeating themselves and reminding him of his recent misfortune. "They were sent by the mining company, or so they said." This was the first he spoke of the incident. "They seemed more like hired thugs to me."

"Government."

"Maybe."

"I never thought they would hurt anyone behind our backs."

"Get used to it. I believe I'm not the last."

"What can we do?"

"Continue fighting. Don't let this stop us. We must remain united. My safety is not as important as centuries of healing. Remember that." And while Juan Romero wanted to listen to the father's words, it was hard for him to separate the present violence from the bigger picture. It wasn't until he read further in his *Milagros* book that he was able to go on. His uncle had written only one passage in the entire book, but it was the one that Juan Romero needed to continue. It seemed simple. He told the story of how a young girl came up to him on the street. She asked him for money to eat. Instead he gave her food. Later that day he saw the child on the sidewalk in front of a house. A large man was hitting her, yelling at her for not bringing home the cash he wanted. When the man finished disciplining her, Juan Romero's uncle ran up to her.

"Are you okay?" She looked up at him and said,

"Yes, because I'm not hungry this time." He realized while what he had done had caused pain for the child, it was also a step towards alleviating her suffering. If he could continue to do that, he was doing the right thing. It was with small steps that the greater good happened.

When Juan Romero arrived at Sofia's café it was bustling. People were worried and stressed about the growing conflict. Men and women came and went to the protest lines, relieving one another at the mining site. Tensions were running higher and the employees at the mine were beginning to lose patience.

"A truck full of workers almost killed us last week," a young man shared. "We've been picketing along the road to try and stop them from taking loads out. We stalled many of the shipments, but haven't yet stopped them. The other day we created a chain and we were singing. No trucks had come or gone. It was Friday though, and those men wanted out of there. A truckload of them came rolling slowly down the road. As they got closer we heard their shouts, insulting us, threatening us. We stood our ground. I was on the left side of the chain, and I remember hearing the driver rev the engine. At first I thought it was to scare us, but I immediately realized it was coming full force at us. Octavio yelled, 'Stand your ground.' It was then that everything slowed down for me. The shouting, the sound of screaming brakes, and the images of bodies flying in all directions. The truck swerved off into the ditch and rolled onto its side. We scattered, heading for the hills to hide. No one was hurt, but the truck had driven up over a rock before it rolled into the ditch and left the transmission on top of the rock. The men were cursing and kicking the truck and each other. Fortunately we all escaped, but their anger was felt even at our own camp several miles away."

"Things are not getting better Juan," Sofia said as she poured two glasses of white wine.

"I know." Juan Romero was becoming increasingly worried. Negotiation attempts with the company had failed, and the government had placed armed soldiers around the mining site's business trailers. "Those soldiers are not a good sign."

"Soldiers never are. They are supposed to instill a sense of safety for the people, but in my experience they instill a sense of fear."

"Sofia," the chef hollered. "I'm going. I'll lock the door behind me."

"Thanks!" she shouted back. "Alone at last. It seems like weeks since I've seen you."

"Alone." She walked over to his chair with the glass of wine in her hand and spread her legs so she could sit on his lap. Her breasts glistened with sweat from a long night's work and dangled in front of his lips. She wet her finger with wine and gently rubbed it across his mouth, drawing his tongue to hers. His hands attacked her body, seeking every opportunity to undo a button or remove a strap until she sat in front of him half-naked in the dimly lit café. His shirt wide open, he pressed his chest against hers, then lifted her up onto the tile-topped table behind them. Her arms swept across the table, sending half filled glasses and empty plates crashing to the floor. They took each other and melted into one. From the table to the floor, to the top of the bar, sitting, standing, lying down, forwards, backwards, and upside down they made love until they could not move anymore, putting the darkness of the night and the times behind them, looking for the light the new day would bring.

CHAPTER ELEVEN

Sunflower

Self appreciation, actualization, opportunity

The noise of clinging wine glasses and bottles of whiskey filled the restaurant. Padre Miguel sat alone, near the window, waiting for Cristian Cruz, a government goon who was the link between the higher ups and the "commoners" such as him. They had set the meeting several months earlier to "negotiate" the contract at the mine, Padre Miguel naively thinking he could convince the mine to do minimum damage while at the same time receiving payment that he could put into the church's work in the valley. He was mistaken. The government had no interest in supporting a valley of what they called "peasants." In their minds the flower industry was a drop in the bucket of monies that through corruption they could inherit, therefore, not a priority.

"There will be no deal Miguel," Cristian blatantly announced.

"We have to work something out Crisitan. Things are getting out of control and I cannot allow my people to get hurt."

"Then make them stop."

"I can't. I can only try to persuade them, but they won't listen. The flowers are important. They will defend them to the death."

"So be it, to the death," his toothy grin emitted a rotten smell. Padre Miguel did not know what else to do.

"There is nothing that can be done?"

"Nothing." Padre Miguel looked down and then stood up to leave. "Unless we can work out access to another community?"

"What do you mean?"

"There are more mining sites, sites that are ripe for the picking, sites without people who believe they have power."

"That's not right," Padre Miguel frowned.

"It's not about right and wrong my friend, it's about money. Those peasants don't know anything. In the grand scheme of things what are they worth?"

"They are human beings."

"That didn't stop you before."

"That was different."

"Not so different. Disappearing a person because she is pregnant doesn't seem very Christian, does it?" Padre Miguel's heart began to pound. He never should have become involved with this man. He knew his actions were unforgiveable, that he was damned to hell for eternity, but he was trying to reconcile this by helping Juan Romero, by serving Aguas Puras.

"May God bless you my son. You will need it." He stood up from the table and began to walk away.

"No Padre, you are the one who will need God's forgiveness. I never pretended I was pure of heart. I've been headed for hell for a long time, but at least I'll not be tormented while on earth." His wicked smile made Padre Miguel's stomach churn.

While Padre Miguel was in Quito, Juan Romero continued their plight in the mountains. The light was warming the early morning sky, burning a rust orange glaze over the peaks. Juan Romero was the only one up. He had not slept at all, and his stomach twisted like the knots of a tree that has spent its life avoiding high winds. The sun rose faster and faster, rapidly bathing the camp with the morning. The air was still and silent, but within seconds of noticing the eerie calm of nature, the explosion rocked the canyon. It sent vibrations straight to Juan Romero's midsection, the pounding of a tympani drum in the back of his throat, followed by the scattering of rocks and debris scraping the side of the mountains, rolling down the hill toward the river, crushing everything in their path. For one instant it was only Juan Romero, the explosion, and then the chaos broke loose. Screams rose up from the tents and people running out, half naked to see what had just happened. The frantic state allowed no one to identify what was going on. Juan Romero stood calmly on the ridge above, observing, peering through the binoculars at the mining camp on the opposite side of the valley. They, too, were oblivious to the recent blast that would leave them trapped for the time being. No other road for vehicles led in or out of the mine. They would have to clear it themselves, and rebuild it, much like during the rainy season at lower altitudes. For the first time in months Juan Romero smiled, feeling although guilty, satisfied at stabbing a small knife into the belly of the beast. He turned and ran down the hill yelling for calm, racing through the camp calling a meeting on the south side. Flurries of questions flew through the air.

"Calm down. Everyone to the south side, now." He slowed his pace and marched through the tents and tarps that were pitched like paint splattered across the mountainous canvas. Upon reaching the south end he stood firmly on top of a small boulder, his back to the sun. "The noise you just heard was an explosion," he announced.

"Where? From what?"

"It was a bomb, detonated on the road at kilometer six. We set it to create a block so trucks can't get through." His words hung in the air like heavy clouds about to release a downpour. Everyone stared blankly at him. "We're in contact with someone who has experience with this kind of work, and I gave the go ahead." Octavio stepped forward amidst the silent confusion.

"I can't say I'm comfortable with this. It is terrorism."

"It's only terror if we kill someone. These attacks are not and will not be designed to target human life."

"I assume this expert of yours will be training us," Gerardo said.

"For what?"

"To prepare for retaliation. To fight back when it does happen. He can't do it alone."

"He's right, Juan Romero. We must know what to do."

Juan Romero was silent for a minute and then said, "You're right. Anyone interested can come talk with me at my tarp. We're not only protesting here anymore. It's going to be more active, aggressive. Peaceful protests will be moved down the mountain near town to avoid violence, if possible. All of those who don't feel comfortable with being here should go. Anyone else may stay. No one is required to do any of it. This is hard and it's going to get harder. Think of your families and your work. Think of yourselves. We need to decide today so we can move the camp. We're not safe here anymore." He turned and went to his tarp. Gerardo and Octavio followed after a few minutes. The three sat in silence while Juan Romero brewed coffee.

"You should have consulted us first," Octavio broke the silence.

"The decision had to be made."

"True, but not at the risk of losing lives, or even livelihoods. You've single-handedly changed the nature of this conflict."

"With the consent of Padre Miguel."

"Padre Miguel is not God, nor is he the only person in this town, Juan Romero." Octavio's voice changed from what was a normally calm, concessionary voice, to that of an older, wiser man clearing the fog for a young counterpart.

"I thought it was the best route."

"You thought without thinking. What happens if they turn even more violent? We may not want to kill anyone, but they do."

"It's a chance we have to take."

"No, it isn't. Death is something we do not choose. It chooses us, and you had no right to pretend to mark our paths towards an unknown destiny."

"Yet if we don't move in this direction, the chances are they might, and at least now we have the upper hand," interrupted Gerardo. They both looked over at the Argentine, sipping his black coffee. Octavio nodded his head.

"You both come from violent histories. Your home countries are designed for this. Aguas Puras also comes from a violent history, but our objective is to not repeat our history. I don't agree with taking the path of such extreme violence, but what is done is done. It's too late." he stared straight into Juan Romero's eyes. "Don't do it again without consulting the others. Do you understand?" Juan Romero acknowledged his understanding by bowing his head and nodding. Octavio stood and walked away, still angry, but in control.

"Do you think I shouldn't have done this on my own, Gerardo?"

"Things happen. People make choices. I for one probably would have done it, but Octavio is from here. He knows more about his people than we do. It's probably best to follow his advice."

"Yeah, you're right. What am I doing?"

"Leading."

CHAPTER TWELVE

Pomegranate

Life and fecundity

The group had grown to 38. Jack had arrived 45 minutes after the explosion. He helped move the primary camp, which they relocated several thousand feet below the mine near a cave. The rainy season was on its way, and they knew life would be miserable and cold for the next few months. Juan Romero helped moved those who initially volunteered and sent Gerardo back with the others. The mining company thought it was a minor earthquake that triggered the landslide that took out the road. It believed this because it was logical, and the area did not have a history of any sort of corporate terrorism, not even guerilla warfare. It had always been a peaceful area, and that is primarily why Maple chose the region. This was fortunate for the group, because it gave them time to regroup, as well as the element of surprise for the second attack. This wouldn't last long. It would only be a matter of time before someone stumbled across the explosives somewhere.

"The lot where the trucks are kept is the next target," said Jack. "The fewer means they have to move the product the more difficult, expensive, and frustrating their work becomes." The mining camp was a series of temporary trailers and tents. The trailers for the bosses, the tents for the workers. Sprawled across the mountainside were trucks and bulldozers, picks and shovels, tools to strip the land of her treasures.

"We blow up bulldozers and trucks, Juan Romero, and we're crossing the line into a new kind of battle," said Octavio. "Why can't we put dead sparkplugs in their trucks, disengage their activity without blowing shit up?"

"I know my friend, but our meager protests have done nothing. Can't you see they see us as a bothersome fly buzzing around their ear, but not a force to be reckoned with? It's time to move forward. If we don't, our water will become poisonous."

"It's too late for that," a feminine voice stepped forward.

"Sofia, how did you find us?"

"I saw Gerardo on the trail up. He told me where you were." Juan Romero regrouped himself and continued with his monologue, trying to ignore his discomfort that Sofia had trekked several days alone and was about to be exposed to his secret violence.

"As I was saying, the water's purity is precious."

"And as I said, we're running out of time, Juan Romero," again Sofia spoke up.

"Say what you've come to say, Sofia. It's obvious I won't be able to finish if you don't." His tone tried to be stern as if to challenge her presence, but was unsuccessful.

"I come to share with you that things are not as tranquil as you believe. I've been sent with a message from Padre Miguel." She held out her hand to pass the folded paper to Juan Romero. He took the letter and opened the sheet. "Read it aloud," she insisted.

Juan Romero,

My trip to Quito was not as successful as I had hoped. It appears that we are on our own and that the fate of our flowers is once again up to us. The town is experiencing something it has been privileged to avoid for its entire history, military occupation. Don't be startled for there has yet to be any violence on the soldiers' part, yet this step by Maple to secure military aid can only mean one thing. They are prepared for a long fight. People are feeling unsettled, anyone would with armed adolescents patrolling the streets. It isn't that we have anything to hide, but the mere presence of these young men generates the natural instinct to retreat indoors. Many do not want to be seen for fear of being approached. These pre-pubescent boys ask the most impertinent questions simply to instill paranoia. Sofia is the only one to keep her doors open after dark. The pool hall does too, only because it is frequented by the soldiers and they ordered Ruben to stay open.

I send this message, not only to inform you of the latest occupation, but also to alert you to the fact that contamination of the water headed for the southern plains has been confirmed. There have been minor cases of nausea, vomiting and a handful of miscarriages. The water was tested and contained high levels of cyanide. It's beginning to leak; it's beginning to penetrate not only the ground and the water, but everything that lives.

Although the situation grows increasingly tense, I urge you to push forward, if not for your grandmother and her traditions, then for the decency of the people of this valley. If we continue to let this global corporate manipulation continue, we will be doing a disservice to all of those who cannot stand up for themselves. Sofia has asked I send this photo sent to me by the priest in Cojines, the town experiencing contamination. Read the note on the back.

Go in peace and with God.
Miguel

Sofia handed over the photo.

"What is it?" Octavio asked.

"Children playing near the river." He flipped it over, but found no note as Padre Miguel had indicated. He looked up at Sofia.

"This is the picture with the message." She held out a second photo. It was of a young boy lying in a bed in a humbly maintained hospital. The note on the back read: "Miguel, the first photo is of the children of my village near the river playing in pools of what they thought was mystical liquid. It turned out it was an illegal dumping pool for mercury. This photo is Ignacio Catarana dying in the hospital. He was so severely poisoned that he has remained in a vegetative state for two months. Stop them before it's too late." Juan Romero said nothing. He merely stood in front of the group, staring at the photo of an empty-spirited young boy. He knew this was more powerful than what he had expected to handle. He was being faced with a situation that impacted social, economic and environmental ideologies, which he, in truth, knew very little about.

"Ideologies mean nothing without people to carry them out," his father once told him. "They are useless rhetoric."

"If we are to step up the pressure, then the parking lot is the perfect target," Jack intervened and broke the uncomfortable silence. Juan Romero took a step back and let his comrade take over the conversation. Sofia took his hand and led him away from the group. They sat atop a pile of large boulders, overlooking the valley.

"Thank you for the message. I would have preferred someone else bring it up though. You shouldn't have come alone."

"I actually insisted," she answered. "There is something else I must share with you," she paused and looked at the man she admired so deeply she couldn't admit it publicly, nor even completely to herself.

"What is it?"

"I'm pregnant." Juan Romero didn't respond. He continued to look out into the night sky. "Did you hear me?" her voice was nervous.

"Yes." He still didn't elaborate, or move.

"You doubt it's yours," she stated.

"Not unless you tell me to." He finally turned to her. "I'm sorry. I'm shocked. I wasn't expecting this at all."

"Neither was I, but I've had time to absorb the idea. You haven't."

"How far along are you?"

"Six weeks."

"And you hiked up here alone?" he criticized.

"I'm pregnant, not handicapped."

"It's dangerous Sofia, that's all I'm saying."

"You needed to know and not via second hand messengers. I'll leave in the morning."

"What will you do?"

"Continue protesting. I've started a blog and we're going to the capital again, this time to Maple's South American offices. We've organized a rally and I think it might help."

"I don't want you there. What if things get out of hand?"

"I will be fine. If I stay I will go mad thinking about you here and the fact that I am not doing anything to stop the deterioration of the one place in the world that has brought me so much happiness and love. I have to help find peace for my friends and now my future family." Juan Romero leaned in and kissed Sofia lightly on the lips, caressing her pale brown freckles.

"I love you," he whispered.

"I'm glad," she answered. They sat in silence for a long while, listening to each other's breath, trying to discern the other's thoughts, making plans for the future. It was the bitter voice of Jack that interrupted their innocent and pleasurable thoughts.

"Juan Romero." He was startled out of his fog. "I need to go over strategy with you if we're going to hit the target day after tomorrow." Sofia took Juan Romero's hand and squeezed it, asking him not to go. He lifted it to his lips and pressed her palm to his mouth.

"My gear is set up at the back of the cave. Go lie down. You'll need your rest." He stood and left the new mother alone, hesitantly walking off with Jack.

"Women are dangerous," Jack commented as he spread the map out on the portable table that was used for everything from holding planning meetings to serving coffee and dinner.

"Especially when you love them," Juan Romero joked.

"I'm serious Juan Romero." He changed his tone. "They are an attachment that inhibits clear thinking, reason, and proper work ethic."

"Sofia is part of this too, Jack, whether you think she should be or not."

"Right now she is, but when this situation becomes more violent, more dangerous you are going to be distracted by her and how to protect her. It's best to let her go before something happens."

"You are too cynical for my taste, Jack."

"I'm a realist." He hung his head over the map and turned his headlamp up a notch. What he had not shared with Juan Romero was his own unfortunate history. It's part of why he ended up as a rogue consultant in South America. In the early 90s Jack had been part of the IRA explosives team in Dublin. His wife and two daughters were aware of his activity with the IRA, but did not know he was directly linked to building and planting bombs. He had been, in fact, responsible for the murders of hundreds of people in Ireland and England. The source of Jack's embitterment was that in early May of 1993 he and his wife were to take their twin girls to Paris as a graduation gift. The trip would take them through London, where Jack decided to help implement a pub attack. It was a small job, which he could do in an afternoon. He would not have to see the explosion through, simply build, place, and arm the bomb. He met the team on a Thursday afternoon and carried out his duties. It was to be detonated that same evening. At around 7:30 his wife and one of his daughters stepped out for a walk to try to find a suitable place for supper. Jack and his other daughter stayed behind. It wasn't long after the two women had left that the phone rang. The bomb, which was scheduled to be blown at 8:03, was not armed. He grabbed a sweater and told her he would be back shortly. He ran downstairs and caught a taxi to a building a block and a half away from the pub. In his haste he did not notice that his daughter had followed him. She, out of the three women, had always been curious about her father's late night escapades, at some level believing he had a lover. Her insatiable appetite for the truth drove her into the street that night.

Jack held the taxi as he climbed three flights of stairs to the remote room where his team could see the pub. It was a simple error in the codes that had prohibited the bomb from activating, and Jack corrected them within ten minutes. Meanwhile, his daughter had ordered her taxi driver to stop on the next block so as to observe her father from a slight distance. When he came down, he sent his taxi straight ahead so he could get one last look at the perfect British pub. As the car passed, he saw the second taxi parked only a few feet from the pub entrance. And then time began to slow as he realized that the passenger was his daughter. Though she had bowed her head as he passed he caught a glimpse of her face. As the taxi turned the corner and accelerated Jack looked down at his watch, 8:02:59. "Stop!" he screamed. The car shook and the driver swerved. Piercing fear, shattering glass, and fire filled the air, followed by utter stillness. He stumbled out of the car and tried to make his way to the blast site, but the taxi was ablaze and his driver pulled him to the ground. There was no saving her. He arrived at the hotel shaky and pale.

When Jack's wife asked where their child was, he turned on the television to images of a burning bar in the middle of London.

"Everyone inside the pub was killed," said the reporter. "The blast even reached a few people on the street, including this taxi. Miraculously the driver lived, but the passenger, who he says was a young Irish woman, did not."

It was then that Jack's wife understood. She comprehended his entire life, who he was, and what he had just done. According to Jack, who rarely recounts the story, she went into the bathroom, threw up, took her purse and her passport and her second daughter and left. She left for Paris and never returned. He spent countless months trying to find her and finally did, living on the Left Bank. He followed her for several weeks until he knew she was safe, then he vanished. It was after this that he went to Colombia. One would think his own pain would have made him change, but the taste of blood was part of his identity and he knew no other way of living.

"I've constructed four bombs to be placed in these four spots," he pointed to four marks on the map. "We will have to get in and out quickly and silently. At the moment there are two guards in this area. If they hear or see us this effort is over. You will take two men to plant the bombs, two as lookouts. You will be in and out in ten minutes. We will place them at 2:30, which is right before the guard change, so we will catch them at the end of the shift, when they are tired."

"What time do we detonate? I don't want people around."

"2:37, but there could be guards there."

"I don't want anyone there," Juan Romero insisted.

"Impossible."

"The guards are switching, so the likelihood of anyone being there is slim."

"They will be far enough away so as not to get hurt?"

"Perhaps."

"They go off after the guards leave. Not a second earlier."

"Your thin skin will be your downfall."

"It's not thin skin. It's compassion. What has ever come of death but pain? All of our freedoms and privileges have come at the expense of death and sacrifice."

"That's the way the world works."

"Not anymore."

"Whatever you want. This is your battle, not mine." Jack turned off the headlamp. "Good night." Juan Romero took his journal and sat with a candle.

Silvia,

Why does life always present itself when death and destruction are the order of the day? Sofia is pregnant and I want to be excited about it, but I find myself concerned. What will happen to innocence in a time when we can barely maintain civil relations with one another? I dare not allow fear to enter into the equation, because even though every new parent experiences fear it goes unspoken. Then there is Jack. This man has no sense of the value of human life. It's as if he has seen death so frequently that it has become part of his daily routine, part of the monotony of his life. This, too, scares me. What if I lose control of all of this? What will happen then? I have faith in Padre Miguel's intentions, yet I don't know if intention alone is enough to hold back the furor. Tomorrow we plant the bombs. This anxiety I've been feeling seems eternal. It began with the planning of the first explosion and has not ceased to gnaw at my stomach like a pack of termites in freshly rotting wood. I'm not wired for these violent approaches. I haven't picked up my camera for a week, and my hands and mind yearn to observe the light. I've never been in a position where I haven't been able, emotionally, to take photos. Thankfully I am conscious of my desire so I can try to reconcile my feelings about the politics and my role as a photographer before I abandon this passion altogether. Hopefully these steps we are taking will yield a positive outcome and we can all leave this behind.

Juan Romero

CHAPTER THIRTEEN

Star of Bethlehem

Joyfully give birth to the new.

Abuela wove the birthing wreath with the same love she had for her own daughter. Sofia had become a special part of Abuela's daily life, even before her grandson had captured the young French woman's heart. Now, with the seed of a new generation blossoming in Sofia's womb, Abuela was as contented as an old woman could be. Somewhere in her mind she knew the child was a female and hoped this would be her prodigy. The heavens had not forgotten her after all. She carefully placed the magnolia in the leaves to lead the child in a peaceful entrance onto earth and give her a sense of safety and joy while walking life's path. The calendula was to enhance the awareness of the importance of earth and nature for the baby, while the columbines provided insight into true identity and one's higher purpose. The spiderwort would give the child the ability to discern the truth, to find clarity in mixed messages and to help her to do so using impeccable organizational skills. Finally, Abuela added the ability to be non-judgmental. At the last moment she decided to add a flower for Sofia, something that wasn't normally done, but her instinct insisted that she must. She placed a single pink Canada Thistle in the wreath. At the time she believed it was to help Sofia process the pain of her mother's death and the guilt she felt for not being with her in the end. Later she discovered it was needed for the trauma she experienced surrounding her new family's loss. Had Abuela known, she would have tried to offset the horror, but she could not.

The party was to begin at dusk, and Abuela had everyone working to honor her first great-grandchild. Sofia had been abducted and taken to the vapor caves where Abuela's friend Alejandra was performing every type of spa treatment available to womankind. Sofia would arrive at the celebration relaxed and open to receive all of the blessings.

The food was an entirely separate situation. With Sofia being the master chef in town, Abuela was in a conundrum. She was so distraught over the importance of the quality of the food that she sent for an old friend in Buenos Aires. Rogelio's family had fled Europe during World War II seeking a new life in a land not plagued by war. He and Abuela had met in Cusco as young adults. They had traveled to the Incan city for the solar eclipse and had bumped into one another three times in the span of two days. Abuela, being much bolder than the shy Italian chef, pointed out the fact and burst into such a boisterous laugh that even Rogelio could not resist giggling. They spent the next week eating cui and drinking very dry imported Chilean wine. Though the entire affair was platonic, it was evident to both of them that their sexual potency was compatible. They had kept in touch over the years and Rogelio agreed to honor Abuela's request.

The dining room table glowed, as it never had before. Each segment of the hand-carved cherry wood was blessed with an exquisite portion of the meal. The appetizer consisted of whole braised garlic on fresh bread and tomatoes stuffed with a fresh basil dressing. Following these exquisite treats was a cream of leek soup speckled with chunks of zucchini. The entrée brought to the center of the table a fat eggplant dish, plump with squash and mushrooms, topped off with a creamy pepper sauce. If this were not enough to indulge the most gluttonous of eaters, Rogelio continued (as if to torture those women pretending to watch their figures) with a dessert consisting not only of the standard French fair of camembert, chevre, and brie, but accompanied, quite scandalously, by a poached peach tart swimming in a heavily sweetened strawberry sauce.

Crystal clinked and china clattered as the food ran back and forth from the kitchen. Wines from all over the world rounded out each woman's glass, filling her with lust, love, and passion. Sofia arrived just as the altar was receiving its final touches. Those who are not familiar with altars often think of them as objects of pagan rituals, however, an altar is a personal sacred space where anyone can offer and receive blessings. In this case, it was a family altar, welcoming not only Sofia, as a new member, but the unborn child into the family. Abuela had built it around the same base her great-great grandmother had made and that had been used for each generation since. The path leading to the altar was aligned with stars. Each woman who attended the ceremony to welcome the new child placed a gift at the base of the altar decorated with photos of several generations of children, interwoven with daffodils, bringing the higher powers to bless the child. A loaf of bread to stave off hunger, a bottle of wine to attract everlasting joy and laughter and, stems of birds of paradise to attract creative energy were only some of the many offerings. Sofia was led to the front of the altar and seated on a hand painted stool. Abuela began to light the candles made with Echinacea extract to boost Sofia's immune system. The other women hummed a calming melody and circled Sofia. No one knew what she was asking for or thinking, but it was none of their business so they didn't wonder. When Abuela was done she took a glass jar from her bag and smeared a lavender salve on Sofia's forehead. The blessing was to pass Abuela's knowledge on to her grandchild. Again, her secret desire for a girl reappeared. What she didn't know was that Sofia, too, wanted a daughter. She placed a crown on Sofia's head and the women left her alone to present her own offerings and prayers.

Sofia felt the silence as soon as the voices of the group had faded into the distance. Her hand on her belly could feel the heat of life in her womb, and she wondered what kind of mother she was going to be. All of her anger and disappointment with her own mother suddenly surfaced, and a sense of fear filled her body. There was a part of her that knew she would not be the same. She had convinced herself she could be more loving, show greater kindness, and comprehend the importance of tenderness, but the power of fear was not easy to overcome. She imagined her mother; drunk from the cheap wine she would mix with water all day long. She would scream at anyone who entered her kitchen without permission. One would think it was because she was protecting her sacred recipes and needed space to explore her creative culinary endeavors, but it was really because she was so inebriated, she didn't know what she was doing. It took Sofia's father 15 years and two burned kitchens to leave her. Later Sofia found out it was because of her father's infidelities that her mother drank. It was the only escape she had. She, because of fear, couldn't leave him, so she sought solace in alcohol. Once he left she threw herself at other men for profit.

The baby inside of Sofia could feel her mother's sadness and let out a laugh that filled Sofia's belly. It was so radiant that it illuminated her naval and warmed her blood. She looked up at the altar and wiped her tears with a smile. Everything would be fine. She left the meadow and the altar and slowly made her way back to the house.

Abuela was waiting for Sofia in the garden when she arrived from the fields. "I want to give you something before we join the other women inside," she said. Sofia stepped from the shadows into the light. "Each generation of women carries a locket." She put her hand on her chest and pulled a star shaped locket out of her pocket. The star represents the mother of this valley, Catalina. She was the first *Hechizada*."

"Died seeking adventure, if I remember correctly," Sofia remarked.

"That's the legend."

"Legend? And the truth."

"I have a series of letters written by Catalina to her lover, which reveal that his intolerance is what really drove her away. He was so obsessed and controlling that he didn't want to accept her ways of life nor her obligation to the valley. He is the one who told Coltamba where she was. He betrayed his love and master. When Catalina died, her mother had the locket made. Inside she placed dried Amaranth to heal her broken heart and Meadowsweet to ensure tranquility and peace in her home. She wore it until her death. The locket was passed from one generation to the next, through mothers and daughters, sisters, aunts, and nieces, sometimes even grandmother to granddaughter. I wish to give it to your baby if you agree she can be trained." Sofia didn't speak immediately. She was filled with more pride than she had ever felt in her life. She had always worked for everything she had. Because her mother had been so unstable she had been on her own for a long time. She left southern France to study comparative literature at the Sorbonne in Paris, only to drop out after two years. She turned to culinary delights while working in a bistro near Sacre Coeur, which is where she met her first Latin American lover. Young and naïve, she followed him to South America only to discover he was married with three children. She made an attempt at being a mistress, but her guilt and understanding that there was no love between them, only companionship, drove her to find herself in the mountains. He, too, felt guilty for having plucked this sweet flower from her native pasture, and in an insensitive attempt to reconcile his feelings gave Sofia money. Had she not been utterly destitute she would not have taken it, but in the end it was the money that helped her buy the restaurant from la *Señora* Moreno after her husband's death. The thick scent of Gardenias hung in the valley the day she arrived in Aguas Puras. She, too, had traveled via bus and then purchased a *motocicleta* in Paso Alto. The first person she came upon as she swerved slowly down the dirt road towards town was Abuela, carrying a huge basket of heavy scented flowers on her back.

"Buenos Dias," the old woman greeted her. She remembered feeling uncomfortable that someone would wave a *moto* down just to say hello, but Abuela had dreamed of Sofia two weeks earlier, and when she heard the motor in the distance she moved into the middle of the road. Sofia saw the thin, fragile frame with a bundle of Gardenias on her back and downshifted. Her aviator goggles and bomber jacket were highlighted by a periwinkle silk scarf, which branded her immediately.

"Buenos Dias," she answered. Her heavy French accent clouded her remedial Spanish, but Abuela could understand her.

"You're here for an extended period of time, aren't you?"

"I'm not sure," an odd question, thought Sofia.

"You cook?"

"How did you know?"

"I didn't. It's just that if you are looking for something to do, there is a café in town." Sofia hadn't considered settling in Aguas Puras so she nodded and smiled, but Abuela was accustomed to bewildered looks so she took a flower from her bunch and handed it to Sofia.

"The scent is so powerful."

"They are from my farm. Once you are settled you should come by for a visit," she pointed to the drive behind her.

"Are you on your way home?"

"I'm heading to town."

"Can I give you a ride?"

"I'd like that."

"Climb on." Abuela lifted her skirt and straddled the seat. She wrapped her indigo blue sleeves around Sofia's waist and held on tightly so as not to lose the flowers. As the chugging *moto* swerved slowly in and out avoiding the potholes, Sofia could feel calmness come over her. It was one that from that moment on she would only feel when she was in the presence of Abuela. Now, today, finally, she was feeling as if she were no longer alone.

"I would be honored to allow Maria de la Luz to be brought into this world to study with you, Abuela. There is no greater path for her to follow." Abuela placed the locket around Sofia's neck.

"When she is born the locket must be hung around her neck. It will protect her regardless of her destiny." Sofia's hand grasped the locket and her heart felt relief. What she didn't know and what Abuela was too frightened to see was that Maria de la Luz's destiny would take an unlikely twist. "May *Pacha Mama* bless this child. Let's go celebrate." The older woman took the younger woman by the hand and led her through the archway, the passage into her next stage of life and in what would later be remembered as the fiesta of Bacchanalian delights, which the females of a small mountain village indulged in until the first colors of dawn crept over the mountains and filled the valley's mist with its sleepy haze. There was only one photo of the event; all the others had burned in the fire that finally robbed Sofia of the final remnants of her life with Juan Romero and Maria de la Luz. It was said to be faulty wiring, but as always the townspeople believed it to be arson. Anything that happened once the protests started was considered foul play. It was a game of chess between the greedy minds of industrial mining executives and savvy "rebels" in charge of organizing the people.

Sofia associated it with closure. The one photo that did not perish was one of Sofia and Abuela, standing in the living room in front of an altar of burning candles. The light from the flash reflected the silver of Sofia's locket, causing it to look like a bright star hanging in the middle of the night.

CHAPTER FOURTEEN

Reed

Purification

The rainy season was beginning to break its pattern of heavy daily downpours. Blue sky made its way through the chemical clouds, the sun pushing from behind the daze the first crop duster created as it skirted the valley.

"It has been brought to the attention of the government that the valley of Santa Catarina is part of a large ring of coca plantations, growing the plant illegally under the guise of flower production," read Juan Romero to a small group of people gathered in Abuela's living room.

"What are they talking about?" asked Octavio.

"It's a ploy," said Padre Miguel.

"They're trying to get rid of us by eliminating the flower crop."

"It's quicker than poisoning the water," said Sofia sarcastically.

"Juan Romero, three of my burros are ghastly ill. What does this pesticide do? How is it going to impact us?" Abuela was beginning to tire. She wanted peace in the valley where she had lived her entire life. She was growing impatient, but even worse, weary.

"I don't know, Abuela." The spraying continued for several weeks. No one could obtain any information about where the planes were coming form. The government denied sending the letter with the coca accusation. In the meanwhile more and more people were falling ill, and the plants were withering away.

Production at the mine had been cut back. Some due to external pressure, but primarily due to a lack of manpower. Many men had left, seeking work elsewhere, preferring to earn lower wages, but being able to work with the security that their lives were not in danger. This became more imperative than the slightly more lucrative wages. Padre Miguel had also solicited the Church for funds for a construction project and lured some of the workers from the mine to the building site. It was becoming more and more clear that the crop dusters were another series of trials.

In a matter of weeks three duster planes managed to poison half of the valley. The fumes were beginning to affect the people as well. As soon as Juan Romero gave the word, Jack acted quickly. He departed for an overnight trip to Cotopaxi province. He had received information that the planes were being housed there. He took a bus at midday so as to arrive in the early evening. Jack armed himself with enough explosives to take the planes out with one blast. When he arrived he found a place to stay in Latacunga. It was cheap, dirty, and not worth the little money the owner asked for, but he took it. He went out to a bar where he was told some of the local pilots hang out. Within a matter of 20 minutes he had identified where the planes were.

He rented a motorcycle from the hotel owner, and at 2:30 in the morning drove out into the countryside. Jack turned up a dirt road that was questionable whether or not it was for vehicular traffic. He went next to the llama farm where he had been told the planes were.

Jack turned on the headlights to illuminate a herd of llamas meandering in the field. Fortunately no one appeared. The guard was so drunk that a volcanic eruption most likely would not have awakened him from his inebriated sleep. It took Jack 30 minutes to plant each bomb and return. He took off on the motorbike, and when he got to the pavement he pulled out the remote.

"Here she goes," and he pressed the button. The planes blew into tiny bits of raging fire balls. He didn't stick around to watch the burning aircraft. The news media reported that the planes were being used to smuggle drugs into Colombia and that it was a special drug enforcement operation. The government knew exactly, however, where the aggression had come from. After that the crop-dusting stopped, but the violence against the people worsened.

CHAPTER FIFTEEN

Queen Anne's Lace

Eliminates illusions of powerlessness and pulls us together when we are scattered or face conflict.

Riding the bus was not as romantic as Sofia had imagined. The roads from Aguas Puras were curvy and wet, and the bus gripped the pavement as if the driver were racing the Indy 500. The swerving back and forth and up and down over the infinitely deep canyons was giving Sofia a sense of profound nausea. Once they stopped descending temporarily and hit a flat piece of road, she stood up to stretch her legs.

"What time is the rally tomorrow?" she asked José. José was a Cuban exile. He fled to Aguas Puras and had become friends with Juan Carlos. His past was not clear, but no one seemed to care. He knew too much about the Castro regime and people thought it best not to know about him, in case anyone came looking for him. He owned a artesian shop in town, which he opened as a working art gallery every Thursday evening.

"10:00 a.m., any earlier and no one will even notice we're there."

"Do you think they'll care?"

"Who knows? Padre Miguel has contacted the press though, so at least we'll get some coverage. He has a friend who works for one of the TV stations. They tend to like the novella aspects of stories, so we need to really embellish, let them know how awful it is."

"It is awful."

"You know what I mean. We need to appeal to the melo-dramatic side of our compatriots."

"I wish people would just see the injustice."

"Life isn't like that Sofia. Life is about drama. We create it, we live it, we die in it. If it weren't for drama what would life be?"

"Simple, sweet, enjoyable."

"Boring."

"I don't know why everything has to be so tragic."

"Because we don't know how to do it any other way. Here, take this." José handed Silvia a piece of paper with the itinerary for the next day. It was International Worker's Day, a perfect time to target an issue that impacted the workers of an entire town, as well as the workers in the mine. Though the miners didn't know it, the small group of protesters from Aguas Puras was submitting a formal protest on behalf of them for exploitation and dangerous working conditions. The Canadian mining company was paying its local labor half the legal wage (although this was more than they would be mak-ing working for other multinationals) and exposing them to the same dangers that it was exposing the valley to by not providing adequate gear for clean up.

There were 114 people traveling to the capital for the pro-test, most of them on this bus that chugged along the wide highway passing volcanoes and farms, meandering through small towns with bustling markets and street vendors. None of them really knew what would happen once they arrived. They simply held onto the hope that something would happen.

The bus pulled up to a small *posada* and dropped off a handful of passengers. Each one of them pulled their back-packs down from the shelf above and aimlessly entered through the front door, not knowing what to expect. Padre Miguel had arranged for everyone to stay in different places throughout the city by contacting a friend of his in the archdiocese. Most of the places were small hotels or bed and breakfasts owned by people affiliated with the church, which in Ecuador was most everyone. The bus went through the same ritual, winding through narrow streets, sometimes stopping on the corner, dropping passengers here and there until it finally arrived at the last destination where it left Sofia and José. A yellow and blue sign hanging precariously above the door read *"Posada Española."* It was owned by Maria, a close friend of Padre Miguel's from Europe. Her family had lived in Ecuador for 40 years, but she had met Padre Miguel while he was on a tour in Italy. Her family had strong links to its homeland, mostly because her father was exiled during Franco's regime and he had trouble letting go. As a poet, he was persecuted and tortured. The moment he was released from prison he fled the country and never looked back. His wife, Andrea, however, would return to see her family once every couple of years. She gave birth in Spain to her first child, Maria, and the young girl traveled with her mother frequently to visit the family. Her father never set foot outside of Ecuador for fear of execution. Padre Miguel and Maria met at a hospital in Italy when she was 24. She was traveling by *moto* with a lover through Europe, rebelling against her life, when tragedy struck. Her wild boyfriend from Madrid took a corner too quickly in the Dolomites and smashed the bike into the side of a mountain. She was thrown from the bike when it hit the ditch, but his body folded-up like an accordion from the impact. He died instantly. She was taken to a local hospital, where Padre Miguel was observing a program to help cancer patients, jointly sponsored and funded by the church and the hospital. When they brought Maria in, she was semi-conscious and rambling in Spanish. The Italian doctors were frantically trying to decode her gibberish beneath the language and strange accent. Padre Miguel immediately recognized the South American dialect and stepped in to assist. He stayed with her through surgery and recovery. They became close friends and never lost contact after that. After the accident, he accompanied her to Spain where she stayed with her grandmother until she was well enough to travel home.

"Bienvenidos," a voice boomed from the upstairs window. "I'll be right down." Sofia and José waited in front of the black iron gate that separated a delicate garden from the noisy street. Maria came rolling through the front door and down the terracotta tile path to greet them. "I've been waiting for hours. What took you so long?" She swung open the gate and embraced Sofia, giving her a big kiss on the left cheek. "Welcome, welcome. *Pasa.*"

"We had to drop-off the others," Sofia replied. "It took longer than we expected. I'm sorry."

"Don't be sorry. You must be famished. Come on in, I've prepared some food." The house was deceiving from the outside. To someone standing on the street it looked like an ugly cement compound, walls cracked and stained from years of rain, but after passing through the heavy hand-carved wood door in the front, the magic exploded. Maria's father had designed a traditional Spanish courtyard with an open-air garden in the center. A flourishing fountain gurgled in the middle of the exotic South American flowers and the exposed hallway of dark red ceramic tile wrapped around the garden in a perfect square. Each room was hidden behind a wood door, but interconnected inside via arched entrances. Iron lamps hung every few feet from a teak ceiling where each piece was woven delicately into the other, leaving just enough light to illuminate the rooms and courtyard. "Leave your things here. I'll take them to your rooms later. Now we must eat." She led them to the opposite side of the courtyard where a large table was elegantly set in the corner, next to a brick oven. The warmth from the baking oven emitted a greatly needed heat, as the evening fog had dropped and the air was once again chilly. "So you're here to protest," Maria wasted no time.

"Yes. They're destroying the valley."

"Nothing new in this country, child."

"It happens frequently?"

"It's not usually the same place or the same people, or even the same thing, but it's always for the same reason— money. I remember about ten years ago a logging company was stripping the rainforest near Puyo of almost all the vegetation. It wasn't even trying to be subtle about it. It was as if they took a super-sized lawnmower to the forest and ran it over. There was nothing left. The parts they couldn't cut they burned. People were finding dead jaguars, monkeys, and charred parakeets scattered across the land. It was horrifying. Nothing ever happened. The company finished its work and left when they had nothing left to take. The area still hasn't recovered, and the local people left for the city to find work. I imagine most of them are living in the *barrio*, not knowing how to function in urban life." Maria placed two bowls of hot potato soup in front of the weary travelers.

"Then there was the oil spill. Remember?" José jumped in, slurping his soup.

"Oh, that was terrible," Maria cried. "How long did that crude oil flow before anyone even knew about it? All of those people died. They didn't even know to get away, and then the fire that exploded."

"But didn't that company get sued?"

"No environmental laws, a corrupt government, a wealthy American oil company and billions of dollars. They are still in court after years of fighting. The *campesinos* won at first, but now the oil giant is appealing. They generated more than 400 toxic pits and spilled more than the Exxon Valdez in Alaska," said José.

"At least you all are fighting. It's not every day that people stand up for what they believe in or to protect something that needs protecting. What time is the rally tomorrow?"

"10:00 A.M" Sofia answered.

"Good. I'll drive you myself. I'd like to see what happens." They stayed eating and drinking until late into the night, listening to Maria's stories, until Sofia could not keep her head from bobbing up and down from exhaustion. The *aguardiente* Maria had served helped Sofia sleep heavily that night despite her nervousness. The down bed Maria had prepared for her, along with the cold night air, pushed her into dreamland without much difficulty. She only awoke because of the heavy knock at her door. "*Hijita,* it's time to get up." Maria was full of energy and so was the day. The sun beamed in on the courtyard and warmed the house. They ate breakfast and packed small backpacks with provisions to cover them for the day. They were expecting a long haul.

The group met in front of the congressional building. No one really knew what to do, but Sofia took over immediately. She had brought a bullhorn and plenty of paper and sticks to make signs, which people started writing on as soon as they were passed out. "*Fuera Maple.*" "Save Our Flowers." Anything and everything was scribbled on the signs, which slowly began to paint the sky in the center of town, bobbing up and down in unison with chants. They walked in a circle, screaming at the men and women dressed neatly in blue or grey suits, trying to climb the stairs to their offices.

The first hour was fairly monotonous, and there was little response to the protestors. At around 11:30 A.M., however, a group of local police officers converged on the plaza, observing the shouts and concerns of the people. Sofia, without saying anything, encouraged the group to increase the intensity of their voices and slowly began moving closer to the government buildings. At this point the police moved in, lining up in front of the steps, with shields in hand. They were not unaccustomed to protests. The country was, in fact, frequently riddled with them because of transportation price hikes, gasoline shortages or increases in cost, rations on certain foods, wages, housing. Everything and anything provoked this small South American country to have a *huelga*, strike, and shut the country down. Roadblocks, burning tires, and the refusal to work were not uncommon, but unfortunately this was different. No one outside the small mountain community was affected, thus little interest in resolving the problem quickly was surfacing. The group spent another two hours trying to get the attention of anyone who would listen. They distributed flyers to passersby, and José even interviewed with a television station that by chance was in the area trying to get footage of a car accident that had blocked passage of the omnibus. Other than that, no one seemed to care, and Sofia wasn't about to push the police line to find out what would happen, not yet at least. The baby inside of her grew quickly, and her swollen belly was transforming itself into a hard, round ball. She was still full of energy, just a little slower, and starting to realize she had to protect the small being inside of her that was occasionally reminding her of its presence with light kicks. The group began to slowly disperse around 2:00, frustrated and tired, but dedicated to return the next day. They repeated the motions of the protests for several days with similar reactions—sympathy but little interest to help stop the mining. People were worried about their own lives. In a country where inflation was hyperactive and food was sometimes hard to find, many of the capital's poor did not understand the urgency of flowers, and while they might listen, they would not act. Those who did not have to worry about food worried about other things, like employment or the safety of their families, and likewise did not seem interested in a small valley of medicinal plants. It was like rowing up river in a slowly leaking boat. Sofia tried repeatedly to get into to see Cristian Cruz, the government representative that corresponded to Aguas Puras, only to be refused, being told she needed an appointment, yet denied an appointment when trying to make one. On the fourth day, the group disbanded and returned to Aguas

Puras, disillusioned by their compatriots and the lack of willingness on the part of everyone in the capital to listen.

"It was pathetic," Sofia told Padre Miguel as they sat on the patio of her apartment. "No one even looked twice at us."

"I should have known. No one cares about what goes on around them if it doesn't directly impact them."

"It was a waste of time," José said.

"Not completely. Now we know what we have to do."

"What? More protests?" José's voice was angry and frustrated.

"Yes."

"Are you insane? It did nothing. All we did was march around like ants in circles, looking busy but with no one understanding where we were going or what we were doing."

"I'm thinking of something that will get their attention."

"What?" Sofia asked.

"We shut down the road that connects the capital with the coast. It runs through the mountains, and without it neither the *camioneros* nor the busses can get through. They won't be happy with that, and people will not get their goods when they need them. We directly impact their lives so that they have to listen."

"Could cause trouble."

"Exactly."

"We'll need a truck or a bus to block the road, tires to burn."

"Manuel has an old school bus parked on his lot. We could ask him for it."

"We should pay him for it," Sofia said. "I'll come up with some money."

And this is how the people of Aguas Puras stopped an entire country for three days. In an effort to raise consciousness and in a desperate cry for help, more than 200 people from town volunteered to haul the bus to *kilómetro 176* and block the road. They arrived at dawn armed with the bus, tires, and gas oil to ignite the fires. Within minutes the bus traversed the two-lane highway and 200 people surrounded the vehicle chanting that the mining must stop. Traffic came to a rapid stop and the line quickly grew. From both sides, cars and trucks tried to make their way to the front, causing a complete traffic jam across the entire road. At first drivers were interested in what was happening, thinking an accident had caused the bus to crash, but as they approached they realized that it was a protest. As time passed they started yelling and screaming, demanding to be let through. Several men even tried to break the picket line, but the men from Aguas Puras were ready. While the women sat on the ground behind them, adorned with wreaths of Juniper and Phlox for protection and unity, the men stood firm, not wavering, holding back a crowd of angry truckers. This back and forth pushing went on for hours until the National Guard arrived, demanding that the blockade be taken down. When they refused the leader of the Guard threatened force.

"You take yourselves out of here or we will take you out ourselves," growled a corpulent man balancing his outdated AK-47, to draw attention to his steal-tipped army issued boots. He tried to stare José down, thinking he could scare the seasoned bureaucrat into submission.

"We stay until you do then," was all he said. The gorilla-like man grunted and spun around on his heals. The night was spent eating and drinking and talking, while maintaining the fires built by burning gas oil in the tires. The soldiers didn't do anything that night except smoke cigars and rotate guard, making sure the crowd didn't get violent. They had created a buffer between the traffic and the bus, and people had resigned themselves to sitting and waiting. Early the next morning the protests began again, and the protestors demanded to see Sanchez. The news of the roadblock had already reached the capital and footage of the traffic jam was running on every television channel. Truckers and civilians trying to get from one side of the mountains to the other were losing patience quickly and didn't understand why the government didn't take these people off the road. While they waited, the tension only grew. The sound of banging pots and pans rang clear through the fields as the protestors played their *cacerolas* as a way to show discontent. The noise was loud and taxing after several hours, grating on the nerves of the young soldiers. At the end of the second day Cruz still didn't show up. Everyone passed another cold night under wool shawls.

On the third morning the soldiers were losing patience and the President realized that 200 people would not easily be taken out, so he sent for Cruz to speak with them. But before he arrived, a small skirmish between the protestors and the soldiers ensued. Santiago, a very young recruit with little tolerance for anything snapped. He couldn't handle the sound of one more stroke hitting the metal and clanging through the air, and he decided that throwing a tear gas grenade into the crowd would stop this. He released the pin and chucked it as hard as he could toward the protestors. When it exploded the soldiers mistook it for aggression on the part of the people. They immediately armed themselves with rubber bullets and began shooting in the air.

"My pots are not bulletproof," shouted one protester, while ducking a barrage of flying fake bullets. Several people were hit and went down as a result of the crossfire, but no one was seriously hurt. It wasn't until the helicopter overhead was heard that the firing stopped. It was Cruz.

When he arrived by air, Sofia knew this was a lost cause. He, like so many of the governments politicians, was so seeped in corruption that the fine champagne he drank as a regular part of his evening dripped from his pours. He would not be willing to sacrifice such luxuries for a small flower village, but she would still try to convince him. He approached the protestors with eight body guards armed with automatic weapons, wearing dark sunglasses, and barely moving their upper bodies. Sofia and José stepped forward.

"You've finally decided to bless us with your presence," she sarcastically said.

"I'm sorry it took so long," he retorted. "I'm Cristian Cruz."

"Sofia Le Franz," she stuck out her hand and he accepted. Julia, a Quechua *Hechizada*, who was quiet and patient just watched. She need not introduce herself to a man she new in her heart was not destined to help her valley. Esperanza had sent her because of her fine ability to determine an individual's intentions.

"Nice to meet you. So, what is it that you need from me?"

"Have you received any of my correspondence?" Sofia asked.

"No."

"Do you know anything about Aguas Puras?"

"Flower region. Quaint little town. Yes, I've been there."

"So you know that the flowers are our livelihood."

"I believe so." His answers were so curt and his expression emotionless. A true politician was standing before them.

"Our livelihood is in danger," she said.

"How's that?"

"Mining."

"Maple?"

"You know them."

"Yes, I'm familiar with them." What he didn't reveal was that he was the individual reaping the benefits of bribery in this entire scandal.

"Then you know that they are illegally dumping chemicals that are leaking into the valley's water supply. It is starting to impact the growth of the flowers and has already done physical harm to several people in the region."

"I didn't."

"I think Mr. Cruz may have heard something about this," added José, "but has chosen not to think about it. Am I right?" José had been around politicians for too long to be fooled by this young representative's oiled back hair and finely cut suit. He looked straight into Cruz's eyes and he knew.

"My affiliation with the company is purely political. I thought it would be an excellent economic opportunity for the people in the valley."

"What it has done," interjected Sofia, "is threaten an entire way of life, and we want it stopped, now." Sanchez looked at José and knew that he had to at least attempt, albeit falsely, to ease the worries of this woman or these people would never leave peacefully.

"I will look into it, Miss. I cannot promise anything, but I will try."

"No you won't." José said.

Cruz simply looked at José and spoke with an answer smoother than the belly of a snake.

"Believe what you must sir, but I promise you, right here and now that I will do everything in my power to stop this mining. I am here to represent and protect my people, not deceive them." With that he nodded his head and turned away. "In good faith I hope you will now go. Contact me in a week and we will talk." José snorted and yelled,

"We're not going anywhere." Three of the bodyguards stepped forward.

"José!" Julia grabbed his arm. "He said he'd do something."

"You believe that rat, Julia?"

"We have to and the reality is that whether or not we believe him, we have listened to what he has said and now we know his intentions."

"We should stay here until he shows us some action," said José.

"Maybe." Interjected Sofia.

"Maybe? Maybe? What's wrong with you?"

"I'm worried, that's all."

"About?"

"Everything."

"It will be okay. We'll stay a couple more days and see what he does."

A couple of days turned into one week and more soldiers. While tensions were high the soldiers were under strict orders not to make any moves, because following the last outbreak the international press had gotten wind of the protest. Any violence would be spread across the world in a matter of minutes.

The pressure was mounting and everyone could feel it. After the outbreak earlier, nerves were fragile and sleep was scarce. Many of those in the traffic jam had abandoned their cars or tried to head back from where they came, but the truck drivers stayed put, and it was their power that pushed Cruz to make a concession. Not only had they become sympathetic with the cause, but their bosses were livid at the loss of thousands of dollars a day, and a strong, forceful lobby pushed the representatives' buttons. On the tenth day of the protest a message arrived from Padre Miguel. *"Cruz has filed a formal complaint with the Ministry of the Environment and spoke to the issue at the last legislative session. It's a step in the right direction. I've received news that Mario Beltran, head of the Ministry, is coming to inspect the site and hear our concerns. Come home."*

While José wasn't convinced a visit from a politician would do anything, he yielded to Sofia and disbanded the protest.

"It isn't the end, but it's a step forward," she said as she tried to get a whiff of the off limits cigarette José inhaled from a distance.

"We'll see."

As the bus made it's way back to Aguas Puras, the people were weary. They were tired of fighting, of begging to be heard and they were beginning to believe their efforts were worthless. Sofia's head was resting against the glass when the bus suddenly swerved off the road. Startled she stood up to see several army trucks surrounding them. Scores of soldiers in black fatigues, heavy black leather boots, and black hoods covering their heads swarmed out of the trucks and up onto the bus. They began pulling people out of their seats. Silvia didn't fight. She had heard of these raids before. They happened often, so she crunched down and tried to hide under her shawl, throwing a bag on top of herself. The screaming and cursing grew overwhelming loud. She covered her ears so as not to hear the brusque voices of the soldiers ordering people to get off the bus. The chaos lasted only a few minutes, and then the leader of the group stopped at the front of the bus.

"Stop this foolishness or we will take the rest of you next." He jumped off the bus and into the front seat of the lead car. The jeeps raced off down the road carrying at least 20 protestors. According to one woman, Citlali, who escaped unnoticed between transfers, the soldiers were going to kill them.

"They were dragging us into the helicopters. I heard one of them say, take them over the ocean, tie cement to their feet, they will never be found." She was in hysterics as she retold the story to Esperanza. Of course, when the townspeople accused the government of such acts of violence, it denied it 100 percent.

CHAPTER SIXTEEN

Magnolia

The first birth; entry and exit on earth.

The day had awakened with bright sunshine, something rare in the valley. It was as if a hole had been opened up in the sky and the sun was shining down in one solid beam of light, covering only this small part of the world. Sofia lay on her side hugging a pillow, her belly swollen and her back tender. She wanted to get up, but was having trouble mustering up the energy it took to lift the extra 30 pounds weighing her heavily to the bed. She hadn't been sleeping well without Juan Romero. Although they had not formally moved into together, when he was in town he stayed with her every night. Abuela had sent his things to the apartment a couple of months earlier without asking questions, and he didn't even notice the change, it was so natural.

Juan Romero was still in the mountains, despite Abuela's advice to come down. The day was nearing when Sofia would give birth, and she didn't want Juan Romero to miss it, but he was too obsessed with terrorizing the bosses that he wasn't able to focus on his own child. Sanchez had sent token inspectors to the mine soon after the roadblock protest, but nothing came of it. Their reports were bogged down in paperwork and would most likely stay there for years to come.

Sofia finally managed to roll herself up and out of bed and waddled to the kitchen looking for a glass of water to quench her dry throat. She gulped it down like an elephant sucking up the first rainwater after the drought. The hotter-than-usual weather and the impending birth were making her very thirsty, even if her stomach was the size of a peanut and she could barely eat or drink anything without feeling as if her intestines were going to explode. It was late and she had to open the café. With most of her employees helping with the protests and the fighting, there were few helping hands. Candice, a young girl whose father was a daisy farmer, began working a couple of months ago and had been Sofia's savior. She was too young to head into the mountains and was more interested in the exotic mysteries of European cooking than the explosive minds of men. Sofia shoved a banana down her throat and threw on the only outfit that still provided comfort—a pair of jeans with the mommy elastic panel and a blush-colored pullover blouse with a lace-up closure at the top.

The café was slow during lunch. Sofia's feet felt bloated, and she could barely stand for more than a few minutes. Once the slight rush slowed she sat down to eat a bowl of soup and a baguette. As she sat she could feel the little one moving. She felt unusually cold as she quietly slurped her soup at the corner table so she wrapped her shawl more tightly around her shoulders. It was then that she saw her mother standing in the doorway. Her spoon fell from her hand into the bowl and she didn't move. The thin, bony woman made her away across the restaurant straight towards her daughter. Her grayish-yellow hair was tied back with a green ribbon, and her brown dress with white polka dots hung like a tent on her skinny frame.

"¿*Ma mere*?" Sofia whispered.

"*Oui mon cheri. ¿Ça va?*"

"*Ma mere, tu est morte.*"

"*Oui cheri. Je sui morte.*" Sofia stared at the ghost of her mother apparently sitting in a chair in front of her; tears welled in her eyes.

"How?"

"Why do you ask, my child? You are the one who called for me."

"I did?"

"Yes. I was perfectly fine, sipping wine and reading Moliere when I heard your voice. This is where you've been all this time?" She looked around with an expression of doubt.

"Yes, this is my home."

"You work here?" Sofia could smell her mother, the smoke from her Gauloises Blondes, the pungent scent of *brie de meaux*, and the Roget Galileo soap that she used to use to scrub her skin.

"I own it mother. It's my café. My recipes."

"I wouldn't have guessed you would be able to do something like this on your own. You are pregnant," she changed the subject.

"*Oui.*"

"When?"

"Anytime now."

"I remember when you came to me. I was so happy. It was winter and it was cold out, blistering cold. Your father kept throwing wood in the fireplace so the fire wouldn't go out. We had to deliver you alone, you know. No one could get to us and we couldn't get out. It's when we lived in Argentiere. You probably don't remember Argentiere. You were so small when we left."

"I remember some things. I remember the mountains. They were so overwhelming. Probably because I was so young."

"No, they were overwhelming. The night before you were born it snowed almost two meters. Your birthday is the night of the avalanche. It was like rolling thunder closing in on the town, but we couldn't go anywhere or do anything. I lay in bed screaming while a wall of snow headed straight for us. François said my screams triggered the slide. Could be true, you were so difficult. The snow sped past the house, in the valley, just below us killed 73 people."

"It's amazing we survived."

"You were a blessing. You always were," her mother leaned in and took her daughter's face in her hands. "It will be fine. Love your child better than I loved you. I never was good at that, but I did. I loved you Sofia." With those words she stood up, turned around and walked back out the door. Sofia sat still, not understanding what she had just seen or imagined, but feeling more relaxed, much more at peace. And then it happened. It was faster and harder than she had expected and she let out a short scream. Candice came running over.

"Are you okay?" Candice saw the tears running down Sofia's cheeks and mistook them for fear, when they were tears of relief.

"Call Esperanza and Carmen to come now."

"The baby?"

"Yes, the baby." She was breathing heavily and the pains in her uterus intensified. "Candice, bring me a towel." Candice looked beneath the chair to see a puddle of liquid that looked like someone had just dumped a bucket of water on the floor. She ran around, hysterically taking plates and shoving the few customers left eating out the door.

"Time to go; here you go, take your food with you." She was in such a state of panic that she was pushing people into the street, plates in hand, telling them to eat in the plaza. She ran to the phone and dialed Esperanza's number.

"Aló?"

"Esperanza? Abuela? It's Candice. Um, um, Sofia, um."

"Candice, what's the matter. Is it time?"

"Yes, time. It's time," she stuttered.

"We'll be right there." In the amount of time it took Abuela to get her coat, pick up Carmen and drive to town, Sofia had already transitioned. The entire town lined the windows of the café, staring in, watching the French woman writhing in pain. When Abuela and Carmen arrived she lifted herself onto a table and had a bottle of Bordeaux in her hand, swigging it to alleviate the pain, or at least forget about it. Candice had constructed a pseudo bed underneath the mother with napkins and tablecloths, but beyond that she didn't know what to do. Sofia wouldn't allow anyone in the café to help her except for Carmen and Abuela, so Candice's extraordinarily large boyfriend guarded the door and kept the onlookers at bay.

Abuela and Carmen came rushing through the door with baskets of materials in hand, prepared to deliver the next generation of *Hechizadas*. Abuela positioned herself behind Sofia, while Carmen checked the suffering mother.

"She's almost ready. That's the fastest I've ever heard of a baby coming."

"What about Luz Cervantes? She delivered in 30 minutes, remember?"

"That's right, but it was her 16th child and she did it in the fields, by herself, standing up. After 15 births you pick up a rhythm. Sofia, you need to breathe and put that bottle of wine down." Sofia chugged one last bit of wine and threw the bottle across the room, sending it crashing against the floor.

"Breathe *mi hija*, breathe." She gently mixed a remedy and had Sofia drink it. "This will ease the pain." Carmen rubbed a salve on Sofia's back and told her to hold steady. "It's almost time to push," she said. "When Esperanza tells you, push." The pain was so excruciating that Sofia felt as if she were about to pass out.

"Okay *amor*, now, push!" Abuela ordered. Sofia did as she was told, screaming as if she were being ripped apart by a pack of wild wolves. After twenty minutes of pushing, breathing, and holding, and pushing again Carmen shouted, "It's crowning!!!"

"Almost Sofia, we're almost there." Abuela placed a cool eucalyptus cloth on Sofia's forehead and gave her a piece of a mango seed with the juicy flesh still hanging on it to bite.

"One more push!"

"I can't," whimpered Sofia. "I can't get it out, just pull it." The two older women looked at each other and began laughing, deep belly laughs that rang clearly through the entire town. Sofia was so stunned by their lack of compassion that she started yelling. "Why are you laughing you stupid old ladies? Can't you see I'm dying?"

"Either you push or you push," Abuela said. "It's too late for anything else. Now do it." Her tone was so forceful that Sofia didn't think twice about the order and gave one last push. In that moment the child came flying out into Carmen's hands. The relief Sofia felt was so great that she didn't think about anything else and fell back into Abuela's arms. Seconds later she heard the cry of her newborn daughter and felt the warm slimy body on her chest. "Here she is," Abuela lifted her head as Carmen helped the baby into its mother's arms. "Maria de la Luz." Her voice trembled with happiness as she saw her great-granddaughter staring up at her mother and then at her. She was small, pink like a baby rat, wrinkled like an old woman, and covered in fluids, but she was perfect. Her black eyes penetrated both of them. The room was silent. Then Carmen turned her head and nodded to the awaiting crowd in the window and they let out a unison cry of joy. The party began, and for three days and three nights the café and the plaza played host to the largest party Aguas Puras had seen in a century.

The news of his daughter's birth arrived when Juan Romero was coming down from the camp. He had missed it, and somewhere deep inside a sharp pain passed through him, reminding him that life was precious and he had just lost one small piece of it. He began running and arrived thirteen hours later. It was the evening of the third day of festivities and he stood on the edge of the plaza gazing across at Sofia, who was sitting in a white wicker chair near the birds of paradise holding Maria de la Luz. The light swirled around her head and the music disappeared. He didn't even notice the soldiers bordering the plaza, watching his every move like an eagle hunting its prey. Everything froze for one moment, and he couldn't believe that he was a father. A hand fell lightly on his shoulder, just like the first day he arrived in town. Without turning around he said, "Is she healthy Abuela?"

"She's the most beautiful child I have ever seen. Even more beautiful than you, which is hard to say seeing as you're my favorite." He turned and hugged his grandmother, holding her tighter than he ever had. She released him and looked towards his new family. He turned and walked slowly with the pace of a cautious jaguar who has just heard something lurking in the brush. He wasn't afraid, just wandering into the unknown. For all of the traveling he had done, and all of the people he had met, this next person was to be the most important person he would ever encounter in his life. As he neared Sofia he stopped and stood just far enough away so he could see the child. He stared, in awe, at this newborn baby girl who would carve his destiny. Sofia finally looked up, sensing someone watching her with more patience and kindness than she had ever known. She smiled at him, her eyes leading him to her. He got closer, standing over the two. She said nothing and lifted her arms to hand him the baby. A gentle cooing sound came out of her mouth. Her hands, tightly squeezed in miniature fists floated near her face and she watched as the new face, one among many she had been introduced to since her journey to the outer world, absorbed the details of her tiny body. He looked different to her. She wasn't sure why he was so tender, but it was similar to the face her mother had when she looked up at her.

LAS HECHIZADAS

"Hola Maria de la Luz. Soy tu papá," Juan Romero whispered. Now she understood. This was the other half. Where had he been for so long? She would have to find out later, but was content that he was finally holding her. She smiled and then fell into a deep sleep seconds later. After sleeping for nine months in a womb it was hard for her to take naps only at the leisure of others, so she didn't. She slept when she wanted. "She's so delicate," he said to Sofia.

"I know."

"I'm sorry I wasn't here."

"I know that too. You missed a good show."

"I want to hear all about it." The two sat in the shade of the eucalyptus trees, babe in arms, as Sofia told Juan Romero her version of the birth of their child. Not once did either of them mention the fighting or protests, nor did they even think about it. Maria de la Luz consumed their thoughts.

As time passed they adjusted to the new schedule and went about their lives, taking the new baby everywhere. Sofia could no longer go to the mountains. She didn't want to. She probably could have left Maria de la Luz with Abuela, but every time the child was out of her sight, a sense of desperate longing came over her and she couldn't tolerate it, so she carried her everywhere. Abuela made her a red sling out of cotton and wool with embroidered Petunias that she tied around her shoulders and placed Maria de la Luz in. This way she could work in the café, do her errands, or simply sit and nurse the baby without much fuss. People got used to seeing her carrying plates of food and drink while hauling the child along with her. "It's not any different than being pregnant," she would say. "She's just on the outside now." Juan Romero did continue his trips into the mountains, even though he longed to stay at home with his child. Every time he left, a piece of his heart was torn. He wanted to be with his family, yet he knew that if the mining didn't stop his family wouldn't exist in the place he too was now calling home.

The fighting had worsened, and much of the mining had halted because normal work could no longer be done. Every day was more dangerous for the workers, who continued to flee to other parts of the country in search of safer employment. Only a third of those who started were left, and the company's equipment was taking a hard hit. They had already lost several bulldozers and a dozen trucks. Jack had convinced Juan Romero that without the violence, the politicians would ignore the situation and nothing would ever happen. When Cruz did nothing and was spotted dining with a Maple executive in the capital, Juan Romero finally understood what Jack was talking about. Corruption runs deep in high places and the good of the people is not part of any conversation that occurs over a 30-year-old bottle of whiskey the kings sip, while sucking on quail bones and poking fun at the peasants begging for scraps. While it seemed that the town was winning the battle, plans to stop the pesky protestors forever were in the works.

Maria de la Luz was 6 months old when the fire broke out. She would remember very little of that night later in life, until the story was retold to her in detail. Abuela was sleeping heavily after trying to recover from a viral infection that had penetrated her body like acid burning through metal, eating every healthy cell she had available. The night was still, the wind didn't blow, and the birds were resting. Even the sounds of the baby breathing were barely audible. Sofia had stayed in town to open early the next morning for the festival. It was to be the first day of the annual Flower Festival, which brought people from all over the country to buy flowers, drink, dance, and learn about the healing powers of the valley through first-hand experience. It was a Mecca for the ill and weak of heart, who flocked to Aguas Puras to be cured. Abuela had already packed up her entire truck with salves and potions, dried herbs and weeds, special baked goods and intoxicating wines.

At around 2:30 A.M. she was awakened to the sound of breaking glass. She and Octavio pounced out of bed. She ran to the baby, while he grabbed his rifle and headed outside. The truck was ablaze. He saw several dark shadows running down the road and fired a round of shots to no avail. He ran to the pump and started screaming for help. Everyone on the farm awakened to his desperate screams and ran into the yard. It was then that he realized that the truck was not the only thing burning. Deep in the fields Abuela's crop was on fire. He dropped the bucket and ran. "Call Benito. Call Benito, damn it, and get them out here!" Everyone stood still, frozen in time, in a state of shock. Abuela held Maria de La Luz and in a shrilling, piercing voice yelled again, "Someone call Benito, *por Dios*, call him." Benito was the town's fire chief. His family had been in charge of the firehouse for five generations. Someone in each and every generation had died a noble death fighting some kind of fire or another. They were insane and would put themselves in situations no human being should be in to save a structure or a human life, even animals. There was the time that the Covar family's stove exploded, sending the roof high into the sky like a shooting star. *Señor* Covar died instantly, but the others were trapped on the third floor unable to get out. Benito scaled the side of the brick house, jerry-rigging a pulley system as if he were climbing the face of the Peruvian giant, Artesonraju and lowered each member via rappel as the building crumbled around them.

Abuela handed Maria de la Luz to Carmen and ran toward the fields. She could not stand idly by while the fire took her life. Side by side she and Octavio carried buckets of water to douse the flames, while the others tossed dirt into the fields. The heat of the blaze burned her face. She could feel the black smoke penetrating her lungs, no one stopped; no one could.

Once they finally got through to the firehouse the men arrived about 20 minutes later. Some of the staff had managed to get the fire in the truck out, but Abuela's goods were all ruined. The rest of them were running water back and forth to the field in a desperate attempt to save the flowers. Benito blazed in with his rusted yellow-green fire truck and made his way to where Octavio was throwing water on the fire. The hose slipped off the wheel like a slick snake ready for the hunt and in a matter of seconds the men had a stream of water dousing the fire.

"To the trenches!" Benito ordered, and his men ran off in unison with shovels in hand to dig trenches around the fire and contain it. Luckily the earth was damp. The hot flames that loved to dance from one plant to the next, consuming them with their devilish desire, were not as active as they could have been. In a manner of an hour the fire was contained, but Abuela lost a third of her crop. She stood in a puddle of ash, covered in mud and smoke, crying.

"When will it stop? When will they go away?" She asked of anyone. No one knew what to say to her and no one said anything. Octavio took her into his arms and held her while she cried. It was the first time he had seen her do so since her husband's death and he realized she wouldn't be able to take much more. She had been punished for her grandson's activism and encouraging him was taking her life into ruin.

Dawn was beginning to break and when Abuela saw the first light she wiped her face and stood tall. She had always believed that each day was a new start and she was not about to stop believing that now. She pulled her hair back tightly into a ponytail and brushed it smooth with her hands. Inhaling, taking in the air of a fresh start she said, "The festival starts today. We can't arrive empty handed. Can someone help me reload the truck?"

"With what?" Octavio asked.

"Estela will have to wait. I have a shipment for her in the storage shed. We'll take that. In the meantime we'll have to redo her order, maybe modify it. I'll call her right now and explain." Octavio looked at Edgar, whose frail frame silhouetted the morning sky. They turned together and headed for the shed. Abuela went to the house to call San Francisco and to gather her things to go to town. "I'll be out in 15 minutes to help Octavio."

He didn't turn back, just sighed and said to Edgar, "How does she do it? How does she always go on as if nothing ever happened? She never seems to tire. Where does that come from?"

"I think you only know that kind of existence if you were born in this valley. Those of us from afar never have had it. It's like they know something that we don't."

"What?"

"That there is always a tomorrow."

"But what good is a tomorrow if you lose everything today?"

"As long as you have your heart you will never lose everything, Octavio." Octavio knew Edgar was right. He was just frustrated, exhausted, and too old to fight any longer. He didn't return to the mountains after that. His life was Esperanza and that would be enough.

BOOK II

Distant Memories

CHAPTER SEVENTEEN

Canada Thistle

**Letting go of pain, guilt or pain
that has been family inflicted**

A taxi sped through the streets of Quito, weaving through people walking in no particular hurry with strides that matched the pulsating energy in the alleys. Catherine sat in the back of the taxi gazing out the window. The volcanoes in the distance called to her. She took in a deep breath of Andean air. It felt heavier to her lungs than the air in San Francisco. It was thick, humid, or maybe just different.

"Señorita, ¿Te pregunté de dónde vienes?" The *taxista* was talking to her but she was so absorbed in her surroundings that she hadn't heard what he was saying.

"¿Cómo?" she asked, using what little Spanish she knew.

"¿De dónde eres?" This she understood and proudly answered.

"Soy de Canadá. Vivo en San Francisco, Estados Unidos. United States."

"What are you doing in Ecuador?

"Do you speak English?"

"Si, un poco."

"I've come to interview a woman."

"You are a periodiste?"

"Yes, I am. *Soy una periodista.* I write for a newspaper in San Francisco," she smiled.

"What are you writing about?"

"Juan Romero Rodriguez."

"Ah, que bien, Juan Romero, era buena gente, good man."

"You knew him?"

"Evrrie one know Juan Romero."

"I suppose you're right." Catherine was beginning to relax. This was her first trip outside of the United States since she had moved there six years earlier. She had just graduated from high school in Quebec and decided she needed a change of scenery so when she was accepted to Stanford she left for California.

The taxi pulled up in front of an old dilapidated apartment building. *"Aqui vive la señorita Rodriguez."* Catherine blankly stared at the taxi driver. *"Aqui, aqui."* He pointed his brown stubby fingers to the pale blue apartment building. She looked up and saw the paint peeling away from the walls and a group of old women sitting on the sidewalk near the entrance.

"47." Relieved that she could understand numbers she pulled out a bill and paid the driver. She stepped onto the curb with her small black leather bag, in which she carried pens, pencils, notepads, an international digital cell phone and her Canadian passport. She pulled out a tiny blue pocket calendar and double-checked the date she had made the appointment. A blue ceramic tile hung above the white door. On it was painted the number 42. She pressed the buzzer once and waited. There was no answer so she pressed several times in a row. The door buzzed open and she entered. 42-C was at the top of the narrow staircase. She gently knocked on the pale green door. As she swung her fist again the door flew open.

"¿Qué quieres?" a woman with long black hair streaked with silver shouted, asking Catherine what she wanted.

"¿Señora Rodriguez?" she inquired.

"Señorita Rodriguez soy yo."

"Hello, I'm Catherine Snyder." The woman didn't reply. "We spoke on the phone." The woman's tanned wrinkled face crinkled around her dark eyes.

"Who?" Silvia immediately switched to English.

"Catherine Snyder. I'm the journalist writing a book about your brother. I called from Miami ... about an interview." Catherine was beginning to wonder if the woman would remember her at all when she said,

"*Ah, si, claro.* I'm sorry, come in. You look different than I expected."

"Excuse me?"

"I thought your hair would be darker, but it's not. It's very light."

"Yes, well my father had light hair."

"I see." Silvia lifted her hand and ran her fingers through Catherine's reddish-brown hair, gazing at it with strange admiration. "*Pasa.* " She waved her arm for Catherine to follow. "Come, this way," she motioned. "Do you want to drink anything? I have cold tea, water, and coffee."

"I'll take coffee please."

"Sit over there, by the window. There is a nice breeze today." Silvia pointed to a yellow wood chair near a table next to the window. The sheer white curtains billowed with the blowing of the mountain breeze. She bustled off to the kitchen. Catherine took her pink knit sweater off and hung it on a hook on the back of the front door. Her hazel green eyes scanned the walls for any hint of Silvia and her family, but there was none. The apartment was bare except for a few pieces of furniture and a lamp. She wandered over to the table and took her seat. "So tell me," Silvia hollered from the kitchen on the other side of the wall, "why write about my brother?"

"He has always fascinated me."

"You are too young to be fascinated by him." Silvia said as she rounded the corner with two cups in her hand. "Sugar or milk?"

"Both please."

"You seem too young even to know anything about my brother." Her voice trailed off again as she went to fetch the milk and sugar. She returned with both and with a small plate of shortbread cookies.

"I have my reasons." Catherine gently sipped the rich coffee. "Yum, this is really good."

"Of course it is *mi amor*, you're no longer in the north. We care about our coffee here." Silvia reached up and pulled the string to turn the ceiling fan on. "So what is it you want to know?"

"Everything."

"How will you format your book? What will the direction be?"

"His life. A biography."

"And you want me to tell you the story of his life? It seems like a large task." Silvia drank her coffee, and her dark, bushy eyebrows rounded upward over her eyes.

"I'm missing information, pertinent information. I am hoping you can fill in the gaps."

"I can't promise anything."

"You are the only person I know who can talk about his family. Everyone else is dead or has disappeared."

"Have you had any luck finding Sofia?"

"No. Are you in touch?"

"No." Silvia looked out the window. Her voice softened. "We aren't in touch. I'm not sure where she is now. The last I heard she had removed herself from everyone. It has been a long time."

"Maybe we can start with the questions I've prepared." Silvia set her cup down on the wobbly table and stood up. She went inside the closet near the front door and pulled out a large brown metal trunk. She took a set of keys from around her neck and unlocked the trunk.

"Maybe we should start with this." She lifted a pile of notebooks out of the trunk and returned to the table. She fidgeted through the pile until she found a red, leather-bound book with gold letters engraved on the front that said *Familia Rodriguez*. "This was my mother's. She kept it as a record of our family." Silvia puckered her plump red lips and blew the dust off the cover. "It's our family tree. It has been passed on from one generation to the next for four generations. It stops with me unfortunately."

"What about his daughter?"

"We don't have any photos of her." Silvia opened the album and Catherine slid her chair around the table to get closer. Silvia lit a cigarette and inhaled slowly. The first page showed a detailed drawing of the family tree starting with Javier García and Graciela Melendez, her great grandparents. "This is my mother's side of the family. I don't have anything on my father's side.

"Who is this?" Catherine pointed to a black and white photo of a young woman with long braids twisted up on top of her head. She wore a delicate lace blouse with silk ribbon trim; her hands were neatly folded in her lap. Her fingers bore numerous thick, heavy silver rings.

"This is Abuela. My dear, sweet, tender Abuela." Silvia gently caressed the photo. "Thanks to this woman I didn't lose my language or culture."

"She is Ecuadorian?"

"Yes. This is my mother's mother."

"What was her name?"

"Esperanza. It means hope. But we called her Abuela. She lived on her ranch in Aguas Puras. We would go every year at Christmas and in the summer to visit her. I'm grateful my mother forced us to go. My life would not be what it is if I had lost my culture."

"Did Juan Romero feel the same way?"

"Juan Romero and Abuela had a special relationship. He came here because of her. They would sit for hours in her garden talking while I played in the river."

"What would they talk about?"

"What wouldn't they talk about?" she laughed. "Abuela was Juan Romero's mentor, the driving force behind whom he was and who he became."

"And these two people, are they your mother and father?"

"*Si*. This is just after they were married. Our pictures were added when we were twenty. Mamá said she'd change them when we were married. Since neither of us had the opportunity to marry, the photos stayed the same. I always thought Sofia should be here, but mamá wouldn't allow it."

"How long were your parents living in the U.S. when Juan Romero was born?"

"Not so long, maybe a year and a half. I remember mamá always saying she got pregnant fairly quickly.

"Mamá always said Juan Romero was a miracle baby."

"Why?"

"Because he brought joy when my father didn't want him. He was overwhelmed with what he thought was going to be a prohibitive financial constraint."

"And you were born?"

"Two years later."

"What was living in Arizona like?" Catherine prodded.

"I liked it, for awhile."

"Until?"

"Until the accident."

"Tell me more about the accident." Silvia looked out the window and paused for a minute.

"Arizona was nice. The community we lived in was decent. We had a nice house with a backyard, which was big enough for a garden. My father was working at the Center for Latin American Studies at the university. He loved it."

"And your mother?"

"She was a high school Spanish teacher. Things were good then. We were happy. Abuela came for my 14th birthday. It was as hot as hell that summer. So hot we couldn't be outside during the day. Juan Romero and I spent most of our time on the covered patio in the back. I would sit with my paints or my dolls and play all day. He would never want to play with me. He was always reading *Mafalda,* the Argentine comic, or looking at photography books my mother would bring home from school. He was an extraordinarily quiet kid. Maybe that's why he liked taking photos, so he could witness life from behind the scenes.

Whenever Abuela was there she would always want to take long walks in the evening to the edge of the desert canyons. The night of my birthday we took a drive out of town together, stopped at the Food Mart on the outskirts of town for a 7-Up and a Snickers—she knew I was a chocoholic. It wasn't the same as the homemade chocolate her neighbor in Aguas Puras would make, but it satisfied me. Juan Romero sat in the back of my dad's red convertible VW bug with his San Diego Padres cap covering his bushy eyebrows, fiddling incessantly with his camera. That car had been rebuilt four times. I think it was somewhere around 35 years old.

Abuela sped down the long open two-lane road, my hair whipped around like the snakes on Medusa's head and Juan Romero held onto his cap as if it were made of gold. We arrived in time to run to the edge and absorb the sunset. Juan Romero climbed onto his rock and watched from behind his camera lens. I cracked my 7-UP and sat next to Abuela as the sun slowly sank and grew into a huge fireball. The canyon walls reflected the orange rays of light and shifted them into blazing red. The ball on the horizon stained the clouds yellow, then pink and finally purple as it secretly snuck out of sight. Abuela began singing. *'Que bonitos ojos tienes, debajo de estas dos cejas, debajo de estas dos cejas.'* It was a song my grandfather would sing to her when he was alive."

"You remember the song she sang?"

"That night I do. I remember everything that occurred the night of my fourteenth birthday. It's as clear as if it had

happened yesterday. It's the night our lives changed forever."
She turned the page in the album. "This is Abuela. Juan
Romero took this photo in the canyon." An image of an older
woman with deep wrinkles in her brown skin sparkled on the
page. She was completely absorbed in a moment of nature's
power.

"She's beautiful." Silvia closed the book and looked
straight into Catherine's green eyes.

"Has anyone in your family ever died?"

"Yes, my mother."

"Do you fear loss?"

"No."

"You should. It's the only way to be able to accept." She
stood up and went to the kitchen for a second round of coffee. "When we got home my mother was in the kitchen cooking dinner." Silvia's eyes wandered as if she were in a distant
place while recalling that evening. "We were in the kitchen,"
she began.

'Let me help, Esmeralda.' Abuela scrubbed her hands and
grabbed an apron. 'What are we making?'

'Pollo de mango,' mamá replied. Mango chicken was my
favorite. 'Gustavo is bringing his colleague home. Dr. Walker,
you remember him?'

'For Silvia's birthday?'

'He insisted.' I saw Abuela roll her eyes, which was comforting seeing as it was my birthday and strange men shouldn't
be invited. She pulled six mangoes out of the basket on the
refrigerator and peeled them so quickly I didn't even see her
pick up the knife. She diced with swift motions of the wrist and
pushed the meaty pieces of sweet fruit into a small glass bowl.

'Isn't he the social justice guru?' Abuela mocked.

'The very one.' My mother's thick eyebrows rose as she
glanced up at Abuela.

'His idea of social justice is living blindly in his posh
neighborhood.'

'Mamá, his neighborhood isn't any more posh, as you choose to describe it, than ours.'

'But you both work … too much I might add. What does his wife do?' Abuela gave mother a few seconds to respond and then gently added 'Nothing. They don't even have children for her to care for.'

'I don't care what she does or doesn't do. I care about what we do and right now we are doing well.' Mamá pounded the dough against a wooden tablet, massaging it to a soft texture. I can still hear the sound of that pounding. 'My family is healthy, well fed, we have a beautiful home, and my children are in school. It's more than most women could ask for.'

'You're right Esmeralda. I don't know why I lose my focus whenever that man's name is mentioned. He bothers me.'

'Silvia, ponga la mesa.' I took out our best tablecloth and put my favorite blue ceramic plates out, the ones Abuela had brought from home. I dug through the drawers for a set of candles that were the same color and replaced the ones that had already burned and dripped our emotions from the night before. 'It's not Dr. Walker's fault, he's ignorant.'

'Yes it is. We are all aware of what is going on around us. The difference between ignorance and enlightenment is the ability to listen.'

'Mamá, where do you hear these things?'

'I am an old woman, *mi'ja*, and I've done a lot of listening. If I ever tell you anything it is this: be aware of who you are, of your surroundings, and of what you have. That's all you need to be happy.' Abuela was always giving us advice about life.

'Hand me the *yerba* for Gustavo's *maté*.'

'How can he drink that stuff?'

'He says the same thing about your *Aguardiente*.' Mother loved to heckle Abuela. They were constantly engaging in friendly banter.

'Bitter hot green tea sipped through a metal straw cannot compare to *Aguardiente.*'

'ALÓ,' my father hollered, his booming voice announcing his arrival. He swept through the kitchen and went directly for my mother. He grabbed her, held her tightly and gave her a long kiss. *'Hola mi amor.'*

'Hola mi vida.' He whipped around in search of me. Typically we would play hide and seek. I would hide under the table or in the garden so it wasn't hard for him to find me. He always pretended like he had no idea where I was.

'And where is my birthday girl?' He looked right passed me. 'Esmeralda, have you seen her?'

'No, I haven't seen her all day. She must be lost.'

'That can't be, not on her birthday, not after all of the gifts we bought for her.' My heart fluttered with excitement. My father was never really able to buy us many things, but he never failed to surprise us on our birthdays. He would always find something that would make our minds race with delight. I was so anxious and excited that I couldn't contain myself, and I leapt out from under the table.

'Aqui estoy papá, aqui estoy.' He ran up to me, lifted me above his head and covered me with kisses.

'Feliz cumpleaños corazón.'

'Gracias papá.'

'Happy Birthday Silvia,' Dr. Walker said from the shadows. His tall, skinny frame emerged from behind my father. His pale skin and orange freckles, splattered across his pointy nose, glowed. I was immediately uncomfortable but answered politely.

'Thank you, Dr. Walker.' He held out his hand and presented me with a small box wrapped in gold paper.

'Open it sweetheart.' My mother nudged me to take the gift. I carefully unwrapped the box that looked too expensive for me to even touch. I lifted the lid and found a shiny gold wristwatch with a blue agate face. It was beautiful and I was drawn to it immediately. I slipped it around my hand and onto my wrist.

'Jeff, that wasn't necessary.' My father was embarrassed. He didn't know at the time that it would be the first in a long line of men and gifts that would try to manipulate me. He let me keep the watch, even though I heard my mother protest later in the evening.

'*Hola papá.*' Juan finally came in from the garden, which for me was a relief. I always felt safer when he was around.

'*Hola hijo.* Where have you been?'

'In the garden.'

'You sure are persistent, trying to plant a garden in the desert.' He smiled and the wrinkles on his skin lit up his blue eyes. My father was handsome. Tall, thick, dark with dynamic eyes that shot through you like a blazing star. His accent was heavier than he wanted it to be, but I loved it. He was so much more exotic than my friends' fathers. 'Juan Romero, you remember Dr. Walker.'

'Of course.' My brother held out his large hand to fearlessly shake the infamous "doctor's" hand.

'Jeff, you've met my mother-in-law, Esperanza.'

'I believe so.' His voice slithered across the room, and Abuela simply nodded her head and continued to knead the dough for tortillas, which she had never made before coming to Arizona. Our family had become an odd mix of Latino customs, a little Argentine, a little Ecuadorian and a little Mexican. My mother handed my father his *maté* and he and Dr. Walker proceeded to the back patio to drink it. Father didn't invite Juan Romero to drink *maté* with them, despite the fact that they drank it together every night.

Dinner lasted for several hours, and everyone ate with plentiful lust. It was as if we knew it was our last supper together. The night crept into the late hours and then into the early morning. I can still smell the *pico de gallo*—an enticing sweetness with a tinge of spicy zest added to warn you not to eat too fast.

The dining room was an extra room my parents had built off the kitchen. Three of the walls were large glass windows, and the fourth opened into the kitchen. There was just enough room for Abuela's dining room table. It was wood with delicate hand-painted ceramic tiles lining the top. A blue candle was always lit as the centerpiece. '*Para equilibrio familiar,*' she would say. My father sat on the east end of the table, my mother the west. No matter how Americanized mamá had become, the superstitions passed onto her through her family history and culture never disappeared. Father was strong and energetic like the day, and she was peaceful and calm like the night. She had only two children because three would be unbalanced and she couldn't risk not having a fourth. She believed deeply in story to explain existence, love, war, everything. Father was simply logical and theoretical. Juan Romero picked up a bit of both." Silvia stopped for a moment and looked up at Catherine, "Where was I? I'm sorry, my mind got sidetracked."

"You were going to tell me how that night changed your life."

"Yes. After dinner everyone moved into the living room for drinks. I fell asleep on the sofa and I was left to sleep there. In a daze I heard the doorbell ringing over and over, like when church bells ring. No one was answering. I groggily wandered into the entryway and opened the door. A policeman dressed in a brown uniform with a gun hanging around his waist stood before me.

'Hello miss, is your mother here?' As he asked the question I felt my mother pull me backwards into her warm belly.

'Can I help you?' She was firm in her questioning.

'Can I speak to you alone Mrs. Rodriguez?'

'*Vete para arriba mi amor, acuéstate en tú cama.*' I was so tired that I obeyed instructions to go up to my loft, but I stopped on the ladder halfway up, halfway asleep, to listen.

'Your husband was attacked Mrs. Rodriguez'

Your husband was attacked, your husband was attacked, and your husband was attacked. That was the last thing I remember hearing, repeating over and over in my mind. Soon after those words left the policeman's mouth my mother began wailing in desperation. Abuela came rushing out, disheveled and in her cotton nightgown. She rushed my mother to her room to dress and then they left. The sun was coming up and they still weren't home. Juan Romero and I sat in the living room staring at the television until they finally returned. I remember as my mother walked through the door I barely recognized her. Her green-grey eyes were swollen shut, and her hair was tied back in a ponytail with big chunks hanging out, stuck to her face.

'*¿Mamá, qué pasó?*' Juan Romero rushed to her side.

'*Ven mi amor.*' Abuela said. She reached out her long skinny arms, calling for both of us to approach. 'Let's go get a cup of coffee Esmeralda.' Abuela led us all into the kitchen and put on a pot of water to boil. My mother sat down, slumping over the table.

'What's going on? Where is *papá*?' Juan Romero repeated the question.

'*Esmeralda, diles.*' Abuela whispered. My mother raised her head slowly and looked at me, then at Juan Romero. Tears welled up in her eyes and her face began to turn red.

'Your father was killed last night.' A pain shot through my heart so quickly I could barely breathe. I looked up at Abuela who was crying. Juan Romero stood completely still. 'He was attacked and shot at a gas station on his way home from dropping off Dr. Walker.' My brother turned away and walked out the front door. I don't know where he went; he never told us. He refused to attend the funeral. I don't think he knew what to do, nor did he understand why humanity could have been so cruel."

"Your brother repeatedly commented that his father's death was the catalyst for his activism."

"Perhaps. I think my father's death was the catalyst for a lifestyle Juan Romero never wanted to accept, which in turn forced him to fight so that others would never have to live through what we lived through."

"What do you mean?"

"My father didn't have insurance. My mother knew. They thought they were young enough, healthy enough, ambitious enough, tough enough to make it through for awhile."

"But he worked for the university."

"As an immigrant, he wasn't afforded the luxuries of 'native' citizens. Insurance was so outrageously expensive that we couldn't afford it in addition to the house and car, and trying to feed and cloth the entire family. It wasn't a priority."

"So what happened?"

"We lost the house and the car. My mother took on two more jobs, so we lost her too." Silvia paused, contemplating the picture on the page and then said, "It's getting late Catherine. I'll fix up the bed for you."

"No, don't worry. I'm staying at a hotel." Catherine abruptly answered.

"No you're not." She stuck her head out the window. *'¡Epa, Ramon!'* she shouted and whistled to a young boy across the street. *'¡Necesito un favor!'* Ramon will pick up your things."

"I should not impose."

"You should not refuse—it's rude," replied Silvia as she went to the back room to make up the bed for her new guest. "I insist. Make yourself at home for as long as you need to." Catherine did not refuse.

CHAPTER EIGHTEEN

Dahlia

Higher development, self worth, dignity

The rain pounded against the freshly painted blue shutters outside Silvia's apartment. It was 4:00 A.M and Catherine lay awake, listening to the tropical drops hit the sides of buildings and the streets below. She pulled the thin cotton blanket up around her neck trying to get warm but couldn't. She got up and pulled the curtain back, scanning the streets for life. On the opposite side of the street she saw a man standing under an awning wearing a brown leather bomber jacket. He had the collar up around his neck, trying to stay dry. He looked vaguely familiar, but she convinced herself she was just nervous. Moving across the room, she was aware of someone watching her below. She stopped and stood in front of the dressing mirror. Her chilled skin glowed through her white tank top and panties. She stood hugging herself, examining her face, her eyes, her hair, and her body.

"What brought me here?" she whispered to herself. She pulled her laptop out from underneath the bed where she had hidden it and connected to an international satellite network server. She began constructing an email to her best friend, George Figare, in San Francisco. George was also a writer, but of a more fantastic genre. He was a columnist for a gay lifestyles magazine and he didn't leave ANYTHING out. His aggressive and boisterous style left even the most outrageous gay man blushing.

TO: gpopilo@digitalcom.satelite
FROM: catherine@digitalcom.satelite
STATUS: Wavering
GMT TIME SENT: 9:27 A.M.
SUBJECT: Information needed

Hello George,

I made it safely here and as luck, or misfortune–I'm not sure which yet–would have it, Silvia Rodriguez invited me to stay at her house. The first few stories she told me were insightful. I hope the rest of my visit is like that. This place is chaotic. It isn't the same kind of chaos as San Francisco, its more like savage chaos. The airport, for instance, is about as big as Pier 39. The place is crawling with 14 year olds with machine guns from the past (I assume they were purchased directly from gringolandia). It makes me nervous that their testosterone could explode at any moment and be aimed in my direction. I haven't explored much. I'd like to get a better feel for the flavor of the city. The volcanoes are practically sitting on top of us—it's amazing and terrifying.

I need a quick favor—Call Sarai and ask her to email me the name and contact info for that professor down here who is a supposed expert on Juan Romero Rodriguez during his time in Aguas Puras. I want to track him down.

I'll be in touch soon.

Kisses,
Cath

Silvia probably had the contact information Catherine was looking for, but she didn't want to ask her for it. She was already slightly intimidated by this woman whom she knew was a fountain of knowledge for this book. Her kindness, although rough around the edges, seemed genuine.

The sun was beginning to rise as Catherine dressed and tied her dark blue raincoat tightly around her waste. She hid her computer again and took a final look out the window. The man was still there. He had been there all night. As she descended the stairs she noticed the lush red and brown carpet down the hallway and the shiny brass ornaments attached to the lights. She hadn't remembered these delicate details from the day before. Things here were not as bad as she had been told, she thought to herself. It was hard for her to imagine anyone not wanting to live in this luxuriously beautiful country. Stories of stern dictators from times past were difficult to believe, but she knew they were true. She had seen the films of the revolutions, the torture, and the poverty. History had written its own political story, which was then distributed throughout the world via the Internet and Real Time Viewers.

After 30 years the tiny country had not drastically changed. In the short time she had been here, she noticed that the people were humble and happy. They were content with peace. She was not used to this. She was used to greed and individualism. The two cultures were so distinct. She reached the last stair and grabbed onto the bar at her waist for balance. The lobby was dark. She hadn't noticed the large leafy plants at the base of the square pedestals sitting in the tiny vestibule either. It was as if new life were being breathed into the air. The morning was filled with utter silence. It wasn't until she neared the front door that she heard a startling voice.

"Buenos dias señorita." She whipped around to find a small pudgy man dressed in a maroon coat with shiny silver buttons. He stepped forward into the light. "I'm Alonso, the *portero*. I'm sorry if I frightened you."

"It's okay, I'm a little jumpy. Nice to meet you. I'm Catherine."

"Did you not sleep well?"

"No, why?"

"Not many people go out so early."

"I have a lot on my mind is all."

"You are not comfortable with *señorita* Silvia?" How did he know she was staying with Silvia, she thought?

"I'm fine, thank you."

"What about the gentleman?" He flipped his head toward the street.

"What gentleman?" she asked, although she knew exactly whom he was talking about.

"He has been asking for you." He jerked his head again, less subtly, in the direction where Catherine had seen the man in a leather jacket.

"Is he still here?" she inquired.

"I don't think so, but he was asking for you. You should be careful. If you like I can make you a *cafecito* here."

"You have coffee?"

"Of course. Café is the essence of life. It is a ritual, a passion, a way to survive." Catherine smiled and relaxed. Alonso went into a closet-sized room and produced two cups, a cloth filter that looked like a dirty sock, and a bag of coffee. "Now all we need is hot water. I'll be right back. Sit down over there," he motioned to a set of brown wicker chairs and a small glass table across the room. Catherine sat gently down and felt her back slip into the chair. Her emotional state seemed so drastic and unstable that she was uncomfortable with herself. Within the span of 36 hours she had been yelled at by taxi drivers, greeted with mistrust by her primary source, then invited to stay, followed, slept very little, and was now sitting in the foyer of an unfamiliar apartment building at 5:30 in the morning drinking coffee with the concierge.

"*Aqui tenemos el mejor café del mundo,*" Alonso appeared and poured the steaming water through the cloth filter. She watched the thick liquid trickle out the other end into the small cups. "It used to be we had to drink only *Nescafé,* but when the coffee market collapsed our government stopped exporting so much and we now have good coffee again. "*¿Azucar?*"

"No thanks, black is fine."

"It's strong," he urged.

"I like it black," she repeated.

"If you say so." Alonso placed the coffee in front of Catherine and returned to his office. "I don't have much, but here is some *pan campesino* and cheese."

"Looks good." Catherine hadn't eaten since the afternoon before and was hungry. She tore a piece of the bread from the loaf and dipped it in her coffee.

"You are here to talk with Silvia." Catherine sipped her coffee and didn't reply. Silvia was fairly famous in Quito for being the sister of a hero as well as for being exiled. It is rare for an American woman to be accepted. Americans were welcomed with mixed sentiments. The tourist income is greatly needed, but the lack of cultural awareness is abhorred.

"Yes. I am," she finally said. "How did you know?"

"Everyone knows. When an American comes to town we make it our business to know."

"I see," Alonso was doing a good job of confusing Catherine further with his hospitality and probing questions.

"What do you want with Silvia?" he asked.

"I want to know more about her. Do you know her?" she turned the questioning around.

"*Si.*" Alonso swallowed his shot of coffee in one gulp."

"And?"

"And I don't know very much about her."

"But you know something."

"A little."

"Like?"

"She is a professor, *Profesora de Danza*—dance."

"I didn't know that. And her friends?"

"People from the university. José. *Muchas personas.*"

"*¿*José?"

"*Su novio creo.* He is also a professor. You cannot mention him until she does or she will know I told you." Alonso turned around abruptly when the door opened. A man in a tattered blue silk shirt stood in front of the main entrance. His silver hair was tightly pulled back into a ponytail. He rang the bell with three short strokes.

"*Momento.*" Alonso called out. He opened the door by pushing a button. A loud buzz rang through Catherine's head. The man turned toward the two coffee drinkers, one dark Ecuadorian and a short American in Levis.

"*Necesito ver señor Toledo.*"

"*Un momento señor. Yo le hablaré.*"

"*Bueno, pero apuráte.*" Catherine heard the words but didn't understand. Her face contorted and her lips twisted into a confused look "*Ya voy,*" she heard Alonso say.

"What's wrong? Why are you hollering?" she asked.

"He's looking for a tenant and he's pushy for so early in the morning. Just give me a minute." Alonso's minute turned into five, ten, and then twenty. She heard Spanish gibberish in the background and was beginning to feel tired. She tried to stand up but her head began to spin. Within minutes she was in a dead sleep in the chair. When Alonso finally got rid of the visitor, she was snoring. He covered her with a blanket from his office and smiled.

CHAPTER NINETEEN

A Yellow Rose

Friendship

Catherine was awakened by the tickle of an Iris petal. Silvia hovered over her brushing the flower back and forth across her face. *"Hola dormilona.* You've been asleep for too long. It's time to get up. Come with me to *el mercado."* Catherine rolled out of bed, vaguely recalling her interaction with Alonso who apparently had helped her upstairs to lie down. She pulled on a pair of jeans, threw a blouse over her head and grabbed her bag. "I'm ready."

"Put some makeup on dear, we're going to *el mercado."*

"Makeup?"

"We're going out into the public. Please make yourself presentable. The image presented on the street is the image of gossip. There is no reason to give the hens ammunition to fuel their clucking."

"Silly," mumbled Catherine.

"But required," answered Silvia. Once on the street Catherine began to realize where she was. She had been so absolutely absorbed with Silvia and Juan Romero's story; she had not taken the time to familiarize herself with her surroundings. The crisp air struck her lungs with surprise and it wasn't until they rounded the corner and Volcán Pichincha loomed in front of her, filling the sky, that she began to sense her surroundings. She noticed the cracks in the buildings and the faded paint. She also noticed her height, how she towered over most of the indigenous women adorned with colorful skirts and wraps to carry supplies. Her pale skin seemed thin and fragile compared to the seasoned brown skin created by the harsh mountain sun and humid Andean air. They made their way to the Trolley bus, which had been in place since the end of the last century, and paid the 4 *Andinos* it cost to ride to the market. The *Andino* was the result of the massive meltdown of the Latin American economy and a spectacular step to revive the Andean states. An economist by the name of Orlando Montemarros had stepped forward shortly after Juan Romero's death in Aguas Puras. It wasn't exactly coincidental; the economies of several pre-Andino states were collapsing simultaneously and struggling to survive in the emerging global markets. The response in Ecuador was to create and push for the new economic/political system, *Andinismo,* which in fact was not so unlike the European system of the Euro. Over the years borders were broken down and a free flow of people and economies developed into a united block. Venezuela, Colombia, Ecuador, Peru, Chile, Bolivia, Argentina, Paraguay and Uruguay became an economic force to reckon with, further developing their rich cultures and finally, after so many centuries of poverty and corruption, a more stable and competitive economic system.

"This is our stop." Silvia made her way to the back door. Standing on the crowded sidewalk Catherine felt the vibrant energy of the block. People were coming and going with handfuls of bananas, potatoes, corn, wheat, mangoes and more.

"Come Catherine, the market is up through here." They walked towards the market where brilliant colors speckled the plaza like an impressionist painting. Catherine stayed close to Silvia, following her through the narrow gaps of the fruit stands, stopping to smell the luscious fruits she had never experienced—the sweet *chirimoya,* the sensuous *guayabana,* and hundreds of different kinds of bananas. Then the smell changed from delightful, mouth-watering fruit to something Catherine couldn't quite identify.

"Shall we eat?" Silvia suggested. "I know the perfect place. Follow me." Silvia led Catherine closer to the pungent smell and into an increasingly noisy and narrow side street. It was then that Catherine realized what the smell was. Strewn out on rows and rows of tables like royal corpses were freshly roasted pigs, being skillfully butchered by well-fed women who were trying to entice market goers into the restaurants located directly behind their tables.

"Venga mi amor, mi corázon, mi preciosidad. Venga a probar," they hissed, trying to seduce the two women into the locale. Silvia smiled and politely turned each one down until she made a sudden stop in front of a tall, thin woman wearing a blue handkerchief in her hair.

"Hola loca," she greeted the woman.

"Hija de puta," shouted the woman in a heavy Argentinean accent. "Where have you been?" she ran around her table to kiss Silvia.

"I've been busy talking about my brother," she turned to Catherine, "this is Catherine Snyder. She is a writer working on a book about Juan Romero."

"Que bien." The woman said. "I am Adriana, come in to eat. I'll have Gerardo prepare *un asado.*"

Adriana was originally from Buenos Aires and had moved with her husband Gerardo, an Ecuadorian, to paint. She was an artist, he had convinced her to marry him and live in Quito. He would open a restaurant, *estilo Argentino,* and she could paint. It turned out that Adriana enjoyed the restaurant business and her seductive mannerisms drew in customers. She would paint in the mornings and play hostess at midday until close. There were times when she would disappear into her art and at times would be preparing for a gallery show, so would not show her face for weeks at the restaurant.

"Her paintings became well known, after the wife of an eccentric American politician became obsessed with a particular painting of a bull," Silvia whispered. "She convinced several diplomats that Adriana was a female Picasso and now it is rare not to find her work in shows across the world." Catherine noticed that the walls of the restaurant were covered with her art, including one of an unusual looking gentleman.

"Who is that?" Catherine asked Silvia.

"My brother. Adriana and Gerardo were good friends with Juan Romero. They lived in Aguas Puras for several years before opening the restaurant. Gerardo was working on one of the flower plantations in order to earn enough money to buy the equipment. He fought alongside my brother."

Adriana sat down with a bottle of Chilean Carménère and poured three glasses full. They finished the entire bottle and had just opened another when Gerardo appeared with a tray full of *chorizos, morcilla*, and steak.

"¡A comer!" he shouted.

"It looks delicious," Catherine said.

"Of course it is," he laughed. "Excuse me," he leaned in to drop the platter in the center of the table. "Anything else?"

"It's perfect," answered Silvia.

"Is this Catherine?"

"Yes. How do you do?"

"Well, sometimes in the bed, others in the shower, and once I even did it—"

"¡Cerdo! Stop verbalizing your alleged promiscuity in front of your wife," interrupted Adriana, trying not to spit out the chorizo in her mouth between snorts. They all began laughing at her uncontrollable giggling.

"So, Silvia tells me you both worked on the flower plantations. What was that like?"

"*Bello*," responded Gerardo. "I don't think I've had a more beautiful job in my entire life."

"Really?" Catherine sounded surprised.

"It was special. Those flowers, with their magic changed lives. They still do. The flowers are enchanting. Literally. That region is filled with mysticism and tradition. Part of both is the flowers. Each plantation grows a specific kind of flower to cure a specific ailment, whether it be physical, spiritual or emotional."

"For example," Adriana chimed in, "the roses were grown to target those in need of rebirth in their lives. Although they are commonly associated with love, they symbolize a much more powerful need in humans. They are the chalice of life and serve as a reminder of the mystical rebirth."

"It was *las hechizadas*, the charmed women, who cast special spells into the soil to force the flowers to emit potent powers to attract those who needed guidance."

"I don't understand."

"You are in love let's say, but your life is absolutely stagnant. The appearance of the rose could mean you are ready for a clean start, ready to embrace that love full force."

"So people would seek out the flower that symbolized their needs?"

"No, the flower seeks them out."

"How?"

"*La señora Estela.*"

"*La señora Estela*? I know a woman by that name in San Francisco."

"So you know her."

"I buy flowers from her all the time. How incredible that you know her. Six degrees of separation I suppose."

"Perhaps. Did you not realize she was from Ecuador?"

"I never thought to ask." Catherine's eyes dropped in shame at her lack of sensitivity.

"Have you ever noticed that you don't know what flower you are going to buy until you arrive at her stall? You could walk through the entire market and NOTHING will catch your eye until you get to her stall?" Catherine considered the notion and conceded that she had often been to the world's biggest flower market and ended up at Estela's. "She is *an Hechizada*," said Gerardo. Her family has been in charge of that stall for generations. She was chosen almost 60 years ago to go and tend the flowers in the north.

"Chosen?"

"Only the strongest willed are sent north to protect the town's interests. There is too much temptation to abandon tradition and culture. The flowers are Aguas Puras. If it were not for the flowers the town would not likely exist. Or if it did it would be a rancorous place."

"The female butterfly floated aimlessly through the wind, searching for a way to solidify her womanhood when she encountered the electric blue male. Her pale brown speckled wings waned in comparison to his magnetic blue. Their wandering spirits united and bliss covered the land; the union was solidified," interjected Silvia.

"Yet to see these wandering spirits alone was a warning, a warning of a preceding death," said Adriana.

"They are the breath of happiness and the loss of a warrior soul," Gerardo said.

"What are you all talking about?" Catherine took another sip of wine and was beginning to feel tipsy.

"The land in the valley is said to be controlled by the butterfly. Souls from the past travel in the flying insects, advising the plants and animals of the pulse of the world. Occasionally, humans too can understand their advice—like in the case of the *Hechizadas*, like Silvia's brother."

"Juan Romero was touched by the butterflies. He could hear them talking, telling him what to do, touching his thoughts and his heart," said Adrianna.

"I'm sorry, but this all seems a little strange," laughed Catherine.

"Strange for you perhaps," Gerardo paused to sip his wine, his eyes staring away from the table in a daze, "But for us it was our reality. There are strange forces at work in this world *querida,* many of which we are never privy to. Some of which affect our lives profoundly and others that have the capacity to destroy us. Don't ignore them. That would be the gravest of mistakes. "The room was silent, each person in a daze of his or her own, contemplating Gerardo's words, when suddenly Gerardo let out a bellowing laugh and said, "But now we eat flan, enough nostalgia."

Several mornings later, as Catherine rounded the corner she saw Silvia across the street, standing outside the bakery. She was talking with a man in his mid-to-late forties. He was tall with his hair pulled back neatly into a ponytail and was casually dressed in blue jeans and a navy blue t-shirt. Catherine slipped into a nearby doorway to observe. They were standing very close to one another and he kept waving his arms about and yelling. Silvia stood perfectly still with a straw bag hanging over her left arm, nodding in agreement. Catherine focused in on the man's face. It was the same man Alonso had been talking to the night she had fallen asleep. Catherine stepped out from the doorway and hollered to Silvia, signaling to her.

"Silvia! Hey Silvia." Silvia glanced up and waved. The man in the blue shirt spun around, shook her hand, and quickly walked off. He turned the corner and disappeared out of sight.

"Silvia, hi." Catherine yelled out as she dodged bicycles and taxis to cross the street.

"*Buenos Dias,* Catherine. Did you sleep well?"

"Yes, thank you. So what are you doing?" Her eyes wandered in the direction where the mystery man had stood.

"Getting bread," she opened her bag to show Catherine the evidence.

"Who was that man you were talking to?"

"A colleague from the university. Why?"

LAS HECHIZADAS

"No reason. I just saw him the other day in the lobby of your apartment. He was asking for Toledo. Are you friends?"

"Sort of. Why all the questions?"

"He just seems odd to me," Catherine again looked in the direction the man had gone and frowned.

"Don't be silly," Silvia grabbed Catherine's arm and began walking. "So are we going to continue talking about my brother or not?" Silvia asked abruptly.

"Yes, I think we should."

"Well then, let's go." She sped off down the sidewalk, Catherine in tow. They didn't stop until they entered a café several blocks away. Silvia sat near the window and asked for two *cortados*. She dug through her bag and plopped some of Juan Romero's journals on the table. "The pain and suffering our nation causes to others is despicable, don't you think?" Silvia asked without looking up from the books.

"What do you mean?" Catherine hesitantly inquired.

"I keep recalling each time we felt the need to intervene with governments for the sake of democracy only to thrust the people into utter despair and chaos. Over and over again the powerful nation we call our own came down like a sledgehammer on a wedge, ripping through the fibers of other cultures. Our own incompetence has led us to self-destruct, nothing else. We always choose war. Think about it. In the early part of the century it was the war against the Arab nations. We chose money and pride over human life. By destroying Iran and Iraq and decimating states like Saudi Arabia we created hatred. This hatred led to more war. All of Africa has been in chaos for more than 200 years. We never helped stop that. Then there is Latin America. Free trade was the excuse back then to "help" the supposed fledgling economies, when all it really was, was a hidden form of imperialism. It's no wonder we keep getting attacked on our own soil. The world is at war Catherine and it always has been."

"I can't imagine life without bomb threats."

"I can."

"What was it like?"

"Filled with guilt actually."

"Guilt?"

"At first I took complete advantage of the fact that I lived in a peaceful place. I didn't relate to those whose lives were always about war. But then, when Juan Romero began to push for change I began to feel guilty. I realized that my country was one of the few where people were actually free, or at least relatively free. That's all over now, isn't it?"

"Not necessarily."

"I would have to say a semi-military state isn't one where freedoms of any sort are recognized."

"Maybe not, but it won't stay like that forever."

"Not unless someone does something about it." Silvia's tone was harsh.

"Someone will." Catherine pulled a cigarette out of her purse and offered one to Silvia. Silvia took the cigarette and placed it tightly to her lips. Catherine lit it. She inhaled deeply and blew smoke out the open window.

"Jesus. How are we going to do any of this?" She mumbled to herself.

"Do any of what?" Silvia didn't answer, she only stared at Catherine for a long minute. Silent. Still.

"Write this book," she finally answered.

"I'll write it, you just give me the information."

"It's going to take longer than a couple of days, Catherine."

"Just tell me how long we need and I'll arrange to stay." A strength Silvia had not anticipated was beginning to shine through.

"This subject deserves undivided attention, and if you aren't willing to turn yourself over to that then you won't be able to do this."

"Give me a chance."

Silvia reached out her hand. "Listen to me carefully," she was stoic. "You stay and you must commit to this. You must promise you will follow through with it." Without hesitation Catherine simply answered, "I will." A shiver trickled down her spine when she said it and Silvia dropped her head.

"This is bigger than you know, Catherine. It isn't just a book. It's my family history."

"I know. At the beginning that's why I was so nervous, but I'm not anymore."

"I must be able to trust you implicitly. There can be no secrets between us. Can you do that?"

"Yes, I can."

"Good," she paused to take a deep breath. "I need to tell you something." Catherine didn't respond. She simply leaned back in her chair and continued to smoke. "The man you saw me with this morning is José Guzman."

"The international diplomat?"

"He was, yes, but he is no longer."

"I thought he was killed when your brother died."

"So do most people, but he wasn't. He has been living here for quite some time."

"What's he doing here?"

"He works at the university. José is Cuban. As Castro got older he became more finicky, more stringent in his ways. José crossed the line by suggesting the press be given more freedoms and when he did he had to flee. He was blacklisted. He came here where he met Juan Romero. He fought with my brother until the end. Fortunately for José, Castro died and the new regime was not interested in him. He, however, chose not to return to Cuba.

"This is fabulous. He will be very helpful. When will we meet with him?"

"He's tense about your project. He hasn't really recovered from Juan Romero's death and lives believing at some level someone is still after him. I'll introduce you at some point, but first I want you to read some of these." She pushed the pile of tattered leather bound books in front of Catherine. They were clean and had brown cords tied neatly around them. "These are the journals. Read them." Catherine rubbed her hand over the images imprinted on the front.

"It's a coyote. He represents the uncertain. He is the trickster. I think Juan Romero chose him as a symbol to remind himself to always watch his back. She stood up and motioned for the check. Silvia dropped Catherine off at the apartment and walked to the market around the corner to pick up a few items for dinner. "I'll be right back," she shouted.

"Buenas tardes señorita," Alonso greeted Catherine.

"Buenas tardes," she replied as she swept passed him toward the stairs. She dropped her things on the table and nestled into the mustard yellow armchair near the window. A cool breeze ran through the curtains. She opened the journal and flipped through the pages. Dates after date of Juan Romero's thoughts were scribbled down in the form of letters to his sister, but she didn't know where to start. Then she saw José's name and stopped to read.

Silvia:

A man came into my life today who I have a feeling will greatly impact my life. José Guzman. He is a Cuban, fleeing from the old revolution. I sometimes wonder if that country will ever exist without some kind of revolution. He has joined forces with us to fight. He told me he couldn't be in a place where people were struggling to save their livelihoods and not help. It turns out that he knows Mariano, my friend from Colombia. He spent some time in his training camps in the early years. His years of wisdom keep him young and vibrant. When he found out I had been there he was thrilled. He immediately fell into our circle and Gerardo accepted him with open arms.

Catherine's eyes swept over the pages, again falling on José's name written at a later date.

José was injured today. A bulldozer almost ran over him when we were protesting. Fortunately it only got his foot, which is broken in several places. He is on his way down the mountain with this week's supply run to see a doctor. I find him so interesting because he is not the kind of man one would expect to stick it out in the mountains fighting a pseudo-guerrilla battle. He was a diplomat, an educated, affluent man with few signs of being able to function outside of a large city, but he does. He transforms himself from an intellectual to a rugged fighter. He and Gerardo have spent weeks planning an academic/physical tactical attack on the trailers that we will initiate next week, so long as he can make it back up here. He suggested that we set a smoke screen in the main trailer to smoke the people out and be able to access their files to find out what their plans are. We would send in men to help put out the fire, disguised as mining workers and have time to pull information about things like shipping schedules, what kinds of minerals they were extracting, and who was working which shift. I think it is ingenious.

There were several more entries describing José's participation in the fighting. Juan Romero had adopted José as his *comandante*. It seemed to take stress off Juan Romero and allowed him to organize the group.

Silvia came in as Catherine was unfolding a piece of rice paper she had found tucked in the middle of one of the journals Silvia had given her. "I've got dinner here. Are you hungry?"

"Famished."

"Let's cook." She saw Catherine holding the paper in her hand. "What's that?" she asked.

"I don't know. I was just about to look at it." Silvia stepped closer as Catherine opened it. "It looks like a letter. It says: 'Dear Silvia, I know we only met for a brief moment but I feel I must express my feelings to you at once.'" Silvia rushed over and ripped the letter from Catherine's hands.

"What is it?" Catherine giggled. "Why is there a love letter for you in Juan Romero's journal?" she egged Silvia on.

"It's nothing."

"Then why can't I read it?"

"Because it's none of your business."

"Who is it from?"

"José."

"When did you meet?"

"I met him here after my brother's death. He was staying with Gerardo."

"So it was once you had moved here?"

"Yes."

"And how long before you started seeing him?"

"Not a very long time. I felt like I knew him the moment we met because of my brother's letters."

"Doesn't sound like you want to talk about it."

"But that's not important right now. It has been a long day and I would like to eat." Catherine let it go, knowing that she could get the real story from Adriana later. She smiled and said,

"That's fine. You'll tell me when you're ready." She was beginning to understand how to work with Silvia and what she could and couldn't get her to talk about. As Silvia chopped Catherine continued to read, backtracking from Juan Romero's notes about José.

Silvita:

Aguas Puras is beautiful. I love the main plaza with the cafés, but the outskirts are what fill my heart with a savage sense of life. The plants grow so lushly that they cover the roads only a week after being trimmed. Can you remember? Abuela's is far enough outside of town that I feel removed. I walk the distance to town when I need to see a friendly face like Sofia's. A rickety bus makes its way down the road and I think of Dominique, the young girl I met on the bus on my way here. She is homeless, wandering, no one to care for her and I wonder why we are permitted to procreate if we cannot nurture? Why are we allowed to throw our children back onto the streets to beg, sell and suffer? Children are lost creatures. They are lost at home, at school and in the eyes of society. We are blind to them.

It is this lack of responsibility that creates all of these situations, and yet we choose to have babies, the ultimate responsibility, to increase the tension and amount of work we must do for others. Children are not animals to be abandoned; yet every day they are abandoned. We don't listen to them. We treat them as objects of abuse, when in fact they are fragile, knowledgeable beings waiting to share what they can. They should not be hungry, cold, scared, or lonely. They should not lack love, tenderness, humor or purity. Even after papá died we were supported. I didn't know it then, but I do now. We were fortunate because many children slip easily through the cracks for no reason. If one person could listen and have the courage to follow through, one child would survive. I don't want to be the person whose ears fall deaf to the needy child. I can barely take care of myself, let alone a child. My ideas go towards work and change. Children are too time-consuming if you are to raise them well and dedicate your full attention to them. If it isn't full-time, you should not bring them into the world.

"Yet he did," Catherine stopped.

"What?"

"Dedicate himself to his daughter 100 percent."

"Not conscientiously. He loved her, but he wasn't blessed with time to raise her."

"How old was she when he died?"

"Less than a year."

"It's too easy to spout off about responsibility and tenderness, but it isn't reality," Catherine thought about her own delinquent father as she kept reading.

As I sit sipping sweet coffee, my trip from Miami to Turbo, Uraba, Colombia comes back to me in bits and pieces. The trip was longer than anyone had expected due to maintenance issues. We had to spend 3 weeks repairing an engine in Haiti that had apparently been rebuilt in Miami. The captain, Orion King, didn't have much money so he purchased used parts from a dealer. They turned out to be faulty and the engine began failing. We passed time doing standard maintenance on the boat and drinking with the locals, starting at around 2:00 every day. When we finally got the engine back up and running we were all so lax about work that it took almost two days to whip us into shape to run the boat again. I found the work tedious and physically tiring and was grateful when the announcement was made that we would land the next day. We docked early and were to be paid later in the evening. I couldn't wait to get my ticket to Ecuador.

We went straight to a bar to find some food and a few cold beers, but everything was closed and no one was around. We heard quiet noises from inside some of the bars and houses and knocked on one door, only to silence the timid conversations that were going on behind it. It was an eerie stillness that seemed abnormal. We saw an old man hobbling down a path between two houses and hollered to him in Spanish. He made no effort to turn around so I ran after him thinking he was hard of hearing. Once I caught up to him he ignored me, waving his hand in my face and repeating "Déjáme en paz. Déjáme en paz." He scurried like a rabbit through the back door of an avocado green house. We didn't see anyone else and after two hours of wandering around gave up and went back to the boat. King had checked in with the guards at a military post in the port and had learned that a fugitive followed by a posse had been through that afternoon. It seems the paramilitary forces had come through, looking to terrorize anyone who knew where this alleged guerilla was. That's all they would say, but we knew how it went. He ran through town, virtually unnoticed, and several hours later the paramilitaries come through, wreaking havoc on the people, accusing them of hiding the criminal, even threatening them. They are worse than the actual villain. If the guy is smart he had a place to go from here and didn't stay very long. The Uraba region in northwestern Colombia is one of the most well known ports of contraband. Legal and illegal economic interests drive the interest to wipe out leftist activity (whether it be drug related or not) in the area. It is a hot spot and I wanted out!

We ate ship food again after dreaming of a normal meal, which made the meal on the boat that much more dissatisfying——rubber corn, overcooked spinach, raw onions and mushy macaronis with Velveeta cheese made my stomach turn. King didn't pay us and we waited for three days before he was able to get our money. The townsfolk didn't come out until the last group of soldiers departed. One small team of three men was left behind to keep an eye on the town for any "suspicious activity." King wasn't able to find many new crewmembers so he decided to leave for Maracaibo to test his luck there. I stayed.

We found a posada run by Alejandra, the mayor's daughter. It was the only place that would take us in following the ransacking. It was uncomfortable to be there, only because the soldiers kept guard 24/7. I wasn't happy, and even less so when Alejandra threw herself at me. I was in the hallway, leading from the bathroom out back to the rooms when she swung her long brown legs around the doorway and stood, her skin glistening from the humidity, in front of me. Her dark chocolate nipples formed shadows beneath her white blouse that hung delicately from her shoulders. Sorry if the description offends you, but I want you to get the idea about how erotic this woman is and how absolutely unavailable as well. So, her long black hair fell heavily in ringlets down her back and her lips were gently pressed together. She stepped up to me and pushed her chest into mine, thrust her hand between my legs and began kissing me. She tore open my zipper and shoved my pants down around my knees. I lifted her skirt and we had sex, standing up, in the hall. She climaxed whimpering and left me half naked in the afternoon light. At dinner I almost choked on the baked chicken when her husband walked in. Mariano. He runs a ranch outside of town.

He sat down directly across from me. As we ate Alejandra began touching me. He rambled on about politics, corruption and murderous tendencies and didn't seem to notice that his wife was giving me an erection. I wiggled a little, which caught his attention. He asked me if I was okay and I attributed it to the rum, said I wasn't used to drinking hard liquor. I quickly changed the subject and started asking questions about the fugitive. Our conversation went something along the lines of:

'What fugitive?'

'We were told there was a man on the run who came through here a few days ago.'

'I haven't heard a word of such a fugitive.' I looked around the table to check to see if any of the others would counter his statement. No one lifted his or her heads.

'The soldiers told our ship's captain they were searching the town for a fugitive.'

'Lies.' Mariano curtly answered.

'What were they looking for?'

'It's their excuse to rob us. They don't come here because of Alejandra's father. I'm grateful for his desire to save his daughter from pain, but it disgusts me that he pays them off. Money is privilege.'

'Mariano is kind of a communist.' Alejandra winked at her husband.

You mock me Alejandra, but you don't understand me. I'm not a communist. I simply believe in equality among people. There is no need for some of us to be incredibly wealthy while others don't have enough to eat.'

'You're interested in reform?' I remember asking.

'Agrarian reform, at least in this part of the world. It could work, but it's not the answer to everything.'

Silvia, in my opinion it is similar to agrarian security. I cannot pretend to be well versed in Agrarian Reform, most simply because I have no agrarian experience whatsoever. I wonder if there are many from our country that can actually defend themselves as producers of food at a basic level. How many farms and ranches are run without computer chips or hormones or pesticides or subsidies? We are slowly killing each other because we don't take the time to care for one another, nor do we appreciate the cost of doing so. Those who do try to work the land suffer if they cannot produce fastest the reddest roundest tomato——never mind that it tastes like water. The flavor of our food, the essence of our beings, the centerpiece of families, has become obsolete. We have lost the desire to appreciate the quality of life as long as we are guaranteed sufficient nutrients. Mariano's idea isn't to change an entire system, rather ensure its survival. Genetically modified foods are not necessary, they are convenient. Mariano points out that to sustain a people they must eat and they should eat well. They must feel worthy by working and what better way to work than for you. They must earn a fair wage for their work and can do so by coming to a consensus within the community. We don't do that.

"I see where he got his ideas. I didn't know he spent time in Colombia. It explains a lot," said Catherine.

"It influenced him a great deal. I don't think he would have moved so quickly in Aguas Puras if he hadn't seen what he did there."

The further I get from home the harder it is for me to understand. How can a nation as wealthy as mine have people die of hunger? How is it that in a nation as safe as mine, there are children who are shot dead in the streets? How in a nation as educated as mine, are there individuals who cannot read? It is inexcusable yet continues to be the norm. What of a government representing our interests—by the people, for the people? Where has our noble sense of truth and dignity disappeared? So many questions that for a long time have gone unanswered.

"This letter came only a few days later." Silvia handed a tattered envelope to Catherine.

Silvia:

I'm starting to lose track of time. My conversations with Mariano spanned several days. I learned that his ranch is run like a government. Everyone who works for him is part of an intricate system. They make as much as he does, live in their own homes and have plenty of money to feed their families. Day in and day out he leaves and every night brings someone different home for dinner. Alejandra and I kept messing around for a week or so, until my guilt no longer allowed me to become aroused. Mariano is a good man and his wife is insatiable. I asked him this evening if I might go to the ranch with him. He refused, stating there was too much going on for him to be able to properly show me around. I am fascinated with his ideas about an egalitarian society. It seems unrealistic and has been proven not to work. Political ideologies come and go. The only stable systems are those that feed off the greed of people and capitalize on the suffering of weaker systems. Historically, powerful nations or systems are those willing to be the most unjust, but it seems to be filtering down more and more to the common man. What is it in our psyche that causes us to reject helping those in need? What is it about power that blinds our conscience and creates beasts within willing to trample over any obstacle in their way? It seems as if the powerful nations never go up against each other because they know it is pointless. There cannot be a definitive winner. The strong choose a weak enemy to ensure victory. The strong thrive on the weak. It is the law of nature. Last night we spoke of this in the focus of social classes.

'It is beneficial for the wealthy classes to band together, build walls and separate themselves from the working classes,' Mariano began. 'Think of them as the essence of society. They are the educated, creative, intelligent, wealthy chosen ones who will succeed in saving countries from destruction and despair.'

'Yet they are responsible for the same despair they wish to avoid.'

'Exactly. Do you know why?'

'Greed?'

'Partly. My belief is they don't really want to prevent poverty, but ensure they do not end up poor. The fear of losing wealth converts them into greed- driven monsters, unable to share and unwilling to sacrifice if it means hindering the progress they are making on their path towards wealth. I see it everyday here. The wealthy landowners or factory owners have no regard for human decency, particularly if it cuts into their profits. Families work, all nine members, 15 hours a day for enough money to buy grains and maybe milk, while the owner lives on the hillside in a mansion surrounded by guards to protect his property from thieves. What this owner doesn't think about is that the thieves are created as a result of the factory. A vicious cycle, true. Avoidable if only we humans used our brains.'

'And government intervention?' I asked.

'They are the worst of all,' Mariano laughed. 'The government's mission is to become more powerful and wealthier than the owners who pay the government off. It is a game of survival, not of consciousness.'

'Many people I know believe in government.'

'I believe in it too. I also believe in cleaning house every few months, if you know what I mean. Sometimes places and systems become dirty, corrupt, they should be changed, cleaned. People are not ignorant. The wealthy and powerful believe we are, but given the appropriate tools we are capable of anything. The first step is to be able to see the truth. The planet has become a series of convoluted lies. The truth is the first step in understanding, the first step to shed the fear.'

'Where is the truth?'

'There are different versions of the truth. The objective isn't to skew this truth, it is to shed light on it. We will all come to our own conclusions, but the truth is always the truth.'

As we discussed this I realized that my photographs are my way of telling the truth. Most of the time I capture an expression or an emotion that exposes what a person is saying or thinking or feeling. Pain, joy, hunger, despair, sadness and much more can be shown in one image. I think I'll pay more attention to that when shooting.

Silvia paused chopping vegetables and said, "This is when he started taking photos without regard for money or time. He dedicated himself to shooting the truth of the people and places he met and saw and sent them home to Shilo, his photography teacher, and to me. In Colombia he sent several rolls a week."

"How long was he there?"

"About a month before he went to Aguas Puras. We started submitting them to magazines. His work was revolutionary, because no one else was ever able to get onto Mariano's ranch and take pictures of the training."

"How did he finally convince Mariano to let him on the ranch?"

"He didn't. He sneaked on." Silvia flipped through the stack of letters and pulled another one out. She shuffled through the yellowing pages "Here. Read this."

I made the most intelligent mistake of my life today. I decided to hide in Mariano's trunk and find out more about the ranch he so vociferously brags about. Once the car parked and the voices faded I pried the trunk open and rolled onto the dirt below. I was afraid to stand because I heard gunshots in the distance. At first I thought I must have climbed in the wrong car, but I looked up and Mariano's bright yellow Fiat was parked just a few feet in front of me. I crawled into a field to the north and lay in the tall grass to catch my breath. The trunk had been hot and the air so thick I was barely able to breathe. I heard a man shouting, but I could barely understand what he was saying. The voice grew louder. I frantically searched for a place to hide. The car was too obvious and I was sure to be seen, not to mention I wouldn't be able to see anything. About 100 feet to my left I spotted an old, rusty tractor and slithered my way under, which wasn't easy with my clunky camera digging into my back. The grass was tall enough to hide in, I thought. I could feel my heart pounding so hard it felt as if it would burst through my skin. I slowed my breathing to avoid hyperventilating. What I saw was not what I had expected. The group of men in green army fatigues was sprinting across the field and then throwing their bodies on the ground as waves of gunshots rung through the air. I kept shooting rolls of film and I could hear the motor on my camera buzzing in my ear, under the banging of machine guns. Out of excitement or stupidity or false fearlessness I sat up to try to get a better shot of a teenaged-looking boy dodging gunfire by leaping behind a rock and I was spotted. I don't know who it was because the butt of the gun slamming against the back of my head knocked me out before I was able to see a face. I woke up in a twin bed in a room painted peach with a green blanket. My camera gear was on the nightstand next to me and it was dark outside. At first I thought I was back at the posada until I heard the rowdy voices of men downstairs. I snuck down to get a better look and was apprehended while peering through the cracked open door.

'Captain, look who I found spying on us again.' The body attached to the husky voice shoved his hand into my back and pushed me into the light. The men laughed when I tripped and almost fell.

'Go easy on him,' the man at the corner of the table said without looking up from his beer. I wanted to say something but my judgment told me it wouldn't be in my best interest to open my mouth. 'Mariano says you're American.' I shook my head yes. 'Says you're traveling, to Ecuador.'

'My family is there.'

'You can see how we might be suspicious of a traveling American with a camera, hiding under a rusty tractor, taking pictures of our men who are armed and participating in military training. Seems like an odd place for a young man like yourself to be.' Once again I didn't say anything. 'Wouldn't you say?' With that permission I blurted out something that sounded much more sarcastic than I wanted it to.

'Wouldn't I say what?' The background noise of slightly inebriated men fell silent and the man at the corner of the table finally lifted his head. The man who had pushed me into this broiling beer bonanza along with two of his cohorts closed in behind me. I could feel the sweat running down the scrapes on my back, burning my skin. In the dead calm of the silence a boom of laughter exploded from the wide mouth of "El Capitan" and the men stood frozen with blank stares of shock on their faces as this well-built man with a thick black mustache released round after round of laughter. With the same suddenness the laughter had begun it stopped, and his pale yellow eyes bore through my own and into my brain. They were catlike, almond-shaped eyes with grey splashes around the pupils. With those eyes he said, 'We're training to fight. That's all you need to know. You can keep your film if you send it out without telling anyone where you were. I want them published. I want them to know we're ready.' And with that I was escorted back to my room. They drove me back to Alejandra's the next morning. When I apologized to Mariano he said very little. I learned they *were guerillas preparing to fight Uribe. Whether they succeed or not remains to be seen. I sent the rolls to you today, separate from the letter.*

"Those are the ones *Time* published aren't they?"

"Yep. This one," she held up a picture of 'El Capitan,' "actually won several awards. Juan Romero didn't care. He was already in Ecuador, fighting with Padre Miguel when most of them were announced."

"Yeah, I've seen them in photography books."

"This is a passage he wrote to go with the images," Silvia handed Catherine a loose piece of paper.

TRUST

Trust is a concept difficult to define. We all crave being trusted and being able to trust yet it seems that forces work against us as we seek trust. It is almost a game of faith that each individual toys with trying to master, yet never fully understands. In the realm of the human spirit we depend on this confusing idea to enlighten us. To seek trust is to seek truth, which brings us peace. If I don't completely trust my neighbor how can I confidently lead an honest existence? I have often heard of people who have lost all faith in society, don't trust government, and reject any sort of community. They pretend to lead full lives, yet it is impossible to do so with such lonely and desperate self-images. We must start by trusting ourselves in order to eliminate fear. Once we have done that we open the possibilities to a more *fulfilling lifestyle. A large problem I see in many societies today is the inability to trust. With good reason, I must add, as historically people and organizations have treated one another poorly, breaking down the existence of confidence and security. Is it possible to stop being malicious and selfish, to stop making excuses by blaming others, and to return to an ideal of basic self-worth and kindness? Probably not. I'm an idealist but I am not as naïve as I once was. There is too much animosity and competition between people to hope for complete recuperation. I would like to seek an answer or a long-term remedy for mistrust and hate without compromising or ignoring the reality, which is that we need a period of time to heal before we can begin again. How long will it take? What steps need to be taken to achieve this? Is it possible? I see it in the combat groups. They trust each other so greatly that they will die to save one another. Is it their cause, or have they been brainwashed? And what is the difference?*

"This time with Mariano really confused my brother," Silvia said. "He was seeing things and comprehending things that went against his nature. He knew that the guerillas in Colombia kidnapped and sometimes murdered people, yet he was sympathetic to them because intellectually he understood their fight for justice."

CHAPTER TWENTY

Opens mother love and love of wisdom of the Goddess.

Catherine and Silvia thumbed through several of Juan Romero's journals as they ate dinner, watching a torrential downpour.

"I've never seen rain like this," said Catherine.

"Isn't it refreshing?"

"It's cleansing. Look how it is rushing through the streets. It has converted them into small rivers, and ridding any filth that previously existed—simply washing it away."

"True. I've always loved the rain here. It penetrates the body. It isn't like rain in the States, or at least not where I lived."

"Arizona isn't exactly Seattle-like weather."

"Hardly."

"Even New York doesn't get this much water."

"No, and even if it did people wouldn't stop long enough to notice."

"Everything here is suspended, as if as soon as the rain starts, people automatically shut down."

"We are waiting for nature to flex her muscles." Silvia gazed out the window as Catherine turned several more pages in one of Juan Romero's journals.

"What are these?" Catherine lifted a small pile of photos from the middle of the book.

"Let me see." Silvia reached out for them. She glanced through the "4x6" black and white photos. "Juan Romero took them. This is Abuela." She passed Catherine a photo of the elderly grandmother.

"She looks so young. How old is she in this picture?"

"I think 74, 75."

"Wow, she looks like she's in her early 60s."

"She always did age gracefully. The mountains and peace of mind her life brought kept her vibrant until right before she died." Silvia brushed her finger across the dark eyes of her beloved relative. "She was such a powerful woman. Look at her elegance and ruggedness." Abuela was dressed in a long denim skirt and a white blouse with embroidered flowers, a gardening apron hanging loosely from her shoulders. A masculine-looking Panama hat shaded her brown skin from the sun and sheltered it from the rain. Her feet were protected from the mud with black rubber boots that reached her upper calf. A large machete dangled from her weathered, bony fingers that she used to slice through the brush. In the other hand was a bouquet of gardenias. "She loved gardenias. That smell is so potent, I can almost feel it right now." Silvia looked across the room and nodded hello to Abuela who was sitting on the sofa sipping chamomile tea. She smiled and winked at her granddaughter. Catherine shot a glance in the same direction.

"What are you looking at?" There was no response and Silvia continued to stare into space. "Silvia?" Catherine took Silvia's arm in her hand.

"What?" She snapped out of her daze.

"Where were you?" Silvia looked back, but Abuela and the heavy scent of gardenias were gone.

"Just thinking," she said unconvincingly. "This is Padre Miguel," she continued onto the next photo. "He was a master orator. This shot was taken during a rally in town after they found out about the mine's existence."

"How did they confirm it was operating again?" Silvia flipped through several more photos and then began laying a series of them out on the table. Catherine glanced down at the black and white photos of tractors and trucks moving piles of dirt and bulldozing trees.

"They had started despite the order prohibiting such mining in the valley. They knew very well that the deforestation and contamination would impact the local watersheds."

"And they were mining gold?"

"Yes."

"And now it is so precious it's prohibitively expensive."

"It was cheap down here, but it has always been valued in the North, and people either don't care or are ignorant about the suffering and destruction it caused to extract it. It's like diamonds in Africa. Even after the horrors and atrocities, the murders and mutilations, people continued to buy diamonds. Why wouldn't they buy gold from a region where the only negative impact the mining had was economic, environmental and spiritual? The mining company understood this all too well."

"How did they find out about the mining?" Catherine asked again.

"Juan Romero found the site by accident. He was walking, taking photos, following the blue butterfly through the cloud forest when he heard the rumbling of machines. He scrambled up the hillside to be able to see into the next valley and what he saw was a large-scale mining operation underway. The site was east of town and high enough into the mountains that it was likely no one would find it. In a letter Juan Romero wrote to me I remember him saying, 'The blue butterfly led me to the spot.'"

"The spirit."

"Abuela told Juan Romero the legend of the blue butterfly just before he discovered the mine, and since the moment he found the site he placed utter faith in the flying guide, especially because the butterfly had already appeared to him.

"What is the legend?"

"The blue butterfly appears in the mist of the cloud forests of the Andes because she was once a child of these mountains. Her name was Isabela, the offspring of an *Hechizada*, Maribel. Although blessed with great powers, Maribel did not make wise decisions with regard to amorous encounters, and her worst judgment in character was Isabela's father." Silvia stopped suddenly, feeling a hand on her shoulder. It was Abuela, telling her the story to pass onto Catherine. "He was an eager and greedy Italian who had come to the South in search of a get-rich-quick scheme. He was a gambler and a drunk and seduced many women in town, including Maribel. She became pregnant and gave birth while he lay with another. Time passed and he came and went, always in search of money. One day when Isabela was nearing one year old he appeared at the door with an empty backpack in hand. He demanded that Maribel turn over the child. She refused and slammed the door in his face. The rain outside pounded furiously and blurred Maribel's view of the Italian's actions. She was virtually blinded, while he could see her every move. Within minutes a rock came crashing through the glass window, shattering it into crystallized pieces and hitting Maribel in the head, bloodying her face and knocking her over. He leaped through the broken window and swept the wailing baby into the backpack, swiftly disappearing into the darkness.

But Maribel was not of weak spirit and within seconds was out the door, machete in hand, pursuing the kidnapper. Her feet beat against the ground rhythmically and her ears sharpened to the sound of her child's cries. Her pace quickened as the rain pounded against her heaving chest. He was not a mountain man and despite his physical strength he had not anticipated such a furious chase from the mother of his child. Isabela was weighing heavy on his shoulders and the storm worsened. He could hear Maribel slashing through the cloud forest with her sharpened machete, howling for her daughter. His breath was short, but he managed to gather enough strength to start up a steep slope. The water ran through the intertwined branches of the thick layer of vegetation, making the ground slippery. He grabbed vines for support and forcefully pulled himself up. The last inches of the slope wore him down. He was exhausted, but then he heard Maribel behind him. She did not sound tired. It was as if she were possessed by something not of this earth, something driving her toward her child.

He tried to identify a route that would lose the obsessed mother and chose a narrow path near the edge of the mountain. It was just wide enough for him to sidestep along. The rain was falling harder, soaking the ground and loosening the rocks to the point that each and every step could be his last. The ravine below was like the open mouth of a famished abyss, eagerly awaiting its next victim. He rounded the corner and reached for the trunk of a gnarled tree, struggling to break through the rock, when a drenched Maribel pounced on the rock above him like a black jaguar after its prey.

'Give me the bag Giovanni,' she hissed. His body trembled from the cold and fear. Maribel held the machete high above her head, ready to slice his throat.

'She is my daughter too,' he contested. Her arm went higher.

'Hand over the bag or I will kill you.'

'You'll kill me either way,' he trembled and slowly removed the bag from his back and held it in one hand. 'Step away and I'll leave her here,' he said. Maribel hesitated but slowly stepped back. Giovanni put the bag near the edge of the ravine and pointed for Maribel to move further back. As she stood to move, her feet slipped beneath her and she fell. The sudden movement startled him and he lunged forward to avoid what he thought was the guillotine-like sword in her hand. As he fell forward his back leg knocked the bag and sent it tumbling down the cavernous ravine. The child's screams were heard all the way in town.

Maribel lunged forward in a desperate attempt to save her daughter, but failed. In an instant the universe stopped. Maribel's breath froze. The rain did not wet her face, the wind did not chill her bones. The air was still. In that moment she raised her *machete* and methodically ran it across her throat, slicing the jugular cleanly. Her blood squirted out of her veins, covering Giovanni's face with a thick liquid, stinging his eyes with her pain. She fell, limp to the ground and the rain washed the blood from her body, into the ground. The wind whipped through the trees, and Giovanni squirmed off the ridge and stumbled down the hill. As he reached the bottom of the hill a group of men came racing up the path and stopped suddenly when they saw him, covered in blood, sobbing. He turned his head and pointed up the hill. Three of the men continued up, following the crushed brush. They found the limp body, wrapped it in several coats and carried it back to town along with the disoriented Italian.

Upon arrival he was taken to the police where he revealed his side of the kidnapping. He painted Maribel as an unfit mother. The truth was that he was to marry a wealthy woman from the capital who could not have children, and without his child she had refused to take him as her husband. The police in Aguas Puras are not traditional and often choose alternative methods of punishment. Although Giovanni claimed he had not killed the mother and daughter, no one could truly ever know. Thus, the police sent him south into volcano country to live in solitude, to await his imminent death at the hands of *Pacha Mama*. He was psychologically tortured by *El Altar*. She would gurgle and burp but never fully release her power, not until many years later when she asserted her beauty by blowing her top and collapsing in onto herself, crushing everything around her, including Giovanni.

As for Isabela, her spirit was transformed into the wandering blue butterfly thanks to the women in town who took her mother's limp body and burned it with rose petals to dissolve her saddened heart and lift her burden of psychological pain. They mixed the ashes with butterfly dust and let them fly above the ravine together where Isabela had fallen to her death. From that moment she was destined to join others in protecting the valley."

"That's a beautiful story Silvia."

"Abuela told it to me," she said putting her hand on her shoulder.

"Is it true?"

"Everyone believes it, so it must be true. Strange things happen in that valley, Catherine, very strange things."

"So after Juan Romero discovered the mines what did he do?"

"He took the photos, developed them and brought them to the church."

"To Padre Miguel."

"Yes. Juan Romero trusted Padre Miguel and was confident he was the man to bring the news to the people."

"The beginning of one man's destiny."

"No, his destiny began long before that, but taking the photos at the mine marked the first time he was conscious of his fate." Silvia turned and put her coat on "I'm going out for a walk. I'll be back later." Catherine nodded then made her way to the kitchen with the journal in hand to make a cup of tea.

Her mind is much more sophisticated than mine. She is constantly thinking about the ideologies behind the reasons we do things. And then there is her subtle beauty. Her auburn hair drops in sweaty ringlets around her neck when she is working. She is shameless in revealing her heavy breasts to the world, sometimes not allowing herself to wear a bra and letting the pale pink nipples show through her white blouse. Her mouth opens and a ring of fiery opinions burst out, torching her burnt orange lips. Her body and her thoughts penetrate mine and push me to the edge of existential bliss.

As Catherine read the journal she was interrupted by a knock at the door. She opened it to find a young man in an Electroex uniform holding a small package.

"Catherine Roswell?"

"*Si.*"

"This package is for you from the United States." She signed, took it and closed the door behind her. She opened the brown paper box and pulled out a headset and microchip. It was an older model of a Panagram Holoviewer, but it worked. She inserted the microchip and an image of her friend George appeared in the distance. His voice was slightly distorted but she could still understand him.

"Hi Cat. I got your message about Juan Romero experts. It was difficult to dig anything up, but I did finally find something that might be useful. There are four formidable people who have done work on him. Three are environmentalists that live here and in Europe, but the other one is at the *Universidad Andina Simon Bolivar*. Here is a link to some of Juan Romero's written work within the gentleman's papers that I found at the cyber library. Maybe it will help you with background." Catherine punched the key word to access the text and pointed the viewer towards the wall so she could read it.

"It is common for an essay such as this to be prefaced by a distinguished colleague or critic in order to give prestige or credibility to the work. The reader will discover that such a preface does not exist in this book for two reasons. One is because it is my journal and two because I find them to be pompous and useless and a way for another person to express his/her arrogance about his/her own intelligence. In an ironic twist this article will most likely not make it very far, thus does not need an introduction.

Now that this matter is cleared up, I can begin this essay by explaining that my thoughts on Capitalism and Democracy have been developed through my experiences within and outside the United States. I intend to share my thoughts with others, but in no way is it an attempt to prove or disprove a theory. In simplest form these are my own personal thoughts.

Capitalism in itself is a valid economic ideology for the human race. It falls in line with human nature to be greedy and egotistical. A capitalist's goal, which is the most profitable, is to take risks that will yield the greatest profit. Most often these risks are taken at the expense of family and community, but not at the expense of the capitalist. This is exactly what I see happening in a small community in Latin America. A community, which has found a balance between capitalism and social conscience, but is being attacked by a larger entity driven by pure capitalism."

Catherine read intently, curious as to how this man, who was raised in a free society could be so critical of the same system that supported him. She continued reading as Juan Romero wrote about how Capitalist ideals were simply the result of the dark side of human nature and how with time it has lost perspective and the ability to prioritize.

"Democracy is theoretically able to work for the good of the people, to provide liberty, equality and freedom for each individual. We are all to have opportunity to obtain happiness whatever that means. The contrary has occurred. We have been plunging into a slow growing abyss called human misery. When hard-working middle-class families cannot afford homes, let alone the "extras" that were once enjoyed by our ancestors, such as toys for our children, a vacation once a year to a National Park, or even a used automobile, this is an indication of a loss of economic stability and the beginning of a criticism of the system. The people begin to blame the political system for not providing what it promised, when in fact it never promised anything.

In turn, the corporations, which are responsible for the stability of the political system whether we like it or not, look elsewhere to exploit human frailty in order to maintain peace in the homeland. They branch out into other systems where they know the people and government are not sufficiently united or organized to fight. Liberty, equality and opportunity are basic values, but for corporations these precepts are not natural and therefore do not exist. Democracy and capitalism are in conflict with one another and it is a wonder they have lasted so long together. Perhaps the rationale behind their union is the government's power to convince the people they are free. Freedom is a privilege and a drug. Those who are free take advantage of the fact, while those who seek freedom are obsessed with doing only that. To keep the state of the nation peaceful its citizens must believe they are free. Convincing them of political freedom is more important than economic freedom. If they are free politically they feel a sense of control over their lives, however false that control may be. Therefore, if they are economically oppressed they can only blame themselves for not fighting the system. This propaganda stops us from genuinely thinking about where the immense wealth earned in our country goes or why it is not distributed more equally. It also stops us from finding out what the corporations are doing to other people in the world. How do these people survive?

To survive one will work and provide for the family, even to the extent of sacrificing oneself to share the wealth. As a capitalist one doesn't ever have enough, while a survivalist who is a democrat can be satisfied. There is no need for children to die of hunger, for mothers to die during childbirth, for human beings to live on the street if you believe in Democracy.

When the market plunged into disaster, only a few were left with any reasonable amount of money. Over investment in technology, housing scandals and inflated values ruined the market, ruined society. I don't know why we don't learn from each other's mistakes.

By nature, Capitalism and Democracy should not be expected to succeed together. Perhaps in a narrow-minded, short-term plan they will. We have seen countries grow, hoard power and money, lose it, and then pretend to bounce back as if nothing happened. We must acknowledge failure—failure to serve the people whom government was meant to care for. Just as the Romans became extravagant and lost perspective on the raw details of governing the people, the U.S. too will face this dilemma. Extravagance of the few cannot sustain an entire society."

The phone rang and Catherine let it, once, twice, four times. It didn't stop ringing, so she finally picked it up.

"*Aló?*"

"Catherine! Why didn't you pick up?"

"Hi Silvia. Sorry, I was enthralled reading something your brother wrote about capitalism."

"He liked writing about that topic. Can you leave that for later?"

"Why?"

"I want you to come down to the restaurant. That's why I'm calling. I thought you might want to eat with us. That way you can talk some more with Gerardo."

"I'm not sure how to get there on my own."

"Take a taxi. There is a card with the address on my dresser. I'll see you shortly." She hung up. Silvia was totally domineering in Catherine's eyes, but Catherine did not feel the need to challenge her. She knew it would create tension between them, and she felt she was gaining Silvia's trust. She grabbed her purse and went downstairs to hail a taxi. An old beat-up black Volkswagen pulled up alongside the curb.

"¿Adónde vas?" the cabby asked. Catherine handed him the card. *"Vamos."* He waved her in. From the moment she sat down he bombarded her with questions. "Where are you from?" was the first that came out of his mouth when he heard her struggling Spanish.

"Canada, but I live in the States."

"Gringa, I thought so," he said in a heavy accent.

"How much further?"

"Soon." Catherine didn't recognize anything but she had to trust he was taking her in the right direction. Almost 45 minutes had passed since he had picked her up. She didn't remember it taking so long with Silvia and that was on the bus. Her heart began beating a little faster and she was feeling anxious, but she didn't say anything. The taxi wound in and out of the streets, stopping at stoplights, rolling the windows up and down as he went past shops and newspaper stands, greeting his friends. She kept a stern face, trying not to show any emotion, but she was scared. Almost an hour and 10 minutes had gone by. She started looking around for landmarks that might guide her, but everything looked the same, old stone, narrow streets, crowded sidewalks. At least she knew they were in *Quito Viejo* because of the buildings. With this realization the taxi stopped. *"Aqui estamos,"* he said pointing to the sign above Gerardo's restaurant. "36 dollars."

"What?!" she shouted. "You've got to be kidding. You drove around for almost an extra hour."

"Scenic route *señorita*." Catherine decided not to fight but only gave him $30.

"Short $6."

"That's all I've got." The driver smiled as Catherine slammed the door and stomped into the restaurant.

"Where the hell have you been?" Silvia accosted her.

"I took a taxi like you told me to."

"That should have taken 10 minutes."

"I'm told it was the scenic route."

"Oh, Jesus" Silvia smirked. "How much did that put you back?"

"Let's just say that it's more than I'd pay in San Francisco."

"Come, have a drink," Gerardo said, winking at Silvia. "We've been waiting for you to arrive so I could start the video."

"What video?"

"The multimedia show Juan Romero put together for the townspeople." Gerardo poured Catherine a glass of Malbec and sat her at a table in front of the stage. "Now that our long lost *gringa* has appeared we can get started. Adriana, the lights." The lights dimmed out as an image of Juan Romero faded in on the stage. The hologram was so realistic that Catherine looked twice to double check it was only light.

"I come to you tonight with news that in all certainty will not please you. I do not want to create chaos or discomfort in your lives, but what I have to show you will change your lives. Per Abuela's recommendation I have begun taking long walks in the forest to clear my head. She says the cloud forest works magic on a lost soul, which I believe I am. She is absolutely right. I found peace while on some of my walks. I found gentle paths and thick eucalyptus to soothe my anxious thoughts. I discovered the power of silence. I sought out the messages of the sweet cool mist. I continued to walk for several weeks, each time allowing myself to go further and to climb higher." As Juan Romero narrated his experiences walking through the Andes, a slide show of magnificent photos he had taken, developed and printed ran in the background. There were images of yellow fields full of tiny orchids, thick shrubs covered forest floors, dense cloud forests, and candid shots of native fauna like an unsuspecting sloth hanging, asleep from a *cínaro* tree.

"On the day I reached the highest I had gone, something sobering happened. I was climbing up *Pico Bonito* when I heard noises that were not natural. I heard clamoring and clanking, motors and voices." As he transitioned from the meditative peace of a tranquil mountain setting an image of an ax propped up against a tree filled the space behind him. Noise from the original audience listening to the newcomer's speech could be heard. "The images you are about to see are the beginnings of a brutal crime against nature, the rape of the virgin forest." The hologram went silent as Juan Romero stepped aside, holding his arms out for the entire town to witness the full-fledged mining operation in action. The pictures of stripped mountainsides accompanied by the sounds of rumbling tractors and metal slamming against rock sent a chill through Catherine's spine. Juan Romero's image was not present, but the sound of his voice was amplified as the images flashed back and forth from the destruction caused by the mining company to the looks of disgust, despair, and anger on the faces of the townspeople.

"Maple Mining has begun extracting gold from the mountains in *Valle Bonito*. They have done so after explicitly being told they could not. They have ignored your wishes (an injunction) and hide their true intentions from you." A strange smell filled the room. It felt like the strong scent of minerals to Catherine. She turned her head to Silvia and received an affirmative nod. It was the same scent of the contaminated water that, if left unchecked, would eventually flow into the flower fields down valley and destroy the flower crops. The smell had infiltrated the room as photos of several holding pools appeared. The mining company was trapping the water and putting it into the pools to buy time. It knew the moment the water was released hell would break loose and a fight would ensue. The stage went black, and then a hologram of Padre Miguel appeared.

"Thanks to this brave photographer we have been enlightened with information to save our village!" Padre Miguel roared. "I think it best to review how dangerous this operation is, for those of you who don't remember the last time this happened. Juan Romero, can you put up the slides of the mines again?" With a laser pointer Padre Miguel began explaining the process. "They begin by extracting the ore from the rocks. This means blasting the mountainside away. It can create pits more than 300 meters deep and two-thirds of a kilometer wide. They then take the extracted ore and transfer it to the leech pads. These are the leech pads," he showed the crowd with the laser light. "The rock heap is then soaked with a cyanide solution that seeps through the pile, leaching out the gold from the ore. The gold-bearing cyanide is then collected from the leach pad and piped into a lined storage pond. That is here."

"Cyanide? That doesn't sound good." Sofia said.

"It's not," he replied. "Although Maple Mines wants us to believe there are no leaks or dangers, there is the possibility for the cyanide getting out into the ecosystem. The gold is filtered out onto carbon granules and the cyanide is sent back to the heap through a storage pond."

"What impact could that have?"

"It's not always clear, but our fear is that the water will be contaminated and that will damage our flowers and put our own health in danger. This kind of mining uses large quantities of water. We cannot trust the mine to be our ambassador of environmental protection. It is not what they are interested in. Regardless, many of you are asking yourselves how this is possible? Didn't we already stop them? Well, after Juan Romero brought me these photos I made some calls and found out that the injunction was quickly lifted when the tune of $2 million dollars was paid. As always, corruption prevails."

"What are we going to do?" a weak voice from the audience asked.

"I don't know, Carmen. I don't know."

This is when Juan Romero reappeared and said, "We're going to fight. We are going to stop the mining by doing whatever it takes. We leave tomorrow to march by foot into our mountains to protect them, to stop their disparagement." At first there was silence and then the sound of two hands meeting one another to generate applause was heard, followed by a second pair and a third until the entire room roared with noise. "Bring yourselves, bring your locks and chains, bring your magic!" Juan Romero shouted. And with that the lights went up in the restaurant as if it were intermission at the theatre.

"I love watching that clip. Especially today," said Gerardo.

"Why today?" asked Catherine.

"It's his birthday," said Silvia. "Why do you think we've gone to all this trouble decorating the place and feasting like we are. Did you not know?" Catherine's face was flushed. She did know and had for some reason totally forgotten.

"I've been completely engulfed in his journals."

"Well, let them go. Tonight is for him, not for you," Silvia reprimanded.

Gerardo stood up in front of the group and with a childlike grin said, "Now it is time for the grand opening of the gallery."

"What gallery?" Catherine asked Silvia.

"Gerardo is opening a photo gallery and in honor of Juan Romero the opening show is a collection of his work."

"Where did he get a hold of the pieces? I thought they were destroyed by a fire."

"Some of them were, but my brother shared everything with my mother and me and sent the negatives to me in New York. I had prints made for a scrapbook. I can show it to you later."

"Why haven't you shared them with everyone before this?"

"I didn't want to. They are extraordinarily personal."

"Still, people had the right to know they existed."

"What people?"

"The world. They are invaluable. It is art. It doesn't belong to anyone."

"They belong to my family and my family decides when and where we want to share the treasures of my dead brother."

"Silvia, if you want me to write a book about your brother you can't hide things from me."

"I'm not. I'm just giving you the information in my own time. If you don't like it then don't write the book." She got up and stood by Gerardo as he continued to ramble, slightly drunk, about his old friend's work. He finally wound down his speech and invited the crowd to join him. The gallery was upstairs in a remodeled storage space above the restaurant. A set of circular winding stairs in the back of the dining room reached up to the gallery. A yellow light beamed down onto the stairs like a ray of light from heaven. Catherine made her way up and through the high arching doorway. The space was a wide-open loft with vaulted ceilings. The walls were painted pale yellow over an old brick. The hard wood floors had been recently refinished and glowed with the warm lighting. An intricately painted labyrinth on the floor led visitors from one photo to the next, sequentially guiding people through the gallery so that the order in which the photos were viewed unveiled a story—the story of a young man's struggle and a village's power to work together as a community. Catherine slowly made her way through the artistically created maze, viewing the powerful black and white prints that had been enlarged to cover the wall space from top to bottom. They ranged from landscapes to shots of the locals. The sixth photo she came upon drew her in deeply, specifically to the tiny child nestled in a woman's breast. Her eyes pierced Catherine and the woman's smile illuminated the room they were in.

"Silvia, who is this?" Catherine asked loudly to draw Silvia to her.

"That's Sofia."

"And the baby?"

"Maria de la Luz, Sofia's baby. My niece."

"They are both so beautiful. This photo feels like—"

"Home," interrupted Silvia.

"Yes. Like home."

"It's because that is what it is. This was a family. Happy and humble, living in an apartment near Sofia's café. I remember when I got this negative and had it printed I cried for hours. My brother had created a beautiful life for himself and he was so far away. She is one month old in this picture."

"Where is she now?" Catherine pushed.

"I don't know." Silvia's lips were tightly pursed and her eyes watered. Catherine did not pursue the subject, feeling guilty. She would wait until the photo was not present. Silvia walked away, wiping her eyes and immediately smiling to greet an affluent looking visitor. Catherine continued down the path, observing and taking notes on the photographs. She was finally able to put faces with the names. The next photo was of Padre Miguel leading a protest march where he carried a sign that read LA TIERRA ES NUESTRA. FUERA TRANSNACIONALES! –THE LAND IS OURS! GET OUT MULTINATIONALS! His eyes blazed like a roaring forest fire; the veins in his head bulged and pulsated. Then there was the image of Abuela planting in the fields. The lens focused on her powerful hands, aged and worn from so many years of tilling and fertilizing the earth. The seeds she held in her hand seemed plump and fertile. The image of Octavio was disturbing after seeing Abuela's serenity. Catherine wasn't sure where he was, but understood he was trying to cut a man loose from chains. The man was unconscious, blood running down his head. He had locked himself to a bulldozer labeled "Maple Mining Inc." Octavio was looking behind him, desperate to free the man. He was unsuccessful for the next photo shows another man in army fatigues standing over the bound man with a pistol in his hand. Octavio was nowhere to be seen. Catherine felt an aching in her belly that she had only felt once before in her life, when she was told her mother had died.

Catherine was already living in the U.S. when she received an urgent email that her mother was ill. She had cancer. It was apparently in the advanced stages and her mother had known for several months, but did not tell anyone. By the time Catherine arrived home her mother was dead. Her uncle, who had been like a father, gave her a laser video her mother had recorded earlier. She put her hand on the locket her mother had given her as a baby. It was filled with dried rose petals.

"*Fuerte, ¿no?*"

"*Si Gerardo*. What happened?"

"This was the twenty-third week of the protesting. They decided that the only way to physically stop the mining was to block the equipment. It actually worked until the site leader decided to hire a group of militia men, ex-military that were part of a radical group in the North that executed innocent people simply for living in a war torn zone."

"*Guerilla?*"

"That's always the excuse. I think they liked to kill. It's disturbing, but I've seen it happen over and over in almost every country. Our answer to stability is violence."

"So, they were hired guns?"

"They showed up at dawn and began shooting protesters. No one from the village had guns. Their intention was to stop the mining, not kill. It was a massacre. Of the 127 souls on that mountain, 63 of them were shot dead on site."

"And Octavio?"

"He escaped, along with Juan Romero. They dropped down the south side of the mountain range. It took them sixteen days to make their way back to Aguas Puras. Everyone presumed they had been victims."

"What happened to the bodies?"

"They were dumped in one of the mines. Almost 12 years passed before we were able to recover them."

"Where were you?"

"I was there." He pointed to the man in the photo, bloodied and thought dead.

"This is you?"

"Yes."

"But—"

"Juan Romero later told me that Octavio saw the man coming and hid behind the bulldozer. As he was about to shoot, Octavio knocked him over the head with a rock."

"And Juan Romero?"

"He was on the other side of the mining camp. Octavio set me free and took me to Juan Romero. They dragged me out of there on their backs. That's why it took so long for us to make it back. Despite the fact that Octavio saved my life when he hit the gunman, the pistol fired and a bullet penetrated my hip, shattering it, rendering me incapable of walking. The pain was so excruciating that when I did wake up I passed out as they carried me down the mountain. They set camp in a cave the first night where we couldn't stay for long, it was too close to the mining camp. For two days they plodded through the forest with me on their backs in search of a safe haven. I was in and out of consciousness. Luckily the bullet went through me and missed my vital organs, but I lost a lot of blood. On the third day Octavio left us hiding in some thick brush near the river. He said he would be back shortly and that we should not move. It was hours before he returned, but he brought several dark-skinned men dressed in bright red cloaks and wool caps. Their feet were covered only with rubber sandals.

"Come here." Gerardo led Catherine by the hand to a photo on the other side of the room. "This is Cotocoatl, he was a Shaman. Octavio knew exactly where he was taking us when we plunged down the mountain into the cloud forest. Cotocoatl was well- known for his healing powers and lived with his people in a secluded inaccessible region of the mountains. The only way in or out was by canoe through treacherous rapids. I was tied to the boat and we launched, eight men, one boat and 27 river km to go."

"How did Octavio know?"

"Octavio is a spirit who has lived in the mountains for an infinite number of lifetimes. His relationship with them is one of wisdom and trust. He knew exactly where to find Cotocoatl."

"This Cotocoatl, does he still live?"

"No. He was 93 when he saved my life and he died nine years later."

"Who is the Shaman now?"

"I believe his grandson was blessed, but I'm not sure."

"What did he do to you?"

"Everything I know about the early moments of my encounter with him comes from Octavio and Juan Romero. I don't recall very much except the vertical mass of the canyon walls towering above me in the canoe, the roar of the water and the voice of a man yelling commands in a language I couldn't understand. When we landed on the riverbank I was so exhausted I could barely keep my eyes open. They took me to his hut, I can still smell the smoke from burning eucalyptus. A woman, Sarai, gave me a potent drink which sent me to sleep for 46 hours while Cotocoatl repaired my injury and wrapped my leg in a healing cloth."

"How long did you stay there?"

"We were there for seven days before I was strong enough to move. Then we had to hike up and over several mountains to access a point on the river that would take us to the plains where we caught a bus."

"That's amazing."

"Yes it is. And it is why I am devoted to both Octavio and Juan Romero. They believed in me and in life."

"Did you ever go back?"

"There was never a need to."

"Weren't you curious?"

"No." Gerardo smiled and kissed Catherine on the cheek. "I must mingle!" Catherine again stood staring at another powerful image taken by this man who started off as an aimless traveler. Cotocoatl's face was expressionless and covered with deep crevices around his eyes and mouth. His skin was dark and the lines paved a path to his brown eyes which seemed to penetrate the camera and look right into the photographer's own eyes. His clothes were slightly ragged but neat and elegantly decorated with shiny beads and embroidered images of mountains, llamas, condors and other symbols from his surroundings. Catherine took notes on each object she saw, thirsting for more information on the significance of each design.

"*¿Vino?*" A handsome young man in an ugly blue tuxedo offered Catherine a glass of wine from a tray. She looked him up and down and smiled.

"*Si gracias.*" Embarrassed by the retro attire he was forced to wear, he blushed and quickly served the wine and bowed his head to the *gringa* then excused himself. She made her way over to a set of overstuffed chairs in the corner of the gallery and settled in, watching everyone interact. Silvia and Gerardo were selling hard. They had invited a handful of select, wealthy collectors and critics. Adriana was in charge of the collectors, discussing the artistic genius of the rebel. The others told stories. With the wine and the heat making its way up to Catherine's head, she felt secure enough to close her eyes and doze off into a contented, half drunken state of Jungian sleep. No one woke her up until morning.

The new day greeted her with the smell of fresh coffee and bright sunlight streaming in through the loft windows.

"*Buenos días amor.*" Adriana was sitting in a chair across from Catherine sipping her morning caffeine. "*¿Café?*"

"Yes, please." Adriana poured the black petrol through a tiny metal percolator. Not much had really changed in South America compared to the States. Life was hard, but simple.

Catherine was starting to appreciate not having to go through 16,000 steps to do even the simplest of tasks, like make coffee.

"I found a letter you might be interested in," Adriana said. "Shall I read it to you while you wake up?"

"From who?"

"Juan Romero."

"Okay."

Adriana pulled an envelope out of her jeans pants pocket and carefully unfolded it so the lilac gladiola petals would not fall to the ground. She began reading.

"Dear Adriana,

We miss having you here. Gerardo is working hard in the fields and I have been walking and taking pictures. You have probably heard by now that we've discovered the mining company has gone forward with operations. I don't know what the next step will be, but I don't think it is going to be easy. I was at Sofia's today reading "La Voz" when I overheard a group of people talking, quite passionately, about the mining company. They discussed whether or not this mine could really destroy everything like the people are saying. They have been fighting for years and now the company says that yes it has gone ahead, but instead of extracting and dumping it will properly dispose of waste and later restore the area. I know that in Peru protests broke out recently over gold deposits. The government there also revoked permits given by a previous president, but not before an immense amount of pressure and documented illness. I fear corruption has already taken over, but I also feel like I have to do something about it. What? Despite reservations we are here. I consulted a set of Milagros Abuela gave to me and drew the coyote. Not exactly a sign of strength, but good advice. He's the trickster, so I should watch my back.

I feel as if I were sent here to protect my family, even though Abuela is the only one left. Maybe I'm protecting it for my future family. There is one woman who piques my interest, but she is French and I'm not sure how to approach her. She owns a café in town. Her beauty and fortitude intrigue me, but my lack of maturity hinders me from moving forward. I'll let you know what happens if anything. Keep us in your prayers. We shall need them.

Your Dear Friend,
Juan Romero

They left for the mountains before I got this letter. The postal service was not so efficient then. Gerardo went with them without telling me. I assumed he had gone when I read the letter. That time was the worst of my life, having the two men you love and adore out of reach for weeks at a time. Never knowing if they will come back. My friends used to say I was too dramatic, but I knew the danger they were putting themselves in. People don't stand up to corporations and government here without seeing bloodshed. It's a natural part of the process."

"When did you hear from Gerardo?"

"He went down the mountain after three weeks and stayed only to help re-supply. He called. We barely said anything. We could feel each other's pain and we both knew what had to be done. After that was when he was almost killed."

"He told me about that."

"Those are the times when you just have to let go of everything and believe that whatever happens is meant to happen. It's like Sofia coming into Juan Romero's life. Tragedy would have never struck had they not met, but she once told me she would not give up the little time they had to love for anything. They fell hard for each other. It was their time. It doesn't happen like that for everyone."

"Like Silvia and José?"

"I guess. How do you know about them?"

"I found a letter, and Alonso might have mentioned something about it to me."

"That damn fool. You can always count on him to open his mouth," Adriana chuckled.

"How did they meet?"

"Through Gerardo. He put them in contact when Silvia was looking for a job at the University. At that time, José was still fairly well connected and set up interviews for her in the Dance department."

"And now?"

"He stopped teaching full time. He's been in Aguas Puras for awhile."

"I just saw him the other day."

"He comes and goes, but he built a house a couple of years ago and has slowly moved into it."

"So they are a couple."

"I wouldn't call them that. They are *amigovios*." Catherine looked at Adriana with a confused expression. "*Amigos/novios*, you know, friends with privileges."

"Oh, I see."

"Truth be told I think Silvia is deeply in love with him, but she can't let herself go. The death of everyone in her family has made her very reserved. Opening up to love again is difficult for her, not on a conscious level, but subconsciously. José is content with what he has as well. They see each other often, when he comes here, and he has his own space. It's a good deal for both of them."

"She won't move to Aguas Puras?"

"Why should she? Her life is here."

"But he is there."

"Exactly."

"I would think she would want more stability."

"It's not for everyone, Catherine. I for one couldn't live without Gerardo day in and day out. He is my rock, my pillar of strength. Other people don't need that or they don't want it. They function alone very well. Silvia has chosen a lifestyle that suits her. Perhaps the future will change her outlook on life, but she is happy."

CHAPTER

TWENTY-ONE

Hawthorn

Hope

Later that same evening Catherine and Sofia were cooking enchiladas. As Catherine diced the onions she wondered about something she had found in Juan Romero's journal. Sofia had written in the final pages. Her despair was so deep that as Catherine read she began to believe Sofia would put her pen down and kill herself.

"What did she mean about loneliness eating you alive? Was she so alone that she couldn't bear the solitude? I have never felt that kind of loneliness. Even now, so far from home, I meet people who are kind enough to share their homes and food with me. People with hearts so generous I can reach out and touch the pulse of giving. Yet I see how it isn't reciprocated. Why do they suffer?" Catherine asked.

"Suffering is a matter of perspective. There are different kinds of suffering. I've seen people living in absolute misery who don't suffer, and others who live luxurious lives, surrounded by people, and they suffer great pain."

"Have you ever been lonely Silvia?"

"Yes," she lowered her head and stirred her chamomile tea.

"When?"

"In New York. I loved being there. I had friends, my life was flourishing, but something was always missing."

"What?"

"Family. I missed my family."

"So why did you leave your mother?"

"Why do most of us leave? It's time. It's time to make our own lives. We just don't realize that we don't have to run from the family to do this. I did. I ran. I ran as far as I could and I regret it. Now I can't go back to her, it's too late for me. With the arrest warrant still valid it is hard as well."

"Perhaps they'll pardon you."

"I doubt it. They don't have a reason. Catherine, I tried to burn down the biggest paper in New York City just because they didn't support my brother. I was crazy."

"Within the social constructs that exist now you are crazy, but stepping outside and viewing it as an act of passion for your brother, to support him and to be a catalyst for change—in my eyes that makes you a heroine."

"Thanks. The truth is I prefer it here. Life is slower. There may be infinite problems, but I don't get lost in the busy shuffle of the day. I have to think about things. I'm not forced to forget. It's a relief. I think my brother felt the same way, about the peacefulness. The part about not thinking, well it never occurred to him. Living in Aguas Puras sparked his need for information. He became obsessed. Listen to this." Silvia began reading from one of Juan Romero's journals.

I picked up a book by Karl Marx. I wonder why in high school we were never exposed to political ideologies other than our own. Democracy, Capitalism, Patriotism. We don't truly appreciate the meaning until we experience another way of thinking, of being. Marx says, 'The Capitalist can live longer without the worker than can the worker without the capitalist.' I have never even begun to think about breaking down the system I grew up in, to question it, but the idea of worker vs. the system is an interesting concept. Everyone around me is always trying to make ends meet, struggling to survive. I had never before thought of us as having a disadvantage, but I suppose we do. Even more-so now, in current times with big business getting bigger and more powerful. Mamá has been working harder for less for years. She is a commodity just like anything else and could expire at any time. What a disturbing thought that humans are expendable. Not a new concept, but frightening all the same. We are all expendable. There are very few of us that are so valuable we cannot be replaced by another. I don't believe that a shift towards Marxist ideals is what will bring the world around, but there must be a better way, a combination of social consciousness, independent thinking, and corporate responsibility.

"He was ahead of his time, especially for one so young."

"Perhaps he wasn't much different from a lot of people who grew up watching the United States try to dominate the world while allowing corporations to rob it blind of its values, morals, and way of life."

"Did he write that before or after meeting José?" Catherine prodded.

"Before. He didn't meet José for another couple of months. José was a dear friend to my brother, despite what you might have heard, and a wonderful advocate for the town. If it weren't for his experiments and ensuing reports to the government on the state of the water, a lot of what was going on might have been kept quiet. He even sent reports to Greenpeace and blew the lid off of the environmental injustices going on in the valley."

"Didn't they end up enemies?"

"No. That's just what they wanted the outside world to believe."

"They?"

"The opposition."

"Why would they need to discredit their relationship?"

"To discredit the idea, not the friendship." Catherine scribbled away. "Can I ask you why you don't tape our conversations?"

"I didn't think you would allow me to. Not after the incident in Miami."

"Those were a bunch of ignorant reporters shoving recorders up my nose two hours after my brother was killed. Wouldn't you have done the same thing?"

"I don't know if I would have grabbed so many of them. I also don't often wear such sharp high heels so my ability to smash the recorders wouldn't have been as successful," Catherine smiled.

"Those were great shoes, weren't they? Made it onto Cristina."

"Cristina?"

"She was the Miami Oprah. That was a long time ago. Go out and get a recorder tomorrow. I promise to behave myself. Are you hungry?"

"Actually yes. That smell has been making my stomach rumble for an hour."

"My mother learned all of the Mexican recipes from Rosa, the woman who owned the restaurant Juan Romero used to work in when he was a teenager. We would hang out there for hours after school and when *mamá* was working, Rosa would

feed us everything from *mole* to *flautas* with spicy red chil-
ies to *sopa de tortilla*. I miss that food." Silvia served up two
heavy plates filled with enchiladas and guacamole and they sat
in silence for a minute, enjoying the smell of the hot steam,
oozing with spicy chili scents and warm ground beef sautéed
with onions. "This is what life teaches you. To enjoy what you
have."

"With all of the years of school I have under my belt
Silvia, I've never learned any of this."

"Any of what."

"How to cook, how to spend time with friends, how to
slow down. I haven't even really learned what politics is. I
have spent my life pursuing stories about politics. I've studied
every system ever invented at some of the finest universities.
I've been to press conferences for people of high rank, but all
I have learned is that I don't know if they are telling the truth."

"Education isn't an institution, Catherine. Have you not
learned that through your writing? Education is experience.
There are levels and varieties of education. Where did you
learn to love?"

"At home I imagine."

"Where did you learn about sexual love?" Catherine
looked away, her skin flushed. The tiny capillaries in her face
filled instantly with blood, brightening her pale skin. "Well?"
Silvia continued to press.

"With a friend."

"Not at university?"

"Of course not. But how does that have anything to do
with politics. Sex and politics have nothing to do with one
another."

"Au contraire my naïve friend. Sex is power; so is politics. We learn by living."

"You're right, but I meant how did your brother learn so
much about politics, how to fight, and how to win? He was
just a photographer."

"You're not listening. He was in the trenches of real life. He took risks that most of us would never take, and he cared. Not many people do anymore. It was also a time when the news was still relatively believable. Now it's a lost cause."

"Why?" Catherine's tone was on the edge of being offended.

"It's controlled."

"It has always been controlled to some extent."

"But it's worse now. Tell me about the process of getting a story run in your paper."

"The editor controls much of what is printed, that's true, but it isn't his fault. He has to follow government regulations."

"Government regulations in the media equates to the death of a free press."

"Most articles are carefully monitored, but we can still contribute what we want."

"Oh, I thought story ideas were handed down."

"They are generally, but if we have an idea we can follow the lead."

"All I am saying Catherine is that you should check the financials of Krocker Communications. I think you'll find it interesting how much money flows from the government into the pockets of the management." Krocker was the parent company to Catherine's newspaper.

"Not uncommon."

"Not anymore."

"You're a pessimist."

"I am a realist. Plus, my thoughts are not my own. They come directly from my brother's writings. He wanted only peace and he didn't get it, at least not while he was alive."

"Some argue he made it worse."

"Initially, they're probably right, because the people had to struggle to break free of the oppressive, destructive business being conducted, but misery didn't exist in Aguas Puras. Those who say the people of the valley were miserable are mistaken.

Misery is when a woman with three children, a job, and assistance from the government doesn't have enough money to live in a home made with solid walls, so she constructs a house with sticks and mud and a tin roof, only to watch it destroyed in the first fierce storm of the season. If she's lucky her neighbors are kind and don't steal the food she has for her children. The kids' teeth are not strong enough to chew tough foods because she hasn't had enough money to buy milk or toothpaste on a regular basis for three years. On top of all of that, she worries that her children will never find a better life because where she lives is an hour on foot from school, and she sends her girls every day, praying they arrive safely."

"Where is this?" Catherine naively asked.

"Most places. Open your eyes. If you are going to write, then write the truth." Catherine didn't respond. She didn't know what to say. Silvia saw the lack of understanding in her eyes. "Finish your food. We're going for a walk." She picked up her plate and threw it in the sink. It was getting dark, and Silvia wrapped a colorful red and blue woven shawl around her shoulders.

"Where are we going?"

"I want you to see something." She opened the front door and stood waiting, without looking at Catherine. Catherine hesitated, but then put her coat on and obediently followed. Silvia didn't speak as they descended the stairwell and walked toward the bus. In silence they stood waiting until a beat up silver and brown trolley bus rolled up. Catherine didn't make a move to get on because of the arms and legs hanging out the sides. Men and women stood on the steps, hanging on to bars on the inside of the door so as to not fall off. The bus was exploding like an overstuffed turkey. Silvia stepped up and began pushing her way through the sweaty throng. "*Permiso, perdón, permiso,*" she repeated. She looked back and screamed for Catherine to get on just as the bus was beginning to pull away. Catherine made a last minute effort to jump up onto the stairs, with arms out in hopes someone would grab her, which they did. It was like being pushed by a wave in the ocean, shoved up and then forward in a sea of unfamiliar darkness. Hot, sticky bodies, humid from the rain, rubbed against each other.

People got on and off the bus, but Silvia didn't move, not that she could. Catherine started noticing a change in the faces on the bus. When they got on, she didn't notice anyone, but now most everyone seemed so different. Different clothes, different skin, long black hair. A woman sitting on the bench directly in front of where Catherine was standing was rocking back and forth, humming and whistling to herself. A strong stench of urine floated up from her lap. She held her dry, cracked hands out asking for money. Her nails were filled with dirt and grime, her clothes hand woven, but dirty and full of holes. Only a pair of thin rubber sandals, which showed her rough, bloated feet, protected her soles from the earth beneath. She held a bag around her shoulder that wrapped across her chest and around her back. Then Catherine realized it wasn't a bag. She was carrying a baby. It did not make a noise. Its face was dirty and it was tiny. Catherine stared, barely able to breathe. She tried to reach into her pocket for money, but it was gone. Someone had pick-pocketed her. She said nothing, for fear of causing problems.

Finally, Silvia began pushing her way back to the door. "*Vamos,*" she ordered, and Catherine stuck to her, trying to take advantage of the space created as Silvia moved through the crowd. When the bus began to slow, she forced herself off the second step and down onto the sidewalk. The street stank of rotten sewage, and Catherine covered her mouth and nose so as not to vomit.

"Come." Silvia began walking. The night had not quite set in, and Catherine could see the outlines of unfinished cinderblock apartments with tin and red tile roofs packed closely together. Half-dressed children with knit wool caps ran in and out of the buildings, while boiling water filled with whatever starch was found for the day gurgled from behind the walls. Block after block was more of the same. Indigenous women, like the one on the bus, sat against the cement walls begging, not saying anything. Children ran up to Silvia and Catherine, fondling them, gazing up with glazed over eyes, pleading for anything. "*Regálame*," they would almost sing, in hauntingly empty voices as their hands searched for treasures in the women's pockets.

"Where are we going?"

"To see a friend." As they rounded the corner three men stumbled out of an entryway reeking of *aguardiente*, pure moonshine, screaming and swinging punches at one another, completely missing true flesh, but capturing big chunks of air. The alcohol was so strong a small match thrown into the air could have ignited a raging fire. A half a dozen children under the age of twelve ran around the courtyard kicking a flat soccer ball and yelling at one another. "*Hola Pedro*," Silvia said to one of the drunken men. He twirled around, struggling to maintain his balance. His eyes were red and swollen. The bottom lid drooped like a dog that had been put under anesthesia.

"Siva? Sat you?" he muttered in drunken slurs.

"Yes Pedro. It's me. Is Alma here?"

"Inside." Just as he replied, one of the other men pushed him from behind and he fell to his knees. He whirled around and grabbed the man by the ankles. Silvia brushed past them and said, "Hey Franco, how are ya?"

"You know those men?"

"They are brothers."

"What are they fighting about?"

"Who knows, they do this every weekend." Catherine stared as they wove passed the two men. "Alma!" she hollered. A robust woman in a tattered, yellow skirt with faded ducks printed on it poked her head around the corner.

"Silvia! *¿Cómo estás?*"

"*Bien, bien.*"

"Pasa." Alma did not get up from the sofa strategically placed in front of the television. Her heavy legs sat firm on the floor like two redwood stumps. The room was dark except for the little light creeping in through the cracks in the plastic roof. The floor was dirt, and the countertop in the kitchen, which was in the same room, was cement.

"¿Por amor y dinero?"

"You know I can't live without my *telenovelas*." She coughed and spit a wad of mucus in a newspaper she held in her hand. "What brings you around? I don't have any jewelry right now."

"I don't need anything. We were just passing through." For the first time Alma looked up and noticed there was another person with Silvia.

"Ump." She grunted without acknowledging Catherine. Alma was not fond of foreigners. Her life experience had placed them as an elite class in her mind, a force to detest for making her family beg in the streets. She frequently saw them with their shiny cameras and bright neon jackets, trekking through downtown, not able or willing to speak her language, throwing dollars around as if they were toilet paper.

"This one's not so bad." Alma looked again. "Are you okay with money?" Silvia asked her.

"No, but when are we? My damn husband spends it all on liquor. That is when he earns any." Silvia pulled a book out of her bag.

"I brought you this," she passed the book to Alma knowing full well that the woman did not know how to read. It was her way of sneaking money to her without embarrassing her.

"Thank you," Alma replied. "I haven't read this one." She didn't know Silvia knew she couldn't read and she never told her. She appreciated the gift she always found in the middle of the book and didn't refuse it. She stood up and moved toward the counter. She cut a small piece of corn bread and wrapped it in a piece of worn cloth. "Take this," she said handing the bread to Silvia. "I just made it."

"Thank you. Well, we should go. I just wanted to say hi since I was in the neighborhood."

"Good to see you Silvia. Come again soon."

"I will. Is Pedro going to work next week?"

"If he sobers up," she snorted in disbelief. Silvia laughed briefly with her. As they made their way through the junk piled near the front door and out of the courtyard they saw Pedro and his brother still wrestling in the grass.

"*Chau* Alma," she shouted back to the house. "*Chau* Pedro." The men didn't stop rolling around.

"Who are they?"

"Pedro cleans at the university. Alma is his wife. I come visit every once in awhile. He invites me to eat and I leave them money when I can."

"They don't have very much."

"That is fairly standard around here. At least they have a place to live."

"But it's one room. Are all those children theirs?"

"They have five and one is Franco's, but they all live together there."

"I can't fathom living like that. It's suffocating."

"For you, because you are used to something different. For them it is a decent upgrade from the streets."

"I can't believe it."

"Get used to it. This is the way most of Latin America is—miserably poor or filthy rich. There are few of us middle classers left anymore." As they began their journey back to the apartment, Catherine noticed the details of the street and the deteriorating buildings that were beginning to crumble around their foundations. Children ran around with torn, dirty clothes and no shoes, and they were skinny. Trash lined the streets and it smelled of sewer. According to Silvia this was the fault of the government. They pushed people into these neighborhoods and didn't give them proper services. With every leader it gradually got worse. While there were brief periods of prosperity for some, most of the time they were scavenging for money for food, or to pay bus fare to get to a job that didn't even support one person, let alone families of six and seven.

CHAPTER TWENTY-TWO

Violet

Faithfulness, humility, modesty

Catherine and Silvia walked through the flower market on their way to mass at the Cathedral. Silvia's thoughts wandered to the night of her brother's birthday party, while Catherine tried to absorb the images of all of the flowers surrounding her.

"He didn't need to die," Silvia blurted out.

"What?"

"He shouldn't have died."

"None of us should die, we just do."

"But what was the point of him fighting when companies all over the world exploit local resources? What was he supposed to do?"

"In the end, the fight was won."

"In one country, in one village."

"It saved the herb that treats emphysema now, and the flower that reminds us to love, and the weed that stops a cough or mends a lonely heart."

"My heart does not yet seem mended."

"Maybe it never will. Especially if you can't let go."

"I miss my baby niece. I never even got to hold her." Catherine handed Silvia a yellow silk handkerchief.

"I think you feel powerless because you weren't here for him."

"I was self-absorbed, thinking I was the most important person in the world. I was so important that I abandoned my family when I was needed. Mother fell ill while Juan Romero was in the mines."

"I didn't know."

"Now you do. I should have gone back to Arizona, but my own addictions to men and work blinded me. Sort of like you."

"What is that supposed to mean?"

"Your obsession with work drove you all the way down here?" Catherine stopped and turned to Silvia.

"My work is my passion. To write is like channeling information from one entity to another so that we become aware of each other. It may seem odd to you that I am down here, but something powerful drew me here. The existence of a special energy is all around me. It's as if I've been here before."

"I know what you mean. I came for the same reason."

"It doesn't make sense to me yet, but I am hoping it will." Silvia took Catherine's hand as they walked past the daisies and lilies and into the plaza. It was crowded with people making their way to the market and to church. An elderly woman in a tattered shawl approached them with a metal box filled with candles. Her rugged hands held out the white candles made from fat, and Silvia gave her two coins. "What are those for?" Catherine asked.

"Prayer candles." The Cathedral bells began ringing as they made their way up the steps and through the immense wooden doors. They both made the sign of the cross using holy water that sat shimmering in a giant stone chalice just to the right of the entrance. The light of the prayer candles behind it reflected upon the water.

They knelt near the back and waited. They stood and knelt and prayed with the rest of the congregation, going through the motions without thought. Oddly, Catherine was able to follow the service and recite her prayers in English simultaneously with the Spanish chorus.

"*Podeis ir en paz.*" With that one last phrase the organ pipes exploded with music and the clergy left the altar. Silvia went to the prayer candles and placed her candle near the front. She knelt down in front of the Virgin Mary and whispered several words to herself. Catherine, too, knelt but didn't know what to pray for. Her mind was filled with thoughts about her book, so many that she felt confused. She finally muttered, "Clarity." Silvia turned to look at her. Catherine smiled and they both stood up. As they left the church Catherine said, "Tell me more about Padre Miguel."

"I only know what I've heard. I've never actually met him."

"What have you heard?"

"He is originally from Spain and was sent to South America as a missionary when he was 23-24 years old. His fate took him to the small congregation of Aguas Puras where he dug his heels in. Some say he was sent there because the church thought it was a safe place to send a progressive and vocal young priest."

"What kinds of things made him progressive?"

"He passed out condoms to unmarried and married people alike, he didn't degrade homosexuals, even spoke poorly about the Pope."

"Things don't change much, do they?"

"Not in the Catholic church. I had a friend who wrote the Pope asking permission to use birth control after her eighth son was born. Ten years later, while she was pregnant with number thirteen, she received consent from the Vatican."

"Choosing between hungry children and birth control has always been one of my favorite discussions."

"In the end I guess Padre Miguel understood that the systems, whether it be government or the church, didn't work and even more so for small rural communities. Abuela tells me that he became the talk of the town quite quickly because of his immediate attraction to Estela."

"The woman in San Francisco?"

"Yes. She was the most beautiful woman in town at the time, single and flaunting it. Imagine how the poor man must have suffered."

"Why did she leave?"

"She was chosen by the spirits, because of her beauty. People were attracted to her the moment they entered a certain radius where her energy field reached. It wasn't just her physical beauty either."

"She had a gentle personality?"

"No. In fact she was quite aggressive, always telling others what to do and offering her opinion when it wasn't always welcome. I was referring to her essence. Her body had the ability to emit the fragrance of the flower essence that an individual desired or needed. It would flow from the pores of her skin and fill the air, enticing people to follow her until their appetites were satisfied. When Reina, the woman who preceded Estela, died, the village had to find a replacement."

"And chose Estela."

"Not before a long process of consulting the strength of the moon and advice from the spirits."

"If she had the essence why did they have to discuss it?"

"Reina never had the essence. Her talent was her soothing voice. Clients were drawn to Reina's stall because of her intoxicating song."

"Oh, I thought they all had the same qualifications."

"In a way they do. They enchant people to listen to Mother Earth's jewels, the flowers and the herbs."

"When did Estela leave the village?"

"*Las Hechizadas* had to act quickly because the stall was empty, but they also knew they had to follow the proper protocol for choosing the village's next representative, or all of the flowers would die before reaching the market."

"Why?"

"The woman who tends the stall is the keeper of life in Aguas Puras. If that person is not destined to nurture the plants, she will eventually abandon the project. The flowers know this so they reject her by drying up their own petals and leaves."

"It all seems like fantasy."

"In our world perhaps, but not in theirs."

"What is the protocol?"

"Seven days and seven nights are spent in the fields with the chosen guardian. At first, it is said, Estela resisted when she was sent for. When her mother locked her out of the house on that first night, leaving her in a hooded cloak under the pouring rain, she went from door to door seeking shelter. Each and every entrance light was extinguished and heads turned away. When she saw that no one was going to take her in, she began to run. Her feet pounded the wet ground, splashing mud up onto her bare legs. The rain fell harder with every step, beating down on her like heavy balls of ice pelting her neck and head. A bolt of lightning struck and sizzled the ground below her, stopping her from moving forward. Abuela says she reached her arms up, threw her head back, and screamed as loud as a child being ripped from its mother's arms. Then she collapsed. She awoke in Padre Miguel's bed, alone, dry, and warm. He was the only human being in town that could not resist rescuing her. When she sat up he was sitting in a chair at the end of the bed with a hot cup of tea. He served it to her, and while no one knows exactly what happened between them that night, Estela went to the *Hechizadas'* cottage the next morning for her initiation. After the seven days and nights had passed, Estela returned to her mother's home to prepare for her departure. She took very little with her, except for a few personal belongings, a crate filled with special herbs, and the book of flower essences that was passed on from keeper to keeper. She still writes to Padre Miguel every week."

"Who will take her place?"

"Her niece is apprenticing with her so as to avoid a gap when she passes away."

"How old is she?"

"I believe Abuela says she is 60 something."

"You keep talking as if Abuela is still alive, Silvia." Silvia stopped in her tracks, turned to Catherine with a serious look on her face and leaned in. "Abuela does not live on the physical plane," she whispered "but that does not mean we do not communicate." She hadn't wanted to reveal this secret to Catherine, but for some reason her heart felt as if she could.

"You're saying she talks to you from the other side?" Her voice sounded skeptical and Silvia immediately felt defensive.

"It may sound insane, but it is true."

"I was just wondering if anyone else talks to you?"

"No, just Abuela." Catherine nodded her head and started walking. Silvia followed.

"You don't believe me."

"Do I have to?"

"No."

"Then we'll leave it as it is. Whatever it is that you do to communicate with Abuela is fine, and it's none of my concern." Silvia was hurt by Catherine's superior air. It was the first time since they had met that she felt vulnerable. It wasn't that Catherine didn't believe Silvia, and she didn't patronize her on purpose. She was afraid. All of the stories about rituals and magic were beginning to make her uncomfortable. It had not been part of her upbringing to think of such things, yet for some reason she was becoming more drawn to the idea that powers unknown to her, unfamiliar to her level of consciousness, were in charge of her world.

"*Ayúdame*," a crackling voice seeking aid rose up from the sidewalk just as Catherine tripped over an old woman wrapped in a multicolored hand-woven wool shawl reached her hand out to ask for money. Catherine fell to her knees and scraped her left shin. She lifted her head and came face to face with someone's abandoned grandmother; sitting bundled up on the sidewalk begging for money. The woman stared straight into Catherine's eyes, piercing her thoughts, unlocking a flood of images about who this person was, why her teeth were falling out of her mouth, how she ended up with tattered clothes and worn out rubber sandals trying to survive on the street at such an old age. Her feet looked swollen and were covered in dust. All of these thoughts raced through Catherine's mind in the few seconds it took Silvia to rush up from behind to help her up.

"Are you okay?" Catherine nodded, still in a daze, reaching into her purse for some money. She knelt down and pressed the bills into the old woman's hand, folding her fingers around the bills and kissed her fist.

"*Gracias Señora*," was all she said, then stood up and took Silvia's arm. They walked in silence for several blocks. Finally Catherine spoke, "Why are there so many displaced elderly people? Women?"

"There shouldn't be, but centuries of corruption yield useless governments.

"There have to be people who want to help."

"Of course there are, but the system is too powerful. It's like my brother." Silvia stopped in front of her apartment building and firmly held Catherine's shoulders. "He died trying to stop mining that was going to destroy a community's economy and poison their water source. He sacrificed too much, Catherine. He lost his wife, his daughter, and his family." The wrinkles on her face, drawn by years of anguish grieving her brother's death deepened. "Most of us would pack up our belongings and go." She took Catherine's hand and led her to the apartment. "He knew something most of us didn't. He knew the valley was protected and its fruits powerful, just as you reminded me. He believed the herbs of that land were indispensable and the people who harvest them are magical. He fought for both human and ecological preservation. He couldn't accept a status quo that disregarded nature and humanity."

"Everyone knows that, Silvia."

"That community would not have succeeded without my brother because it needed a leader. He was the person who was not afraid to stand up against international interests. Padre Miguel was one of those individuals too, but he did not have the ability to actually fight, because of his position in the church. He was a superb orator and able to rally the *pueblo*, which he frequently did, pushing Juan Romero forward. It was as if they were participating in a mini-revolution where the oppressed rise up and claim what is rightfully theirs. It hasn't happened at a nation-wide level though. There are no leaders. There is no cause and we have become complacent, thinking nothing will ever happen to us."

"But you aren't complacent. You never were. You responded to him." Catherine said.

"Fairly soon after the first trip to the mine, yes." Silvia answered.

"And did you do everything he asked?"

"I did my best. I contacted several organizations and showed the photos to a number of magazines. It took me almost a month to get anyone to pay attention, but finally a woman from an organization called Tierra Watch returned my calls."

"I've heard of them."

"You have because of the Aguas Puras project. Once she agreed to look into it, the struggle began drawing international attention. It was a positive experience all around. She actually knew Estela. She bought flowers from her often. Juan Romero got the pressure he needed on the government, and she got the recognition she needed for future fundraising."

"What did they do?"

"Primarily a letter writing campaign, and facilitated as much media coverage as possible. Most of it was in newspapers, but there was one report done by an American journalist who sold the story to the major news channels. That helped with inspiring emails to government officials."

"How long did they campaign?"

"They continued to work with my brother until the end, and then after his death tried to go after the culprits."

"I understand they were never found."

"Everyone knew who sent them, but no one could prove it, nor could they prove who actually did the killing."

"So they let it go?"

"Not initially. There were protests and vigils and threats, but in the end Abuela stopped all of it."

"Why?"

"Peace. She just wanted peace."

"But not bringing them to justice seems like never being able to find peace."

"That's how I feel, but she did not. She refused to tell me why she did it. To this day there is a part of me that wants to know."

"Do you think the influence public knowledge had over the situation helped?"

"I think more people would have been killed, and it would have taken longer to resolve. Maybe even never have been resolved if it weren't for the public knowing. I also believe the shareholder activism was the final straw. Here," Silvia passed Catherine a letter. "Read this."

Dear Sirs:

I am writing to protest the presence of Maple Mining in Aguas Puras, Ecuador. In the two years the company has been mining in the central valley it has repeatedly abused the land, the law, and the people. It is my understanding that in the process of extracting ore for gold you have virtually stripped the mountains of all vegetative life. Once lush vibrant sponges are now desert-like. The leach fields surrounding the mines are leaking toxic materials into the water, which not only is what the local people use as potable water, but if levels increase, could cause the community's irrigation for its flower industry, one of the few that doesn't use harmful pesticides, to be ruined. These flowers are healing remedies for many, and if they are destroyed it will be a great loss on many levels. What is going on in this community can be labeled as eco-terrorism. This company is violating Mother Nature and no one cares.

As a shareholder I would like to formally request a full investigation into Maple Mining's practices in this community. If I am to support mining it cannot be that an atrocity occurs each time I contribute a dollar. While I am not normally an activist, I must speak out on this subject.

Sincerely,
John Rowday III

"This is just one in a huge stack of letters the mining company received from its shareholders. The early 21st century was a time when shareholder activism was an emerging idea. It wasn't as common as it is now."

"It seems to dictate corporate policy today."

"To some extent, but during the time when Maple Leaf was exploiting this area, it was just beginning. Tierra Watch actually ended up taking on the cause, not because of the pictures, but because they held shares in the company. It had a horrific track record in all of North America, and they had purchased a large chunk of stock a couple of years earlier. Aguas Puras was added to the list of places to focus on."

"A coincidence."

"Synchronicity."

"It took a long time for them to actually get anything accomplished."

"That's why I think Abuela let it all go. She didn't want to use proper procedures to achieve justice because she believed it would result in the same corruption everything always has. Corruption is inherent in our lives here. It's blatant, it's part of what we do everyday. Go to the grocery store, pay off the attendant to make sure the car doesn't get stolen, send a letter, bribe the postal worker to actually meter the mail so it will have a chance of being mailed, take a drive into the country, slip the national guard $10 to let you continue down the road. It's nothing new. It's always been like that. Abuela knew the judges in her district had already been paid off. 'Wasn't it obvious?' she would say to me. 'How do you think they made it as far as they did?' I would always shrug my shoulders in ignorance. 'Bribery. Corruption *hija*, corruption.' Later I found a section in my brother's journal that shed some light on her perspective. Here it is." She passed the book to Catherine who opened the marked page.

The townspeople apparently had passed an ordinance banning any and all types of mining in the valley, and for that reason believed they had put a halt to the project. They were shocked at my news and it has been almost 16 weeks since our initial encounter with the mining company. More people have joined our fight, but they continue mining. The things they get away with are despicable. I always knew that large companies fled the north because of rules and regulations, but I never contemplated the utter lack of moral consciousness. Why is it that one nation realizes the deadly harm chemicals and toxins can cause to human life, takes action, educates the populous and the corporations, then pushes for new, cleaner technologies, but the corporate mastermind ignores all of this. A simple move solves all of its headaches—fair wages, environmental regulations, workers' rights, benefits, everything.

This mining company has taken over the political system in this country. Our meager fight is not the only one in this region. A story about mercury poisoning further south regarding a different company, reached us via the lips of one yucca farmer who left after his family died and his land was destroyed. "A truck crashed on the road to the city," he said. "Streams of silver liquid flowed and froze onto the road. We knew it was mercury, the stuff they used to take the gold out of the ore they mine. Pablo, a man who worked anything he could on the black market had been known to buy it from the same truck driver to sell to gold diggers deep in the jungle. When he saw this he began yelling, "Gather as much as you can. I'll pay high price for an entire bucket." People desperately swept the poison up into their arms, running home in hopes of earning more in one hour than in a week's worth of work. The next day a group of men dressed in suits came to town, offering cash to anyone that would help clean up the remaining mercury. It was swept into puddles and with their bare hands the workers put the mercury into plastic bags. Pablo's wife was pregnant at the time and a few weeks after the spill she lost the baby and her own life. She bled to death.

We could not get any more information from him, but he stayed to help us. " I'll do anything to stop them from doing any more damage to my country," he told me. Padre Miguel heard from sources in the church in Quito that Maple has convinced the higher-ups that they have every intention of backing the country in its fight to protect its borders from further invasion from its southern and northern neighbors. This paranoia comes from ancient arguments over small pieces of insignificant land, but politicians love to embellish and feed on the fear that someone maybe, might, could possibly invade. Someone told the government that the company has important political contacts in Canada and the U.S. that would be able to help in times of need. According to this same source the company has filed a lawsuit that challenges the ordinance Aguas Puras passed and until it goes to trial they are free to work. I am beginning to feel desperate and angry, yet I know I must remain focused. Even conversations with Sofia have become stressed. I sometimes stare at her but don't really see her. The woman in front of me is the woman I am falling in love with yet there are times she still didn't understand me. I believe in change, change for the greater good. It's not a vision of socialism or communism, not democracy or capitalism, but more of a social movement toward a type of fragmented globalism. It's a world that agrees to cooperate and care for one another while maintaining its own cultural wealth. Business for me is the catalyst for *this globalization. Business moves economies and governments. It is the key to peace and war.*

"It was soon after this that they began shipping colored postcards with stories about the town's struggle with the flowers. Estela would arrange bouquets and shrubs with the card stuck in the petals of the flowers. All of the images were taken by my brother," Silvia said.

"Is that what increased the letter campaign?"

"One-thousand fold. Tierra Watch was flooded with emails from Estela's customers. You see, once you buy one bouquet from Estela you never buy from anyone else, so her customer base exceeds 200,000 people."

"Wow. And the repeat customer was because?"

"Of the healing power of the flowers. No matter what was wrong with your body, mind, or spirit, Estela had the right flower for you."

"On whom did the letter campaign focus?"

"There were three primary targets: Maple, the Ecuadorian ministry of the environment, and the U.S. Congress. They figured that if Congress was bothered enough they would pressure Maple interests in the States and therefore be able to in turn push for change in Ecuador."

"Did it work?"

"It was a slow process. The flood of letters started about four months after the initial protest and in the meantime the violence began to escalate."

"Padre Miguel?"

"That was the beginning, yes."

CHAPTER

TWENTY-THREE

Eyes of Mary

Helps to change a given perspective so that we see gifts inherent in difficult situations

The buzzer rang and Silvia got up from rummaging through Abuela's trunk to answer. *"¿Si?"*

"Hola Silvita. Soy yo, Adriana."

"Hola. Pasa." She opened the front gate for Adriana to come through. She propped the apartment door open and went into the kitchen to put water on for *maté*. "Do you like *maté*?" she asked Catherine.

"What is *maté*?"

"It's a very strong, very bitter green tea. Adriana always brings it over when she visits. It's a ritual in Argentina."

"I'd love to try it."

"¿¿¿ Aló???" Adriana peeked her head around the corner. Her fashionable, red- rimmed sunglasses balanced on the bridge of her nose.

"Venga Adriana. Adelante."

"Hello Catherine. I didn't know you were here."

"Yes, and very much looking forward to trying this *maté* stuff." Adriana laughed.

"What horror stories are you telling her?"

"That the green and yellowish herb that smells like straw is wonderfully sweet and delightful," Silvia giggled.

"Bring the water!" Adriana pulled out a gourd from her bag that was elegantly decorated with pictograph art. She set the gourd and a bamboo straw with tiny holes at the bottom and one opening at the top, on the coffee table. Silvia came out of the kitchen with a tray, carefully set up for *maté* drinking. A small blue ceramic teapot was the center of attention surrounded by a tiny bowl of sugar and a plate full of miniature croissants topped with a sweet sugar glaze. Adriana added a bowl topped off with the bitter green tea that looked like a mixture of leaves and sticks. She filled her gourd with the tea and gently manipulated the straw or *la bombilla* into the dusty hay-like bowels of the tea.

"With or without sugar?" she asked.

"I think I'll start with." She lifted the gourd and carefully poured the hot water over the loose leaves. It sucked the moisture up like a dried out desert soil, thirsting for enough water to help its habitat survive. She poured more until the leaves floated and the water nearly reached the rim. She turned the gourd so the *bombilla* faced Catherine and handed it to her. *Yerba maté* is a caffeinated tea made from the leaves of a holly plant harvested in pre-Hispanic times along the Parana-Paraguay river system. By the 1770s *maté* was a popular social drink throughout the Andes and now is a common household drink.

"Don't move the *bombilla* or you'll get leaves with your tea." Catherine sipped the hot concoction and cringed. "Bitter?" Both Silvia and Adriana laughed. Catherine nodded yes and with a perplexed look on her face handed the *maté* back.

"I suppose it's an acquired taste," she said.

"You'll get used to it."

"So what's all this?" Adriana poked her head into Abuela's trunk.

"Abuela's things. I've never entirely been through this trunk. Catherine and I were exploring."

"Mind if I help?"

"No."

"Here, drink up." Adriana passed Silvia the maté and dived into the pile of antiquated memories her friend had kept secret for so long. She pulled out a stack of photos tied neatly with a pink ribbon and dried sage.

"Look at these, Silvita," she nostalgically cooed. She handed Silvia the photos one by one. "She looks so young and vibrant."

"She was close to 60 in these pictures."

"A little lovin' will do that for a woman," Adriana smiled.

"What are you talking about? I thought your grandfather passed away long before this."

"You haven't mentioned Octavio?" Adriana glanced at Silvia.

"Abuela's farm hand?"

"I'm sure his hands were good for more than picking flowers," Adriana snorted.

"A little respect Adri. She is my grandmother." Silvia looked up and across the room. She saw Abuela sitting in the window watching the three curious women unravel the secrets of her past. "Besides, it wasn't like that."

"What? Hot and passionate?" Embarrassed, Silvia tried not to look Abuela in the eye. "Well, yes, it was hot and passionate, but they truly loved each other. Plus they had to keep it a secret."

"Why?" Catherine asked.

"Several reasons, I guess." Abuela twisted her hair with her finger, lost in thought about the times she spent with

Octavio, longing for him to pass to the other side. Silvia heard her melancholic whispers and relayed the story as she always did when Abuela wanted to ensure the truth was spoken. "Octavio was from a family of cattle ranchers. His father actually had considerable land holdings and was a successful businessman. If events would have unfolded differently that sweltering summer night, Octavio might have never met Abuela."

"What happened?"

"Octavio was the eldest of four sons, three of whom were obsessed with their father's wealth. Octavio, being the eldest, was in line to inherit the majority of his father's holdings. While the other sons were well off, they never forgave their father's favoritism and despised their kindhearted brother, who often would show what they believed to be poor business sense by giving significant amounts of money away to the church or directly to the impoverished. Octavio's mother had died while giving birth to his youngest sister, and his father Julio, had taken a second wife, Lucia. She was plain, but caring. The brothers were indifferent towards her, but Octavio always treated her with respect. As time passed, Octavio's brothers became more and more jealous and were resentful of taking orders from him. He was, at that point, in charge of running the ranch on a daily basis. They began to think of unmentionable ways to destroy their brother's credibility, but none of them ever followed through, until one night when Ricardo, the second eldest, came home drunk and horny. Julio was gone for the night, having traveled to another ranch to discuss business with an old friend. The air was heavy and humid, almost too thick to be able to inhale. Ricardo's shirt was already damp from his own sweat and blotches of whiskey he had spilled on himself while taking shots at the bar in town. As he stumbled through the garden en route to his own home that his father had ordered built, he noticed Lucia sitting in a wicker chair, her hair bundled up atop her head, her hands passing a damp cloth along the nape of her neck to cool her skin. In what was a matter of seconds, Ricardo approached his father's young bride and grabbed her around the neck, covering her mouth so she couldn't scream. There was no moon, and the light from the porch was too far away to illuminate her attacker's face. Lucia came from a town near the northern border with Colombia. This was not the first time a man in her village, wreaking of bourbon or whiskey or any other moonshine available, had taken their anger out on her, believing that an act of animalistic, undesired, unsolicited copulation would ease their pain. The previous two times she had fought, bloodied her attackers with nail wounds or bites, and ended up with bruised ribs, a broken jaw, and a dislocated shoulder. She never shared her personal horrors with Julio. There was no reason to relive the past, now that she was happy and safe, or so she thought. This time she lay still, not even tensing her body. She looked up in the sky and focused on the Southern Cross for guidance. Her eyes lost their ability to focus as this man pleasured himself in not much longer than it would take him to use the toilet. As he rolled off of her a gasp came from the bushes, and then the pitter-patter of little feet. Rosalinda, the cook's daughter, had seen the mistress raped. She screamed for help and with the first screech that escaped her throat the man stumbled to his feet, but not in time to avoid a large stick striking the back of his head. Lucia's skinny arm carried the fury of a woman scorned, and she knew now she could attack because he would flee, and he did.

'*Señora*,' came the screams of Javier, the cattle manager. '*Señora Lucia!*'

'*Aqui estoy.*' Lucia sat on her knees, bent over, covered in dirt and dripping semen. She rocked back and forth. Javier lifted her head to find tears flowing like a waterfall crushing the rocks below. Her eyes were swollen and bitter with disgust.

'Who did this to you, *Señora*?'

'I could not see.'

'Rosalinda?' The child hid behind her mother's skirt, but she could not speak. They took Lucia back to the house and prepared a hot bath. Javier sent a band of men out to look for the devil who had taken *el patron*'s wife. They found no one, of course, except for Julio's drunken son Ricardo, passed out in the ditch on the road leading to his house. They threw him in the back of the truck and took him home.

Julio arrived the next day, greeted with the horrific news of Lucia's attack. He was furious, demanding to know how this bastard had escaped. 'We searched the property immediately following the incident, sir. The only person we found was Ricardo, your son, drunk and asleep on the side of the road. He was on his way home.'

'Send him to me.' Ricardo arrived at his father's study shortly thereafter.

'You wanted to see me.'

'I assume you have heard what happened to Lucia.'

'Yes sir.'

'Did you see anyone else along the road last night in your stupor?' Ricardo, convinced that the young girl had seen him, had concocted a story that would not only erase him from doubt as Lucia's attacker, but that would eliminate his brother Octavio's presence from the family forever.

'Father, I did not want to involve myself in this atrocious misfortune, but as I look into your eyes I see the sadness and fury, and I cannot withhold the information I have from you any longer.'

'What do you know?'

'Octavio brought me home last night. He dropped me at the gate at the head of your driveway. We waved goodbye and I saw his car head down the road. The truth is that I was very drunk, and after passing your house on my way home I decided to stop for a smoke. I am embarrassed to say I fell asleep in the ditch.'

'I, too, am embarrassed by your antics,' his father grunted.

'This morning when I was in town with Octavio I found this under the floor mat.' Ricardo had somehow taken Lucia's lace handkerchief from her pocket and had produced it for his father. His father's face turned pale white.

'What are you telling me?'

'How else is he going to get a hold of her handkerchief, father?'

'You are accusing your brother of rape, Ricardo. Do you realize what you are saying?'

'It's not the first time.' At this point Ricardo launched into a monologue of fiction about the licentiousness of his eldest brother and his violent nature with women. His creativity even surprised him and sent his father into a sickened state. He went to bed and did not show his face for 36 hours. When he did it was to banish his eldest son forever from the farm. Octavio said nothing except,

'You will one day know this was not me, father.' He turned and left with the clothes on his back and the beat up blue pickup he still drives today. When Lucia heard what had happened, she cried enough for all the women on the ranch. Although Julio was her husband, she was in love with Octavio. She pleaded with her spouse, 'It could not have been him.'

'Ricardo saw him my love.' He tried to console her, wiping her tears, but she would not allow it. Her pain rang clearly through the air, haunting the minds and spirits of everyone within miles. On the third day of her mourning, Julio found her again in the garden, in the same place she had been the night of the attack. 'Why do you torment yourself, Lucia? Why come here?'

'I'm trying to remember. I need to remember.' And it was then that Rosalinda appeared from behind the secret bush. 'Rosalinda, what are you doing hiding behind those bushes?' Julio demanded.

'She's not hiding. I knew she was there. She's always there.'

'I must tell you something, *Señora.*'

'What is it dear? Come, come sit with Lucia.' Rosalinda climbed up onto Lucia's lap and touched her swollen cheek. 'You need not cry *Señora.* It was not him.' Lucia caressed Rosalinda's long black braid and tilted her head in the way one does when trying to jog the brain to clarify comprehension. 'Look on the backs of the men's necks, remember?' Lucia gasped and hugged the child; kissing her forehead with such force it left a red mark.

'Send for Javier. I want him to check all the men.'

'What ridiculousness do you speak of Lucia?'

'The night of my rape, Julio, I dared not move for fear of further abuse. I laid still, enduring humiliation, praying for an end. Then in a moment sent from God I found my inner strength and fought back against this man with a brutal whack to the back of the neck. I broke the skin. The blood on the stick told me that much.'

'Why did you not share this with me before?'

'In my grief and shock I had forgotten until Rosalinda reminded me.' Julio immediately got up from the bench and marched straight to the house, ordering Javier to examine the necks and shoulders of every man on the ranch. After hours of a thorough search Javier found nothing.

'Bring Ricardo to me.' Ricardo was not aware of the massive hunt for the bruised culprit and went willingly to his father. Had he known, he most likely would have fled, for he understood his father's fury. Yet, because of his euphoric state of newfound wealth the ignorant son went blindly toward his destiny.

'Take off your shirt,' his father ordered.

'What are you talking about?'

'Take off your shirt Ricardo, or I will have Javier do it for you.' Ricardo complied. Javier stood behind Ricardo and simply nodded his head yes. 'Take him to the field and whip him,' Julio bluntly said. Ricardo went into a panic.

'What? Javier? What's he talking about?' Three of Javier's men took hold of Ricardo as he squirmed and screamed, 'I demand to know what's going on.'

'You will never show your face in this house again.' And in that moment Ricardo became complacent, for he understood that his father knew. Javier took the boy he had seen born in the fields and sent the other men away. He whipped him until he could not stand and then said,

'I suggest you pack your things and go.'

'Where will I go?'

'I don't know. Where do you think your brother went? I'm surprised your father let you live. The pueblo will not be so forgiving.' When Ricardo returned to his house he found it locked and guarded.

'You are not allowed to enter this house,' said the one sitting in a chair in front of the door, a rifle across his lap.

'I only need a few things.'

'All you will need is in there.' He looked at a small backpack at the edge of the stairs.

'No.' Ricardo regained some of his arrogance momentarily. 'I need some other things.'

'All you will need is in there,' the man repeated. Two more men stepped forward to stand on either side of the chair. They, too, were armed with rifles. Ricardo leaned down and picked up his backpack, turned, and began walking down the road to his car. But again, it was guarded by armed men. He kept walking. The afternoon heat beat down on his broad shoulders that slouched forward and followed his bowed head as he made his way away from the house. Once his figure disappeared on the horizon, no one ever saw him again. It is said that he was seen working on a ranch in the North, but it was never confirmed. Julio tried to reconcile with Octavio, but Octavio's pride and profound suffering caused him to stay away from his father and his family's ranch. Though they knew of each other's whereabouts, neither Octavio nor Julio spoke to one another or about the other again. It was shortly after those trying times that Octavio arrived in Aguas Puras, still a relatively young man, still single, looking for work. He met my grandfather Romero, who hired him to work the flower fields under Abuela's command.

Abuela and Octavio worked together for close to 15 years. They became good friends, and their relationship was completely platonic until a couple of years after grandfather died. Look, this is a picture of the three of them on New Years Eve, 1992. It seems like so long ago," Silvia sighed.

"What happened after Romero died?" Catherine asked.

"Abuela said that for a while she felt nothing except numbness. 'My body felt tired, old, numb,' she would say. 'I might as well have been the one to die.' She and Octavio shared their grief for the loss of a man who had greatly impacted both their lives. More than two years passed before either of them finally admitted they were interested in one another. Abuela was 58, Octavio 48. They were playing chess in the living room, just as they had done every evening for the last 18 years.

'Your move, Esperanza.'

'Sorry. I was thinking of something else.'

'May I ask about what? You seem different.'

'I think it's fair to say I feel different.'

'About?'

'I don't feel sad anymore.'

'About Romero?'

'Yes, and about being alone. I have begun to realize that I don't have to be alone.'

'Technically you're not alone. I'm here.'

'That's exactly where I'm headed. You're here, I'm here. We're both alone.' Abuela blushed right before she shared her next thought. 'I like you Octavio. You're good company.'

'That's it? Good company?' he smiled.

'You're attractive too, I suppose. Don't make me embarrass myself. I barely have the courage to mention this.' Octavio stood up, stepped around the table, leaned in and kissed Esperanza with the passion of his entire life. He had, unknowingly, held a place of not only tenderness in his heart for this woman, but of raw lust. It was at that moment that their love affair began and lasted in secret until my brother showed up to provoke unrest."

"Why then?"

"Because Octavio became one of Juan Romero's most trusted men, his mentor really. He volunteered to be in charge of the 'enviro attacks.' This caused Abuela immense stress."

"Cancer is the evil that clings onto the human worries," chimed in Adriana.

"Pancreatic cancer. She died quickly."

"I'm surprised she wasn't able to heal herself," said Catherine.

"I think the accumulation of all of her life's sorrows finally caught up with her. When you live to be 90 you witness a lot. She tended to absorb the ills of others, trying to cure them with her recipes."

"The flowers?"

"Yes, the flowers and the herbs and the potions and salves that she made to conquer physical and emotional traumas."

"Don't you have her recipe book, Silvia? I remember seeing it once," Adriana asked.

"Yes, I should, but I haven't seen it for awhile, probably since the last time we looked at it."

"Maybe it's in the trunk." Adriana began searching.

"Didn't I keep it out last time?"

"Who knows? What color was the cover?"

"Sage and yellow." Adriana kept digging while Silvia served more hot water and changed the tea.

"I'm feeling jittery, I don't think I want anymore," said Catherine.

"O.K. What about pastries?"

"No thanks."

"Here it is!" exclaimed Adriana.

"Give it to me," Silvia demanded.

"Relax. I just want to show Catherine some of the recipes. My favorite is the mango-mint cleanse."

"Fine, but Catherine, you cannot copy any of them down. They are a family secret and I intend to keep them such."

"But you let me copy some of them," Adriana always had a way of putting Silvia in an awkward situation.

"True," Silvia retorted, "but you're not writing a book about my family."

"I wouldn't share them in the book."

"I can't be sure of that Catherine. I'm sorry." Silvia had come to a point in her life where she had learned to trust very few people, and especially young, ambitious writers. Anyone, in her experience, who was interested in her brother always asked for more than they should. One example was when she was living in New York and met a handsome Italian man in a café/wine bar. She had been sitting with her glass of Malbec, reading the *Times,* when he approached her. Their conversation began simply with standard strangers asking each other questions. "What do you do for a living? Are you originally from New York? Are you married?" The conversation changed, however, when he expressed an interest in dance. Silvia's monotone responses to his mundane advances changed drastically. "I'm a dancer," she said. It turned out he had seen her perform the night before. What she didn't know was that he had been to the performance specifically to track her down. Two weeks later, after a substantial amount of passionate lovemaking, he made off with one of Juan Romero's more favored prints. He ended up selling it on the black market for $75,000. Ironically, it was an image of Octavio with an AK47 Jack had purchased from the Colombians. It is said the picture is again in South America, but Silvia lost track of it. It's the only copy, because it came from a roll developed in Aguas Puras, the negatives of which were stolen when Juan Romero was attacked.

"Maybe after the book is published," Catherine pressed.

"Maybe," she blankly answered, thinking of her Italian lover/thief.

Adriana flipped through the book, pulling out cards and folded pieces of paper, scavenging through it like a child on Christmas morning. "I love how she sketched everything and dried samples. Look at how beautiful it is." She slid over next to Catherine and placed the book on her lap. "It's a journal of her recipes." Adriana was right. The years of creating and compiling recipes had unconsciously driven Abuela into a creative venture. With each word and drawing she had developed a piece of art unique to her own style. Accompanied by the delicately colored drawings were brief stories, pertinent tidbits, anecdotes about why the recipe was developed, for whom, and what the results of the treatment were.

"His head ached after several days of fever," she wrote. "The lime flowers were not enough on their own so I added crushed, dried chamomile to the salve and had him rub it on his temples for seven days and seven nights. Without chamomile it would have taken twice that time."

"Every recipe has a special note," said Catherine. She was a true healer.

"That is what *Hechizadas* do, Catherine. That is why it was so important to preserve the tradition and ensure the practice. It isn't just economics; it is history, thousands of years of history."

"Water is sacred in the valley and has always driven the healing powers of these women. They say it is because of Catalina, Valiente's daughter."

"The princess who was slain?"

"That's right."

"Do people really believe that?"

LAS HECHIZADAS

"Read this and decide for yourself." Silvia took the book from Adriana's lap and turned to the front inside cover. Carefully pasted inside was a piece of rice paper folded in the shape of a pair of woman's hands. Silvia unfolded the hands to reveal a drawing of the same woman's palms. Written in calligraphy were the words that inspired not only Abuela, but also hundreds of women before her.

There is a time for progress, a time for rest, and a time for fighting. As women in this valley our fights are few and far between, but when we decide to rise up they are vicious and pointed. We will not surrender until we have accomplished what we set out to do. Use the time of peace to heal the wounds of war that others suffer for they do not see what the future brings and do so from the roots of the earth.

"These are the words that bind the women of the valley," said Silvia.

"Why aren't you an *Hechizada,* Silvia?" Adriana held her breath. This is a question she never dared ask. She wasn't sure why, perhaps because her upper-class Argentinean upbringing didn't condition her to take risks, yet that would defy the artist in her. Perhaps it was the fear that Silvia would have a nervous breakdown once she started confronting the huge loss she felt by not being a part of the rich culture and tradition her grandmother had wanted to pass down to her mother and then to her. Most likely it was the knowledge that once she started asking questions she wouldn't be able to stop. Deep down she was delighted for Catherine's presence and lack of history with this family.

"It was too late."

"Why?"

"According to Abuela a woman must be initiated before she turns 25. When she approached me I was still of age, but foolishly turned her down for my dance."

"That doesn't seem foolish. Dance was your passion."

"It was, but I regret passing the opportunity to maintain tradition," she paused. "In the end, though, it didn't matter."

"Why?"

There are no other women in our family to continue with flower harvesting. I am not able to have children."

"I'm sorry, I didn't know."

"It's not something I ever made public. I was embarrassed, then saddened. Plus, I never met the person with whom I wanted to have children."

"And Juan Romero's daughter?"

"She's dead."

"Presumed dead," interrupted Adriana.

"Enough Adriana. We've been through this before. The child was murdered."

"I just——"

"No, end of discussion. I will not speak further of this." Silvia took the book and placed it on the left side of her bookshelf in the same section she had recently cleared to store her brother's journals. Catherine looked at Adriana with a pleading expression. She gestured that they would talk later. Catherine was curious. This was the first she had heard that the child may not have been killed.

CHAPTER

TWENTY-FOUR

Alyssum

Worth beyond beauty

Adriana and Catherine sat in a café just off the main plaza in Old Town. Catherine had waited a week before she was able to tie Adriana down to have coffee and talk.

"Why do you think Maria de la Luz is alive?"

"Intuition I suppose. Hope even, that those monsters could not kill an innocent child."

"Then why didn't they look for her?"

"They did, but they didn't find her."

"Why didn't he leave when she was born, or stop the fight?"

"Would you have? He was the leader of this whole movement. His ideas were infectious, and he was becoming obsessed with them."

"Do you have any other writings? I mean other than his journals?" Catherine knew that Juan Romero's political writings went deeper than what Silvia had already shared with her. It was a combination of these writings, which were primarily opinion pieces, and his photos that drew acclaim from the international community. His vociferous views caused mixed debate in places like the U.S. Congress and the EU Parliament. People began using them as reference points to introduce new legislation regarding multinational corporations operating abroad.

"A few." Silvia in fact had all of them, but she had not shared them with very many people. She was planning on publishing them as a collection, but because of selfishness had not yet taken any steps to do so. A good number of his political essays had been published in English and Spanish, as excerpted pieces in magazines or newspapers, but Silvia possessed the original texts. "Here is one that I like because of his insight about the struggle of working people." She lifted the pages and began to read:

"Throughout my young life the rhetoric I have heard has principally been about the dangers of corporate wealth. Little emphasis has ever been placed on the weaknesses of government to control the power held by corporations. Even following recent financial debacles in developed nations where entire corporations were found guilty of doctoring records, illegally moving monies through subsidiaries, and allowing the executives to take off with hundreds of millions of dollars in assets without blinking, no one does anything. While most of us don't directly feel the impact of these disasters, we can appreciate the residual disgust left in the empty cubicles, by unknowing, hard working people who were flat out cheated. Their life savings squandered by CEOs on homes in ski resort towns or the Caribbean, on frivolous trips to frivolous places without recourse to recover any of it. What do these people do with their lives after having everything stripped from them? Where do they go? Whom do they trust?

The common corporate worker is not so unlike the people here, in Aguas Puras, who dedicate their lives to work only to have any benefits taken from them, if they ever had them to start with. Corporate exploitation has taken on a new *definition in the North, but the essence of it has not changed— pay workers nothing, give them nothing, and they will not ask for anything for fear of losing their jobs. The only difference in modern corporations is they <u>pretend</u> to provide when really an employee is like the ball on a roulette table that is forced to run in circles until it finds the big payoff and then is dumped for the blackjack table. The men working for Maple are not doing so because they believe in any principles. They work for $6 per day because they have to feed themselves and their families. The families who live and work in Aguas Puras don't have to degrade themselves and do this to survive. They own businesses, land, and make profits to lead productive healthy lives. They may not be multimillionaires, but they are solid citizens and they are sane. When did the world come to this? That poverty and extravagance learned to coexist and are passively accepted as the norm? Why? The human ego is so powerful that it does not comprehend truth. It blinds our eyes from pure compassion. We have our momentary lapses of guilt where we reach out a helping hand, but our ego always returns to remind us of self, the most significant of beings, me. Until society rids itself of the human ego none of her systems will work gracefully, because a system is a partnership, and only true selflessness can oil those fine engines. Thus, necessity vs. ego—can there be a resolution?*

"He was more of a philosopher than the politician they wanted to paint him to be," said Catherine.

"'Dangerous communistic-style rebels' I think is what the Senator from Georgia once called his words," smiled Adriana.

"With cameras as guns."

"If only it were so simple. If only someone would actually have come down here to talk with him. Word spread fast after the second bombing. They initiated six in that same number of weeks, so you can imagine how startled the Canadian, American, and Ecuadorian governments were. The soldiers cracked down."

Interestingly, the order didn't come from the government. It came from Maple's CEO Frederick Kane. Kane had experience operating in the southern hemisphere including Indonesia, South Africa, and South America and was infamous for his brutality. In Indonesia he had ordered an entire village burned after months of unrest in the area and claims their fish, the main staple, were being poisoned by mining activities. Nothing was ever proven, but the locals knew.

Girlain, the man Kane put in charge, began paying the soldiers to more severely interrogate people on the streets and, in some cases, enter and search their homes. He paid an unusually high amount for the soldiers to scare Abuela a second time. Early on a foggy day, dawn was breaking and Abuela made her way to the kitchen to boil water for her morning tea. The *La Belle Sultane* rose in her window gave her a breath of timeless energy as she deeply inhaled its luxurious fragrance. Her mind had been unsettled in recent days because she had not heard from Octavio. He had made it a habit to send a message with the supply crew, but none had come. Abuela was having trouble concentrating because of it. Estela had sent a request for yarrow and gardenias. One of her regular clients was in need of a way to heal his liver and open his mind. The alcohol and hallucinogens were killing him, Estela wrote, but he claimed he needed them to play his music. Abuela was preparing to pack the box that very day.

She poured the steaming water over the mint herbal bags she had tied herself. She set the pot down on the stove and turned around, slamming into a brick wall of a man dressed in dark khaki green fatigues. Her breath stopped for a moment.

"Esperanza?"

"*Sí.*"

"We're here to ask you some questions." The man stepped one-half step to her left to reveal three additional soldiers with automatic weapons hanging from their shoulders. Though her heart quickened, Abuela was able to pacify her fear. The calmness in the old woman agitated the soldiers.

"I think you should sit down."

"I prefer to stand."

"As you wish. So long as you answer the questions."

"I'm sure I will be of little assistance as I do not know very much about your line of work; unless I'm mistaken and you've come for a remedy. Is something wrong?"

"With me no. I do find it odd though that you know nothing about the goings on of your grandson and your ranch hand. They are guerrillas, conducting illegal activity, yet you know nothing."

"They do not work for the mine. That is the only group around here that I know of that is conducting illegal activities." The soldier leaned into Abuela. His breath stank of whiskey from the night before and his skin of putrid sweat. Abuela felt his shoulder push against her side.

"Where are they?" She did not answer. "I said, where are they?"

"I believe Juan Romero is out taking photos. Octavio is selling crops for me further north. That's his job."

"Flowers?"

"That's right."

"To who?"

"In the markets, to different clients, just as he has done for the past 25 years." He turned to the three statues standing erect in the corner and jerked his head, signaling them to initiate the search. They leapt like hungry coyotes on their prey, tearing through drawers, leaving everything they touched marked with their gun-powdered hands. Their lack of grace began to gnaw on Abuela's nerves, but she showed no emotion. The crashing of drawers, shattering of ceramic hitting the floor, fluttering paper interrupting the morning breeze filled the house.

"We know you are aware of their true whereabouts. I suggest you cooperate."

"I told you where they are." With that sentence the man raised his arm above Abuela and, like a sledgehammer, brought his clenched fist down and across her face, knocking her to her knees. Not a sound came out of her.

"I repeat, where are they?" Her gentle mauve eyes looked up and into this pathetic man's face.

"I repeat, I've told you all I know." The grimace on his face worsened and he raised his hand once again to strike her. She smiled and said, "Beating an old woman will not ease your pain, or your anger." Her frankness only infuriated him further, and he hit her several times until she fell to the floor and did not move.

"Nothing sir. Just a bunch of herbal remedies," the soldiers reported, not flinching at the sight of a bloodied grandmother.

"Let's go."

"Shall we leave her sir?"

"Pick her up, tie her to the chair." The men leaned over Abuela and saw that while her body was still, her eyes revolved in circles. They stepped back, frightened that the woman was having a seizure.

"Captain, she's dying!" The heavyset captain bent over, sticking his face as close to hers as he could. He saw the movement in her eyes. It was like a swarm of African killing bees buzzing around a white cloud-filled sky. A soft hum surrounded Abuela's head and caught the soldier's subconscious, lulling him into a gentle daze. Just as his heartbeat began to slow and his thoughts began to wander, Abuela's body suddenly jerked. Her eyes froze, pupils dilated, staring straight at the man who had ordered her bound to her own kitchen chair. The rigid and rapid movement, along with the pair of now frozen eyeballs startled the captain so much that he screamed, something he never imagined he, as an official of the Army, would do. The other men leapt back. The captain tried to regain his composure but was finding it difficult to breathe. Beads of sweat formed on his brow and his thoughts were blurred. He managed to pull himself together long enough to press his fat, hairy fingers against the woman's neck to find her pulse. He found nothing. The room was absolutely still except for the groping fingers desperately seeking the slightest hint of life. The other soldiers, without realizing, were holding their breath.

"She's dead," he proclaimed. It wasn't until he looked up that the men released their breath and stood dumbfounded. The captain lifted Abuela and set her in the chair. "Tie her up." The men looked at each other, not understanding their superior's orders. "Move!" he shouted. They jumped to her side and with a purple silk scarf they had found in her drawer they pulled her arms behind the chair and tied a loose knot to secure her limp wrists. When they were finished they stepped back and stood at attention awaiting further orders. The captain turned and exited the house, his job unsatisfactorily completed. "What a waste," Abuela heard him mutter as he closed the door behind him.

She couldn't help but smile as she patiently waited for sufficient distance to be opened between her house and the ignorant men who believed they could break her. Once she felt certain that they were gone she sat up, slipped her slender wrists from the silk scarf, and stepped into the bathroom to clean up. She cleansed her cuts with a yucca soap to wash away the impurities and rinsed with tea tree oil diluted with rose water. She spread aloe on the wounds. As she combed her hair Liliana knocked on the door.

"*¿Señora?*" Liliana had been working for Abuela for a short time as the cook for the men and women who worked in the fields. She was originally from central Mexico. Abuela had met her on one of her journeys north, on her way to visit Esmeralda. Liliana was running a *mango/jicama* stand. It was a small, white cart with a yellow umbrella propped up to protect her from the scorching sun. She sculpted the mangoes to look like blooming flowers, then would place them on sticks and sprinkle them with lemon juice and chili pepper. The single mother mastered the carving knife with so much skill that she could even produce images similar to the sun with the *jicama*. Abuela was enchanted by Liliana's ability to weave such a powerful trance that the line to eat mangoes and jicama was always halfway around the block. People would wait hours to receive her food art.

Abuela spent several weeks in Liliana's village and they became good friends. Several years later Maria, Abuela's previous cook, died. Abuela sent Liliana an invitation of employment, offering her room and board plus a healthy salary. Liliana remembered the somewhat eccentric woman who left her an 18 months' supply of Amaranth to cure her broken heart. Her husband had left her and their daughter Andrea when Liliana was pregnant. She never heard from him again, but some say he died in the Sonora desert trying to cross the border to the United States. His tongue was smoother than silk when it came to sweet talking Liliana into his amorous web. Had it not been for his mulatto-colored skin and lime green eyes that sparkled like emeralds, she might not have been so easily wooed. If Abuela would not have sent the invitation with a human courier and offered to pay all of Liliana's moving expenses, the young artist probably would not have gone.

"¿Señora?" she repeated. Abuela opened the door. Liliana gasped, covered her mouth, and then gasped again. She placed her small hands on Abuela's cheeks "What happened, *Señora*? Who did this to you?"

"Help me make my tea Liliana. I haven't had a chance to drink it." It is hard to say whether it was fortunate or unfortunate that Liliana was the person to first find Abuela. Her reputation for embellishment was grand, thus the story of her mistress's beating quickly reached the town. Before anyone knew it, the rumor had grown and a tall tale of her death fell on Octavio's ears. The thought that Esperanza had been beaten and left for dead sent her lover into a fury. He let loose and attacked an outpost of soldiers guarding the onsite offices. He blew the entire place up. He was like a wild, rabid animal racing around in search of soldiers to harm. Juan Romero had to gather several men to contain him. They cuffed him to a tree until his rage finally passed. In a fit of desperation and sorrow Octavio broke down, sobbing, and confessed the secret love affair to Juan Romero, who at first was shocked but then relieved. He, too, was in a state of shock that anyone could have harmed his grandmother, but instead of rage, a deep depression came over him. He stopped eating and didn't come out of his cave for more than 48 hours.

"It's good to know she was well loved," he told the broken man. "She was lucky." Two days later a letter arrived with the supply run. It was from Sofia, telling, for what she believed was the first time, the story of Abuela's attack. The first line read. "My love, don't be alarmed by what this letter will reveal to you, for in the end Esperanza is fine."

"Esperanza is fine," he mumbled. "Esperanza is fine," he repeated dumbfounded. Tears ran down his face, because for the first time since the news of this loss he let himself feel what was inside of him. His grandmother, the woman he adored most in the world, was alive. He ran through camp yelling, "Esperanza is fine," poking his head into tents and under tarps in search of Octavio. When he finally found him he whispered "She's not dead," and they both sat together in silence, their heads bowed, crying.

CHAPTER

TWENTY-FIVE

Honeysuckle

Free of nostalgia or regret

Silvia was at the gallery with Gerardo, which gave Catherine the space she needed to spread out. She had been in Ecuador for four weeks and had been randomly jotting notes in her electronic note pad, but had not had the time to go through them. She actually despised the mini version of the computer because she was so visual. She needed to see the bigger picture and had a really hard time doing that while clicking through each screen. Luckily, her friend George had given her another useless mini-gadget prior to her departure, or so she thought. The "Petite Printer" as it was so quaintly named, turned out to be the perfect tool for organizing Catherine's thoughts. By attaching it to her note pad she was able to print out sticky-backed strips of narrow paper with her notes scribbled on them. She began hanging them up all over her room like scrolls, each in the order she thought the ideas could be formulated into the book. Oddly, she had lost track of why she was researching this man's life. Ironically, she had initially been drawn in because of her own family's almost insistent dislike of Latin America.

LAS HECHIZADAS

Catherine had been raised in Montreal. She was an only child. Her mother was a teacher, her father a banker of French descent. They were a humble family, living and working, leading an honest yet uneventful life. They seemed to be a tolerant bunch, but whenever anything about the Hispanic community came up in the news, or her father had to interact with a Spanish-speaking person he would grumble, "Why don't they go back to where them came from." Her mother would flash him one of her "Keep your mouth shut," stares and he would change the subject.

When Catherine came home one evening after spending the day at Musée des beaux-arts de Montréal, she gathered up the courage to breach the unspoken subject. "I went to the museum today to see the Frida Kahlo exhibit," she stubbornly announced. Her mother continued to sip her soup, but lifted her eyeballs to get a better look at her father.

"Why?" was all that was said.

"She's a fascinating woman. She experienced so much pain at such deep levels and shared them on canvas. Isn't that amazing?"

"It's not normal," her father insisted. "None of them are normal."

"None of who father?" Catherine's mother cleared her throat and warned her daughter not to go any further.

"They aren't cultured, they have no real civilization, they are savage," he raised his voice.

"For God's sake father. You sound like someone from colonial times."

"You don't know."

"And you do?" she scowled. Just as her father was about to retort, her mother stood up, pounding her fist on the table.

"That's enough. Neither of you has any point to make that is of value, so why don't you just stop."

"Mother, I just want to know what his problem is."

"Whatever it is Catherine, it's his, not ours, so leave it alone." Catherine resented her mother's orders. Her father

264

had no reason for being so nasty and prejudiced. She and her father rarely agreed, and in fact didn't have very much in common. She felt as if with each passing year they grew further and further apart. In her mind the man who raised her was her father, but her heart never connected with his. Perhaps it was due to his prolonged absences; he frequently traveled to visit his family in France or for work and when he was home he did not pay much attention to either her or her mother. This coldness could be seen in her mother's deep depressions. She would fall into states of such sadness that she would spend hours staring out the frost-paned window watching the snow fall. The melancholy was so profound that it drove Catherine into the streets. She hated going home after school because she couldn't handle the crying and grey faces. While some might think this sad, it in fact was a blessing for the aspiring young writer. It was so cold that she found refuge in a small coffee shop near McGill University. It wasn't anything special, or chic, but she could afford a cup of coffee, which gave her permission to linger for hours. She would scribble in her journal, describing the woes of a young teenager. These insignificant ramblings gave birth to poetry, which eventually led to the short story. These times were good for Catherine because they helped her turn a normally depressing situation into a creative force and gave her the courage to approach the school newspaper to see if they would print one of her stories. While the editor wasn't interested in printing fiction in the paper, he did take the time to read the story and convinced Catherine to join the team. This was the exposure that launched her into journalism. At 23 years old she had already published one book on immigration in the United States and had a column for a major newspaper. Once she left Montreal for the States she had only made it home a handful of times. When her mother passed away there was no excuse to draw Catherine back. She saw her father when he flew into San Francisco for business, and if he happened to be in Montreal alone during the holidays she would visit. In recent years he had been traveling with his new girlfriend, a woman half his age from London, who Catherine suspected had been with him even before her mother's death.

She held a snapshot of Juan Romero up to the light. It was the same picture she had discovered in the newspaper's archives when researching an article on Tierra Watch a year earlier. It was the organization's 60th anniversary, and she was doing a profile for the Sunday magazine. She had come across an article written 25 years earlier about the group and its most recent cause—a small flower growing community in South America. She remembered being drawn in by the dark skinned man with long dark hair, wondering what would make a young person from Arizona fight to save the livelihood of a community. At the time she didn't know his family was rooted there, but with time she had uncovered more and more.

She went over each piece of scrap paper she had jotted ideas down on and tried to formulate them into more comprehensive thoughts before entering them into the electronic notebook. Catherine's mind was filled with ideas, yet there was a part of her that felt this book was leaving out the magic. "Journalism is truth, not magic," she imagined her editor saying. "There is enough sensationalism out there. We don't need to add to it." She knew this to be true, but her heart yearned for more of the magic. Then she did something she hadn't done since she was a teenager. She took up her pen, an antiquated writing tool at best, opened her paper notebook and began writing the book.

"The valley is speckled with vibrant colors created by nature's paintbrush. From above, its canvas is so powerful it's easy to believe it could be the work of Proserpina." Catherine stopped suddenly, sensing something, thinking it was the fresh evening breeze. She bent her head down again into the notebook and continued to write. Abuela stood near the window, gazing toward Pichincha with a subtle smile. Catherine stirred the froth in her coffee cup, trying to imagine what it must

have been like to have to fight Maple Mining. Why had she never heard about the crop dusting? Everything else had been clearly documented. Even some of the abuse was reported in American papers, but just like most news that goes unnoticed, it wasn't sensational enough until Juan Romero's death. Even then because he had been living in a country considered by most of her compatriots as "developing," the violence was accepted, overlooked, almost expected. Spraying plants and people with poison and potentially lethal viruses goes unnoticed in the northern hemisphere. It wasn't the first time nor would it be the last. She recalled the movement in Columbia to eradicate cocaine through crop dusting. It killed off not only the drug production but every other kind of production as well. Ironically, the cocaine keeps coming. She was starting to feel sick to her stomach. Her thoughts whirled like a hurricane force wind through her mind. What would this story's purpose be? Society had changed very little since his death more than 22 years ago. And despite a certain amount of peace it came at the expense of violence.

Catherine was an eternal optimist, but since her arrival in the South her lighthearted ignorance had begun to betray her. She, in fact, was often so optimistic that her own positive attitude would interfere with her work and in her relationships. Her long-term boyfriend, Pete, finally left her after what he termed irreconcilable differences in opinion about the world.

"You're just too damn happy Cate," he would say. "The world is not your favorite flavor ice cream topped with mounds of chocolate sauce and whipped cream. It is shit." Between her optimism and his pessimism the two of them were constantly arguing. His main points finally sunk in after they had broken up. It's always after the break-up that one finds wisdom in his/her partners, asinine ways, but then it's too late for the relationship, but not for the individual. Her incessant arguments with Pete molded her thinking, and although he does not know it, pushed her to write this story. She never forgot his pessimistic words. They are what drive her to this very day. She stopped and took in the air floating in from the streets.

She finally was starting to enjoy the foreign place she had landed herself in. The language, the smells, the streets, and the food were all developing into a mosaic of thought about how she would tell the story of a man who sacrificed his world for the benefits of others. She opened the next journal and twirled her pencil as she read.

Things are not as they seem. We work for the simple freedom of being able to make a living, and the interesting part is that so are the people we fight. None of us wants to be doing this, but it is as if we had no other choice, no other path to choose than to conquer and destroy one another. I sit in this camp with the peaks watching over me, trying to imagine the end. When is enough, enough? When is it time to stop? I believe we can only stop when Mother Nature is no longer being raped. It is she that needs us now. With Sofia being pregnant I am constantly thinking about what our new baby will face in a world where pollution and corruption is standard. I am afraid for her future, for my own. Padre Miguel has stopped receiving threats, but others have come like notes on doors warning families that they are next. Last Wednesday Señor Garza was badly beaten and left on the edge of town. He was found by Silvio, the barber, who thought Garza was drunk again and had fallen asleep on his way home as he often did. The threats haven't intimidated us enough to stop protesting and to stop fighting. It's not the same as a war between people and government, like so often occurs in these lands. It is a fight between people and business, something that is more frequent in places that prosper, but rarely happens in places where no one is exactly sure where the next meal comes from. Aguas Puras is exceptional in that way. This community has always flourished despite the struggles of its country or leaders. It has done so with its flowers. Perhaps we fight in vain, but we fight for something called tradition. This is what capitalism and government don't always comprehend. In the short-term minds of the executive, the bottom line is what matters most. I have my doubts that the local government, for example, orchestrated the crop dusting. It is more likely a strategy implemented by the mining firm and carried out by goons. We have discovered where they are fueling up and a new attack has been scheduled. The pilots have a makeshift landing strip about 50 kilometers from the main valley. We're planning to get rid of the pesticides. It is the least confrontational way to stop the crop dusting. Some want to sabotage the planes, but it will only create more reprisals, and Padre Miguel gave strict orders that it was time to stop the brutality, even if it is only a one-sided effort. Abuela is working up a mixture of essential oils to replace the chemicals. She's diluted them with water because there are several 20-gallon drums. We're going out to the landing strip tonight to replace chemicals with this fertilizer she has concocted, so instead of killing everything we will be giving the flowers a nice boost. From what we have heard there are only two men on guard, which we can handle.

LAS HECHIZADAS

Far from my home, my mother and my
sister, I wonder why my father left and took
her away from her family. What was it that
drove him North, virtually fleeing a place that
could provide for the both of them? Was it
that it wasn't enough? Is it ever? We push
ourselves to the brink of physical and emotional
exhaustion seeking answers that are not going
to come until we slow down to listen, yet
slowing down is hard to do in a place that
imposes fierce competition for everything.
Work for money to buy a house and a car one
cannot afford, which leads to more work and
less time to enjoy the home. It is a constant
circle of ambition. No one has an answer to the
questions of my father's past. Mother, on the
other hand, seems transparent. She fell in love.
This is as straightforward as a shooting star
blazing in a new moon sky. It hit her, blinded
her, and set in motion a series of events that
she could not control. It must be genetic, for
I too have found myself in the tangled love
web. It intoxicates me, simultaneously leaving
me stupid, irrationally overjoyed, and afraid.
Love leads a person into foreign places, to do
unfamiliar things, to experience life in ways never
imagined. This is what must have happened to my
mother. But why do I speculate? Why have I
not asked her? Fear, I suppose, or discomfort.
We never discussed matters of the heart after
papá died. Not like she and Silvia do. Once he
died I replaced him in many ways. She looked to
me for leadership. I was able to give it to her
temporarily. My soul, however, knew that my
path was not to stay in Arizona, so I abandoned

her. At one level I think it was like a knife in her stomach to lose the second man in her life, yet on the other hand it had to be an opportunity for her to start anew. They are both fine. They write and with time the sound of desperation in their words has minimized. Mamá stopped working 4 jobs, sold the house, and bought an apartment she can afford. Silvia is doing well in New York; her dreams will be fulfilled in a city infested with bodies and drive. I could not survive in a place without air, but in her last letter, she seemed content. Her excitement about publishing my work in the newspaper was thrilling. I can't wait to see it.

As a future father I worry I will not know how to create a path for a child that will bless me with love, freedom and open his eyes to dream. All I ask for is the strength to try. I am scared.

CHAPTER TWENTY-SIX
Water Hyacinth
Balance and non-judgment

Silvia was packing when Catherine arrived from the market with a bag full of vegetables and yellow tulips popping out of the top.

"Where are you going?"

"We're going to Aguas Puras."

"When?"

"Tonight. Start packing your things."

"When did you decide this?"

"This morning. Gerardo offered us a ride. He's going to visit some friends. I thought it would be a good idea for you to see where all of this actually happened." Catherine eagerly nodded and put the bag on the counter. She rushed to her room and began stuffing her bag with clothes, pencils, paper, and her computer. She was planning on going to Aguas Puras on her own because Silvia had not mentioned anything, and she thought it was for emotional purposes that she never went. She didn't want to cross any lines. The buzzer from downstairs rang like a horn.

"Hurry up Catherine! Gerardo's here."

"I'm coming. Give me two seconds."

"You've had 30 already. Get a move on." Catherine zipped a glance across the bed and through the room, hoping she wasn't forgetting anything, and turned the lights out.

"I'm ready." She stood in the living room with her bag slung across her shoulder.

"Good." Silvia finished stuffing her bag, grabbed the keys, and headed for the door. "Turn the lamp off," she hollered as she pulled the door open and twirled around the corner. Catherine stumbled to find the switch, but finally did and ran out the door, slamming it behind her. She leaped down the stairs and blew a kiss to Alonso.

"Chau!"

"We'll see you in a few days *linda*." Gerardo, Adriana and Silvia sat in Gerardo's 2001 Volkswagen Beetle. The second generation of the enduring convertible was as classy as any car on the road. The fresh red paint sparkled in the afternoon sunlight.

"¡Suba!" Gerardo shouted. "We're off to the land of wonder!" He smiled and opened the door, pushing the seat forward to help Catherine in the back. "Give me your bag. It goes in the front." Catherine climbed in and the idling engine gurgled, waiting the relief of the accelerator. Gerardo loaded the car and they were off. The pot hole riddled pavement caused Gerardo to jerk the car around as he wove in and out of traffic laying on the horn every few minutes to get the attention of bus drivers and mad taxi jockeys. Catherine could barely breathe, she was so anxiety-ridden from the traffic closing in around her, blowing black smoke in her face and blaring a different kind of music with each passing vehicle. She finally pulled her violet scarf over her face, slunk down in the back seat, and kept her eyes closed until the sounds she heard were those of wind rushing over the windshield and the voices of her car mates. She lifted the veil and inhaled. The air was soft, and her surroundings had changed from high-rise buildings to the lush green countryside she imagined when she gazed out

of Silvia's window into the distance. There was trash littering the sides of the roadways, and occasionally she would get a whiff of burning garbage or wood or grassland, but the intense chaos of the city was gone.

"How far is Aguas Puras?"

"It's about five hours," Gerardo answered. "We'll get there in the morning. We're going to stop over at a friend's house in a town called Baños. There are hot springs we can soak in tonight and adjust to the slower pace of life before we delve into Aguas Puras."

"Can't we stop on the way home?" Silvia asked.

"Why are you in such a hurry?"

"I'm not."

"Then we'll go at my pace."

"Yes sir, *capitán*!"

"He wants to stop so we can eat. His friend Mario is a fabulous cook, and it's rare to pass up an opportunity to eat with him. Last time we were there he roasted an entire lamb for us. We showed up at 2:00 in the afternoon, and he prepared a Christmas feast for us. He is also an avid wine drinker." Adriana rubbed her fingers through Gerardo's hair and smiled. Her gaze was one of utter adoration. She was in the kind of love that was all encompassing. She loved the disheveled hair that wound around Gerardo's head like a dirty mop and his sweet drunken breath after a bottle of wine. She adored the way he yelled and carried on with customers in the restaurant, and the way he held her at night like a porcelain doll, not wanting to damage or lose her, yet not wanting to smother her either. She longed for the dances they shared, alone, after closing shop, just the two of them rocking back and forth to everything from tango to boleros, even American country songs when they felt like being goofy.

It hadn't always been like that. They had gone through some trying times when they first moved to Ecuador. She wasn't completely convinced she wanted to be there, and he wasn't completely convinced he could make her happy. She was much younger than he was, by almost 14 years, and his insecurities were often played out as angry acts of macho immaturity. When she wouldn't come home for dinner because she was painting in her studio, he would assume the worst and believe she was sleeping with another, so to get back at her he would do just that. He slept with whomever he could find that would accept him. At first she didn't know, but then he could no longer handle the torment and helped her discover him by accompanying a woman friend of his to a café across the street from Adriana's studio. They sat in the window, directly across from her window and he held the woman's hand, caressing her arm, kissing her neck. The fiery Argentine artist was not one to tolerate infidelities and knew that he had been doing this for some time. Why else bring her to introduce to his wife? She marched across the street covered in paint, without taking her smock off, paintbrush in hand, and stormed in through the front door. Gerardo saw her coming and stood up in defiance. Adriana punched him in the face and splattered orange paint all over the woman's gown.

"¡Hijo de puta!" she screamed in irate style. Her heart felt enlarged, and when she realized that the man that had led her so far from her home, her friends, her family and had used her, she stopped screaming, put the paintbrush down and left. She did not go home from the studio, but took the first flight back to Buenos Aires where she showed up at her sister's door in Congreso and cried for three days. On the fourth day she sent a letter to Gerardo, telling him where she was and that she was not going to return. She didn't know what to do with herself and for the next couple of weeks drove her sister crazy by cleaning the house, cooking, and making herself altogether too available to do everything. A week later Gerardo appeared with his tail between his legs, begging for forgiveness. He had to stay for two months to seduce his wife into accepting him again. It was as if they had to start over, from the beginning and eliminate all of the fear and mistrust from the start of their relationship. Everything and anything they were feeling was put on the table during long visits at the bars and cafes of San Telmo, or walks near the Tigre River. Adriana missed her home, but she loved the old fool so much that she could not deny herself his companionship. She did finally go back to Ecuador with him, but the struggles they had faced gave them both a renewed vision of what love was—it was foolish, it was painful and it was a lot of work, but it was worth every fraction of heartbreak it brought to one's soul.

"There's Cotopaxi, Catherine."

"It's so beautiful. It's not as big as I thought it would be though. How high is it?"

"We're higher than you think. Don't let the colors fool you." Gerardo laughed. He was right. They were driving at high altitudes, but the landscape was as green and vivacious as a fresh spring meadow back home.

"Everything down here is so much more intense," Catherine commented.

"In what way?" Silvia asked.

"It's greener, bigger, and more spectacular."

"I noticed that too when I first came here. I don't notice it so much anymore."

"How can you not? It's so obvious."

"Twenty-two years away from a country can make one feel as if she is suffering from amnesia."

"I forgot."

"I forget too. Don't worry. I don't want to be there. This is my home; this is where my family is from."

"Speaking of family, will we be able to see Abuela's ranch?"

"Of course. Why wouldn't we?"

"I didn't know if it was still in the family." Catherine saw Gerardo look at Silvia through the rear view mirror with a warning.

"Didn't I tell you Sofia still lived there?" Gerardo said innocently, as if he hadn't concealed any information from her new friend.

"Sofia lives in Aguas Puras?" Catherine looked at all three of them in shock. "I thought she was—"

"Dead," interrupted Gerardo.

"Well yes, or missing. Silvia said she didn't know where she was. I assumed no one did."

"You assumed wrong."

"Why didn't you mention this, Silvia? What are you afraid of?"

"It's not you she's afraid of Catherine, it's Sofia."

"Why are you afraid of Sofia?" Catherine turned her body towards Silvia.

"I'm not afraid of her!" She whacked the back of Gerardo's head.

"They haven't spoken."

"Since when?"

"Since Abuela's funeral."

"Why?"

"Abuela left the farm to Sofia not Silvia and she's mad about it."

"God damn it Gerardo, shut your mouth."

"Well you were," intervened Adriana. "I don't know why you don't just tell her."

"I'm not mad anymore. I was never really mad, just hurt."

"You thought your family should keep the farm."

"It seemed logical to me then."

"And now?"

"I've come to understand why Abuela did it. I didn't know anything about the ranch or the town, or even how the flower market worked. I hadn't been to Aguas Puras since I was 11. Sofia had made her home there and was a very important part of my grandmother's life. She was also the wife of my brother, the mother of my niece. She deserved to stay in

Aguas Puras more than I did. Abuela thought that she needed a new home, a permanent place that she could grow old in and be happy." Silvia looked up to see Abuela sitting on the top of the back seat, her bony legs, covered with old fashioned one-piece pantyhose and Velcro sneakers, dangled down the seat. Abuela knew her granddaughter was going to have trouble letting go of something that she felt belonged to her, but Sofia was just as much a part of the family as Silvia, and she was present. Silvia wasn't one to run a farm, or live in a small town. Even when she was exiled she didn't visit the farm. She had gone once to visit her grandmother but stayed in town, showing no interest in Abuela's house. Abuela stuck her arms out to the side to feel the wind penetrate her clothes and tickle her skin. It had been ages since she had ridden in a convertible. "I still would have liked it, ouch!" A swift kick banged her leg.

"What's wrong?" Silvia rubbed the side of her leg.

"Nothing."

"Seems like you were being selfish."

"When you have lost your entire family you tend to become selfish. I wanted something of them for myself."

"Even if you didn't really want it," Adriana said. Abuela smiled. She liked Adriana. She was feisty and straightforward, just what Silvia needed to keep herself grounded.

"But I did."

"You probably would have sold it by now *mi amor*," Adriana laughed. "You never would make it up there. It's too isolated for you."

"I know," she whined like a small child. "I thought I could adjust."

"Are you unhappy where you are?"

"No."

"Then your Abuela was right to give it to Sofia. Let it go already." Silvia put her hand on Abuela's lap and gave it a squeeze. "I will. I just miss them."

"We all do *corazón*." The car began descending a winding road and Gerardo let it fly. He was eager to make it to Mario's house before dark. "Slow down *idiota*!" Adriana screamed and laughed. "You're always trying to scare us." The steep mountains crept closer to the edge of the road, so close that Catherine could see the cavernous drop with no apparent bottom. They swerved back and forth, dropping further and further into the valley, as the mountains grew taller around them. The mountains were lush and green, splattered with tiny plots of varying crops planted by the locals. Small waterfalls cascaded down the sides of the hills, sometimes crossing the road. Catherine could see the river in the basin below. Patches of brown rock and dirt were also scattered across the mountainside. Though she couldn't see it, she knew that Tungurahua, or "the throat of fire," as the Quechua call it, was just around the corner. The towering volcano erupted briefly in the late 20th century and then released her fury in the early 21st century, causing a national disaster. The town was rebuilt and was once again starting to flourish. The locals had a flare for attracting tourists and turning their disaster into a must-see sight in the country.

The car bounced along the brick street as Gerardo rolled to a stop in front of a salmon-colored house, decorated elegantly with an exquisite garden boasting colors from every palate. The lights inside glowed like warm candlelight through the small square- paned windows that covered the front of the house. Gerardo lazily walked up the front walk, stretching his legs as he made his way to the door. He knocked and the door squeaked open. *"¿Alo?"* The smell of roasted garlic floated heavily through the air. *"¿Mario? ¿Estás?"* No one answered, but Gerardo heard banging in the kitchen and loud music blaring from the radio. He poked his head around the corner to find his overweight friend bouncing in delight, singing along with the radio and throwing pots and pans here and there, elbow deep in chopped vegetables and *carne mechada*.

"¿Aló? ¡Loco!" Gerardo shouted. Mario spun around on his heals to reveal his graying mustache stained with red wine and tomato paste splattered all over his apron.

"¡Gerardo! ¡Amigo! ¿Qué haces aquí?" He opened his arms and moved towards his old friend in one slow, rolling motion. He wrapped himself around Gerardo like a boa, squeezing him tightly. They patted each other firmly in forceful macho style, pounding the other's back, bouncing each other up and down.

"I've come to eat! Why else would I be here," Gerardo answered.

"You're timing is impeccable. I'm just finishing shredded meat in a light tomato sauce with rice and salad."

"I have some other friends with me."

"Bring them in. You know there is always enough for everyone." Gerardo waived the women in from the front door and left them to bring in his bag. They found him, glass of wine in hand, already boisterously laughing at Mario's ancient jokes.

"Good evening," ventured Adriana.

"¡Belleza! How are you? It's been so long. You are more beautiful than ever. It's as if angels have been sent from heaven. And who are your timid friends?" Mario leaned around trying to steal a glimpse of the two divas standing behind his loyal friend's wife.

"This is Silvia and this is Catherine. Catherine is from up North so she doesn't speak much Spanish."

"Yet," interrupted Catherine. "I want to learn."

"Well, good for you. It will make our lives much easier. But for now we will communicate in choppy English and Spanish. *¿De acuerdo?"*

"De acuerdo," she answered.

"Consuela!" Mario hollered. *"Consuela, ven mi vida."* Consuela was Mario's life partner. They had never married because neither of them believed in marriage as a modern ritual. Mario was afraid that the piece of paper binding them in marriage would only ruin the passionate love they shared, while Consuela was too afraid to marry because of the bad luck in her family. Every woman in her family who had married had done so more than once. Not one had ever made the first marriage last. Some were lucky to only have two, some, like her great aunt Margarita reached an astronomical 17 husbands. Several died, others cheated on her, and others were drunks or bums or losers, in her words. She was never satisfied. Consuela believed it was a curse and thus refused to fall into the trap that would ultimately doom her relationship with Mario. She came from the South, near the border, where life was hot and savage, dusty and difficult. Law was hard to find, except for the law of the land when men took matters into their own hands. Her mother ran a small *burdel* in the town of Macará, an alternative crossing place to Huaquillas-Tumbes. While many think the life of a prostitute is dangerous, it was the most profitable and stable profession in that area. Conchita, Consuela's mother, had been in business for 33 years, pleasing passersby and locals alike. Her only rule in life was pay before pleasure. She learned long ago that men who don't want to pay up front wouldn't want to pay after. Joaquim, a heavy black Brazilian man from Bahia, served as her doorman, and unless someone was so drunk that they found courage in the depths of their bowels to stand up to him, Conchita rarely had problems with anyone defying Joaquim.

"Si mi amor. Aqui estoy." An extraordinarily tall, thin woman followed the voice through the corridor. Her bleached out white hair blended with her translucent skin that hung from her bones like a potato sack. Her eyes, bloodshot red and blue like a sun-faded denim shirt popped out of her skinny cheekbones. Catherine couldn't help but stare at this rare albino woman.

"Gerardo and Adriana are here and they've brought some friends."

"Fabulous!" She swept around the room in her neon yellow sundress that was worn through in the backside and kissed everyone on the cheek. *"Welcome. ¿Cómo estás?"* She stopped at Adriana and held her arms out. "Let me look at you. Wow! You look better than ever, gorgeous." Adriana blushed.

"You say that every time I come."

"Is it my fault you become more beautiful with every visit?" Consuela had a way of making other women feel downright drop dead gorgeous. In spite of her disturbing physical appearance, there was an aura of sexual prowess that surrounded her, that gave her a confidence not many women have, and that rubbed off on others.

"Come, let me show you your rooms. Adriana, you and Gerardo can take the guesthouse. There's no one there. Silvia and Catherine, follow me." She led them upstairs and down a long narrow hallway with squeaky wood floors. She opened doors on either side of the hallway. "This is yours, Silvia" she gestured to the left. "And this is yours Catherine," she gestured to the right. "The bathroom is right down the hall. Feel free to wash up if you like." Catherine stepped into her room to find an elegantly decorated room with fresh cut roses on the nightstand. The bedspread was hand-woven lace, and a pair of French doors opened up onto a large patio. The moon had risen and shimmered on the patio below, lighting up the avocado tree in the center of the garden. She could hear a waterfall close by. She changed her clothes and washed up, then went downstairs to find the crowd still huddled in the kitchen, drinking and talking, picking at Mario's food.

"A comer." Mario announced upon Catherine's arrival. "Everyone to the dining room. We will eat a civilized meal." They all wandered into the dining room where the round table was carefully set with a dark red tablecloth and sky blue ceramic dishware. A round candelabra illuminated the glasses, and the room was filled with the sweet smell of sandalwood incense. They sat as Mario served the soup and then

the main dish. Catherine was so hungry that she barely spoke. She slurped her soup and devoured her meat. When she had cleaned her plate she barely realized she had finished, except for the sudden full feeling that rounded out her belly. The group chatted about old times and new, reminiscing about the days of partying in the city.

"And this trip is for what?" Mario finally asked.

"We're going to Aguas Puras."

"What a beautiful place," he responded. "I'm surprised you're going, though. When's the last time you traveled there?"

"It's been awhile."

"Have you been since Juan Romero was killed?" They all looked down, ashamed to have to admit in front of Catherine that they had not.

"Gerardo? You haven't been either?"

"No dear, I haven't."

"Why? What keeps you all away? It has been more than twenty years."

"It gets harder every year to go back. When Abuela died I thought of going, but the restaurant and Adriana's art."

"No excuse," Silvia said.

"Don't talk missy, you aren't much better." Silvia shut her mouth.

"The truth is that I don't know if I will be able to handle seeing everything and everyone again. When he died I ran. I ran as far and as fast as I could, for fear of being the next victim. They were looking for us, hunting us like animals. It was frightening."

"And later, when the government changed."

"Time goes by faster than you think, Catherine. I don't have an excuse, but we're going now so that's all that matters."

"Catherine is writing a book about my brother," Silvia told Mario and Consuela.

"Great! How is it going so far?"

"It's somewhat difficult to tell you the truth. Getting information out of this crowd is like trying to pull secrets out of a spy."

"There are many secrets that shouldn't be revealed. Be careful what you ask for." Mario laughed loudly and the others chuckled uncomfortably."

After a long evening of drinking and storytelling, the crew wandered up to their respective rooms one after the other, disappearing slowly like sloths into the forest. Catherine had fallen into a heavy sleep, but several hours after she had laid her head on the goose-down pillow, she was awakened by a strange squealing noise. At first she thought it was an animal, but the louder it got the clearer the noise became. It was accompanied by grunting and pounding, then heavy breathing. She realized that she was listening to Mario and Consuela having sex. Her doors were open and their room was across the courtyard on the opposing balcony. She stood up to close the doors but when she got close to the balcony something stopped her. She froze and couldn't help but listen to their lovemaking. As her eyes adjusted to the dark she could see where the noise was coming from. The two dichotomous body types were thrusting and twisting outside on the balcony, pushing and pulling like two savage animals fornicating in the wild. Catherine was not embarrassed and stood there until they simultaneously climaxed and collapsed on top of one another in utter exhaustion.

The next morning Consuela winked at Catherine across the breakfast table, and when they were packing up the car gave her a wet kiss in the ear and whispered, "I hope you enjoyed it." Catherine was so flustered she simply nodded her head yes and jumped into the car.

"Good luck Gerardo," Mario hugged his friend.

"Thank you. It was good to see you Mario."

"You as well. And you can bring that young beauty around anytime," he smiled.

"You dirty old man."

"What's new? I may be old, but I'm not dead."

The group headed out of town in silence, each thinking about different things.

The car chugged up a long narrow mountain road into the mist. Gerardo stopped to put the top up and pull sweaters out of the suitcases.

"It gets chilly during rainy season up here." While Catherine had experienced the frigid side of the equatorial climates, this mist was colder, eerier. It was so thick that she couldn't see past the plants that crawled out onto the side of the road. The humid cold penetrated her skin and left her shivering.

"We're pretty high, that's why. Wait until we drop back down into the valley. It will warm up," said Silvia. It took almost three hours for them to climb up and around the winding road that extended a mere 100 kilometers. Near the top they broke through the clouds, and the rocky terrain jutted out around them. As they crossed the highest point they passed through a hand-constructed rock archway which read: *"Bienvenidos a La Valle de Las Flores."* To the right was a church, also built of stone.

"Should we stop?" Gerardo asked.

"Yes, I think she'd like this. I want to light a candle in the chapel," replied Silvia.

"This chapel was built by an elder from Aguas Puras. His name is Juan de Divinidad. He built this archway and the chapel by himself using pieces of glass from bottles and stones he collected from the mountainside."

"Alone?"

"Yes, alone. He said that a vision came to him that he had to build a welcome point for the land his wife treasured so deeply. She was an *Hechizada*. Some say he felt powerless next to her so he invented a project for himself, something that would record his life in the history books alongside his wife's. So he began collecting stones and bottles and carrying them by hand to this spot." Gerardo pulled over and parked the car on the side of the road. They walked up the stone path toward the chapel. The doors were open. A dim light came from inside. An older man sat at the back of the church with a box of candles. Silvia dropped a coin in his bucket and took the candles.

"Vaya con Dios," he said, trying to stand but wobbling so intensely that Silvia had to help him back down before he fell.

"Gracias, usted también," she answered. Catherine copied Silvia and responded the same to the gentleman's etiquette. He once again tried to stand. His face was old, covered in wrinkles, protected by a round bolo hat with a colorful band just above the brim.

"How old is he?" Catherine asked.

"I don't know, but he was here the last time I came and he was old then," Silvia said. "They stay until they die, protecting their ancestors' work."

"He's related to Juan de la Divinidad?"

"Yes, I think he is a great-great-great-great-great-great-great nephew." Silvia made her way to the front of the church, walking down the center aisle. Catherine followed. Each pew and bench was made from the same stone and glass as the structure. The floor, too, was made of the same material. The windows that lined the walls were carefully designed images from the Catholic religion, made from melted colored glass. The altar was also made of stone, but covered with a white silk cloth and adorned with a silver chalice. A picture of Juan de la Divinidad and his wife Carolina was propped up on an easel near the front.

"Is that him?"

"Yes, as a young man. He started building the church when he was 73. It took him 24 years to finish. The day after he did, he dropped dead. They found him in his bed holding a handful of stones and blue glass, dead."

"How sad."

"Not really. He finished didn't he?"

"True." The two kneeled in the first pew, quietly praying for different things and at very different levels. While the young journalist asked for specific things, the older dancer had learned that asking for anything but guidance was a moot point. So in her mind she simply said, "Guide me through these times and help me understand what it is that I should do." She stood and left Catherine to pray alone. When Catherine finished her conversation with God she sat and absorbed the peaceful ambience of the small chapel. She hugged herself, noting the cold of the high mountains, and wondered what could have provoked a human being to build a chapel entirely out of stone. She stared at the photo in front of her, hoping it might talk back, but it didn't. The old man simply stared at her. "Odd." She said to herself.

"What is odd?" a creaky voice from behind asked. Startled, she turned around. The guard they had encountered at the entrance sat directly behind her.

"You scared me."

"I didn't mean to."

"It's okay. I was just thinking that it's odd that a man would build a church with only stone and glass and for no apparent reason."

"He had a reason. God told him to."

"How is that possible?"

"In a dream. He instructed him how to build each and every corner using glass and stone so that the structure would be sturdy and admired."

"It's hard for me to believe."

"You don't have to. The dream wasn't meant for you." The man brushed Catherine's bangs from her forehead and said, "But don't worry, your time will come." He smiled to reveal his toothless mouth. He stood and went back to his post at the door. His assurance that she, too, had a destiny sent a chill through her spine, but at the same time comforted her. She made the sign of the cross and exited through a side door. Gerardo was standing by the car smoking, and Adriana and Silvia were sitting on the steps of the chapel. The fog had thickened and hung heavily over the mountains. The silver stillness was so quiet it was eerie.

"You ladies ready?" Gerardo shouted. "Let's go."

After reaching the highest point the road would go they began descending once again, via numerous switchbacks and curves. Every few kilometers a thatched mud house with a red tile roof would grace the hillside, regardless of the inclination of the mountain. The people in this area would build where they could, walking up steep slopes to reach their abodes. Their cheeks were red from their overactive capillaries, and they covered themselves with woolen shawls to protect themselves from the cold. As they got closer to the valley the sun began to break through the fog, and the hillsides transformed from rocky tough terrain to lush fields of vegetables and, further on, thousands of different kinds of flowers. The meadows were like Monet paintings, splattered with pastels and vibrant reds, oranges, and purples.

"It's so beautiful," Catherine said in awe.

"I know," said Gerardo. "There isn't anywhere like it in the world."

"I had no idea," she said.

"Not many people do, even after Juan Romero's photos."

"But his photos never depicted this beauty."

"Yes they did, but those didn't sell. It was violence that sold then, not peace. He has an entire series of nature photos that were never given proper merit."

"Do you still have them?"

"Silvia does. We're going to put them in the gallery later."

"I'd like to see them."

"Anytime my dear, anytime." As the valley widened so did the road. Gerardo picked up speed and zoomed through the flower fields. With the top down a plethora of scents penetrated Catherine's olfactory system. Before she could recognize one scent, a new one was floating into her nose. Gerardo downshifted to take a sharp hairpin curve and then the town appeared suddenly. "Here we are." He zipped around the corner and down a side street lined with brick and adobe buildings. The windows were covered with decorative iron bars, and the doors were painted bright blue, yellow, and pink. The streets were bustling with people on their way to market to help unload the flowers from the trucks onto the train. The trucks came to town on Wednesdays to unload the week's merchandise, and everyone pitched in to secure the boxes on the cargo car of the train headed for the capital. Gerardo stopped in front of a two-story red apartment building near the plaza and hopped out. "Be right back," he said.

"Where is he going?" Catherine asked.

"To see if Sandra is here."

"Who is Sandra?"

"She owns the inn. She's a friend of ours from the old days." A few minutes later Gerardo waved the women in. "Sandra's not here, but they've got room for everyone. Bring your stuff." The group settled in and decided to take a nap before inquiring for Sofia at the café. Catherine had trouble falling asleep, so she wrote in her notebook, describing the trip, Mario and his wife, and her impressions of the valley. She finally dozed off in a big yellow velour chair near the window, with her pen and book in hand. She was awakened by a knock several hours later.

"Catherine? It's Silvia? Are you there?" Catherine heard Silvia calling in the distance. It took several knocks before Catherine realized that she was not dreaming.

"One minute." She groggily got up and opened the door.

"Hi. Were you sleeping?"

"I dozed off, yes."

"I couldn't sleep. I am too anxious. I want to get out. Do you want to go on a walk?"

"I want to go to the loading dock," Catherine said.

"Ok. Let's go. They are still working."

Silvia and Catherine wandered through the streets, stopping every few minutes to chat with someone. The news that Silvia was in town had spread quickly and by the time they had made it into the streets, only a few hours after their arrival; everyone in town knew Juan Romero's sister had returned. The train station was only a few blocks from the Inn and was the engine of the town that afternoon. Before she even saw the activity, Catherine heard the shouts and movement from around the corner. The immensity of the work was more than she had expected. Lines and lines of people loading crates on different cars crowded the train station. Boxes were marked by the kind of flower and organized accordingly.

"Gladiolas, red, white, purple, and yellow in car seven!" shouted a tall man with a long dark beard. "Daisies in car five! Roses in cars eleven through seventeen."

"Roses seem popular," Silvia said to the man as she smiled.

"*Por Dios,* it's true! The little one has arrived! How the hell are you?" The big man released a bellowing laugh, picked Silvia up, twirled her around and planted a huge kiss on her open mouth as her legs dangled in the air. After a long while they stopped and he put her down.

"I'm fine, and you?"

"Better now that you're here. It's been awhile."

"It's not my fault you haven't come to see me."

"It's been busy. I haven't been able to get away. What miracle brought you here?" Silvia turned to Catherine.

"José, this is Catherine Snyder. She's the one I told you about. She's writing a book about my brother." As soon as he reached his hand out Catherine remembered. This was the man who had been lingering around Silvia's apartment when

Catherine had first arrived, and the same man Gerardo and Adriana had told stories about.

"Nice to meet you, José. I've heard a lot about you."

"Surprised to hear that!" He mocked Silvia by goggling his eyes at her.

"Not from Silvia, don't worry. She hasn't lost her knack for hiding everything. Gerardo and Adriana filled me in."

"That sounds more like it. It's a pleasure to meet you."

"Likewise."

"Where are you two staying?"

"We are four," Silvia corrected. "Gerardo and Adriana came with us."

"Fabulous. You can all stay with me."

"We got rooms at Sandra's Inn."

"For tonight, but after that you're staying at my house. No arguments." Silvia had hoped he would offer, but had not wanted to impose on José before. Although their affair had been known for several years, she was not completely comfortable bringing Catherine into the circle. She and José had always been informal and open. 'You have your life I have mine. There are no expectations was their motto, and she didn't know if Catherine would understand.

"No arguments here," Silvia smiled. "We're going to go to Sofia's for dinner. Will you join us?"

"Sofia's?" his voice interested in this strange twist of events from a woman who didn't want to have anything to do with her brother's lover.

"Catherine wants to meet her and well," Silvia looked down, "It's time I get over myself."

"Nice to hear a change in attitude," he said. "Does she know you're coming?"

"No, but I imagine she knows we're here."

"Probably. How 'bout I meet you over there. I think I'll stop by a little early to prepare her."

"Prepare her? Does she need it?"

"It's only fair. You don't need to surprise her. She deserves to be allowed to act as gracious as possible." He smiled and kissed Silvia. "Now get out of here. I've got to get back to work. Good to meet you, Catherine."

"José, can we stick around and watch? I'd like to ask some folks some questions."

"You can do whatever you want, just leave me be. I've got to finish up if I'm going to prep the feisty French chef."

"Silvia?"

"Sure Cath, let's go." They walked off and Silvia was quiet.

"Are you okay?"

"Nervous, I suppose. I hadn't really thought too much about Sofia until this trip. It's like opening old wounds."

"Wounds that don't seem to have healed. Maybe it's a good idea. You can close this chapter once and for all."

"Yes, you might be right." The two walked through the corridor, stopping and talking with almost everyone Silvia recognized. Even though she had spent very little time in Aguas Puras, everyone remembered her from her childhood, from the stories her grandmother had told, and as the little sister of an important man in the town's history. It was easy for Catherine to ask questions and find stories from those willing to tell them.

"When the flowers started suffering, a lot of us began to deteriorate," one man told Catherine. "We were losing hope that the mine was going to win, but Juan Romero came, every week that he wasn't in the mountains, and helped load the train. There was a time when we had only 50 crates to load, because the flowers were so sick, but he was so positive that day. I remember him taking photos between loading crates and talking with everyone. He kept our spirits up. We almost lost it all, but he wouldn't let us give in. Today we are running almost 500 crates. If it weren't for his persistence, I think many of us would have given up." Many of the stories were similar, of positive motivation and of courage. There was a woman of about 80, named Faviola Benetti. As she labeled the crates she told Catherine the story of her son who had died while fighting in the mountains.

"It took me a long time to forgive Juan Romero for Carlos's death," she began. "I was so angry when I heard that he had been placed in a group to plant dynamite under the bulldozers. What I didn't know was that Juan Romero was in the same group, and that Carlos saved Juan Romero and several other people when he threw himself in front of a bullet."

"What happened?" Catherine asked.

"They planted the dynamite in the early morning. Normally the men didn't arrive until around 8:00 a.m., but for some reason one of the men had stayed in the office the night before. No one knows why. Perhaps he was paid to stay to look out for trouble, because he saw the boys. He came flying out of the trailer with a rifle and began screaming like a madman, demanding to know who they were or he would blow their brains out. None of the four boys spoke. The man fired the rifle into the air. They still didn't speak. According to Juan Romero time froze in that moment, because the man aimed his rifle and began firing. The first shot missed and the boys scattered, but the man quickly cocked his gun and fired a second time, straight at Juan Romero. Carlos screamed and leapt towards Juan Romero. The bullet hit him in the head. He died instantly. The boys ran into hiding. In the meantime the man collected Carlos's limp body. It was delivered to my door with no explanation at 2:00 in the afternoon."

"That's awful."

"No, the awful part is that he was only 18. He didn't have the chance to live life, and neither did Juan Romero."

"But they did a great thing. Look at where you are now."

"True, but I sometimes wish for him. It's selfish to wish the destruction of a society over one individual's life, but I admit that I do have those kinds of thoughts. I miss him, but at least he was alone. I couldn't bear what happened to Sofia. Poor child." The old woman shook her head.

"Yes, it's sad to lose your family."

"And not really know if you lost them."

"Excuse me?"

"Let's go," Silvia interrupted. "We should get back to pick up Gerardo and Adriana before dinner."

"Wait,"

"What do you mean, *Señora*?"

"That Sofia's daughter was supposedly killed, but they never found her body."

"Is that true?" she turned to Silvia. Silvia said nothing.

"They tore her from her mother's hands and she heard gunshots, but they didn't leave the body for her to grieve over as they did with Juan Romero. Some say she never died at all. They say she is alive, living elsewhere in these parts."

"Maria de la Luz?"

"That's what they say, but rumors run wild like cheetahs in Africa." She rolled her eyes at Catherine.

"And what do you say?"

"We've never been able to find her. They found traces of her blood and clothing alongside of a road outside of town. There was a considerable amount of blood on her outfit, so much that it is hard to believe she would have survived the gunshot."

"The baby was shot?"

"We assume. Catherine, I don't want to talk about this right now if you don't mind." Silvia was nervously looking around, very uncomfortable with Faviola and the fact she had revealed to Catherine something Silvia was not prepared to discuss with her. "Can we please go?"

"I'm sorry; this must be hard for you to talk about. Yes, let's go." Catherine turned to Faviola and took her hand. "Thank you, *Señora* Faviola. You've been a great deal of help."

"Good luck with your story," she said. "And with Sofia when you see her." She winked at Silvia. Silvia forced a smile and grabbed Catherine by the arm, pulling her away from Faviola. They didn't speak the entire way back to the inn.

CHAPTER

TWENTY-SEVEN

Aloe

Healing

The rain had set in and was softly drizzling over the town, but Silvia was sweating as if it were 100 degrees with 90 percent humidity. She kept wiping her forehead with a blue handkerchief Gerardo had lent her. "Relax, Silvia. Everything is going to be fine. Sofia is an adult."

"I feel guilty. I should have kept in better touch with her. Technically we are family. I just could never accept her."

"I know. She knows too."

"I have been immature."

"What's new?" Gerardo winked.

"Thanks."

"The truth often bores into our hearts to give us a reality check."

"I don't need anymore holes in my heart, thank you very much." Silvia stopped in front of the café, wondering if in fact José had been able to speak with Sofia. The truth was that she didn't know what to expect from her sister-in-law. It had been awhile since they had spoken, and after the way Silvia had behaved following Abuela's death, Sofia had no reason to communicate with her. Gerardo took her arm and pulled her toward the door. It was busy. The restaurant was packed with locals enjoying Sofia's fare. It had taken her almost a year and a half to recover from the incident. She had stayed with Abuela, who nurtured her back to health. She spent the first three months without speaking. She would cry for hours in Abuela's arms, sleep, eat, and then cry more. Abuela knew that nothing would heal her except for time. How Abuela managed to care for her and not go crazy herself no one knows. Her inner strength and perhaps Octavio are what got her through.

Silvia stood in the entrance, frozen, unable to move further into the restaurant. Gerardo saw Sofia first and immediately embraced her. *"Hola preciosa,"* he said, holding her face in his hands. "You look fabulous."

"You too, Gerardo," she gently smiled, looking over his shoulder at the three women standing behind him. "Hello Silvia." She stepped passed Gerardo and held out her arms. "It's good to see you." Silvia started to cry.

"I'm sorry. I'm so sorry."

"For what? Come." Sofia stepped forward and held her beloved's little sister. More than twenty years had passed, yet the pain was still there. Neither of these women had really ever been able to let it go. They stood holding one another for several minutes, and then Sofia wiped the tears from Silvia's cheek and turned to Adriana. "Welcome Adriana. How are you?"

"Good Sofi, I'm good. You?"

"Pretty good," she answered.

"Sofia, this is Catherine. She's from the States and is writing—"

"A book about Juan Romero," Sofia interrupted. "I heard." She didn't sound pleased or displeased, more neutral. Catherine took this tone of indifference as a warning.

"Pleased to meet you," Catherine stretched out her hand, but Sofia did not return the gesture.

She simply said, "Same," and turned to take Silvia's hand. "Are you hungry? Let's sit down and I'll have Carmen prepare something for us to eat." Silvia was relaxing. No wonder her brother loved this woman, she thought. She was kind. José arrived shortly after the group sat down.

"Well? How did it go? Do you hate one another?" he laughed. Silvia shot him a warning look.

"Unlike most of you, Silvia and I know that the only thing standing between us is the lack of time we have spent together. Once we share our stories and understand who the other is, the jealousy will disappear and we will be friends," Sofia said. "Now shut up and have a seat. We're just about to toast." Silvia liked the way Sofia addressed José. No one else could ever get away with being so audacious, but because of who she was to his dear friend and to Abuela, he let her say whatever she wanted, whenever she wanted.

"To peaceful and happy reunions," Sofia began. "May this be the first of many family gatherings," The group raised their glasses and cheered. Catherine sat quietly, observing, understanding that now was not the time to ask Sofia any questions about anything. Stories of good times from the old days came out, but no one touched on any subject that would set either of the two women off. They ate and drank until late into the night, laughing, dancing, and telling jokes. It was as if nothing had ever happened.

The next morning Silvia and Catherine drove out to Abuela's, now Sofia's, farm. Sofia had insisted that they come for lunch to visit with Octavio. Silvia was nervous, but Catherine was so excited she could barely contain herself. She asked one simple question, but Silvia snapped so ferociously that Catherine didn't open her mouth for the rest of the drive. Luckily, José acted as a tour guide and explained to Catherine where they were, whose farms were whose, and what kinds of flowers were grown where. When they turned up the dirt road that led to the house, Catherine was stunned. It hadn't stopped raining all night, and the water shimmered off the plants and flowers that willingly opened their petals to get a drink. An archway covered in vines and tiny purple violets introduced them to the entrance of the farm. Large eucalyptus trees lined either side of the road, providing a narrow path leading visitors straight to the house. A large sign with Spanish tiles read *"La Finca Juan Romero."*

"She changed the name," Silvia said.

"Abuela did, a long time ago. She wanted to leave him something."

"How come I never noticed?"

"You weren't paying attention." Silvia looked down. It was true. She wasn't. She was so self-absorbed about her brother's death that she hadn't even noticed the details and actions taken in his memory.

"This is amazing. It's enchanting."

"Yes, it is." Silvia took a deep breath. José wound around the path, through the meadows of lavender until he finally arrived at a large wooden gate. On it was a carving of an indigenous woman with her head thrust back and her chest forward, arching her back, screaming toward the heavens, and clutching a small bunch of calla lilies in her tiny hands.

"Who is that?" Catherine asked.

"Catalina."

"The woman who started it all."

"That's right." The gate swung open, and an older man stood slightly hunched over.

"Buenos Dias," he said from underneath his wide-brimmed hat.

"Hola Octavio. Soy yo, Silvia." Silvia got out of the car and walked around to give her second grandfather a hug.

"Mi hija. ¡Que sorpresa! What are you doing here?"

"Didn't Sofia tell you we were coming?"

"I don't know. I forget everything nowadays. She probably did." He waved José through and walked Silvia to the house. "What brings you to Aguas Puras? It's been so long."

"I brought a woman who is writing a book about Juan Romero. She wants to interview people, and she wanted to see the town for herself."

"A book, eh? That should be interesting."

"I suppose."

"You don't like the idea?"

"It brings up old feelings, revisits old pain. I don't know if I want that now."

"No one ever wants it, but sometimes it's necessary, even unavoidable."

"I know."

"What's the young girl's name?"

"Catherine Snyder." Octavio looked at Catherine. She reached out her hand.

"Encantado," he said and shook it.

"Nice to meet you."

"Come Catherine," José interrupted. "Let's give them some time." He took her by the arm and led her away.

Silvia and Octavio walked to the main house via the garden Abuela had dedicated most of her life to. Every curve of every path and every edge of each bush had been hand-carved by Silvia's grandmother for close to 80 years. The house looked better than it had the last time Silvia was in town. She remembered it being so sad and lonely, but now it had a new light surrounding it. It was happy to have Sofia living there. Octavio opened the door for Silvia, and they left their shoes in the mudroom. "It's been a long time since we've seen each other, Octavio. I apologize for not coming sooner."

"You're here now and that's all I care about. The present is where we live." She leaned over and kissed his cheek. "Thank you for loving Abuela. I should have told you that a long time ago."

"No need for thanks. It was an honor to be able to love such an incredible woman." They crossed the threshold into

LAS HECHIZADAS

the house to find José, Catherine, and Sofia already drinking red wine.

"You made it!" Sofia smiled. I see Octavio already has you under his spell. You look much more relaxed than you did last night."

"I am."

"Good. Make yourself at home. You are welcome to anything in the house or on the farm. It is just as much yours as it is mine."

"Thank you, Sofia. I was thinking I might walk into the fields. I haven't done that since I was a child. I need some time to think."

"Whatever you want. We'll be here. It will give me some time to talk with Catherine. I'm sure she's about to explode. We haven't let her interrogate me about my husband, and it has been almost 24 hours." Sofia laughed and put her hand on Catherine's shoulder. "Am I right?"

"I am a little anxious, yes," she embarrassingly admitted.

"Can I go with you?" José asked Silvia.

"No, I want to be alone."

"Why don't you help me," Octavio suggested. He knew all too well what it meant when women wanted to be alone. "I have some heavy bags to lift onto my truck and I'm an old man. I could use a pair of young hands." José acquiesced and followed Octavio back outside. Silvia, with her bag still in hand, turned around and went to put on a pair of rubber boots.

"We are finally alone," Sofia jested.

"Yes. It's odd to be able to actually meet you. I have heard so much about you that I feel as if I know you, yet I really don't know anything about you."

"I am a legend."

"In Silvia's words, sort of, yes."

"I am the woman who stole her brother's heart. She sometimes forgets that he is the one who in fact stole mine. I never expected to fall in love with him, but I did. It was the most wonderful and the most awful thing that could have happened to me in my life."

"How can you say that?"

"I say that because the universe gave me a special gift, a family, and then took it all from me in less than a minute. Life is hard and unjust at times. I knew that before, but I didn't realize she was so genuinely cruel."

"Would you be able to tell me what actually happened? Every time I bring up the subject it gets changed. No one wants to say anything except that Juan Romero was killed."

"It's not that they don't want to, it's that they cannot. I was the only one there that night, and I don't speak of it often. Other people in his family have only heard an abbreviated version that I shared with Abuela. They came, they shot, and they kidnapped. That is what they know."

"Why haven't you ever told them?"

"I couldn't talk about it for a long time. It wasn't until after Abuela died that I understood that I was the new messenger. Silvia chose a different path from what her grandmother would have liked, but it was the right one for her. I, in a way, became her replacement."

"Are you an *Hechizada*?" Catherine sounded shocked.

"No, no. That's not what I mean. I don't come from the correct bloodline. My daughter did, but that doesn't matter anymore. What I mean is that I took over Abuela's role as a community healer, but in my own way. Instead of through the flowers it is through my cooking. I also, of course, have kept this farm running. I pay for it to stay a float. There are several *Hechizadas* who come and work the land to produce the right kind of flowers and we then export them, just like before. We stepped into our role in the wheel. We are no longer leaders, but we didn't give up either. I couldn't. Especially not after what Juan Romero sacrificed for this community. It's my duty to stay here and make sure that as long as I live this farm is a working flower farm."

"Will you tell me what happened the night Juan Romero died?"

"Yes. You should probably know a little more about us first."

"Silvia has filled me in quite a bit."

"I'm sure she has, but what she didn't know was that we were married. No one knew that except for Abuela and Padre Miguel."

"When?"

"We married shortly after Maria de la Luz was born. It was in secret, in Padre Miguel's chambers at the church. Abuela was our witness. The day was finishing, adding the final touches of light to the evening sky when we arrived. I wore a blue cotton, sleeveless dress with white rosebuds embroidered around the borders. Juan Romero wore a pair of brown khaki pants and a bright green button-down shirt. Abuela made me a bouquet of Ivy, Forget-Me-Nots, Lilies and Lilacs. She never did anything without thinking about its deeper meaning and implications."

"They represent?"

"A long lasting marriage, true love, and fertility. We wrote our own vows. I still have them in my journal. Juan Romero was a poet of sorts, and he helped me to come up with something I wasn't embarrassed to share. Words for me have never come easily. Plus, what I wanted to share with him came from my heart, not my head. It's difficult to tap into one's heart and express what is there."

"Tell me about it. I've been writing for years, but the straight facts have always been easier for me to report than the creation of art through love, or pain, or joy. It's very hard."

"We did it. We stood in front of a huge, round glass window with a fire lit in the sky behind us and made one promise to each other, that we would never betray our love."

"Why did you do it in secret?"

"Juan Romero was afraid."

"Of?"

"That if we were married they might come after me. They had already attacked Abuela and the farm because she was all he had. With the baby he was even more suspicious and afraid that they would try to use her to get to him."

"He was right."

"Not really. They never gave him that chance. They simply killed him and took her. We never had the opportunity to negotiate." Sofia looked down and took a deep breath, trying not to cry. "They raped my soul of the two people I loved." Catherine put her hand on Sofia's arm, but didn't say anything. "I'm sorry, it's just that sometimes I feel as if it happened yesterday."

"It must feel like that. I can't imagine losing my husband and daughter in such sudden acts of violence."

"People thought I should have been prepared. They said I knew it was coming. Why does that mean that it should be any easier?"

"It doesn't."

"We had been married for eight months. Maria de la Luz was becoming a beautiful child. She was healthy, happy and so amazing. Her eyes sparkled when I spoke to her. It was as if she had always been in my life. What I mean is that she had been waiting to come into my life. She knew me better than anyone. At least I felt that way."

"And was Juan Romero around a lot during that time?"

"He was here off and on, in-between trips to the mountains. His longest stint was three weeks. After coming down and seeing how much she had changed in such a short time, he was really upset. He told me he was confused. He wanted to be with us, but he needed to be fighting."

"Did he change?"

"Somewhat. He stopped going for such long periods. He started going for only a week and a half, maybe two weeks at a time. Jack pressured him to stay, but he was strong-willed and tried his best to ignore him."

"Didn't he have other people to fight?"

"Of course he did, but no one else could lead."

"What do you think was the catalyst for the assassination?"

"I don't know for sure. There were rumors that it had been in the works for months. That's how things happen down here. You are hated for believing what you believe, fighting for what you believe, or even talking about what you believe. If these beliefs go against the hierarchy of power, violence is the ultimate end. Saying that, Juan Romero was the perfect target. It could have been anyone who did it. The mining company is the most obvious, but I never ruled out the government. It had its own interest in the mining as well as in the land of this valley. It is one of the few areas in the country those corrupt bastards have never been able to completely conquer and control. It saw the fighting as an opportunity to divide the community and reunite them in the way it saw fit—to benefit its own agenda."

"No one ever admitted to murdering him?"

"Never. The uprising afterwards was so strong that fear rocked the very foundations of both the corporation and the government. They dared not cross the line of arrogantly accepting responsibility for killing a hero. In essence, they created a martyr, which is hard to justify as an evil entity."

"I heard about the uprising."

"People across the country burned buildings, rioted, protested and went on strike in outrage for what happened. I hadn't realized how well known Juan Romero was. Our protests, letter writing, and media coverage both here and abroad had created a web of passive supporters until the day he was murdered. It was then that they stood up and said enough is enough."

"Is it true he was shot?"

"Yes, ten times in the head. It was obscene." She stopped again and refilled her wine glass. She looked out the window for a long moment, gazing at the fields, wondering if he was listening to her. "We were coming home from the café after a long night. He had come by to eat and brought the baby with him. It was late, but we were not afraid of walking the two blocks from my café to the apartment. Nothing had ever happened before and it was Semana Santa."

"What does that mean?"

"Easter Week. There were people everywhere in the streets the entire week, celebrating. They would dance, drink, and socialize until very late in the plaza. It wasn't as if we were walking alone in a dark, unsafe, unfamiliar town. We crossed the plaza and stopped to talk with Jaime Miranda. He was trying to convince us to buy a plot of land out here, near Abuela's. We were actually considering it, and in fact that's what we were talking about when a brand new black Toyota Landcruiser pulled up beside us. Seven or eight men jumped out. They were dressed in dark clothes with masks covering their heads. They had machine guns hanging diagonally around their shoulders. I felt someone grab me and start dragging me away from him. All I saw was white light coming from the middle of the truck and loud banging noises. I didn't know what it was. I now know it was the light from the guns. The shots rang clear in my head—they still do to this day. I saw Juan Romero slump to the ground, reaching out to me. When I looked down he wasn't moving. Maria de la Luz was screaming. Then seconds later she was ripped from my arms. I ran after the man, able to cling to the back of his shirt. Then I felt a blow on the back of my head, like someone had hit me with a chair. I fell hard and the car sped off into the darkness. I was able to crawl to Juan Romero. Blood covered his chest and face. I couldn't recognize him. They tell me that I was howling like a lonely wolf, abandoned in the forest. I don't remember my cries. Someone pulled me off of him and carried me across the street. They tried to revive him, but he had died instantly. The bullets had cut through his body like a knife through butter. I saw the white sheet draped across his body, and the blood continued to flow onto the pebble stone sidewalk."

"Then what?"

"I stayed with his body at the doctor's office until they came to take him to the morgue. I couldn't leave. I didn't know what to do. I told the police what I had seen, and they began the search for Maria de la Luz."

"What happened?"

"Nothing for a long time."

"But they found her."

"They found a baby girl's body near the river several weeks later. Her face was indistinguishable, but it was wearing the same clothes. We accepted that it was Maria de la Luz. The sick bastards murdered our child for no reason."

"Why does Adriana say she didn't die?"

"She doesn't want to believe it."

"But is there a reason?"

"I guess since we could never confirm that it was her body. Another baby from a town several miles from here had gone missing a couple of weeks earlier and the rumor was that it was her, but the clothes were Maria's. People wanted to believe that our pueblo's baby could not be dead. People began saying she had been kidnapped."

"Was there evidence it could have been a kidnapping?"

"No. Plus no one ever asked for a ransom, which made Adriana think it was a kidnapping, like the ones that happened in Argentina during the dirty war when the babies were taken and sold. She was influenced greatly by those times and refused to believe that Maria was dead."

"And Abuela?"

"She was a rock. If it weren't for her I would not have made it through those times. I was on the verge of suicide myself. Maybe it was better for her that she had to take care of me, or she might have fallen apart herself."

"And Esmeralda?"

"She came down for the funeral, after a lot of convincing on Abuela's part. She initially wanted his body sent back to Arizona, but Abuela refused. The funeral was here. It was the most spectacular show of love you have ever seen. The church was filled with flowers to heal our souls and food for the entire town. People stood and read poems, sang songs, and told stories about their beloved Juan Romero. Esmeralda just sat and cried the entire time. It wasn't until after the funeral and the gathering that she even allowed me to speak with her. She called me over to the corner where she had been sitting for hours. Her face was swollen, and she held a photo of our baby in her hands. 'She was beautiful,' she said to me. I took the photo and began to cry. She held me for a long time before I could stop. I wanted her to know how much I loved her son. In the end we were able to talk about him and about the light he had brought to both of our lives. This is a woman who had lost her husband, her son, and her granddaughter all before she had turned 50. She was torn apart. She didn't know how to go on."

"But she still returned to Arizona."

"Eventually. She stayed here for a while. We became good friends. We wrote until the day she died. I don't think she had much to live for after Juan Romero died. She continued to work and started painting to pass the time. She came for several visits, which healed her relationship with Abuela. While she was never able to completely show her mother the remorse she felt for leaving, or admit to her that she had been wrong in abandoning her family, they finally understood one another's choices and could live with them."

"How did she die?"

"She had a heart attack a couple of years ago. She was 70 I think."

"Young."

"Relatively. Especially since Abuela lived into her 90s."

"Silvia doesn't talk much about her mother."

"She feels guilty, just like with everything else. She thinks she should have stayed with her mother, or at least have gone back to her following her brother's death. There's something you should know about Silvia. She has always been running from the truth, but desperately wanting to discover it. That's why you're here I would imagine. While she doesn't really want to have her brother's life exposed, if you do it she has access to emotions that she can't tap on her own. She wants you to dig up the past and share it with her so that she can deal with it."

"Did she come to Juan Romero's funeral?"

"No. She never said why either."

"And you never asked."

"No. I figured she would tell me if she wanted to explain, but I don't think she even knows why she didn't come. "

"I didn't come because I wasn't invited," Silvia curtly said as she stood in the doorway.

"You don't need to be invited to your own brother's funeral," Sofia retorted without looking up.

"I wasn't invited to, or for that matter even informed about his wedding. Why should I worry about going to a funeral?"

"That was different. Our wedding was private for a reason, and that reason wasn't because we wanted to hide it from you."

"Do you know what it's like to find out that your own brother has married and chose not to tell his only sister?"

"No, I don't."

"It's not nice," Silvia scolded. "In fact it is upsetting."

"Get over it." For the first time since they had reunited Catherine saw the tension that had made everyone else so uncomfortable and worried about them speaking.

"Seems like you should both get over it," Catherine interrupted. The two women stared at her, shocked that she would intervene, perhaps because no one had intervened before. Everyone had always just let them have at it, playing their petty games until they stopped speaking to each other and went their separate ways.

"This is none of your business," Silvia cut Catherine off.

"No, it's not, but as an outsider it seems like the two of you would be good friends if you could let go of your jealousies of one another."

"We're nothing alike," Sofia said.

"But you must have something in common for Juan Romero to love both of you so much." They looked at each other, frustrated with this girl's intrusions.

"He loved us for different reasons."

"I'm sure he did. Now you both live in the same country, only hours from one another and you can't even be friends. That's sad. Fighting over nothing seems like a waste of energy."

"It is," Sofia sighed.

"I'm tired to tell you the truth." Silvia's eyes watered up.

"As am I." And with that they stopped arguing. They didn't make a conscious decision to become friends or even to stop bickering, but it happened. Catherine sat still for a minute and then offered Silvia a glass.

"You'll join us then?" she asked, holding up the crystal goblet.

CHAPTER

TWENTY-EIGHT

Lily of the Valley

Return to happiness, purity

"What do you want me to do with this thing?" the brusque voice from the back of the truck desperately asked. "She won't shut up."

"I don't know what we're supposed to do with her. Hold on until we get to *el jefe's*." The black car raced through the hills out of town, screeching around bends, leaving rocks and dust in its trail. Maria de la Luz did not stop crying. They tried everything from bouncing her to covering her mouth with their hands to singing and yelling at her, but her screams just got louder and louder. While she didn't know that her father was dead, she knew something wrong had occurred and that these men were not the people she was supposed to be with.

"Do you think he's dead?"

"If he's not you are," said the driver. Then there was silence. After driving several hours toward the flatlands the car turned up a long dirt driveway. The lights were on as they got out of the car. "Give me the kid," the driver said. "You all stay here." He walked up to the front door and pushed the heavy wooden slab open. His boss sat in a chair with his back to the door, in front of a fireplace. Cigar smoke curled around his head.

"Well?" the man with a foreign accent asked.

"It's done. Here is the baby like you asked."

"Take her clothes off."

"Excuse me?"

"There is a change of clothes for her in the hallway. Take those clothes off and put the other ones on her."

"Yes sir." The bulky, uncoordinated man lacked the finesse to change the child quickly and fumbled with the score of buttons and snaps covering the infant's outfit. When he was done he took the baby back to the sitting room.

"Put her in the cradle." He did as he was instructed and then stood waiting. "What do you want?"

"Payment, sir."

"You'll get it, but not here. It's not safe."

"Understood."

"There's one more thing. We've had some luck."

"What's that?"

"In the bag near the door is another infant. It's dead. Put the child's clothes on her and dump her by the river near Aguas Puras."

"I thought we weren't going to kill any children."

"We're not. This baby was found dead yesterday near the mine. No one knows who the parents are or how she got there. She was in the back of one of our trucks. Could be that some-one left her there. I don't really know. I don't really care. This way no one will come looking for her."

"What are you going to do with her?"

"None of your business."

"Yes sir." And with that statement the man turned, leaned over to pick up the bag and clothes and left. When the door closed *el jefe* picked up the phone and dialed.

"Hello Stanford," he said in English. "I have a surprise for you." He paused as he listened to the other person's questions.

"Yes, I have found a baby. She's a beautiful little girl. Her parents were killed in a terrible accident and there is no other family. You'll have to come down here to do the adoption papers, but everything looks like it is in order. Congratulations." The conversation continued for a few more minutes until the men agreed on the details of the transaction—$150,000 for the adoption proceedings to be paid directly to Shawn Girlain, the Canadian who had fought Juan Romero to the death. He was not about to let his mine go under. Maria de La Luz was shipped out of the country six days later. No one knew she had gone. No one knew she wasn't dead, and no one on the other side knew the truth about where she came from. To them she was an abandoned third world child with unfit parents and an opportunity of a lifetime.

CHAPTER

TWENTY-NINE

Fleur-de-lis

Flame of light, life and power

Silvia stood in front of the long dressing mirror braiding her hair in preparation for the party. Tonight was the anniversary of her brother's death. Every year Sofia threw a huge party in his honor for the entire town. While she was alive no one was going to forget him. Silvia noticed the silver streaks in her hair and thought how quickly the years had passed. She was now entering her middle years, when she should be stronger and wiser, but she didn't feel stronger or wiser, she felt lost. Her entire life had been about trying to find her way to something, whether it be dance, or love, or her family. She never felt contented with any of it. She always wanted more. Unlike her grandmother she was unable to live in the present and enjoy her life. Each and every day was a new excuse for her to procrastinate or be depressed or angry. It started with her father's death and never ended. Her self-pity had consumed her. As she stood, brushing powder over her deepening crow's feet, she understood that the time for all of that was over. Catherine may be a pest, but she had forced Silvia to reexamine her life inadvertently. Being in Aguas Puras was filling her with a sense of peace she had not felt since she was a child, hiking in the desert with her brother, throwing stones deep into the canyons.

"Silvia? Are you ready?" José pushed the door open and peeked around the corner. "You look ravishing," he noted.

"Thank you." A glow came over her and she smiled. He walked in and pulled her into his arms.

"Did I ever tell you that I love you?"

"Did I ever tell you?" she replied. He grinned and kissed her gently on the lips. He too noticed her calmness. Normally she squirmed or avoided the subject of love; for her fears wouldn't allow her to completely open up to him. He knew that this trip would be hard for her, but she reacted the opposite to what he expected. She was actually softening up. The power and beauty that was her femininity, rolled together like honey sticking to oats. She was aglow.

"Shall we?" He offered out his arm and she took it. They made their way to the garden where the party had already begun. Thousands of orchids hung from vines bordering the inner walls of the garden. Tiny sparkling lights and brilliantly lit red torches illuminated the shadows. In the corner a group played Andean flute music and strummed their guitars. Long banquet tables were decorated with luxurious foods such as blackberry brie, quinoa breads twisted into long braids, rice, beef, a hundred different salads, blood sausage, wines, fruits, and more. At the end of the garden a *lechón,* sweet tender pork, roasted on a grill. The flames leapt up at the small pig, cooking its juicy fat to a crispy exterior while leaving its interior tender and sumptuous, dripping with liquids. Silvia looked around for familiar faces and saw Gerardo and Adriana standing in the corner, holding one another in a slow romantic dance. As she glanced around, the faces became more recognizable and her heart was content to see so many people at the party. Then she saw Octavio, sitting on a swinging bench near the bonfire.

At first she thought the shadows were deceiving her, but after looking a second time she realized they weren't. Sitting next to him was Abuela, holding his hand softly in her lap. He was talking and she was listening.

"Poor Octavio," said José.

"What?"

"He's talking to himself again. Ever since your grand-mother died he sits alone and talks to himself."

"Has anyone ever listened?"

"No, we all have too much respect to bother him."

"I see. Will you excuse me for a minute?"

"Sure, would you like a drink?"

"Yes." Silvia crossed the garden and stood far enough away so she could hear him, but so that he wouldn't notice her.

"She seems better. I wouldn't worry so much. Yes, I know tonight is the night." He paused. "If it is meant to be they will work it out. We can't intervene."

"Hello Octavio." Silvia stepped up. She leaned in and whispered in his ear. "Send my love to Abuela." She kissed him on the cheek and smiled, then turned and walked away. Octavio was shocked.

"I assumed they all thought I was crazy," he told Abuela. "You never told me you talked to other people. Oh, I'm the only one that talks back, eh? Well great. I hope she doesn't tell anyone. Then they'll really think I'm crazy." Abuela caressed Octavio's hair and kissed his forehead before she got up to leave. "You're leaving? Why? You don't want to be here. That's beautiful; leave it to the living to solve the problems. Thanks." She strolled off into the fields, not looking back, praying that the evening would end in joy and not despair as so many other evenings had in the past.

Catherine appeared on the path, dressed in a silver strap-less gown and a black shawl with silver stars. The tassels hung down around her waist, and her hair was swept up into an elegant twist. She too had been nervous about the evening. The energy in the house was so explosive during preparations that she couldn't concentrate on writing her notes. People were whirling around the kitchen, trimming hedges in the garden, pounding hammers to hang lights and build stages, and engines roared as they raced up and down the road to the house. She had offered to help, but Sofia would not have it. "Enjoy your time; it is precious," she said. But Catherine couldn't, so she simply stared out the window, watching the people work like a colony of ants. In one day the entire garden was transformed into a magical stage fit for a king.

"Catherine," Silvia called to her, waving her hand. "Come join us." Catherine made her way across the crowd to a large round table in the corner where Silvia and her crew had installed themselves with several bottles of champagne and large plates of food.

"You look spectacular!" commented Gerardo, who was already lighthearted from the bubbly.

"Thank you," she replied.

"Have a drink." José poured Catherine a glass and then raised his own. "To Catherine. That her quest to finish a book on the man we all love so dearly be a tremendous success."

"*¡Salud!*" They all shouted.

"Where is Sofia?" Catherine asked.

"She's running around. The hostess of the party never sits to enjoy her own labor. I think she is probably preparing the readings as we speak."

"The readings?"

"Every year she reads a different passage from one of Juan Romero's writings. She has just about finished his book, so I guess I'll have to share his journals with her for next year," said Silvia.

"Which one is she going to do this year?"

"Fear, I think," said Octavio. And as he said that, the music stopped and the lights around the garden dimmed. A jingling of bells rang clearly through the crowd and everyone froze, already familiar with the routine. They took their seats and looked up at Sofia, who stood in a blazing red gown, adorned with sequined daisies.

"Good evening everyone. Welcome to our annual dinner in honor of Juan Romero. As you all know, each year I do a reading from his book *Life Through My Eyes*. This year I am going to read a passage about letting go of fear." A screen behind her lit up and the slide show began. Slowly, images of Juan Romero's family and friends faded in and out as Sofia read. "Although I am not very old I know one thing, which is that life is never permanent. It fluctuates from good to bad, from love to anger, from illusion to disappointment. Theoretically we should be able to adjust and adapt to the new scenarios life presents us with, but often we resist. We resist for good reasons or for no reason at all except to rebel. We morph into the change like chameleons looking for protection or we fight it like a savage lioness protecting her kill. Either way it happens. I have found that the resistance is driven by fear, and that we have not discovered how to let go. With the fighting I have experienced this fear, and it has driven me to stop operations, or change my mind without reasonable rationale. This is inexcusable. Fear is the basis of all errors the human race has been faced with, and until we overcome it none of this will be resolved." Sofia stopped and looked around. She turned to watch the remaining slides as the volume of the music went up. The plucking of the guitar strings grew louder and their beauty touched the souls of those present. When the last image faded out she turned back to the microphone and said, "Remember to live your lives without fear. Thank you." The crowd was still until Octavio put his hands together to applaud the show. Others followed. Sofia wiped the tears that always came when she saw her husband's photographs and sat down with Silvia and the others.

"That was beautiful," Silvia commented.

"It always is. His images say so much more than his words, but I feel the need to include the writings."

"It's the combination of the two," said Catherine. Sofia turned to Catherine, her eyes tracing a path from the young woman's eyes to her chin, neckline and finally resting on her chest. She frowned, squinted, and leaned her head closer.

"Where did you get that?" Sofia hissed.

"What?" Catherine replied innocently.

"The necklace. Where did you get it?" she insisted.

"I have had it all my life. My mother gave it to me when I was little." Sofia reached for the star pendant hanging from a silver chain. Catherine quickly covered it with her hand.

"Sofia, what's wrong?" Silvia cautioned.

"That pendant. It's Abuela's." The entire table looked at Catherine accusingly.

"No it's not. I told you I have had it my whole life."

"On the back is a Juniper bush engraved in the silver ... for protection. Flip it over." Catherine froze and didn't remove her hand. She knew that in fact there was a tiny Juniper engraved on the back of the pendant, but how did Sofia know that? "Turn it over," Sofia demanded. Catherine slowly removed her grip and rolled the star over onto its back. Sofia moved closer and everyone held their breath. "See! It's right here! Take it off!"

"No!" yelled Catherine. "It's mine, I swear." She pulled away from the enraged Sofia. "I told you, my mother gave it to me when I was a baby."

"That is impossible. That necklace was given to me for Maria de la Luz before she was born. I haven't seen it since her death. It has been passed down for generations through the *hechizadas* and was meant for my daughter. Where did you find it?" The two women continued their angry banter, not considering that there could be an alternate response. Octavio had been silent since the moment Sofia began attacking the young Canadian writer and finally interrupted. "Unless it really is her necklace, Sofia." Everyone shifted their gazes from the bickering women to the seasoned old man.

"What are you talking about Octavio?"

"What if she is telling the truth?"

"That's impossible, because that would mean she is my—" Sofia's words froze. "Don't be ridiculous Octavio," Silvia blurted out. "This woman is not who you say she is."

"Why not?" interjected Adriana, who was the only one all along that believed Maria de La Luz was never murdered.

"It's preposterous," added Gerardo. Catherine still hadn't picked up on what the group was trying to discuss and sat dumbfounded in her chair with both hands clasping her necklace.

"Perhaps, but what other explanation is there?"

"She found it. She stole it," said Gerardo.

"Why would I steal a necklace that was mine?" Catherine asked.

"Because you are obsessed with my brother and would do anything to get a story. Oh, you're sick Catherine. You are truly sick."

"I don't understand," Catherine pleaded. "I've done none of what you say. This is mine. Look." She struggled to pull her purse out and dug for her wallet. Then she pulled out a picture of herself as an infant. "This photo, it's me," She handed the photo to Sofia who took the picture and gasped, putting her hand over her mouth so as not to scream. Tears welled up in her eyes and rolled down her cheek.

"Dios mio," she said. "Look at this picture Octavio. Whom do you see?" Octavio took the picture and nodded his head.

"It does look like her."

"Like who?" Catherine pleaded.

"Like Maria de la Luz." Catherine's hands dropped to her side.

"I'm sorry Sofia. That's just not true." Her heart ached. She knew Sofia had never believed her daughter was dead, but this was absurd. "Look, I'm in Canada, with my parents," she said.

"It's true," a voice from the darkness chimed in. Again the group turned in unison.

"Padre." Octavio stood up and took his hand. "Come sit." It was Padre Miguel. His posture had shortened and his frame thinned, but it was still the same man who had pushed Juan Romero into defending the valley. He looked tired and ready for some rest.

"For those of you who don't know me, I'm Padre Miguel." He greeted the table and wobbled into a chair.

"What are you talking about?" Sofia shot the demand his way. He did not look at Sofia, only at Catherine whose nerves were on edge. She could feel her heart racing and her hands trembling.

"You are so beautiful," he said. "I'm glad you grew up to be as strong as you are."

"Miguel. Stop it. What's going on?" The priest sat still for a long moment and said nothing while each and every face stared in anticipation at him. Finally, he broke the silence.

"Maria de La Luz was never murdered."

"I knew it!" Adriana shouted.

"Shut up Adri!" Silvia shut her down.

"She was merely kidnapped," he continued.

"And how do you know this?" Sofia asked.

"I helped kidnap her."

"What?" Sofia gasped.

"I didn't actually take her away, but I kept quiet. I knew they were going to go after Juan Romero."

"And you said nothing?"

"I couldn't. They had me in a bind. I was told if he was gone they would stop, or at least minimize the work."

"And you believed them?"

"I had no choice. They were killing my congregation. Slowly they were poisoning us. We wouldn't have survived much longer."

"Bullshit." Sofia screamed. *"¡Hijo de Puta!"* she shouted even louder.

"I'm sorry Sofia, I had to."

"You did not!"

"They had Abuela."

"What?" Octavio asked.

"They had taken her and were holding her hostage. They had threatened to kill her. I just thought they were going to kidnap Juan Romero and send him away. I didn't know they were going to shoot him. I couldn't let her suffer."

"She never said a word."

"She made me promise I wouldn't either. They held her in a cave at the base of the mountains. It was less than 12 hours, but what they did to her in unspeakable. She confessed to me how they raped her, beat her and tortured her with the news of her grandson and new great-granddaughter. I do not know how she survived"

"Her inner strength is not of this world," Silvia answered.

"She would have never chosen what happened." Octavio said.

"She didn't. I did. I have had to live with this my entire life. After his death I could barely speak with Abuela, but she still treated me the same way she had before. I didn't deserve it."

"And me?" Catherine asked.

"When I found out what happened I went directly to Shawn Girlain."

"Son of a bitch," said Gerardo.

"He assured me you were not dead and that you had been sold to a couple in Canada. As proof so that I would not tell, he sent pictures of you to me every year." He pulled them out of a shoulder bag he was carrying. "I meant to tell you sooner

Sofia, but there was never a good time, until now. I saw Maria de la Luz in town today. I thought I was having a heart attack. I followed you and when I was close enough, I was able to confirm it was you. I've stared at those pictures over and over, praying that you would one day return."

"Why does that matter? There is no 'good time.' You ruined my entire life, you bastard." Padre Miguel held his head low and pulled several envelopes out of his bag. He pushed them across the table to Catherine.

"Open them," he said. "I think you'll recognize them." Catherine looked around and her eyes fell on Silvia. After all of this time digging and investigating, trying to find the "truth" for her story she suddenly didn't want to hear it. Silvia nodded her head to encourage Catherine. Although she was in shock, she still needed proof. Catherine carefully tore open the envelope and pulled the photos out. One by one she looked through the images of herself as a child, growing up in the north.

"Well?" Sofia insisted.

"These are photos of me." Sofia's head fell onto the table and she began sobbing.

Then she got up and ran off toward the fields. Gerardo stood up to go after her.

"Let her go," said Octavio. "Give her space."

No one else moved until Adriana stood and took Catherine's hand. "Come on Catherine." She led Catherine away from the table and into the house. Gerardo looked at his old friend in astonishment.

"Were you ever going to tell us?"

"I thought it was best that no one found out, but when I heard she was in town I knew it was my chance to free myself from the burden."

"Free yourself?" Silvia asked in disgust.

"I have been living with this for more than twenty years. I wanted to make it right."

"It's a little late."

"It's never too late."

"My brother was killed because of you! He trusted you. He fought because of you." She stood up and towered over the fragile priest. "You are the most disgusting human being on the planet," and she raised her hand to slap him. Gerardo quickly grabbed her and dragged her away from the table.

"Esperanza knew you were involved?" Octavio pushed for more information.

"No, she would have never let me sacrifice him for her."

"Nor would I."

"I'm sorry."

"So am I."

CHAPTER THIRTY

Red Poppies

Eternal sleep and oblivion

Catherine found Sofia sitting under a eucalyptus tree on the other side of the sunflower field at dawn. A circle of marigold petals and eucalyptus leaves surrounded her. Catherine sat down next to her and didn't say anything for several minutes.

"I called my father last night," she began. Sofia did not answer. "He admitted to me that I had been adopted."

"From?"

"From Ecuador." Sofia turned and looked at the young woman sitting next to her that was nothing like she had imagined her daughter would be like. "He and my mother couldn't have children. At the time he was doing business with a mining company based in Toronto. He had become friends with Girlain, who convinced him adopting a child from here would be the most compassionate thing he could do. Plus, it could happen immediately, and with enough money my father wouldn't have to go through the cumbersome process of filing several years' worth of papers."

"He paid for you."

"Yes." Catherine swallowed and felt a rock-sized lump stick in her throat.

"Adriana was right."

"Amazingly."

"I never even thought it could be a possibility." They again sat in silence. "You're my daughter."

"I suppose so." Catherine stared out into the morning sky, dazed and numbed by all that was happening.

"I don't know what to do. I spent most of the night staring at the night sky, crying, and asking Juan Romero for guidance. The only thing I heard was 'Trust the process.' What does that mean?"

"I guess we don't do anything except let ourselves figure out what is supposed to happen."

"We wait and we try to get to know one another." Sofia took Catherine into her arms and they both cried for a long time, not saying anything else.

The breakfast table at the house was just as quiet. José and Silvia had not made an appearance until Gerardo and Adriana were almost finished eating. Octavio spread raspberry jam on a piece of bread and dipped it in his coffee. Silvia absentmindedly stirred the yolk of her over-easy egg around and around on the plate.

"Can it be true?" Gerardo finally broke the silence.

"She talked with her father last night," said Adriana. "I was there."

"And?"

"He did pay for a baby from Ecuador."

"Can it be possible? Such a coincidence?"

"It's not a coincidence," said José. "It's the way things happen around here. It is fate. It's as if the *Hechizadas* called her to San Francisco, called her to Estela, knowing somehow, all along, that she was alive."

"I can't believe it." Silvia began to cry. "All this time she has been alive and none of us knew. None of us were able to take care of her, to raise her, to be true mentors for her." She began crying again.

"It's not your fault," said Adriana.

"I know, but it isn't fair."

"She's here now."

"But will she stay? We are not her family. She has a life. She doesn't remember us."

"Maybe she will now."

"Does it matter?" Octavio asked. They all looked at him as if they didn't understand where he was coming from. "If she stays, will that heal anything?"

"I think it will," said Gerardo. "She is Juan Romero's daughter. She is part of him."

"Yet she knows nothing about him, or his mother."

"But she will. Her mother is still alive. She will have to stay."

"She has to do nothing of the sort—her life is not here, it is in the North. She is not one of us, not even partially Silvia," Octavio said referring to Silvia's biculturalism. She can't even speak Spanish," his voice was harsh.

"What's wrong Octavio? Why are you so angry with her? It's not her fault."

"I'm not angry at her. I'm angry with Padre Miguel."

"We all are. No one can believe it was Padre Miguel who sold Juan Romero out."

"It would have happened anyway," Gerardo said. "They used him to get to Juan Romero more easily. If Padre Miguel would have refused Abuela would have died and then they would have killed Juan Romero at a later date. It was inevitable." Gerardo was right and they all knew it, but the idea that a loyal confidant would betray you sunk deeply into each individual's mind. Trust was hard to come by. As they sat in the kitchen, wondering where Sofia and Catherine had wandered off to, Edgar's son Felipe entered the kitchen. Felipe had taken over his father's job after Edgar developed Alzheimer's and could no longer work. He still lived with his son, but was so disoriented all of the time that it wasn't safe for him to work. Felipe was young and strong and had a good command of the workers on the farm. Thanks to his efforts the farm continued to run almost as smoothly as when his father was in the fields.

"Buenos Dias, Felipe," Octavio greeted him.

"Buenos Dias," Felipe answered. He continued to stand in the doorway until Octavio said, "Come in Felipe. What's the matter? Why are you acting so strange?" Felipe looked down at the floor and held his hat in both hands in front of him. "Are you okay?"

"No sir. I've been sent to tell you that Padre Miguel is dead."

"What?" They all gasped and looked at Felipe in shock.

"He hanged himself last night at the church."

"What are you saying Felipe?" Octavio stood up and slammed his fist on the table.

"I'm sorry sir. The cleaning crew found him this morning when they went in to clean."

"And a note? A letter."

"Yes sir. It was addressed to you. Here it is." Felipe pulled an envelope from his back pocket with Octavio's name written in black ink on the front. "I didn't open it. It is addressed to you, sir." He handed the letter over.

"Thank you Felipe." Octavio took the letter and sat back down. "You may go. I know there is a lot of the work in the fields today."

"Yes, there is. I'll be near the roses today if you need anything."

"Thank you." Felipe nodded his head and politely dismissed himself. Octavio opened the envelope with a knife and began reading to himself.

"Aren't you going to read what he says?" Silvia asked.

"Yes, in a minute. I want to read it myself first." The group waited patiently as Octavio finished a first reading of the letter and then made himself more comfortable to read it out loud.

Octavio,

It is with a lighter heart that I now choose to pass to a new plane. While everyone will say that I have sinned by taking my own life, I am at peace and it is time for me to go. I regret very few things in my life, but one of the only things I never forgave myself for was not speaking up about Maria de La Luz. I did it because I thought it was the best for everyone. I would not have done it if I knew that the people would go so crazy after Juan Romero's death and assault the mining operation the way they did. In a way, however, that would have never happened if he had not been killed. The rage that boiled in their blood during the time when they pillaged everything could never have been replicated. In the end the mining stopped and we were able to continue. Even Sofia went on. There were times when I saw her crying in the plaza, or walking alone with an empty look on her face and I wanted to tell her what I knew—that her baby was safe and healthy and growing into a beautiful woman, but something stopped me. Maybe my own fear of death, but now I do not fear it, I long for it. I ask that you please forgive me and that you tell Sofia and Maria de La Luz that I am profoundly sorry for never revealing this secret. I hope that they will be able to find one another again.

Yours Forever,
Padre Miguel

Octavio put the letter on the table and leaned his head into his hand to support the confusion in his mind. "He was tortured."

"He should have been after what he did."

"I understand why he did it," Gerardo said.

"How?" Silvia said with disbelief in her voice.

"Did he have another choice?"

"He could have snuck Juan Romero out of the country."

"True, but how do we know that they wouldn't have continued to work and killed us all in the end. We're here because of Juan Romero's courage to fight and Padre Miguel's ability to see the future."

"And later? After the dust had settled? After everything had gone away?"

"I don't know, but it's over now. What can we do?"

"Start over," said Adriana. She was the only one who truly understood what this meant. Her grandmother had lost a child during the dirty war to similar circumstances. She was one of the women who marched in the Plaza de Mayo until her death, looking for Adriana's aunt. She never found her, but the family had to move on. Adriana's mother had to grow up a single child, marry, start her own family, and trust that everything would work out. If she hadn't, Adriana would not exist.

"It's harder than you might think," said Silvia.

"Yes it is, but it is possible if you want to do it. The question is, do you?"

"Of course. I just don't know how."

THE LAST CHAPTER OF
A NEW BEGINNING

Iris

Faith, wisdom, hope

As the old woman planted the last gladiola bulb she looked up at her granddaughter. "Silvia never had to make the choice of how to start over because Catherine made it for all of them. Upon discovering that her father wasn't really her father she was almost relieved. She immediately understood why she had felt the way she did her entire life and couldn't believe that her destiny had led her to the truth. It was such a profound time for her that she decided to change her life completely and not return to San Francisco. She made a drastic change, in synchronicity with her father's personality. The natural path for her to follow was to stay in Aguas Puras and train. It was not too late for her, as she had not yet reached 25. The *Hechizadas* embraced her with frantic felicity, showing her the traditions and secrets of their culture without hesitation. She moved in with Sofia so that they could get to know one another and soon after, they burned the pages of notes she had compiled over the last year for her book. She no longer needed to write about a distant man in a distant land because she had to write about her father. It wouldn't be until after Sofia passed away that Catherine, who returned to using her birth name, began writing the story of her family.

Silvia stayed with them for the first six months, and the circle of power was revived. She returned to Quito to her apartment, understanding that her path was not the farm, but her work in dance and teaching. She made a monthly trek to the valley to stay with her newly reunited family. Octavio, finally feeling at peace, died in his sleep. It is said that he can be seen dancing in the fields with Abuela under the full moon."

The granddaughter smiled because she knew that this story was that of her grandmother and that it was now her duty to pass in on. She put her hand on top of her grandmother's hand and together they buried the bulb. Deep in the dark earth a red Gladiola, the fire, the spear bread life and would fight to keep tradition in the valley alive.

~El Fin